Ultimatum

www.penguin.co.uk

Ultimatum

Frank Gardner

BANTAM PRESS

LONDON · NEW YORK · TORONTO · SYDNEY · AUCKLAND

TRANSWORLD PUBLISHERS
61–63 Uxbridge Road, London W5 5SA
www.penguin.co.uk

Transworld is part of the Penguin Random House group of companies
whose addresses can be found at global.penguinrandomhouse.com

Penguin
Random House
UK

First published in Great Britain in 2018 by Bantam Press
an imprint of Transworld Publishers

A CIP catalogue record for this book
is available from the British Library.

ISBNs 9780593075814 (hb)
9780593075821 (tpb)

Typeset in 11/14.5 pt Palatino LT Std by Jouve (UK), Milton Keynes
Printed and bound by Clays Ltd, Bungay, Suffolk.

Penguin Random House is committed to a sustainable
future for our business, our readers and our planet. This book
is made from Forest Stewardship Council® certified paper.

1 3 5 7 9 10 8 6 4 2

For Amanda

'Sabr talkh ast, valikan bar-e shireen dārad.'
'Patience is bitter, but it has a sweet fruit.'
PERSIAN PROVERB

Prologue

'SALAAM, ALI-JAAN. IT'S me.' The voice, thick, gravelly and unmistakable, came over the encrypted line as tinny and distant. 'So. It's all in place?'

'It's all in place.'

'No changes?'

Ali didn't answer straight away. He removed his earpiece, tipped his head back, closed his eyes and wiped the palm of his hand over the stubble that covered half of his face. Still in his thirties, but already the coarse hairs that crept up his cheek were grey. He sighed. *How many times had they been over this, he and the man at the other end of the line, whose name could never be mentioned?* He replaced the earpiece and spoke into the mike. 'No,' he replied patiently, 'there are no changes. Everything is exactly as we discussed.'

'Good. Because you know—'

'Yes, yes, I know. So much is riding on this.'

'So much? *So much?* Are you playing with me, Ali-*jaan*? Have you forgotten all the meetings in Qom? The pledges of loyalty? The instructions? This is everything! Everything we have ever worked for. Remember, we are just the facilitators here, nothing more.'

Ali waited for him to finish. He closed his eyes once more and pinched the ridge of flesh between his eyebrows. So many weeks

1

of planning, so many contingencies to think of, so many what-ifs. By God, he was tired. But the other man was not done yet.

'So, Ali-*jaan*, I am counting on you. We are all counting on you. No mistakes. Nothing left to chance.' It was part question, part order. 'Are you certain you can do this?'

'Yes,' said Ali, abruptly, just a hint of irritation creeping in now. 'I am certain.' A pause. 'And if they don't accept the ultimatum . . .'

'And they won't, we already know this.' The gravelly voice was stern now, authoritarian, unflinching. 'We carry it out, without hesitation. This is a lesson they must learn. Our government is weak and it cannot hope to survive this. A new era is coming, Ali-*jaan*, and it will be our time. I will see you on the island.'

There was a click and the line went dead.

Chapter 1

THE PITCH. THE proposal. The moment of truth. That split second when the man or woman in front of you realizes with a start exactly what you're suggesting. That they should risk everything, maybe even their lives, their families, to betray their own organization, their own country, to steal a secret and hand it over to British intelligence. Get it right and you might reel in a big fish, a top-access agent, who keeps on giving, propelling you into the upper echelons of MI6, perhaps retiring gracefully to the shires with a knighthood, a valedictory lunch with the PM and some quiet recognition from your peers. Get it wrong and you're toast.

When Luke Carlton arrived for the rendezvous that morning in the back room of the café he had just four words reverberating in his head: 'Don't screw it up.' This was their third meeting and his contact was nervous as hell – that much was obvious. The man was sitting at a table in the corner, visibly sweating, perched half off his chair, twitching like a bird, glancing repeatedly behind him at the door, as if expecting trouble to come flying through it at any second. A television set, mounted on the wall, was tuned to a football match with the sound turned down. Luke held out his hand and gave him what he hoped was a reassuring smile. The hand he gripped was damp and slippery.

'I shouldn't be here,' said the contact.

The man's shirt collar was frayed, his suit jacket old and

stained. He definitely needed the money, or he probably wouldn't have turned up. 'Well, thanks for coming anyway,' said Luke, breezily. 'Can I get you something to drink?'

The man shook his head. 'I haven't much time,' he said.

'No, of course,' said Luke. 'So, er, have you had a chance to think about what we discussed, the last time we met?'

'I'm not clear on what you're proposing,' he replied, shuffling his chair closer to Luke's. 'Please. Tell me what exactly you want from me.'

Here we go. Deep breath. Take the plunge. This was the watershed moment when Luke would shift from one dimension to another, from legit to illicit. He reached into the inside left pocket of his jacket, drew out an unmarked envelope and put it on the table, keeping it covered with his hand. 'I'd like to offer you a job,' he said. No reaction. Okay, keep it going. 'A job that pays good money.' The man's eyes flicked down towards the envelope. Luke kept it covered. 'In here,' he continued, tapping the envelope with his fingertips, 'is something to get you started. Think of it as a welcome present from my employers.'

The man looked perplexed, his brow furrowed. 'But I still don't understand,' he protested. 'What is it you want me to do?'

Enough. Surely we've been through this already. It was time to stop beating about the bush. Luke needed to lay his cards on the table. 'I need you to . . .' he hesitated. He had to phrase this just right. There could be no misunderstanding. The contact was watching him intently now, waiting to hear how he would finish the sentence. His eyes, keen as a hawk's, met Luke's. 'I need you to get me the passcode for the state security data files.' There. He had blurted it out in one breath, as if expelling some toxic object from his system.

What happened next took place in a dizzying blur. Before Luke had a chance to react he saw the contact reach beneath the table. Suddenly a high-pitched alarm was sounding and the door crashed in. Two bulky figures dressed in uniforms he didn't recognize came barrelling through the open doorway and lifted Luke out of his chair, then pinned him hard against the wall. It was too late to resist: one already had a hand clenched around his balls while the other held a baton to his throat.

The 'contact' rose slowly from his chair, took out a handkerchief and wiped a layer of shiny theatrical grease off his face, then folded it away, tucking it neatly back into his pocket. He sauntered over to where Luke stood, restrained by both arms, and smiled affably. 'Better luck next time, Carlton. I'm afraid that was a failed pitch. You showed your hand much too soon.' He patted Luke on the shoulder and nodded to the two 'guards' to let him go. 'There's tea and biscuits in the debriefing room when you're ready. They'll play back the tapes to everyone in there.'

Luke's shoulders slumped. He was not used to failure.

'Listen,' the 'contact' added, 'practically everyone fails this part of the course the first time round. You'll get another shot tomorrow.' He left with a wink, calling over his shoulder: 'Nobody said agent running was easy.'

Chapter 2

OUTSIDE IT WAS drizzling. Not enough to bring out the umbrellas in force, just a slow, sad seepage from the colourless November sky, turning the stained pavements of Whitehall wet and sleek. Sir Charles Bennett disliked November: it came too late in the year for a warm weekend in the Mediterranean and too early for the ski season. But this November, as Britain's National Security Adviser, he had rather bigger things to worry about.

'Let me bring you all up to speed,' he told the room, which was full of concerned faces. 'Iran . . .' There were some knowing nods. 'Or more specifically,' he continued, 'the Strait of Hormuz. This is threatening to turn into a full-blown international crisis. Already this month the US Navy has recorded three hostile approaches towards their vessels by Iranian missile boats in the strait. One got within six hundred metres of a US warship and only stopped when it was fired upon.'

He paused, aware that all eyes around the table were focused on him, from the PM down to the Cabinet Office minute-taker, a young lad in a blue checked shirt and no tie, fresh out of university.

'And, yes, you might be thinking, So what?' resumed Bennett. 'Surely we've been here before. And we have – under the previous US administration. But things are very different in the White

6

House now. The current administration has made it abundantly clear it sees Iran as the number-one enemy.' He could see the Foreign Secretary waving, trying to catch his eye. Geoffrey Chaplin was a notoriously ambitious member of the Cabinet and Bennett did not welcome this interruption. 'Yes, Geoffrey? You wanted to say something?'

'That is not, I should point out, a view shared by this government,' said the Foreign Secretary. 'We reopened our embassy in Tehran just over two years ago. In fact, I was thinking it's probably time I paid a visit there. Pour a bit of oil on troubled waters, so to speak.'

'Thank you, Foreign Secretary.' Bennett moved on to his point: 'So, we are getting dangerously close to a flashpoint in the Gulf. The Iranians have test-fired a number of ballistic missiles this year and Washington has very publicly "put them on notice", whatever that means.'

'What does it mean, precisely?' asked the Prime Minister, who tried never to miss the weekly National Security Council meeting.

Bennett turned for help to the woman on his right, Jane Haslett, the Permanent Under Secretary of State for Foreign and Commonwealth Affairs, an absurdly pompous title. 'Jane? Any clues?'

'Prime Minister, we're still trying to decipher the smoke signals from Washington,' she replied, 'but our best interpretation is that the White House has drawn a line in the sand, so to speak.' There was a short silence, and even the young graduate paused in his minute-taking to look up.

'Meaning what, exactly?' said the PM.

'Meaning,' replied the FCO Chief, 'that the next major provocation they see coming from Iran will be the cue for a military response. There are certain figures in the Pentagon – and I'm not going to name names – but some people in Washington are just itching to have a go at the Iranians.' Further down the table the Minister for International Development groaned and covered her face with her hands, shaking her head in despair.

'The problem is,' continued Jane Haslett, 'there are also certain people in Iran, some of the so-called hardliners, who seem to want exactly the same thing.'

'What – war with the United States?' asked the Home Secretary, incredulous. 'Why would they possibly want that? It would be suicide!'

'Yes . . . and no.' A career diplomat, Jane Haslett had spent a lifetime evaluating all the options, all the angles, yet never quite committing herself to one course of action or another, just in case it turned out to be wrong. 'They don't want all-out war, of course not, but they know it won't come to that. Russia and Turkey will step in and stop it before it goes too far. No, what they want is an end to peace. They don't like all this rapprochement with Europe – they don't even like the Vienna deal, the nuclear pact that saw the sanctions lifted. Isolation suited them just fine. They made a lot of money out of those sanctions, which gave them extraordinary power.'

'So, Prime Minister, if you'll allow me?' Bennett held up his hand. 'I think we should focus today on what this actually means for *this* country. And I have to tell you that the latest Joint Intelligence Committee assessment makes for pretty grim reading.' He opened a file on the table in front of him and took out a thin pile of documents, each bordered with a scarlet edge and marked 'Strap 2 Top Secret'. He held them up vertically, tapped them once to shuffle them into line, then passed them down the table. 'These are all numbered and we expect them back when we finish here.'

'Strewth,' someone muttered, as they started to read.

'The headline point here,' said the National Security Adviser, speaking as they read the document before them, 'and it absolutely cannot leave this room, is that if even a *limited* conflict breaks out between Iran and the US, we can expect the IRGC, the Iranian Revolutionary Guards Corps, to mine the Strait of Hormuz and make it impassable to shipping. That strait . . .' he paused for emphasis '. . . is the world's most strategic chokepoint. Over sixteen million barrels of oil pass through it every day and it's where at least thirty per cent of our oil comes from. So, what does that mean for us here in Britain if it's blocked for any length of time?' He was now looking straight at the Home Secretary. 'It means a chronic fuel shortage, disruption of food deliveries, then hospitals, factories, lifts, generators all going without power. In short, it means the lights going out.'

He rarely showed emotion but now he was picking up tempo, enunciating every word, every syllable. 'You can forget about switching over to renewables if this happens. That won't be enough to bail us out. Let me be blunt. If war breaks out in the Gulf, and the Strait of Hormuz is blocked, people are going to die. Not just over there but right here in Britain, in our hospitals and in our homes. Which is why . . .' again, the pause '. . . it must be our number-one priority to stop it happening.'

Chapter 3

Shahid Beheshti airbase, Iran

WHEN IT CAME to certain things, such as how he took his tea, Karim Zamani was fastidious. No glass was complete without the addition of *nabot*, the uniquely Persian sticks of crystallized sugar, tinged yellow with saffron. Wearing the dark green uniform and gold braid of a senior officer in the Sepah, the Iranian Revolutionary Guards Corps, he held the teaspoon between the tips of his thumb and forefinger and slowly twirled it, the scalding liquid swirling around the tulip-shaped glass, which had been handed to him moments earlier on a patterned saucer. It was an oddly dainty gesture for a man who wielded such power, such influence. He blew on the tea and took a sip. No, still too hot.

Placing the glass on the small table beside him, he turned to his host, the investigations officer. Through the cracked, stained window of the room in which they sat, the sun streamed in, glinting off Zamani's rectangular spectacles and picking out the flecks of grey in his neatly trimmed beard.

'How serious is the problem?' he asked quietly, regarding the man with unblinking eyes.

The other was about to answer but had to wait as the roar of an aircraft engine rose, then fell, outside the window. An ageing

10

US-built C130 transport plane, cannibalized for spare parts during the long years of sanctions, was lumbering into the air.

'It could have been very serious,' the investigations officer replied, 'but we have everything under control now.'

Zamani said nothing. How many times had he heard that glib line from his subordinates? How many times had he checked up on them only to find it wasn't so? How many times had he been forced to make an example of them so they would never lie to him again?

'We discovered all three had secret social-media accounts,' continued the investigator. 'Under false names, of course. They were using a proxy server in Dubai, thinking they could hide by going through VPN.'

'VPN?' questioned Zamani.

'Virtual Privacy Network. I'm told people use it to hide what they're up to online. But we caught them all the same.'

'And how,' Zamani asked, as he picked up his glass of tea again, 'did you manage that?'

'Our Chinese friends have been most helpful. You remember the ZTE monitoring system we bought from them a few years back?' Zamani looked blank. The acronym meant nothing to him. 'Well, it's more than serving our purposes. We can pinpoint users right down to the room in their house, intercept their text messages, see everything and everyone they're accessing online. I tell you, Karim-*jaan*, it's like we're standing over their shoulder and they can't see us!'

Karim Zamani finally took another sip of his tea. It had cooled just enough to drink but a thin curl of steam still rose from its surface.

His host now came to the point. 'So, the three we caught, they were importing some dangerous ideas and spreading them here on the base. By God, Karim-*jaan*, it was like a cancer.'

'What kind of ideas?' Zamani enquired softly.

'Dangerous ones. A threat to our national security. Misguided, liberal, Western ideas. Foolish delusions about democracy and free speech. Questioning the wisdom of the Supreme Leader.

11

These are ideas that could threaten the Jumhuri Islami, the Islamic Republic. They were even messaging people in the US, in London, in Germany . . .'

'And in the Zionist Entity?' prompted Zamani, using his organization's expression for the State of Israel.

'We haven't found proof of that yet. But I am certain they will confess to it in good time.'

'Make sure they do,' said Zamani. 'And where are they now, these three *kha'in*?' Already he was calling them traitors. 'Have they been processed yet?'

'We have carried out initial interrogations, naturally. But we'll be sending them to the Revolutionary Court for trial.'

Karim Zamani stood up, smoothing the creases in his tunic as he did so. 'I would like to see them,' he said abruptly.

The smell hit them the moment the heavy steel door was yanked open. Sweat, fear and faeces. Three things that come with the territory for those unlucky enough to see the inside of a Sepahi holding cell. The prisoners were sitting in a row against the opposite wall, still wearing their military uniforms but stripped of their ranks, their knees drawn up close to their chests, their ankles shackled to chains fixed to heavy iron rings on the wall. On the ceiling, a single neon striplight, blotched grey with the collective bodies of long-dead insects, fizzed and flickered but never went off, day or night. No windows. In the corner an open toilet bucket hummed with flies.

Karim Zamani stood in the middle of the cell and surveyed the men, the investigations officer at his side. 'Which one is the ringleader?' he asked.

The other man pointed to the figure sitting on the right. He was a good-looking young man, or he might have been before the purple bruises had so disfigured his face. When he raised his head to look up at them, Zamani thought he saw something flash in his eyes. What was it? Defiance? Arrogance? No matter. They all had that when they were first brought in. It rarely lasted more than a few days, a week at most.

12

Zamani walked over to him and crouched down to his level. He took the man's jaw in his hand, exerting just enough pressure on his bones to cause him pain. Zamani stared straight at him for some time, saying nothing, then turned back to the investigator. 'Break his bones,' he said quietly. 'And make the others watch while it's done.'

Chapter 4

South coast, England

'WELL, CONGRATULATIONS TO all of you. You've made it this far so give yourselves a pat on the back.' The training director stood at the far end of the long room, facing his students with both hands thrust into his trouser pockets. To Luke, it looked like contrived nonchalance.

'My name is Jim Donaldson – and that is my real name by the way.' He gave a short chuckle. 'I'm your course director on the agent-running course. First off, a bit of background about me . . .'

Luke cast a discreet glance around the room. He knew first impressions could be deceptive but he was pretty damn sure no one else here had the same sort of operational experience he had. Iraq and Afghanistan with the Royal Marines, then places he could never talk about from when he'd done his four years with the Special Boat Service. All that followed by a horrendously dangerous mission on contract for SIS, the Secret Intelligence Service, in Colombia. How many others here, he wondered, had ballsed up their practice pitch like he had just now?

Now that he had joined the Service, as a full-time case officer, Luke was surprised to find what a steep learning curve he was on. Of the three career streams he had had to choose from – reports officer, targeting, and agent running – there had never been any doubt as to which one he would head into. His psych assessment profile had been unequivocal on that. It had to be agent running. The sharp end. The most difficult and dangerous job in human intelligence work.

'Luke Carlton,' it had read, 'has exactly the right temperament and aptitude for recruiting and running agents in hostile environments. He is recommended for Category 1 operations.' It was the path that everyone with him in this room had also been selected for. The young man on his left had introduced himself that morning. Ginger-haired, freckled, well spoken, a 2:1 from SOAS in Middle Eastern studies, he was wearing a green gilet over a checked shirt, fawn trousers and polished brown brogues. All a bit *Horse & Hound*, thought Luke, but the woman on his right was intriguing. At thirty-seven, Luke had reckoned he would be the oldest trainee on the course but she must have been a good five years older, her bare, muscular arms coated with a liberal scattering of tattoos. 'Spikes', read one, in a florid purple italic. He wondered what special skills had brought her to this room today.

'I take it,' Donaldson was saying, 'that you're all familiar by now with what we like to call the intelligence cycle.' He had finished talking about himself and was on to his main brief. He looked around the room, hands still in his pockets. 'Whitehall sets the requirements, our targeting officers identify the potential agent, we work out a way to get you in front of them, you try to recruit them and if you're successful . . . *if* you're successful . . .' Donaldson looked meaningfully at the first row of faces just in front of Luke '. . . then the material you produce will go to a reports officer who will make their own judgement of whether it's credible. Then he or she will send the final version to Whitehall. Are we all clear on that?'

'And what if they don't think it's credible?' It was a man in the third row, late twenties, sitting just behind Luke. A Brummie, Luke guessed from his accent. Sideburns, gold stud earring, cheeky smile.

Donaldson took his hands out of his pockets, placed them

on his hips and grinned. 'That's a fair question, young man,' he replied. 'These days, there are strict Chinese walls in place between agent runners – that's you – and the reports officers. If something doesn't smell right about the product you're sending them, they'll send it right back to you, believe me.'

Luke heard the door open behind him and turned in his chair to see half a dozen of the training staff file in and take their places against the wall at the back, arms folded across their chests. He knew exactly what they'd been doing: watching him and the others through CCTV cameras from a monitoring room upstairs as they made their practice pitches. The 'agents' were there, too, all retired intelligence officers acting their parts. They must have been writing up their appraisals just now, so ritual-humiliation time was coming up.

'Anyway,' Donaldson was saying briskly, rubbing his hands together, 'let's move on.' He surveyed the room, as if searching for something in the rows of faces that stared back at him. 'Cover profiles. Your alter ego. Your "legend", as our friend John le Carré would call it. I believe you've all had a chance to talk these through with your team managers and the security advisers.' Luke looked around for reactions. No one had had this conversation with him yet. It wasn't supposed to be scheduled until next month.

'Brendan!' declared Donaldson, projecting his voice a little more than usual. He was looking straight at Luke.

'That's right. Fellow in the second row. Yes, you, sir. Brendan Hall. How well d'you know your cover?'

Luke couldn't help it: he laughed. 'I'm sorry,' he said, trying to keep a straight face. 'I don't think you mean me. I'm not Brendan Hall.' What a ridiculous cover name, he thought. Who would choose that? It sounded like a stately home.

Donaldson's face clouded. The false bonhomie, the practised nonchalance were gone. 'So you think intelligence work is a bit of a joke?' he shot back. 'A bit of a laugh, is it? Well, let me tell you, your cover story is everything. It's what you live by. It's the difference between a successful agent runner and – and a total failure!'

It could even cost someone their life. Just think about that for a moment. If you can't maintain a convincing cover, you're no use to us in the field and furthermore—'

Donaldson stopped in mid-flow. A woman in a charcoal business suit had come up to the front of the room and was now whispering something in his ear. Both were looking at Luke as she spoke.

'Ah. It seems,' resumed Donaldson, his tone towards Luke rather more conciliatory, 'that I've been a little premature in your case. I do apologize. If I could ask you to step outside the room, please, some people from Vauxhall Cross are waiting to see you.'

Chapter 5

LUKE FOUND ANGELA Scott outside the lecture block. She was standing, facing out to sea by the Napoleonic fort's low wall next to the cannons, a place that had seen generations of trainee spies pass through. Hunched into the collar of her Halifax Traders windbreaker, she was taking a long drag on a cigarette. Luke could not remember ever seeing his MI6 line manager smoking, but then again, this was a woman who kept her private life strictly to herself.

'Cover names,' Angela said, as he walked up to her. He watched her turn her delicate freckled face towards him and smile in greeting. Pale, interesting, dedicated Angela. Forty-one, unmarried, half a lifetime devoted to the Service and someone he trusted completely.

'Yes. D'you want to explain what that was about in there?' said Luke. 'I thought we weren't discussing mine till next month.'

'We're not, you're right. Don't worry about that for now. We've got something more important to discuss.'

She was wrapped up against the November chill while he was still in his shirtsleeves. 'Hey!' she exclaimed. 'Aren't you freezing?' As if to emphasize her point, a gust blew in off the English Channel, whipping the hair across her forehead. Angela stubbed out her cigarette, flicked it over the sea wall and looked at him questioningly. 'We can go inside, if you'd prefer?'

'I'm fine, thanks,' he said, as a blast of sea spray splashed across his cheek. 'It reminds me of my time in the Corps.'

'Here's what's going to happen,' she said. 'In a couple of minutes a man will come through that door and join us out here. He's called Graham Leach and he's our Head of Iran and Caucasus.'

Luke glanced instinctively at the door he had come through but it remained shut.

'He's come down here to see you, Luke, and the job he's going to ask you to do is not without risks. I'm here to remind you, as your line manager, that you don't have to accept it if you don't want to. We're not the Stasi. Okay, here he comes now.'

Leach shut the door behind him and strode over to join them. Luke immediately clocked the faded purple scar below his right eye. In another time, another age, it might have resulted from duelling, and it gave him a certain swashbuckling appearance. Later he'd ask where it had come from.

'Graham Leach.' He held out his hand and Luke gripped it. 'How's the course going?'

'So-so,' replied Luke. 'Not sure I impressed anyone this morning with my pitching skills. But I'm guessing you haven't come down here to talk about that.'

'No, I haven't. In fact, we're pulling you off the course.' Leach caught the look on Luke's face and quickly reassured him. 'It's all right, we're not failing you. We'll put you on the next one. It's just that something rather urgent's come up, let's call it an opportunity, and we'd like you to be involved.'

'I'm listening.'

'The Service has been tasked to increase its penetration of Iran.' Luke kept a straight face. Of course he knew exactly what that word meant in intelligence terms, but even now, after all these months of working for MI6, it still made him smile. 'Penetration' made him think of sex. 'I'm talking specifically here about the IRGC,' Leach continued. 'You're familiar with them, I take it?'

'The Revolutionary Guards. Yes, I am,' Luke said. 'We had a few close encounters with their boats in the Gulf when I was serving as a Royal Marine.'

'I'm sure you did. Well, we're picking up signs that a hardcore element within that organization is hell-bent on sabotaging the 2015 nuclear deal. The fact is, it's set back their nuclear ambitions by fifteen years but now it's under threat from both sides. Washington doesn't like it and wants to rip it up, and in Iran the hardcore revolutionaries don't like it. They're trying to trip up the moderates in their government and undermine anyone who's looking to open up Iran to the rest of the world. Especially since the election in May. Plus they seem to be spoiling for a fight with the US Navy right now, which would clearly be disastrous for everyone.'

Luke turned his face towards the breeze as it blew in off the grey chop. A trawler was making heavy progress through the swell, its bow rising and falling. He had done time on ships in seas like that, clinging to a slippery bulkhead, and didn't envy the men onboard. He turned back to face Leach. He was still waiting for the punchline. 'So where do I come in, sir?'

Leach gave a short, embarrassed laugh. 'Come on, Luke. You can drop the "sir". You've been with us long enough now to know we don't do formality.'

'Sorry. Old habits.'

'We need to know more about what the hardliners in Iran are up to.' It was Angela who spoke this time. 'We have agents there, obviously – we wouldn't be much good as a service if we didn't. But the Chief wants us to get someone placed upstream who can tap right into what the hardliners are thinking, what their next move is.'

'And you've found someone?' Luke looked from Angela to Leach and back again.

'Yes,' she replied. 'Targeting have come up with someone perfectly placed – *if* we can get close to him. Karim Zamani is a very senior official in the IRGC, the Revolutionary Guards. He's also on their Supreme Committee for Peaceful Nuclear Development.'

Luke was getting seriously cold, standing by the sea wall in his cotton shirt, but he was damned if he was going to admit it. 'You do know,' he reminded them, 'that I don't speak a word of

Farsi? That I've never been to Iran? And that I'm quite probably on some list of theirs from my time in Special Forces?'

Angela laid a hand on his arm. 'Yes, we know all of that, Luke,' she said soothingly. 'Come on, I think it's time we continued this conversation indoors. You may be hard as nails, but Graham and I are absolutely freezing out here.'

They found a side room and sat down at a circular table.

'Oh!' said Leach, noticing Luke's missing finger for the first time. 'Mind if I ask what happened there?'

Luke gave a weary smile. He had had to tell this story so many times. 'Afghanistan,' he answered. 'I lost the middle finger to a Taliban bullet in a firefight. Could have been a whole lot worse.'

Leach looked impressed.

'Can I ask how you got the scar?' Luke nodded towards the purple line just below Leach's eye.

'This? Kinshasa. A long time ago, on my first overseas posting. Just a misunderstanding.'

Nothing more was said but an unspoken connection had been forged between the two men.

'Right, well, back to Iran,' continued Leach, briskly. 'Zamani himself is not a good target for us. He's fiercely loyal to his masters in the Sepah, the Revolutionary Guards Corps. It's in his blood. But his family are a different matter.' He nodded at Angela, who produced a thin sheaf of photographs from her bag and passed them to Leach. He selected one and handed it to Luke. 'This is his wife, Forouz Zamani.'

Luke tilted the photograph to avoid the reflective sheen from the neon light on the ceiling. The face that looked back at him was that of an attractive woman in her forties, with intelligent brown eyes. Perhaps a little work had been done here and there: the nose seemed a little too delicate for the rest of her face.

'She comes from a very well-connected family,' Leach went on. 'Business interests right across the country, so plenty of money there.'

'What does she do with it?' Luke asked.

'She collects art,' said Angela. 'Persian art, mostly. And she travels a lot on business. Berlin, London, New York, the Gulf.'

'They sound an oddly matched couple. She's hardly the revolutionary zealot,' Luke remarked.

'She's quite the opposite,' said Leach. 'We're hearing there may be serious strains in their relationship.'

Luke pushed his chair back from the table and folded his arms. 'Okay, so I'm guessing where this is going,' he said. 'You want me to get myself in front of her and try to recruit her?'

The pair from Vauxhall Cross smiled and shook their heads.

'Good guess, but no.' Leach handed him a second photograph. 'This is the person we want you to recruit. She's his daughter, Tannaz Zamani. She's twenty-two, attends Tehran University, she's the apple of her father's eye, and she absolutely hates him.'

Chapter 6

Tehran

THE PARTY WAS strictly word-of-mouth, invitation only. Parked in the leafy side-streets of north Tehran, off Fereshteh Street, the drivers of the imported luxury 4x4s sat patiently in the dark while their passengers lost themselves in another world inside the darkened three-storey house. The drivers kept their engines running, watching, wary, ready with the denial story in case the Gasht-e-Ershad, the morality police, came banging on the window and asking awkward questions.

It was a substantial mansion set in substantial grounds, built in the 1900s, its creamy walls fronted by imposing faux-Roman columns and a flight of wide, sweeping steps guarded by a pair of stone lions. There were domed cupolas, balconies and balustrades. It had once been home to a wealthy family with close connections to the Shah, long ago departed for a different life in Santa Monica. Back then, in the 1970s, before the seismic upheaval that was Iran's Islamic Revolution, the lights would have been blazing late into the night, the sound of Western music – the Bee Gees, Blondie, Boney M – spilling out into the street, neighbours dropping by to join in. Not these days. You could still have fun in Tehran, a lot of fun, if you moved in the right circles, but you had to be careful and you needed to know which parties to avoid. All it took was for word to get out to one wrong person and you could land yourself in a whole world of pain.

Pulling up in a taxi, Tannaz shuddered to think of what had happened to her friend Farah, swept up in that police raid back in April, carted off in a windowless van to the detention centre at Vozara. Still wearing that designer dress of hers and the earrings, questioned, humiliated, searched in the most intimate, invasive way imaginable, then weeks later forced to sign a confession to immorality. She was out now, with a stern caution, but everyone agreed she had never been the same since.

Tannaz chose her friends carefully, perhaps even more carefully than most, given who her father was. Coming to this party was far more than a social call: it was a deliberate act of rebellion against him. She loathed what he stood for, all those killjoy religious rules and telling people to cover up in public. She was sick of hearing how the Islamic Revolution had cleansed Iran in 1979 and how terrible life had been under the Shah. What did she care? The Shah had been dead for fifteen years by the time she was born. And yet, despite everything, she knew that her father, Karim, loved her, doted on her in his way. It was as if he saw in her what had once made him fall in love with her mother. She shuddered, repulsed by the thought.

Tonight it was a trusted crowd – she would know everyone – but still she chose to come by taxi. The family driver was not a risk worth taking. She let herself out of the rear door and pulled the black folds of her *chador* tight around her face. There had even been stories of the Gasht-e-Ershad hiding in the shadows outside parties like this, quietly taking pictures and, days later, presenting them as irrefutable evidence in a police interrogation room.

Outside the blue-painted steel gates she pressed the buzzer twice, then once again. The agreed signal. A tiny window with a grille opened and a man's clean-shaven face peered out at her. There was a pause, then the gate slid back just far enough to let her slip through. Once inside the inner courtyard she swept the veil off her face and let it hang loose across her shoulders. Two

24

young men with walkie-talkies nodded to her in recognition. They pointed over their shoulders to where a single, fat candle cast a flickering pool of light onto the path. Encased in glass against the chill evening breeze, it had been planted in a bucket of sand. Tannaz strode past it in her Valentino sandals. She knew the way. She had been there before. If she stood still, which she did now, and held her head to one side, she could just make out the faint sound of voices laughing from upstairs. And music. Not the Bee Gees, these days: 'Saturday Night Fever' had given way to Beyoncé, Rihanna and, more often, Iranian singers, like Kiosk and King Raam, now trending in twenty-first-century Iran.

Tannaz pushed open the door on the ground floor, removed her *chador*, and handed it to a boy in a Led Zeppelin T-shirt. Revealed in her strapless black minidress, split right up the thigh, and her metallic leather sandals, she was like a different being. Down a carpeted corridor, the music pumping louder now, then through another door – and suddenly she was in a world of kaleidoscopic lights and sinuous, gyrating bodies, dancing, twirling, embracing. A young DJ was nodding rhythmically to the music at a deck, earphones on, eyes shut, a sweet smile of contentment on his face. That would be Rami, she thought, stoned again.

From out of the shadows friends emerged and hugged her wildly, dragging her straight onto the dance-floor. Someone offered her a shot of vodka, and she tossed her hair to one side as she knocked it back. A boy with gelled hair and a designer leather jacket draped an arm around her, planted a wet kiss on her cheek and offered her a joint. Tannaz laughed, waved it away, then changed her mind, took a long drag and handed it back. The boy blew her another kiss, then wrapped his arms around his boyfriend's waist, their hips grinding together in time to the music.

Upstairs it was a different scene, more chilled, less manic. As Tannaz went in search of a bathroom she found herself stepping over slumped figures in the corridor. Through an open doorway, several of her friends were sprawled on cushions. Between them, on the table, lay a small mountain of coke. Not her thing. There was a queue outside the bathroom so she moved on, making her way upstairs to the top floor. There was a master bedroom, she remembered, with an ensuite. Probably, she thought afterwards, she should have stopped and turned the moment she heard the sounds but she really, really needed the loo so in she went.

She froze in the doorway. How many were on the bed? Five? Six? Seven, even? With all the thrusting and groaning and gasping, it was hard to tell. The room was a blur of intertwined limbs, of hairy buttocks and heaving breasts, shiny with sweat in the yellow glow of the bedside lamps.

'Tannaz-*jaan!*' someone called. 'Come and join us!'

'*Goh khordi.* Oh, shit.' Her mobile was going off in her bag. She turned away and pulled out her phone. Her father. At this time of night. Not good: four missed calls and a text: *Where are you? Nana is unwell. Come home now or I will send someone to find you.*

Tannaz knew exactly what that meant. Two minutes later she was outside, back in her all-enveloping black *chador*, flagging down a taxi in the street. No one would have guessed she had come from an orgy. She crammed a stick of menthol-flavoured chewing gum into her mouth and spritzed a squirt of perfume on her face to hide the smell of alcohol. The driver caught her eye in his mirror and grinned knowingly. She averted her gaze, staring intently at the lights of north Tehran as they flashed past the window. How long could she keep up this secret double life, this lie? Free-spirited, hedonistic, party-going twenty-two-year-old by choice, conservative citizen of the Islamic Republic of Iran by birth. Her father would kill her if he knew what she got up to and, she reminded herself, he was not just anyone. He was a very senior officer in the Revolutionary Guards. He was Karim Zamani.

Chapter 7

Parchin Military Complex, Iran

DRIVING SOUTH-EAST OUT of Tehran down Highway 44 or, rather, being driven, Karim Zamani squinted up at the early-morning sun. Slanting low over the powdery, ochre-coloured hills, streaked red with ore and dusted with the first snows of winter, it glinted off the golden domes of a roadside mosque. He liked winter. It reminded him of his childhood, growing up in the foothills of the mighty Elburz Mountains. Old enough, just, to remember standing shoeless by the side of the road, watching the convoys of rich people's cars going past, heading up to the ski resorts of Shemshak and Dizin in their furs and aviator sunglasses. The Shah's people. The enemy. Long gone now but what had replaced them? Another elite, the new rich of Tehran in their Lexuses and Porsche Cayennes, clogging the weekend roads out of the capital. Karim Zamani disapproved of this flagrant display of affluence, with its connotations of Western cultural decadence. And then there was his wife, Forouz, elegant, fragrant Forouz, her curious obsession with art and all the costly visits to galleries in Europe. Some of her tastes were anathema to him but he tolerated them because her family were rich and powerful, and she had defied them to marry him when he hadn't had a pot to piss in. But his daughter, Tannaz? Now she was a worry. He had resisted allowing her to attend Tehran University. And now look what was happening. He was convinced that, as he had feared, she was mixing with the wrong sort of people. He should have her followed, or married off, or both.

Karim Zamani put aside these thoughts as he sat up in the back seat and placed the braided peaked cap on his head as they approached the first gates. He was wearing his dark green dress uniform, the gold wreath and crossed-sword epaulettes on his shoulders denoting his IRGC rank of Second Brigadier General. It was a rank to be respected and even now, after all these years of service to the Islamic Revolution, he felt a twinge of pride each time he put it on.

A large sign read in Farsi and in English: 'Parchin Military Complex. No photography'. ID check, three armed guards, weapons lowered as they recognized him, saluting him smartly and waving his car through. Down a dusty road beside a chain-link fence, guard towers, red-and-white-striped barriers, speed bumps, more security checks, and then a smaller, narrower road, unpaved, hugging the contours of the mountain, leading away from the main complex until it reached what might, at first glance, have been taken to be a natural cave. It was no cave. A reinforced-steel door sealed the entrance to a tunnel bored deep into the rock face. No guards this time, but Karim Zamani understood what he had to do. Slowly, carefully, knowing he was being watched by hidden cameras, he stepped out of the car and walked to the steel door. He reached inside his jacket and pulled out a small digital LED device, then peered closer at the flickering green numbers displayed on the screen. He keyed them into a console on the side of the door. For a moment nothing happened. Then, quietly, it slid open. He nodded at the car and it drove off to park in the shadow of a nearby cliff.

Inside the tunnel Zamani adjusted his eyes to the semi-darkness. The sodium bulbs embedded in the walls at intervals gave off a half-hearted light as if nearing the end of their useful life. He walked on, down the empty tunnel, and stopped at a door. Another console, set into the wall, this time with an iris scanner. He removed his spectacles, placing them carefully in the pocket inside his tunic, then placed his hands on the console and leaned forward slightly, bringing his eyes level with the scanner. Four seconds later there was a discreet click and the door opened to reveal two armed guards wearing gloves and off-white face masks. They spoke into a radio, then handed him his own pair of protective gloves and a mask. Flanking him, side by side and saying nothing, they went down in the lift together. Down and down they descended, into what felt like the very core of the Earth. The lift had no sides and seemed to scrape the surface of the exposed rock until it stopped with a jolt and the guards clanked open the mesh gate.

Zamani stepped out into the subterranean corridor and smiled. The team were all assembled, waiting for him, expectant and deferential in their white lab coats.

'*Khosh amadid, Rais,*' said the man in front, the chief scientist, stepping forward to greet him. 'Welcome, Commander.'

Zamani moved down the line, greeting each one in turn, telling them how important their work was in the service of the nation. He resisted the temptation to look at his watch. With so many responsibilities in the Revolutionary Guards Corps, he was always pressed for time. But then he remembered. Time was of little importance on this visit. This was a strategic project that transcended all timetables.

They moved down the narrow corridor in single file, turned left, through another doorway, more guards, weapons clasped tightly to their chests, and on down a passageway until they came to a door marked with a large yellow-and-black triangular nuclear hazard symbol. The chief scientist stepped forward and slotted his electronic pass into a reader. The door opened into a control room where more men in white coats were working at a bank of computer terminals. After the catastrophe of the Stuxnet virus, a piece of computer malware developed by US and Israeli scientists, introduced via a USB stick that had wiped out around a thousand of Iran's nuclear-enrichment centrifuges at Natanz, everyone in the room had had their backgrounds and family connections exhaustively checked and rechecked. The project under way down here, hundreds of feet below the wrinkled deserts of northern Iran, was such a closely guarded secret that almost no one in government even knew it existed.

When they were all assembled inside the control room, the scientists looked at Karim Zamani, waiting for him to give the order to begin.

'Run the sequence,' he said quietly, then stood back, arms folded, waiting and watching intently. All faces turned towards a chamber, separated from them by a thick glass screen. On the other side a long, thin ballistic missile rested on a metal stand. It was painted in khaki camouflage but marked with the Farsi letters spelling the word *Zolfaghar*. A serial number was stencilled on its side, B-313-92-05, and next to that the tricolor of the Iranian national flag: green, white and red. But where the business end of the missile should have been, at the pointed tip, there was a gaping hole, a cavity waiting to be filled. That was as it should be.

Now a remotely controlled robotic vehicle on caterpillar tracks moved slowly towards the front of the missile. Its rear was held down with heavy lead weights for balance while from its front protruded a small crane. Beneath that, hanging by chains, was a white cylinder the size of a diminutive barrel, the black-and-yellow triangle stencilled on the side denoting its radioactive content. Painstakingly slowly, centimetre by centimetre, the cylinder was positioned over the cavity in the missile, then lowered until it was settled into its new home. Immediately, tumultuous applause broke out in the control room, and the chief scientist beamed with pride. He turned to address Karim Zamani. 'We are close now, very close, to completion. Just a few more weeks of tests and then everything will be ready, God willing.'

A strange, almost beatific expression had come over Zamani's face. His normally stern demeanour had given way to something else: he looked almost happy, as if he finally felt himself at peace with the world. Those who didn't know him might easily make the mistake of thinking him a humourless man, a man incapable of kindness or generosity, but that was far from true. He would see to it now that every single person working on this project was amply rewarded. When he spoke, his rich, gravelly voice carried a note of triumph.

'You are doing magnificent work here,' he told them. 'What you have achieved already, in this blessed laboratory, is a symbol of our struggle against the shackles imposed on us by neo-imperialist and Zionist powers. Powers that would seek to humiliate and belittle us. When, soon, your work here is complete, we will show the world that the Islamic Republic of Iran is nobody's servant. We have an absolute right to nuclear power.' Zamani paused, searching their faces, then raised his voice in a crescendo: 'And, by God,' he thundered, 'we have a right to *become* a nuclear power. My brothers, this warhead you are creating here *is* that power.'

The applause lasted for several minutes in that underground chamber, unheard by the world, more than a hundred metres above. Everyone present had a smile on his face, including an individual who was not smiling inside. Someone who was deeply disturbed by what he'd just witnessed. Someone who knew he needed to get word of this to those who should know, even if that meant risking his own life.

Chapter 8

NO POT OF coffee, no tray of biscuits, no rambling preliminaries. Just straight down to business. Eight were sitting round the boardroom table on the sixth floor at Vauxhall Cross, the cream-and-emerald Thameside monolith that served as the headquarters of Britain's Secret Intelligence Service, MI6. The last to arrive, Luke took his place beside Angela and kept a respectful silence: he had been officially on their books for less than a year.

As the man in charge of Iran and Caucasus, Graham Leach was in the hot seat and the first to speak. He cut straight to the chase. 'Black Run has broken cover.' He let that sink in around the table.

Luke, nonplussed, leaned over to Angela. 'Black Run?' he whispered.

'One of our agents inside Iran,' she whispered back. 'He's been sending us grade-A product.'

Grade-A product? He wondered how they came up with these terms. It made MI6 sound like an iron-ore smelting plant.

'He had eyes on Echo Sierra two days ago,' Leach was telling the room. 'At Parchin.'

'Oh, Christ,' said someone, quietly.

Again Luke had to nudge Angela for a translation. He had

32

always expected to find himself in a world of codenames at SIS, just hadn't imagined he'd have to guess whom they referred to.

'Echo Sierra,' answered Angela, 'is Karim Zamani. It's in your briefing pack.' She shot him an admonishing look.

'It gets worse,' Leach was saying. 'Echo Sierra didn't visit the main complex. He went straight down to Tunnel Six.'

'Tunnel Six?' interrupted a bearded Scotsman in a short-sleeved shirt, nervously tapping a biro on the table. 'The one they claimed was abandoned? Is he absolutely certain?'

'A hundred per cent,' said Leach. 'He was there in person. So, given what we know about Echo Sierra's role on the nuclear committee, this leads us down a number of possible paths. None are good.'

'Any more detail?' asked the Scot. 'Any more flesh you can put on the bones?'

Angela scribbled something on a sheet of paper and passed it to Luke. 'Dr Ken Paterson,' it read. 'Scientist. Head of Counterproliferation.'

'Yes, and no,' Leach was saying. 'The burst transmission Black Run sent suggested he's got plenty more to tell us. But he wants to do it face to face. He's got sketch maps, descriptions, names. We might even get our hands on a thematic diagram.'

Paterson's pen-tapping was becoming louder and louder, almost frantic. 'What I want to know,' he said, 'is if he can give us solid proof the Iranians are cheating on the Vienna Agreement.'

Luke looked from Paterson to Leach and back again, like a spectator at a Chinese table-tennis tournament.

'That depends,' said Leach, 'on whether we can get someone to him ASAP.'

'Well, for God's sake, let's just do it!' said the Scotsman, looking around the room in exasperation, as if he were being refused the most trivial of requests.

Listening to this, it occurred to Luke that he had entered a world where people lurched seamlessly from one ongoing crisis to another. Was this the way his life would be for the next twenty years? An endless succession of last-minute apologetic phone calls to his girlfriend, Elise, as he missed yet another dinner at home, a weekend with her parents, an art-gallery opening, a party they were supposed to go to together? He was meant to have left that life behind when he'd finished with the SBS and couldn't see her putting up with this for long.

'It's not quite as simple as that,' replied Leach. 'Getting someone to him inside Iran is not straightforward. Black Run thinks he's being watched. And he probably is. The Revolutionary Guards have stepped up their game on counter-espionage in the last six months. But we've come up with a plan.' The Head of Iran and Caucasus looked around the room. No one interrupted him.

'It didn't get much publicity at the time but Iran has recently concluded a visa-free agreement with neighbouring Armenia. That means their citizens can cross the joint land border with minimal fuss. It's under a lot less surveillance than the Azerbaijan crossing. So . . .' Leach paused for effect '. . . we've advised Black Run to take two days' leave, then cross into Armenia discreetly. There is a way. He'll show up in Yerevan and meet whoever we send for the debrief.' He sat back, waiting for questions.

'Nice,' said someone at the far end of the table. 'So who are we sending?'

Leach rubbed the tips of his fingers across the scar below his eye before he spoke. It was a trait Luke recognized from his own injuries. Often when he was concentrating he found himself unconsciously rubbing the soft, fleshy stump where his middle finger had once been.

'Under normal circumstances,' Leach replied, 'we'd send Faisal Rizki from Dubai Station. Black Run is his agent and he developed him. But his wife is expecting and he can't travel right now. There's Jensen in Ankara, but he's already down at Gaziantep on the Syrian border, so we'll have to deploy from here.' Everyone round that table knew the Service had undergone a massive uplift in headcount recently. It was still training intakes of new and untested junior case officers while a lot of the more experienced hands, with twenty-five years' service behind them, had jumped ship, preferring to spend their final working years earning a lot more money for far shorter hours out in the commercial

34

world. So now here they were, apparently struggling to find anyone to send to Armenia to meet a key agent with vital intel. This was not something anyone in the room would have wanted the Cabinet Office to know.

'There is one other thing I should mention,' said Leach. 'Even though it's Armenia, and technically a neutral country, we should still expect hostile surveillance from the Iranians. And that's on top of the exisiting threat from the Russians. They consider this their backyard and they've still got three thousand troops stationed in the north of the country. Anyway . . .' He laid his hands flat on the table. 'Angela? Would you like to take over, please?'

'Sure. Thank you, Graham.' Angela leaned forward, cleared her throat and addressed the meeting. 'For those of you who haven't yet met him, one of our recent new faces, Luke Carlton, is sitting beside me.' Luke gave a cursory nod. 'Some of you may remember him from the Colombia job he did for us while he was on contract.' There were murmurs of approval. 'Well, Luke will be going to Armenia to debrief the agent.'

When everyone else had left the room Angela asked Luke to remain. 'Want a coffee?' she asked. 'I can order some up.'

Luke sat back and shook his head. She was regarding him with a coy expression, which he found quite irritating. 'Any reason you couldn't have given me the heads-up I was going to Armenia?'

'Come on, Luke, you're a big boy. You knew that was why you were here. And, no, I couldn't tell you before,' she looked at her watch, 'because it only got signed off upstairs twenty minutes ago. They wanted to send someone from Legal Affairs with you, so you can thank me for talking them out of that.'

Luke grunted and stood up. 'I'd better go and break it to Elise that I'm off travelling again. Never an easy conversation.'

'No,' concurred Angela, 'but I think it might be a little less contentious this time.'

'Why?'

'Because,' said Angela, choosing her words carefully, 'your

girlfriend has a very good reason to go to Armenia herself. She works in an art gallery here in London, doesn't she?'

Luke's eyes narrowed. 'I don't see that Elise's work has anything to do with my debriefing one of our agents coming out of Iran.'

'Then you're not using your imagination, Luke. Come on, try a little harder.'

Luke chewed the inside of his cheek, a habit he'd picked up in Afghanistan.

'All right,' said Angela. 'I'll spell it out for you. Yerevan is awash with art galleries. It's the perfect cover. You go as a couple.'

'I think we'd better discuss it, Elise and I. You know she may not want to do it.'

'Oh, I think she does.' Angela remained sitting.

'Really? And what makes you so sure?' He was trying hard to keep the irritation out of his voice now.

'Because, Luke, we've already spoken to her. It fits in perfectly with her work at the gallery and it's all expenses paid, by us. You'll be in Yerevan by tomorrow evening. Two-day trip, nice and clean. Don't worry, you'll get a full security briefing before you leave this building and, remember, there's always a back-up team here to support you.'

'Angela, I don't give a flying fuck about the back-up team, I just don't want my girlfriend involved. I thought I'd made that pretty clear.'

'You probably need to talk to her about that.'

There was something about the calm, unruffled way Angela spoke that set alarm bells ringing in his head. His boss seemed very sure of where she stood on this one. Luke walked over to the window and stared down at the Thames. The deeper he got drawn into the world of espionage, the more he wanted to shield Elise from it. And yet now, the very person – all right, the only person – who really mattered in his life was being drawn inexorably in.

'Do me a favour then, will you?' he said. 'After this mission, just leave Elise out of it. She's off-limits, okay?'

'Of course.' Angela smiled sweetly and got up to go.

And why, Luke thought, do I not believe that for one minute?

Chapter 9

'NO! SERIOUSLY? NO fucking way!'

In the two years since Luke and Elise had moved in together she had never seen him so worked up. He had hardly said a word in the taxi on the way to the restaurant that evening. Sitting opposite each other in a softly lit booth at the back of the Electric Cinema diner on Portobello Road, they were supposed to be having a romantic treat, a chance to draw breath from their hectic schedules. But it had not gone as planned.

'So you can imagine,' Luke said, 'I was a bit lost for words when the office told me they were trying to rope you in to helping them. Bloody cheek. Hope you told them where to get off.'

'I didn't,' she replied. 'I think it's a great idea, don't you? Come on, Luke, I've not been away for months. I could use a break.' She reached across the table and put her hand over his. 'Luke, I'm on your side, you know I am. I want to be helpful. And, well, as it turns out, I can be.'

And that was when he had lost it, regretting his outburst as soon as the words left his lips. 'Elise,' he said, 'I just don't want you mixed up with those people. At all. Why would you want to get involved with secret intelligence work? You're an art dealer, for God's sake, and a bloody good one. You've already got a perfectly decent career.'

Elise sat back in her chair, her earrings flashing briefly. She regarded him with a wry smile. 'So that's how it's to be, is it?' she said. 'You get to be the all-action hero while I have to mind my own little business in the gallery?'

'No!' he protested. 'That's not what I meant.' It was exactly what he'd meant. But Luke's motives were born not out of vanity but the need to protect what was most precious to him, yet he lacked the tools to explain without coming across as patronizing. 'Elise . . .' he began. Now it was his turn to reach across the table: he took both her hands in his. 'I just don't want you mixed up in any more danger. After what happened with the Colombians I'd have thought you'd have had enough . . .' He searched for the right word. 'Enough jeopardy?'

Elise tossed back her dark hair, removed her hands from his, and searched in her bag for her lighter. 'Look, you can relax. It's not as if they're asking me to undertake any work for them. I'm not joining MI6, if that's what you're worried about. But this is a trip I'd really like to do and I just can't see the downside.'

Luke said nothing.

'I need a cigarette,' she said, getting up and half turning to squeeze past the next table. 'Keep me company?'

Luke followed. He smiled at their waitress as they passed her. 'It's all right,' he reassured her, 'we're not doing a runner.' But behind his smile, Luke was uneasy. Elise seemed to have made up her mind about this trip and now things were moving in a direction he didn't like. There were few things he loathed more than not being in control of his own situation and now was one of those moments.

Chapter 10

Agarak–Meghri border crossing

THE LIGHT WAS already draining from the day as the battered, wooden-slatted truck changed down a gear and filtered into the queue of vehicles lining up to cross the border. Iranian plates, Iranian driver, Iranian pistachios stuffed into sacks and loaded into the back, no space to spare. On the wild, barren mountainsides that crowded in on all sides, the weak sun lit up the spaces between long, purple shadows that reached, like fingers, up the gullies and towards the saw-toothed peaks.

The temperature was dipping close to freezing, and inside his unheated cab Kaveh, the driver, shivered. It wasn't just the cold, it was the thought of what would happen if they caught him. Was he mad taking on this job? Yes, probably. But this year's harvest had been disappointing and still the government seemed to be milking him and his family dry. They needed the money. As the queue lurched forward in fits and starts he tried hard not to think of the man hidden in the back, curled up like a giant foetus and probably shivering half to death, breathing in the chill, diesel-fumed air with several hundred ripe pistachios piled high on top of him. But six million *tomans*? That was about two thousand dollars. Good money. Half paid in advance, half on delivery across the border. Just think about the money, Kaveh.

It was all over in minutes. Across the river bridge, up to the Customs house, a cursory inspection from a yawning Iranian border guard and some bored questions, just going through the motions. Where are you heading? Yerevan. What's in the back? Pistachios. Where will you sell them? Wherever I can get the best price! Then God be with you. A quick stamp of his papers and he was through. And how sweet the air smelt on the Armenian side of the border.

Kaveh wound down his window, breathed in lungfuls of it and accelerated towards the border town of Meghri. Now all he needed to do was locate that patch of waste ground they'd told him to head to, just past the boarded-up warehouse on the left, and then he could get rid of his illicit passenger, wash his hands of him for good. Six million *tomans*. Thank you very much, that will do me just fine. By tonight he would be in Yerevan, bedding down at the hostel on Amiriyan Street. Maybe go out and treat himself to a glass or two of Ararat cognac, perhaps look for a woman. Armenian girls were supposed to be hot for Iranian men – that was what all his trucking mates told him, and Kaveh had yet to go with one. Then tomorrow he'd sell the pistachios, drive down to Areni and load up with as much semi-sweet Takar Reserve red wine as he dared take into Iran, decanted into innocent-looking one-litre Coke bottles with the tops screwed on tight. Yes, this was going to be a profitable round trip.

At the junction, he turned left, switching his vehicle's lights on to full beam as he looked left and right for the warehouse. Already he was on the edge of town and the place was practically deserted. The warm glow of lamp-lit windows in family houses had given way to empty farmyards and bare, wintry orchards. There was no traffic behind him and the only people he passed were a pair of old men, clinging to each other as they moved along the road, muffled up against the cold. There. That had to be the warehouse. It was exactly as they had described it to him: grey and rectangular with stained, slatted walls and smashed-in windows. He drove past it onto the waste ground, a flat expanse of nothing bordered by bushes, and pulled up. He switched off the ignition and the engine gave one last judder.

Kaveh jumped down from his cab, rubbing his hands together, then moved round to bang twice on the side of the truck, informing his passenger that they had arrived. He hauled himself up onto the tailgate and climbed over the sacks of nuts. The last of the daylight was almost gone now but he could just make out the ones he was after. They were piled up at the back, one on top of another. Humming an old folk song, he began shifting them, pausing to call out the man's name and getting a muffled grunt in return.

As if endowed with a life of their own, the sacks began to move and an arm in a green padded sleeve appeared, then another. 'Help me up,' gasped the figure beneath. Kaveh did as he was asked. The sooner he was shot of his human cargo the better. When the man stood up, he rubbed his joints, then embraced his driver. He reached into his jacket and handed him an envelope bulging with 50,000-rial notes. Payment in full. Kaveh stood there, counting the money in the gloom. He didn't ask the nature of his business and the man hadn't offered to tell him. Kaveh had no idea how his stowaway was going to travel on, let alone get himself back across the border into Iran, but that wasn't his concern. He patted him on the shoulder, his way of saying 'Now go, get off my truck', then helped him lower himself, slowly, painfully, from the tailgate to the ground. He disappeared into the night.

Black Run had arrived in Armenia.

What neither man noticed was the faint green glow of an infrared surveillance device some distance off. Someone was observing them from the edge of the waste ground, photographing, recording, preparing to transmit the information to those who needed to know.

Chapter 11

Yerevan, Armenia

'IT CERTAINLY LOOKS pretty from up here,' remarked Elise. They were flying into Yerevan at night and she had the window seat, resting her chin on her hand, Luke beside her. With the Air France Airbus on final approach, she gazed down at the twinkling lights of the Armenian capital, patches of snow clearly visible, lit by the yellow light of the streetlamps.

In the arrivals hall it was swelteringly hot: the radiators were on at full blast to compensate for the cold outside. From somewhere there was the faint but unmistakable smell of onions. An announcement was being made on the tannoy, in heavily accented English, as Luke and Elise joined the queue at Immigration.

'It's like they're all in uniform,' she whispered. Luke could see what she meant. They were surrounded by a sombre crowd of men wearing black leather jackets, all spilling off the Aeroflot flight from Moscow. Immigration officers, in dark blue uniforms, silver-braid epaulettes and vast, sweeping Soviet-era caps, milled around the hall. Nobody paid the two art dealers from London any attention.

The security team in Vauxhall had concluded it would be best if no one met them off the plane. Their cover should be maintained around the clock: they were to be on their own. Passports stamped, taxi hailed, Luke and Elise were out in the night, being driven past piles of dirty, half-melted snow and giant signs that read 'Russia–Armenia Expo 2017'. The Soviet Union might have disintegrated in 1991, before either of them was even into their teens, but this Caucasus country was still very much in Moscow's sphere of influence. Yet staring out of the taxi window at a derelict factory beside the road, it appeared to Luke as if the Russians had left in a hurry. Now he was looking at a garish hoarding for mobile phones beside a rusting hulk of an abandoned oil tank lying on bricks, weeds creeping up its sides. Even with the cab windows wound shut, the sharp tang of petrol fumes and pollution in the air stung the back of their throats.

'You do take me to the nicest places,' said Elise, giving his hand a squeeze.

'You volunteered for this, remember?' he reminded her. 'I'm just doing my job.'

'Smartarse,' she replied, blowing him a silent kiss.

They pulled up outside a low-rise, ivy-covered grey stone villa, one of the few relics of Yerevan's nineteenth-century architecture to have survived the current urban-planning blitz. Cheaper and more discreet than the modern hotels, it had been carefully chosen by the Security people at Vauxhall. A line of triangular concrete bollards sealed off the forecourt from the road. Luke noticed that each one was spray-painted with a stencilled Kalashnikov assault rifle and the words 'Defend Yerevan' in English. A curtain twitched, a light came on in the hallway, and the door opened to reveal an old lady, muffled up in a shawl and scarf. She spread her arms wide in welcome as Luke paid off the driver and they grabbed their bags. She bustled about them, muttering in Russian, escorting them to their room and drawing their attention to the woven carpets and hand-painted ceramics that hung from the rough-hewn stone walls. Unbidden, she fetched them steaming bowls of potato and mushroom soup, then hobbled off down the corridor, leaving them in peace. Luke locked the door behind her, then he and Elise sat cross-legged on the bed, facing each other, as they ate their soup with hunks of coarse bread.

'I could get used to this,' said Elise, stretching out a foot towards the inside of Luke's thigh.

'So could I,' he replied, but he was preoccupied. Somehow this just didn't feel right. It was as if time had been suspended, the real world left outside on the pavement. He was in Armenia on a mission, his first as an agent handler. He had to get it right, and there were still too many variables to worry about. What if the agent didn't show up? Or he changed his mind? Or decided he didn't want to be debriefed by Luke but by someone else? Luke was used to operating on his own, or with a small, highly trained team, certainly not with his girlfriend at his side. He wondered why on earth he had agreed to this plan.

He got up, walked over to the window and peered out into the darkness. They were on the ground floor and he looked across at the shovelled snow piled up on the edge of the pavement. A dog stopped and lifted its leg, then trotted on. A car passed by, stereo blaring, two lads singing along, then a police car. The sounds of the city receded as it settled down. Elise had finished her soup by the time he closed the curtain and came back to the bed. He kissed her forehead and stroked her cheek but his mind was elsewhere. Somewhere out there an Iranian agent had crossed the border to meet him. An agent with vital nuclear secrets, who was prepared to risk his life to betray his country to MI6. Luke could not escape the thought that a hell of a lot would rest on his shoulders tomorrow.

Chapter 12

Yerevan, Armenia

'OH, LOOK,' SAID Elise. 'Someone's pushed an envelope under our door.' She bent down to retrieve it, then turned it over in her hand but there was nothing to say who had placed it there. Luke was standing a few feet away at the washbasin, halfway through brushing his teeth. He froze. How had that happened without his noticing? Someone had crept right up to their door in the night, or in the early hours of the morning, shoved something under it and he had slept on oblivious? That wouldn't do at all.

Toothbrush still in his mouth, he took the envelope from her and opened it carefully while Elise stood behind him, resting her chin on his shoulder and planting a kiss on his cheek. Inside was a single sheet of headed paper, printed with the logo of the Yerevan Museum of Russian Art but otherwise blank.

'That place is on my visit list for today,' she remarked. 'Hang on, something's written on the back.'

Luke flipped it over and there, scrawled in the bottom left-hand corner, was a single line of words: *Geghard M. Chapel. 1200 today. BR.*

Immediately Luke felt a frisson of tension: Black Run had made contact, the debrief was on. Midday. In just over three hours' time.

'Geghard M.,' he said to Elise. 'That must be Geghard Monastery. Does your guidebook say how far away it is?'

She went to her bag and took out *The Lonely Planet Guide to Georgia, Armenia and Azerbaijan* and ran her finger down the index. 'It says allow about an hour by taxi,' she said. 'Looks nice. I'll see if the old lady can make us a picnic.'

Us? Luke regarded her curiously with his eyebrows raised. 'Sorry, 'Lise, but this isn't an "us" kind of trip. I'm going alone. We can go back together another time.' Or not, he thought. He made a quick calculation in his head. 'Look, I don't know what the mobile signal's going to be like, up there in the mountains, but if I haven't made it back by five I need you to call this number. It's the British Embassy out-of-hours switchboard. Ask to speak to Jane. She'll know who you are.' He passed her a card with the number on it. 'But I'll be fine,' he added brightly. 'A debrief is pretty straightforward.' That, he knew, was complete bollocks. Nothing was ever straightforward in the world of espionage, which was exactly why he didn't want her mixed up in this.

'O-kaaay,' said Elise. She didn't sound convinced.

From just outside their bedroom they heard floorboards creaking as someone approached. Silently, Luke moved up to the door and whipped it open. It was the old lady bringing them breakfast: omelettes, plums, bread, homemade jam, and coffee in a little painted ceramic jug. Muttering in Russian, she moved past him and placed it on the dresser, then turned to leave but Luke blocked her path. He showed her the envelope that had been pushed under their door and turned the palm of his hand upwards. Had she placed it there last night? She shrugged and waved it away, still speaking in Russian, as she moved past him. Luke didn't like variables. He would have much preferred to know if she was working for the Service or not. When the door was shut, he started pulling on his clothes, wolfing down the breakfast at the same time.

'Slow down,' Elise pleaded, 'or you'll get indigestion.'

'Probably,' he replied, 'but I need to get up there well ahead of the rendezvous and scope the place out.' It wasn't the way he liked to do things. Back in Afghanistan he'd have had a crew in place watching the site for hours, maybe a drone flying top-cover overhead, jamming the mobile signals that could trigger any hidden IEDs, plus a whole back-up team on call, ready to be flown in by chopper if things went pear-shaped. By contrast, this mission was feeling distinctly lonely.

Luke didn't want to have to make contact with the British Embassy on Marshal Baghramyan Avenue unless he absolutely had to. The Security team in Vauxhall had been quite emphatic about that: the building would almost certainly be watched, they had told him. SIS also had to assume their Yerevan Station Chief was being shadowed wherever she went, by either the Russians or the Iranians, or quite possibly both. No, Luke needed to stay off the grid and keep low.

'Well, at least take this,' said Elise. She was standing in front of him in her T-shirt and underwear. She handed him her guidebook. 'I know you think this is old-school but if there's no mobile signal in the mountains you might just need it. I've bookmarked it at page one forty-nine for you. Tells you all about Geghard Monastery. God forbid you absorb a bit of culture while you're up there!'

Luke pulled her closer and kissed her. 'Thanks, 'Lise. You're a star. And, honestly, don't worry about me. I'll be back by last light. Then we'll go somewhere nice for dinner, I promise.'

'The last time you said that you pulled an all-nighter,' she reminded him.

Luke rolled his eyes. 'Yeah, okay, fair point. This time it'll be different.'

Chapter 13

Yerevan, Armenia

ALONE IN THE front seat of the taxi, being driven uphill and east-wards through the dun-coloured suburbs of Yerevan, Luke watched the wintry landscape slip past. Towering tenement blocks, long, low factory buildings, a giant metal Soviet hammer-and-sickle tipped onto its side and left abandoned in the snow. As the images flashed past, he considered his situation. He was unarmed, unless you could count the Swiss Army penknife in his pocket. It wasn't that firearms were hard to come by, here in the southern Caucasus, it was just that Vauxhall Security had assessed the risk for this meeting to be 'Category 4 – Low to Moderate'. So it had been decided, by others, that it wasn't worth the hassle of arming him for Armenia. Great, thought Luke. If anything goes wrong I'm in the shit.

'A rat!' his driver announced, breaking into Luke's reverie. They were the man's first words since Luke had clambered into the old yellow Lada he'd flagged down on Mashtots Avenue. Luke scanned the road ahead but it appeared to be rodent-free. The driver was pointing now, his arm outstretched and obscuring Luke's view, the car starting to veer off-course as he took his eyes off the road. And there it was, just across the border in Turkey, sheathed in snow and towering over everything, the celebrated five-thousand-metre-high mountain of biblical fame, a conical white massif that dominated the landscape for miles around.

'Ararat.' The driver grinned as he gunned the engine. Picking up speed, they pulled away from the winter smog of Yerevan and headed high into the hills.

They made good time. An hour after leaving the capital the road levelled out and they pulled into steep, wooded Geghard Gorge, leading to Geghard Monastery. Luke had been able to track their progress on his encrypted Service phone using the Atlas app, which worked pretty much like Google Maps but without giving away your location to someone you didn't want to know it. He knew they'd be watching his route in Vauxhall too, some nameless operator sitting at a console, following the pulsing blue dot as it moved across the digital map of western Armenia, then firing off a report to the Mission Controller upstairs. That was if the operator hadn't wandered off on a tea break.

The driver pulled up, yanked on the handbrake and drummed his fingers impatiently on the dashboard while Luke counted out his fare in Armenian *dram* banknotes. He got out and did a quick 360-degree check of the car park as his cab pulled away. He was alone and early, which was just how he liked it. The parking spaces reserved for the summer tour buses stood empty, covered with a thin layer of snow. No one else had come to visit the monastery today, yet somehow he felt claustrophobic, a sense of being hemmed in by the towering cliffs on either side. The gorge was a dead end, a geological cul-de-sac with nowhere to run to if things went wrong.

In the silence left by his departed taxi Luke glanced up at the mountainside above him. It was pockmarked with dozens of caves where, according to Elise's guidebook, monks had once hidden in contemplation. A weak, watery sun was trying to break through the clouds, casting fleeting shadows across the gorge but offering little warmth. It was, he thought, an odd place in which to debrief an Iranian agent when they could have met, unnoticed, in any one of a dozen crowded cafés in Yerevan.

49

Luke took out his phone, coded in a sequence of numbers he had been made to memorize before he left London, and seconds later the screen filled with the photograph of a man's face looking straight at the camera. Luke put him probably in his late thirties. His expression was neutral but his skin was unusually pale for an Iranian – possibly Armenian-Iranian, Luke reckoned – and his eyes were surprisingly light in colour. This was the man he would be meeting, MI6's agent inside Parchin. This was Black Run.

As he studied the image, recommitting it to memory, he considered for a moment the extraordinary risks the man was taking in working undercover for British intelligence. If his cover was ever blown he would meet his end – after a lengthy and painful interrogation – with a rope around his neck and swinging from a crane as a crowd jeered beneath him. Or perhaps it would be an unseen and anonymous death, in a prison yard at Evin, with a bullet in the skull. Either way this man had a serious set of *cojones* and Luke respected him for that.

Luke checked his watch: still thirty-five minutes to go before the rendezvous. He found a boulder beside the road, brushed off the dusting of snow on its surface and sat down, rehearsing in his head the sequence of phrases they would need to exchange to validate their identities. It didn't sound so different to him from all those old Cold War clichés of the rolled-up newspaper under the arm, the brush-past in a railway station and a muttered sentence, like 'It is always cold in Minsk in winter.' When he moved off, walking uphill towards the gates of the monastery, his eyes flitted over the mountainside above, scanning its crags and gullies for escape routes, hiding places and potential ambush points. It was a habit he had picked up in the SBS that had never left him. A gust of icy wind blew down the valley, prompting him to turn up the collar of his jacket as his boots crunched on the snow-covered paving stones.

The huge stone entrance to the monastery was impressive. To Luke, this place looked more like a fortress than a religious retreat. A high dry-stone wall joined it to the mountainside, making it hard, if not impossible, for any intruders to get past it. But the gate was open and, inside, an arch was set in another arch. Above that he saw a triptych of religious symbols, embedded in the wall in a frieze. A solitary pine tree stood guard to the right, the wind hissing and sighing through its swaying branches. A man was sitting alone on a wooden stool just inside the gate, rubbing his bare hands together to stay warm. Luke slowed his pace. Could this be Black Run? No, he didn't match his description. The man caught sight of Luke and immediately picked up an accordion and began to play, then nodded his thanks as Luke walked past him and dropped a banknote into his upturned hat on the ground. The hat, he noticed, was empty.

Luke stood on the edge of the monastery's main courtyard, his senses on full alert. After all the months of induction and trade-craft training he had been through with MI6, this was, he realized, with a jolt, his first time back in the field since Colombia. He had better not screw it up. His eyes took in the scene before him: a large cobbled space enclosed by a high wall, a square blockhouse building of pale, weathered stone, with vertical, arrow-slit windows, topped by a conical turret. That must be the chapel where he was due to meet Black Run. Three figures in his field of vision, and none looked like his contact. A monk, bald, bearded and cassocked, hurried past at a stoop, nodding to Luke in brief greeting. Then a pair standing in the centre: an Asian tourist in a fluorescent yellow cagoul, filming himself on a selfie stick, while a figure in an anorak held onto his arm, trying to get his attention. A tour guide, Luke guessed. He moved closer to the pair, catching phrases in the wind.

'. . . fourth-century World Heritage-listed site . . . named from the spear that pierced Christ's body . . . crucifixion.' From what Luke could see, the tourist wasn't listening, more interested in adjusting his selfie stick.

Time check. Sixteen minutes to the RV. It was time to enter the chapel – he had found it earlier, listed in Elise's guidebook as the Chapel of St Gregory the Illuminator. From inside came a low, melodic chant, the sound of a choir in full voice. Glancing back to check he was not being followed, Luke stepped inside, adjusting his eyes to the near darkness and the flickering shadows cast by a dozen candles. Could Black Run be one of the choir? Disguised in one of their floor-length brown cassocks? That would be ingenious. And weird. No. He dismissed the notion: its members were young men, barely out of their teens. He slipped past them, unnoticed, aiming to get himself into position in the shadows, somewhere he could watch the doorway. To his left he made out three side-chapels off the main hall, supported by stone columns lit by thin grey shafts of daylight from somewhere high above. He ducked into the first. Empty, but no cover. Then the second. Perfect. He would tuck himself behind the pillar in the far corner. Best check the third chamber in case his contact had shown up early.

Luke crossed the threshold and stopped abruptly. Someone else was in there. Someone sitting close to the far wall with their back to him, propped up against a column with their legs stretched out in front of them. It was an odd pose for a winter afternoon in a freezing cold monastery in Armenia, one that made no sense for either a tourist or the man he had come to meet. Something was wrong.

Luke moved up behind him and said quietly: 'Excuse me, but do you have a charger for an iPhone 6?' It was the prearranged validation phrase, the harmless exchange of words that would confirm that this was his man, or not. Silence.

Luke knelt down and started to repeat the question, louder this time but his voice trailed off. The floor around them was wet, and even in the dim light he could see the man's jacket was saturated, stained dark and glistening with fresh blood. Luke gripped the man's shoulder and his head flopped uselessly to one side. He could see it now in all its horror: the vivid red gash that extended right across the throat from one ear to the other.

Cursing under his breath, heart racing, Luke held the tips of two fingers to the side of the man's neck, just behind the point where the killer's blade had begun its work, searching for a pulse he knew wouldn't be there. Nothing. The dead man's pale eyes stared back at him, as if fixed on some distant point far beyond Luke.

He already knew who it was, already felt the sick blow of defeat, like a kick to the back of the head, yet he forced himself to take another look. And it was him. It was Black Run.

Chapter 14

Tehran

TANNAZ ZAMANI WAS in spa heaven. Her university lectures finished for the day, the manicure done, her nails immaculate, she was treating herself to a luxurious, sensuous foot massage. Zohreh's beauty salon, just off the northern, more fashionable end of Valiasr Street, was lit up from the outside with winking purple neon lights, as if advertising some non-stop party within. But Zohreh's salon was strictly for women only, and in the tranquil interior Tannaz reclined in comfort, ignoring the steaming cup of Shiraz tea placed beside her.

The TV on the wall was running pictures from some weighty UN debate in New York, then cut to dramatic footage of the Iranian Navy carrying out manoeuvres in the Gulf. Missiles streaked across the screen and a uniformed white-stubbled officer was making a defiant speech to the camera. But the sound was turned down and she didn't catch a word of it. Instead, her manicurist was wittering on about the joys of cosmetic enhancements.

'You know, Tannaz-*jaan*, I do admire how you've done your eyebrows.'

Tannaz touched them self-consciously with her fingertips. She had hairs woven in there permanently but had resisted the temptation to copy others who had gone for the full tattoo effect.

'Have you met Dr Vahid?' the manicurist continued pleasantly. 'If you're ever thinking of a nose job, he really is the best in Tehran. Everyone's doing it now. Many of our best clients here use him.'

Tannaz's eyes popped open and flashed in anger. She sat up in the padded chair and spoke sharply to the surprised manicurist. 'I don't need plastic surgery and I don't want Botox. You should know I am perfectly happy with the body God gave me.'

'Oh, no, I wasn't suggesting . . .' The girl trailed off and she resumed her work in cowed silence while Tannaz sat back and scowled, her good mood evaporated. Impatient for the nail polish to dry, she picked up her phone and began scrolling carefully through her messages. One from that boy Ramin – she deleted it. Then there was a text from her mother, and her heart sank. She would be going on at her again to come and meet some eligible bachelor, someone she had zero interest in. But, instead, a smile spread over her face as she read on. Tannaz put down her phone and touched her manicurist tenderly on the shoulder. The girl recoiled, wary of another rebuke, but her client had already forgotten their earlier exchange.

'Be happy for me!' Tannaz said. 'Mama is taking me to an art exhibition in Abu Dhabi!' She clapped her hands and looked up at the ceiling. 'Yes!' she exclaimed. 'Finally, a break from this place.'

Chapter 15

Geghard Monastery, Armenia

LUKE MOVED FAST. He leaped back from Black Run's lifeless corpse and whirled round, ready to face the killer. The pool of blood at his feet had yet to congeal, the murder just minutes old, so whoever had done it could not have gone far. In fact, he might still be here in the chapel. Heart thumping, Luke paced quickly round the dark recesses of the chamber but it was deserted, save for the shapeless bulk of Black Run's body slumped beside the column. And then he remembered. There was a reason why the agent had asked for this meeting in person. He had something to hand over – a file, a document, a trove of data – some vital piece in the jigsaw of intelligence that MI6 was trying to build on Iran's covert nuclear programme. Luke dashed back to the body and searched through Black Run's pockets, fingers scrabbling, but all he came up with was a handful of empty pistachio shells. If the agent had brought anything with him to this debrief it was gone. Which meant only one thing: the killer had stolen it.

Something had changed in the way the choir were singing: there was finality in the pitch of their voices. They were coming to the end of their session. Any minute now they would start to disperse, then someone would find the body and it would all turn to rat shit as he got fingered as the prime suspect. He looked down. The dead man's blood was all over his hands and there were dark droplets on the front of his jacket. Luke would have a hard time explaining that to the Armenian police with no diplomatic cover to save him. He bent down quickly and shifted the dead agent's body, concealing it behind the column to buy himself extra time, then walked past the choir, still with their backs to him, and out of the door into the courtyard.

It was empty. The guide, the tourist and his selfie stick had departed. So now he had a choice to make: get back to Yerevan as fast as possible or go after Black Run's killer. If he called it in to Vauxhall Cross, he knew exactly what the response would be: 'Safety first, Carlton. Remember the risk assessment. Remove yourself from the scene of the crime and stay out of sight.' And Luke knew that that was probably the most sensible course of action. Yet he was damned if he was going to admit defeat. Eight years as a Royal Marines officer, then four in the secretive Special Boat Service had taught him to seek out the unusual, to surprise his opponent with the least expected course of action. His agent debrief had been thwarted, in the worst way imaginable, and there was nothing he could do to change that. Yet he could salvage the mission if he tracked down the killer, found out who had sent him and retrieved the stolen file. He would call in to Vauxhall Cross and break the news that they'd lost Black Run. But only once he had finished this.

It was starting to snow, thin, dry flakes falling like feathers from a sullen sky. That meant there would soon be footprints. His, as well as the killer's. The chapel behind him had fallen silent. Luke crossed the empty courtyard and went out through the stone gateway. The accordion player had gone, and for a moment Luke wondered if he could have been responsible for Black Run's murder, but he dismissed the idea. Why would the killer hang around?

Outside the monastery's fortress-like walls, Luke dropped out of sight into a gully. He was trying to put himself into the killer's mind – 'Red Teaming', they called it in the Service – imagining what he would do if he were the killer, and then it came to him.

The mountainside was pocked with caves, each one a perfect hiding place, somewhere to go to ground and wait for the coast to be clear, then slip away, probably under cover of darkness.

From deep inside his jacket Luke took out a miniature pair of binoculars, compact enough to fit in the palm of one hand. Only 8x25 magnification, but that was enough to let him scan the mountainside intently for the slightest movement. It took him less than a minute. A man was scrambling up the slope in a hurry, his dark clothes partly obscured by the falling snow, loose rocks skidding down from where he'd missed his footing. Luke kept the binoculars trained on him, noting his position and waiting to see which cave he chose. From somewhere down in the valley he could hear a vehicle changing gear as it came up the hill. That would be the transport for the choir, he guessed. Good. With any luck they'd bugger off before anyone found Black Run's body in the side-chapel.

The figure in the viewfinder had stopped and turned towards him, looking back down the mountain. For a moment he seemed to Luke to be looking directly at him, as if willing him to follow. Then he turned back and vanished inside a cave. Getting up there without being seen by his quarry wasn't the issue. As a former Royal Marines Commando, Luke had sailed through the gruelling eight-month mountain-leader course in Scotland and Norway, learning how to scale the most daunting rock faces and survive in sub-zero temperatures. No, the issue here was that the killer in the cave had a serious blade on him, possibly even a firearm, and Luke had a Swiss Army penknife. What he wouldn't have given right now for a silenced Glock or a Sig Sauer pistol.

This was madness, a one-man mission against unknown odds. He could almost hear Angela at Vauxhall Cross telling him to let it go and abort the mission. And he didn't even want to think of what Elise would say. But, fuck it, he'd see it through.

Luke put away the binoculars and made a rapid assessment of the route he was going to take: he would use the dead ground out of sight of the cave's entrance. Then he set off up, his breath frosting, his fingertips gripping the snow-dusted rocks as his boots sought toeholds. When he reached a point halfway to his target he paused to catch his breath and listen. Silence from the monastery below and, in the car park outside the gates, he could see that the bus to take the choir home was still there. Not a good sign. The longer those people stayed, the greater the risk they'd find Black Run.

Without warning, a large bird soared right past him, an eagle perhaps, making him duck instinctively. The bird passed so close to him that Luke could hear the muted hiss of wind sifting through its outstretched wingtips and saw the creature's head swivel left and right as it searched the ground for prey. Was he prey too? Was he being drawn into a trap? Spurred on towards a fatal encounter by his own bloody ego? For a second time he stopped to question the wisdom of what he was doing. He was at the point of deciding to jack it in when a sound pierced the stillness of the valley, freezing him to the spot. Police sirens.

Chapter 16

DR KEN PATERSON never liked crossing the river to Whitehall. With his scientific training and years spent closeted in secret labs at the Atomic Weapons Establishment in Aldermaston, Berkshire, he liked to deal in facts, not policies, certainties not nuance. But as Head of Counter-proliferation at MI6 he was finding that an inordinate amount of his time was taken up in crossing Lambeth or Westminster Bridge, attending meeting after meeting in Whitehall. Today was one of those days. This would be a sensitive encounter, just him and Nigel Batstone, the Director of the Foreign and Commonwealth Office's Middle East and North Africa Department.

In earlier times the two men might have discussed their business over a leisurely dinner at the Travellers Club, a short stroll away across the park in Pall Mall. They would probably have thrashed out their differences as they reclined in stiff leather armchairs, tipping a discreet nod to the barman for another glass of vintage Armagnac. But twenty-first-century Whitehall wasn't like that. Both men were overworked, with cluttered diaries and busy families, so they had scheduled a meeting on the first floor of the FCO for 0930 hours.

Wearing his customary tweed jacket with leather elbow

patches and a knitted woollen tie, Paterson sat in the back of the chauffeured car, his hand resting protectively on the locked case beside him. Behind its combination keys sat the Parchin File, a condensed version of everything MI6's Counter-proliferation Division had gathered so far on Iran's suspected illicit nuclear programme. They drove through Parliament Square, past a motley collection of anti-war protesters, with handwritten banners, then a short way along Whitehall and swung left into King Charles Street. An elderly security guard peered at the number plate and looked down at his list, then ambled over to pass an upturned mirror on the end of a pole beneath the car's chassis. He checked beneath the bonnet and in the boot, then nodded them through. The steel barriers slid into the ground, allowing the car to pass.

A young researcher, fresh-faced and mustard keen, despite her absurdly low salary, escorted him from Reception across the courtyard, through a doorway and up the magnificent sweep of staircase to the first floor. Paterson had arranged to meet Batstone in the Entente Cordiale Room, a vast, ornate, almost palatial chamber that smacked of former glories long past. The FCO mandarin was already there, sitting – rather awkwardly, Paterson thought – in front of an empty unlit fireplace and beneath an enormous gilt-framed portrait of King George V, resplendent in his dress uniform and ermine cape. Paterson marvelled at how, after all these years, the place still gave off echoes of Empire.

Batstone's PA came in bearing a tray of coffee and tiny cartons of UHT milk. She took his coat, then left them to it, closing the door softly behind her.

'Thank you for making time to see me,' Paterson began.

'Not at all.' Batstone gave him a forced smile. 'So, what can I do for you?' He could be urbane and charming, but Paterson strongly suspected this was not a visit he would welcome. Head of Counter-proliferation at MI6? He could almost sense Batstone's scepticism, even before he opened the locked case at his side. Everyone knew things were at a sensitive stage right now with Anglo-Iranian relations. The FCO and the more pragmatic technocrats in Iran's Foreign Ministry had worked hard to repair the damage done after that mob had invaded the British Embassy in Tehran in 2011. Channels were kept open with the Iranians despite the worsening tension between them and the US Navy in the Gulf. Paterson had done his homework and he knew the last thing Batstone wanted at this stage was a new complication introduced by the spooks on the other side of the Thames.

'It's about Iran,' he began. 'I know it's flavour of the month in this department but on our side I have to tell you we're having some serious concerns.'

Batstone gave a strangled laugh, more of a snort really, and got up to fetch himself a teaspoon. 'Well, I wouldn't describe it as our flavour of the month.' He went back to his seat, stirred his coffee and scowled as a rogue drop landed on an immaculate white cuff. 'We have concerns of our own, naturally, about events in the Gulf. We're giving the Americans our full support in the Security Council. But, that said, we do believe the current crisis will blow over in time and our policy is very much one of *engagement*. The gravitational pull is what you might call "constructive ambiguity". It's a risk-based approach,' Batstone continued, the modish Whitehall jargon tripping off his tongue with practised ease, 'and, going forward, it's vitally important that the moderates are seen to be rewarded for signing up to the Joint Comprehensive Plan of Action – the nuclear deal.'

Paterson stared back at him for a long moment. As a trained nuclear scientist he was more than used to jargon. But this? This was another language to him, alien and unhelpful. 'Constructive ambiguity'? What a load of nonsense. In his book, either something was or it wasn't. 'Rewarded for what, exactly?' he said patiently.

'Well, let's review it, shall we?' Batstone suggested. He was known to take a patronizing tone with people who couldn't see things as clearly as he expected them to. It was a long-established trait. Some would call it a flaw, but Paterson thought he was probably unaware of it. 'Since that deal was signed in Vienna,' Batstone continued, 'Iran has reduced its stockpile of uranium by ninety-eight per cent. It's also closed down two-thirds of its centrifuges, and has stopped enriching uranium at that under-ground place – Far-something.'

'Fardo,' said Paterson, helpfully.

'Yes.' Batstone seemed to be making a conscious effort to soften his tone. 'So I do think we're in a good place now. And, of course, the PM is keen to see some positive spin-offs from the deal.'

'Of course. I can appreciate that,' said Paterson, finally reaching for the briefcase he had brought with him and twirling the combination locks. 'But my team would also like to make you aware of some disturbing developments at Parchin.'

The Head of FCO Middle East and North Africa sat back in his chair, as if trying to place some distance between himself and whatever was about to come out of the case. He crossed his legs and threw his visitor a wary glance. 'What sort of developments?' he asked.

'We believe,' said Paterson, 'with seventy-five per cent certainty, that an element of the Revolutionary Guards Corps is covertly working on something banned by the Vienna treaty, something deep in a tunnel at Parchin that they haven't declared.' He looked meaningfully at his host.

'Right. Could you be a little more specific?' said Batstone, irritation now creeping into his voice.

At first Paterson didn't answer. He pulled out a sheaf of papers from the briefcase, some with diagrams and satellite images, then passed them across to Batstone. 'There's a tunnel down there which they declared to be out of service,' he said, leaning forward and pointing at a circled area on a laminated satellite photo. 'But the fact is it isn't. What's more, there's something going on down there they don't want us to see.'

'Which is?'

Paterson hadn't expected to have to spell it out but now he looked Batstone straight in the face. 'It is our estimation,' he said, 'that work is in progress on weaponizing a nuclear device.'

'Christ,' said Batstone. 'You mean a warhead?'

'Possibly, yes. Their missile programme is racing ahead – they've even put satellites into space.'

Batstone got up and walked over to the window. A moment later Paterson joined him. There wasn't much of a view, just the blank grey walls of the Treasury opposite and a few bare trees below in St James's Park. The glass was grimy and stained with rain splashes. With FCO budgets under constant pressure the cleaning contracts had been one of the first casualties of the cuts. He could see an elderly commissionaire standing in King Charles Street, remonstrating with a white van driver. An untidy jumble of scaffolding lay piled on the pavement – there seemed to be a never-ending succession of half-finished building works going on.

'I hate to say this, Ken,' said Batstone, 'but haven't we been here before with your Service? I mean, with Iraq and the whole WMD debacle? You'll forgive me if I'm coming across as a little sceptical.'

'No, no, that's completely understandable,' replied Paterson. He had anticipated this. 'But we're expecting some hard evidence of their activities to come to us out of Iran any day now. We . . . um . . . we have a very well-placed agent who's had first-hand eyes on what I've just described to you.'

'I see,' said Batstone.

Paterson could tell from his tone that he wasn't convinced.

'You do know, don't you, that the Foreign Secretary plans to visit Iran in the near future?' Batstone went on. 'We obviously don't want any spoilers ahead of that visit. It'll be the first by a UK Foreign Secretary since the US and Iranian elections. I can't emphasize enough how important this is for Britain. If anyone's going to defuse the tensions in the Gulf then it falls to us.'

'I was aware that a visit was possible,' said Paterson, 'and that's exactly why I'm here today. Given our concerns about their covert nuclear activities, don't you think it might be prudent to put the brakes on this rapprochement with Tehran?' The conversation made him feel as if he was trying to swim through marmalade.

Batstone cleared his throat and moved away from the window. 'I hear you,' he replied, diplo-speak for *All right, you've made your point and I totally disagree with everything you've just said.* 'And your views are duly noted. But I'm sorry, Ken, without some solid proof of these "covert activities" you mention I really can't see how you would expect us to change course. I'll say it again: we *need* to engage with the Iranians. I think we're all agreed on that, are we not? And the Foreign Secretary's visit is very much a part of that constructive engagement, which is enshrined in policy now.'

Paterson followed him back to the fireplace, making some effort to hide his exasperation. The meeting was clearly over. 'Just give us a few more days,' he said, 'and we'll get you that solid proof. In fact, it should already be on its way over to us.'

'Good,' said Batstone, briskly, buttoning up his jacket and moving towards the door. 'Then I look forward to seeing it when it comes in.'

Chapter 17

Geghard Monastery, Armenia

THEY'D HAD A name for the tunnels, back in the Corps. Marines called them 'the Smartie Tubes', a distant dark memory that still haunted Luke sixteen years on. Yard after yard of twisting, painful, subterranean darkness, the gravel and pebbles digging into his joints as he crawled blindly forward on his elbows and knees beneath the gorse and heath of Devon's Woodbury Common. It was just one small part of the Royal Marines Commando endurance course that he had had to do as a recruit, all those years ago. Going first or last wasn't so bad – at least that way you didn't end up trapped between the man in front and the one behind. But the corporals had put Luke in the middle, sandwiched between two barrel-chested men who were at risk of getting wedged. Halfway, there had been an unexplained blockage and the line of men was stuck. Their breath came in short gasps as the panic spread among them, like a contagion, each man fighting to contain the terror that this was where his life would end, suffocating quietly in the dark. Eventually they had emerged, breathless and panting, but for Luke, the realization that all his exits had been cut off, all his options removed, well, that was a situation he vowed never to get himself into again. Ever.

And yet here he was now, cornered at the wrong end of an Armenian gorge, his options crumbling away from him.

Escaping to Yerevan down the road he had come by was no longer possible because the police were there. Go back into the monastery? Out of the question. He was committed now: he had to go forward. He could see three police vehicles racing up to the gates, lights flashing, sirens blaring. The cops would start questioning the choir at any second now, firing questions, taking swabs and photographs, gathering forensic samples from Black Run's supine body. Luke was certain that when they found no obvious suspects on the premises the search would begin in earnest. They would fan out across the gorge and start checking the caves and crags. There would be dogs, helicopters with searchlights, and lines of young men eager to be the one who caught the murderer. He didn't have a lot of time.

The snow flurries had stopped but already, in the mid-afternoon, it seemed to be growing darker, the mountains closing in on him, the wind tugging at his clothes. From his vantage-point behind a boulder halfway up the slope, Luke glanced back over his shoulder to check no one was behind him, then set off uphill again. With the contours as natural cover, he needed to stay out of sight of both the monastery below and the cave ahead, where his quarry lay hidden. It took him nearly twenty minutes to reach it, approaching on the balls of his feet for the final few yards. Just before the entrance he stopped and removed the Swiss Army penknife from his jacket, eased open the largest blade and locked it in place. Two inches of forged steel: it wasn't much but it was the only weapon he had. Not quite, he remembered. From his other pocket Luke took out a thin metal ballpoint pen, a leftover from some tedious London conference he had sat through months ago. He closed the fingers of his left hand around it to keep it concealed inside his fist and held the locked blade in his right. 'By Strength and Guile': that was the motto of his old unit, the SBS. He'd need both for what was coming next.

*

He was short, much shorter than Luke, but heavily built. The man was turned away from Luke, his powerful shoulders hunched forward as he peered out from the cave's entrance, looking down the hill, his head swivelling left and right, like that of the eagle that had swooped past only minutes earlier. Was he empty-handed? Luke couldn't tell. No time to hesitate, no time to think, he knew he would get only one shot at this. He exploded out of cover and barrelled with full force into the figure in the cave, slamming him against the bare rock face and kicking his legs out from under him. The man let out a roar of pain and surprise as he went down, arms flailing as he tried to grab Luke and pull him down with him. *He's a wrestler. He knows the moves – got to stay out of that crushing embrace.* Luke twisted free and stepped back quickly, away from his grasp, but his adversary was recovering fast, rising up first on one knee and then the other. *Was that a smile on his face?* Luke made a snap judgement of the distance, then caught him full on the chin with a front thrust kick straight to the head. No groans this time, just the sick, hollow crunch of Luke's boot as it connected, fracturing the jaw in two places. He watched the man slump, heavily, on the uneven floor of the cave, his skull making a crack as it landed on a protruding rock. Then he was motionless. Luke was on him in an instant, about to press the blade of the penknife against his windpipe before he went through his pockets, when suddenly his world changed. He couldn't breathe.

What the fuck? Gasping, his hands went to his neck, desperate to tear away whatever was wrapped around his windpipe. His feet struggled to find purchase as he was dragged across the cave floor. *Why hadn't he seen this coming? Of course there would be two of them – why wouldn't there be?* It was standard protocol for a covert IRGC hit team, one to do the dirty, the other to watch his back and clean up any mess afterwards.

Luke knew all about strangulation. More than once he'd watched in silence as the life-force drained out of a man's eyes while his own fingertips pressed down relentlessly on the carotid artery. Nothing personal, just getting the job done. Now it was his turn and the stats were screaming in his head. Ten seconds to blackout, five minutes to brain death. *This is it, Luke Carlton. You've got to get out of it.*

As the training kicked in, Luke's body went through the drills. He jerked his chin downwards and hunched his shoulders, trying to relieve the pressure on his windpipe. It bought him two seconds at most. His adversary knew his business and immediately tightened his grip. Luke could feel his sight blurring and he was starting to see double. The pain around his neck was excruciating. And still he hadn't glimpsed the man who was inflicting it. The penknife! He had almost forgotten it. *Got to stay conscious.* Luke swung his right arm round behind him and drove his fist sideways into the leg of his unseen opponent, expecting resistance as the short blade pierced the flesh.

Nothing. His hand was empty. The knife had fallen from his grasp the moment he was jumped from behind. Through all the pain, the fear and the mounting dizziness, Luke knew these could be his last few seconds alive. And now there was a sudden clarity to everything, as if all his senses had been sharpened. He caught a glimpse of his opponent, his face swimming briefly into focus: narrow, hawklike features, dark eyebrows meeting in the middle, jet-black stubble, hair thinning on top. This was the man who was working to end Luke's life. *Well, fuck you, you're not having me.* The fingers of Luke's left hand curled tightly around the slim metal ballpoint pen. This was his last throw of the dice. With everything he had left, he jabbed it hard at the man's face, aiming for the eyes. He missed, the nib of the pen hit just below the right cheekbone, but the shock made his assailant loosen his grip for a vital second.

Luke squirmed free, twisting his body 180 degrees. Then he was up and launching himself at the would-be strangler. Luke's right arm shot out, driving the heel of his hand into the cartilage of the man's nose, catching him off-balance. Then he drove home his advantage. With his opponent momentarily confused, Luke pistoned out his left arm with the ballpoint extended in front. In just a fraction of a second it pierced straight through the ear drum into the cochlea and beyond. Luke opened his hand wide so that it was flat, then slammed it down hard on the protruding metal pen, forcing it into the man's brain. In his moment of death, as he slid to the floor, he wore an expression of surprise, even curiosity, as if losing a fight were a novel experience for him.

Luke felt nothing. No pride, no satisfaction, not even relief, though that might come later. He had won this round, but others would come after him, he was certain of it. And now a new sound was reaching his ear. A sound that told him he was still in deep, deep trouble.

Chapter 18

Above Geghard Monastery, Armenia

DOGS. A PACK of them. Luke could hear them baying somewhere down the mountain from the direction of the monastery. Dobermanns? Belgian shepherds? What the hell difference did it make? Once they got to him, they would tear his throat out in seconds. He had to get away from this cave, fast. Put as much distance as possible between him and them. Find some running water, then cross it. Throw them off the scent. Vanish.

His pulse still racing from the fight, he put his hand up to his throat and touched it warily. Where the strangle cord had nearly throttled him, his neck was on fire and he realized he couldn't swallow. That was the least of his problems. Luke knelt down, placed one hand on the dead Iranian's ear and with his other he quickly pulled out the silver biro from where it had pierced his brain. It made a hideous sucking noise as it came out. No time to wipe it clean, no time to hide the bodies, not even time to update Vauxhall. He flung the pen out through the entrance and down the slope, hearing it clatter against the rocks. Sure, they would find it eventually, but by then he would be long gone. He hoped. Luke checked the coast was clear, then bolted from the cave.

What was it Angela had said back at Vauxhall Cross? It's just a simple debrief, Luke, don't sweat it. Go over to Armenia, take

Elise with you for cover, get the intel and get out. That had turned out well, hadn't it? Here he was, marooned in a mountain gorge in the south Caucasus, bodies piling up around him and a pack of slavering dogs about to be let off the leash to find him. He had no means of defence, no diplomatic immunity, no excuses and no alibis. And that was if the cops got to him before the dogs did.

Keeping his silhouette low and staying out of sight of the monastery, Luke moved quickly away from the cave and began to traverse the mountainside, his boots searching purchase on rocks that slipped and skidded under his weight. His eyesight had already adjusted to the dying light of the winter afternoon, and in the gathering gloom he could just make out where the gorge ended in a steep, wooded ravine. If there was running water anywhere in this godforsaken place it had to be there. He stopped and listened, shivering briefly as the temperature fell, his bare hands clenching and unclenching to keep the blood flowing in the cold air.

Yes! There it was! Somewhere in the semi-darkness he could hear the gurgle of running water. A mountain stream. It had to be. He stumbled down the slope and through the trees towards it, bare branches whipping at his face, rocks tripping him. The sound of rushing water was growing louder, and suddenly he was at its edge, looking at a full-blown river that surged past him in its headlong dash down the ravine. He cocked his head to one side, listening intently for the baying of the dogs. When he couldn't hear them he pictured them racing towards him, panting with anticipation, saliva streaming from their jaws as they closed the distance. He had no time left.

Luke took a deep breath then launched himself into the river. The icy cold hit him hard, leaving him gasping, his legs burning as the snow-fed waters swirled and pulled at them. He waded deeper, aiming for the dim shape of a rock halfway across, holding his phone above his head to keep it dry. It was nothing he hadn't done before as a young Royal Marine, when he could feel the Arctic wind of northern Norway slicing through him, yet this was worse, far worse. It wasn't a test, it was real. There was a manhunt on and he was the prey. He could picture it now, his sorry face plastered on the front page of *Armenia Today*, beneath the words: 'Foreign Serial Killer Caught Escaping!' Even the thought of it made him angry because it hadn't been him who had slit Black Run's throat up in the monastery: it had been the hitman sent from Iran. *Yes, okay, Luke, but face it, you did kill that one and his back-up, didn't you?*

He looked down as he waded deeper into the river. The frigid waters were above his waist now and he could feel his legs numbing with the cold. But he was nearly at the halfway rock, just two more strides and he'd be there. In the rush to reach it, he didn't bother to test his footing on the riverbed. Bad mistake. With no warning, the gravel and shale beneath him fell away. Luke lost his balance, falling head first into the rushing torrent as the submerged current swept his legs from beneath him and he felt himself being pulled under. He fought for air, fought to keep his head above the churning foam as it propelled him at breakneck speed down the mountainside. With no helmet to protect him he knew it would take only one collision with the rocks to knock him unconscious and then it would be over. Slam! The current smashed his body hard up against a protruding rock but his shoulder took the brunt, not his head, and there, lit by the phosphorescence of the water, was a low-hanging branch. His feet found solid ground on the riverbed and he stretched out his hand to grasp it. Deafened by the roar and crash of water all around him, he lunged at the branch, his ice-cold fingers made contact and he hauled himself out of the water. He was across.

Now what? Luke's phone was waterlogged and useless to him. He couldn't even be sure if the Tracker chip embedded inside would still be working. For all he knew, he had gone completely off the Vauxhall Cross grid. He could picture it now, Angela standing over a monitor back in the operations room, frowning as the data analysts tried in vain to retrieve his vanished signal on the screen. No one would be riding to his rescue out here.

The temperature was still dropping, it was dark and he was starting to shiver uncontrollably. Got to keep moving, got to get the circulation going before hypothermia set in. Luke beat his chest a couple of times, wrapped his arms around himself and slapped his sides, then set off downhill, keeping the river on his right. At least the compass in his watch was still functioning and showed him heading west. He tried to recall the map he had studied for those vital few minutes before he had left Elise that morning. He remembered there was some kind of tourist attraction just a few kilometres west of the monastery, an Armenian temple. No one would be there now, not at this time of year and not in the sub-zero darkness. The place should be deserted. But if he could find some shelter there he could hole up for the night and mingle with the next coachload of tourists in the morning. It wasn't much of a plan.

It took him nearly an hour to reach the temple, working his way along the riverbank, stumbling between boulders, stopping once to crouch low when a convoy of police cars went past on the road above, blue lights flashing. He shuddered. Jesus, it was cold. His clothes were still drenched from the river and he knew hypothermia could be a killer. He needed to focus on finding shelter. Ahead of him he could see the temple, could just make out its columns silhouetted against the faint sodium glow from the distant lights of Yerevan. He approached slowly, measuring each footfall, pausing and listening. It was when he was just five metres away from the outline of a hut that he stopped in his tracks.

Someone was calling his name.

Chapter 19

Tehran

DISGUSTED. YES, THAT was the only way to describe how he felt about his domestic situation. How had he let it come to this? How had he, Karim Zamani, rising star in the Revolutionary Guards, managed to lose control of his family? He sat at the head of the family dinner table in their house on Hafez Street and stared in disbelief at his wife. She glared back, saying nothing, her face a mask of defiance. Their relationship, he knew, was in terminal decline, their differences irreconcilable. In fact, he realized, it had probably passed the point of no return some time ago.

To his right sat Parviz, their dutiful thirteen-year-old son, keeping his head down, like the smart boy he was, spooning rice into his mouth as quietly as he could and just occasionally sneaking a glance at his mobile under the table. His sister, Tannaz, sat at the other end of the table, in the spot where her father liked to place her so he could look directly at her while he was eating. She got up and took her plate into the kitchen. There was no question of where her loyalty lay in this argument – with her mother – but the atmosphere in the room was so toxic she was doing her best to stay out of it.

'Explain to me again, dearest,' he said to his wife, speaking slowly, sarcastically, in a tone of mocking affection, 'why you feel the need to fly to . . . to Abu Dhabi?' He spat the last two words. He could feel his anger mounting as a vein began to pulse in his temple but he managed to keep his voice even and controlled. Just. 'Is it not the case that you could visit any art gallery in the world – anywhere? And you choose Abu Dhabi. I simply cannot see the reasoning. Don't you watch the news? Read the news-papers? Don't you know how tense things are in our part of the world? Yet you choose now, of all times, to pay a visit to those uncivilized Bedouin on the wrong side of the Persian Gulf?'

'You're always telling me things are sensitive,' his wife shot back. 'When are they not? But that's your world, not mine, not ours. My God, it's not as if I'm suggesting you come with us!'

'Us?' Karim Zamani stood up abruptly, his chair nearly tip-ping backwards behind him. 'Who is "us"?'

Forouz Zamani sighed, in the exaggerated, theatrical way that always annoyed him. Was she doing this to provoke him? She knew he didn't approve of these artistic excursions yet she per-sisted in making them.

'Us,' she replied quietly, 'your beloved daughter, Tannaz-*jaan*, and I.' He looked up sharply, glancing at Tannaz who stood frozen in the kitchen doorway. She was carrying a plate of fresh pomegranates, their ripe red seeds glistening in the light that hung from the ceiling. His face softened as he studied her, remembering her as the child she had been only yesterday, his ray of light, his angel. She had grown up so fast, and now he had to worry constantly about the company she was keeping.

'I don't know why you're getting so upset about this,' con-tinued his wife. 'Tannaz will be with me the whole time. I'll keep an eye on her, I guarantee it. There will be no dishonour to this family.'

Karim Zamani clenched his hands behind his back and began to pace around the dining room. Anger built within him. What was wrong with him that his own wife was flying in the face of his wishes? With his fellow officers in the Pasdaran, the Iranian Revolutionary Guards Corps, he was feared, respected, honoured and decorated, but here within their family home on Hafez Street he felt his authority slipping away, like sand through his fingers. He had married above him. That had been the trouble all along, of course. All that money and influence her family had. That, and her breathtaking beauty, the way she would look up at him so coyly from behind that fringe of hair. He had been smitten back then, no question about it. Everything about this woman had impressed him. But now? Now he wished he'd married the carpenter's daughter from Shemshak, the village he had grown up in. At least then he could have counted on total loyalty and obedience.

'Do you understand,' he addressed his wife, putting his face close to hers and still speaking deliberately slowly, as if to a very small child, 'that every time you cross the Persian Gulf to the Arab side those people are monitoring you? Documenting your movements? Noting where you go? I'm telling you, Forouz, they have spies everywhere. Have you forgotten who you're married to?' He scowled at her, willing her to back down and abandon her crazy plan to go traipsing round art galleries in Abu Dhabi at this time of tension.

Forouz shrugged and gave him a hollow laugh. 'So what if they are? Let them follow us. We have nothing to hide. Maybe we'll leave them the bill and they can pay for our cappuccinos at the hotel!' She turned away from him, picked up a cut segment of pomegranate and began to scoop out the succulent seeds with a spoon.

With sudden, blinding ferocity, Karim Zamani snapped. He lunged forward and knocked the fruit out of her hand, sending the spoon clattering to the floor and splashing the crimson seeds across the top of her dress, like a spray of blood. His wife screamed once, then clamped her hand to her mouth. She stared at the table in silence.

'Forouz!' He shouted her name, facing her square on. 'You think all this is amusing? You think my job is some kind of a joke? You don't stop to consider for a moment how this makes me look? My wife and my daughter running around abroad, flirting with strangers, while I'm working day and night here to defend the Revolution?' He opened his arms wide and looked up at the ceiling, as if to ask: Oh, God, what have I done to deserve this?

77

'We would never dishonour you,' she whispered.

'What?' he shouted back. 'Say it louder!'

'I said, we would never do anything to dishonour you.' When she raised her eyes to meet his he could see they were wet with tears. He found this curiously calming.

'Very well,' he continued, quieter now. 'I have to go to Qom for a few days so, tell me, who's going to look after Parviz while you're away?'

'He'll stay with my parents in Elahieh, I've already made the arrangements. They will spoil him, as they always do.' He could see her attempting a smile. It was pitiful, really, and he chose not to return it.

From the kitchen next door came the ceramic clatter of plates being rinsed under a tap, and from outside in the street, the evening call to prayer floated over the rooftops, gentle and melodic, rising above the crash and din of Tehran's traffic. In the house of Second Brigadier General Karim Zamani, senior officer in the Army of the Guardians of the Islamic Revolution, the Iranian Revolutionary Guards Corps, nobody spoke any more that evening.

Chapter 20

Garni Temple, Armenia

SOAKED THROUGH, TEETH chattering, eyes darting to left and right, Luke Carlton was already on full alert when he heard his name called in the dark. He braced, about to duck back into the rock-strewn ravine. Those bastards. Armenian security must have worked out that this was exactly where he'd run to, the only shelter for miles around. Of course it was. *You bloody idiot, Carlton, what were you thinking?*

A split second later, he recognized the voice. It was Elise! What the hell? Was he delirious? Was he imagining this? What was she doing out here? Hadn't he left her safe and warm in a hotel room back in Yerevan?

'Luke!' There it was again, her voice, urgent, insistent. He scanned the darkness ahead of him until he saw her, a shapeless form moving uncertainly towards him, a pencil torch in her hand. He flinched instinctively as she rushed the last few feet and flung her arms around his neck, then held on tight. On the run for hours, he still felt very much the hunted prey.

'Elise,' he murmured, when they had caught their breath. 'How did you find me?'

'Tracker. The embassy was monitoring your movements.' She

put the palm of her hand on his chest. 'Christ, you're soaked through! Let's get you into the car.'

'Wait. What car?' He stood his ground.

'The embassy one – they brought me here,' she replied, pulling at his jacket. 'Come on, we don't have time for this.'

They picked their way across the stony ground, Elise leading. Somewhere in the darkness a dog barked. Through a gap in a wall and out the other side and they reached an empty car park. Empty, except for a solitary vehicle with its engine running. A Range Rover. Well, that's not obvious, Luke thought. Why not fly a bloody great Union Jack from the aerial and play the National Anthem while you're about it? In the faint glow from its tail-lights he could see the red-and-white number plates, with a D. Diplomatic plates. Would it get them through the checkpoints? They'd soon find out.

'You're down here,' Elise said briskly, holding open the back door for Luke and pushing him gently in. 'Going to need you to lie flat, then I'll put this over you.' She reached into the back for a coarse woollen blanket as Luke lay down and struggled to contort his six-foot frame into the gap behind the front seats. This was bloody uncomfortable but he wasn't complaining. For the first time in hours he wasn't freezing, and it was dry. Safe? Too soon to tell. He felt the front seat compress next to his head as Elise got in and closed the door behind her. They moved off immediately and he hadn't even had a chance to see who was driving.

Luke's mouth was full of dust from the blanket but he had so many questions he just couldn't stay silent. ''Lise? Fill me in. What's the situation?'

'The situation . . .' She was smiling, he could tell. He knew her voice so well. 'The situation is that you seem to have caused an almighty shit storm! The Armenians are going berserk. The embassy is going to have to get us out under diplomatic cover.' He felt her hand reach round behind the seat and touch his shoulder.

'Checkpoint ahead.' Another disembodied voice, a man's this time, the driver's. Luke laid his head sideways, flat against the thinly carpeted chassis, and pulled the blanket tighter over him. He could hear the Range Rover changing down and slowing to a stop, the sound of an electric window winding down and an exchange in Armenian, interspersed with the word 'diplomat'. Luke held his breath and kept very still as a torch beam flickered briefly round the interior of the car. He heard a lengthy rattling sound as something was dragged across the tarmac – a chain spike barrier? More exchanges in Armenian and then the engine revved once more. They were through.

'So, how did you know?' Luke turned to look at her. Beyond the round Perspex window, the lights of Yerevan receded beneath them.

Elise took a sip of vodka. 'How did I know what?'

'That I wasn't going to make it back by five.'

'Ah. Just a hunch.' Elise looked up at the Polish stewardess and held up her glass for a refill. Seated side by side in business class on the 04.40 Lot Airlines from Yerevan to Warsaw, they were possibly the only passengers still awake.

'That's bollocks, 'Lise. How did you know?'

'I didn't,' she replied. 'Not until a woman from the embassy told me. She came and found me in the art gallery and we drove straight from there. I think they must have been monitoring the police channels or something. So . . .' She rested her hand on his arm and moved her face closer to his. Amazing. They had gone through all this and still she had that delicious fragrance about her. But Elise's expression was serious now. 'Do you want to tell me what went on up there in that monastery?'

Oh, sure. I found my agent with his throat slit from ear to ear, then fought for my life with two thugs in a mountain cave. I ended up driving a pen into a man's brain. More vodka?

'Not really, no,' Luke replied, wiping the tiredness from his eyes. 'We've got thirteen hours to kill in Warsaw before our connection. Let's leave it till then.'

Elise nodded, put her head on his shoulder and closed her eyes.

Thirteen hours to kill in Warsaw. He knew exactly what was coming next. There'd be the initial debrief with the Head of Poland Station, the obligatory 'interview without coffee', the encrypted report flashed back to Vauxhall with snide personal observations. 'Subject displays no remorse for what's happened. Recommend further psych profiling and a period of compulsory leave', etc., etc. Then the summons into Vauxhall and more debriefs. Various figures would express their disappointment. Perhaps there'd be a pitying look from Angela before the dreaded word: reassignment.

But what did he expect? A simple agent debrief had turned into a bloodbath. Three dead bodies and not an ounce of intel to show for it. That was a pretty crap scoreboard by anyone's reckoning. No, whichever way you cut it, this op had turned into a complete and utter fuck-up. Perhaps, after all, it was time to consider an alternative career in investment management.

Chapter 21

Tehran

ON THE ROOF of the Shahrbani Palace a flurry of snowflakes swirled around the red, white and green flag of the Islamic Republic of Iran. With each blast of icy wind that blew straight off the Elburz Mountains it twitched like a living thing. It was a grand, imposing building that dated from the 1930s, long before the Islamic Revolution. It had columns and balustrades, tall trees outside, a glittering interior within, and now it housed the Ministry for Foreign Affairs.

But today its grandeur was lost on Morteza Hosseini as he took the entrance steps two at a time, stealing a glance at his watch as he reached the top. He was late. He was a small, neat man in his early forties who liked to keep impeccable timing. As Deputy for Legal and International Affairs at the Foreign Ministry, he knew this meeting could not begin without him. With his degree in political science from a US university, his internship at a bank in the City of London and his fluency in English, Arabic and German, there were few people in the ministry with a skillset to match his. And while of course, as everyone knew, the final decision would always rest with the Supreme Leader, aided by his closest advisers, Hosseini's input was vital. Like many of those he worked with at the Ministry of Foreign Affairs, he would be considered by outsiders as 'a moderate', a pragmatist, eager to see Iran regain its rightful place on the world map, old enmities forgotten, new alliances forged. The hardliners hated him.

'So the question we have to address today,' he told them in the meeting room, 'is do we need good relations with Britain?' There were murmurs and glances. To some sitting at that ornate carved table, Britain was, and always would be, the Little Satan, the junior partner in crime to that most enduring of Iran's foes: America, the Great Satan. The role of MI6 and the CIA in overthrowing Iran's democratically elected Prime Minister in 1953, and helping the Shah to power, would never be forgotten or forgiven. Others saw it differently.

'Let us consider this question carefully,' the Deputy continued. 'Because remember, my friends, Britain is leaving the EU and our friends are in Europe. For example, I have more than two hundred applications for lines from European banks sitting in my computer.' Those who knew Hosseini could recognize that he was playing devil's advocate. To some he had confided that his years spent in London as a young man were some of the happiest of his life – he had even developed a fondness for English Breakfast tea, thick-cut Oxford marmalade and watching soap operas like *EastEnders*. His friends liked to tease him that he was practically an Anglophile. His enemies saw that as a weakness to be exploited.

'Why am I asking this question?' He looked around the room, one eyebrow raised inquisitively. 'Because we have been approached by the British Embassy with an interesting offer. Something that could provide us with an opportunity to extend our reach across the Persian Gulf and dilute the Western alliance with those Gulf sheikhdoms.' He pronounced the last two words dismissively, as if Iran's oil-rich Arab neighbours were just a temporary annoyance.

'My friends,' he continued, 'I will not pretend that this doesn't come with its own dangers, and we must keep our eyes open at all times to the machinations of those who would do this great country harm.'

They waited expectantly for him to finish but Hosseini paused while a glass of water was fetched.

'Gentlemen,' he resumed, dabbing his mouth with a napkin, 'it has been suggested that we host a visit from Britain's Foreign Secretary.'

Immediately he registered the murmurs of surprise and a few scowls of disapproval. He had been expecting that. There would be many, he knew, who would say this was surely not the time for such a visit. But he held up his hand for silence. 'As I say, the final decision rests with the Supreme Leader and, as always, he will do what is best for our country. But I must tell you that, in the interests of progress, of modernity, and of strengthening Iran's position in the world, I am going to recommend that we approve this visit.'

The meeting broke up with those present dividing themselves into two factions. Hosseini stood near the door, accepting the handshakes and congratulations of some, while others gave him only the most cursory of nods as they filed out into the corridor. He ticked off the names of the dissenters in his head and found they matched exactly the list he had had in mind. No surprises there: Iranian politics could be confusing to outsiders, but if you knew your way around them, some things were reassuringly predictable.

Outside the ministry the temperature was hovering just below zero – Tehran's climate tended towards scorching in summer and freezing in winter. In the icy breeze that swirled around the courtyard there was no one to notice a muffled figure as he walked quickly to a secluded corner. He was one of those who had declined to shake Hosseini's hand after the meeting broke up. Checking first that no one was peering down at him from the windows of the Foreign Ministry, he dialled a number in Qom, eighty miles to the south. The man at the other end of the line was intrigued to hear what he had to say and thanked him. The Circle, the Dayere, had expected to be kept up to date with every development. This was important and worrying news.

Chapter 22

Qom, Iran

AS THE CAR sped southwards down the Persian Gulf Highway from Tehran to Qom, the spiritual heartland of Iran's all-powerful clergy, Karim Zamani felt a deep contentment. He was leaving behind all his domestic troubles and drawing closer to this holy city of domes, minarets and boundless wisdom. Qom always felt like an all-embracing mother to him. Zamani was a military man, not a religious one, but as a guardian of his nation's Islamic Revolution he drew strength from the religious convictions of the ayatollahs and other clerics in Qom. He had always admired their wisdom and piety. He knew that their profound knowledge must come from long hours spent hunched over texts in seminaries, sitting cross-legged in poor light, reading centuries-old curling, yellowed pages through thick-lensed spectacles. That was dedication, that was devotion, and that was something he, Karim Zamani, could personally identify with.

His appointment was in an unremarkable building, constructed in the post-Shah era, with pale, austere walls and dark, smoked-glass windows. It stood slightly apart from the others in the street and was surrounded by an imposing ten-foot-high wall, topped with razor wire and interrupted only by a steel grille gate. High up on the wall a camera swivelled towards the chauffeured car as it drew up to the gate, which, seconds later, swung open. The raised barrier behind them was lowered and Zamani's car was ushered into the inner courtyard.

Just three days had passed since the unfortunate events across the border up in Armenia, three days in which Zamani and his immediate circle had had to come to terms with the loss of two of their finest, most trusted covert operatives, men who had killed across three countries with impunity, vanishing into the ether afterwards. They had carried out their duty with honour, silencing the filthy traitor who was about to spill the country's innermost secrets to its enemies, and they had paid for it with their lives. That can happen when you put together a rushed operation like this. But the worrying question was, who had dispatched his men in that cave? Yes, there was much to discuss today, Zamani told himself, as he stood up, straightened his tunic and headed for the ground-floor entrance.

The hall was bare, save for a large portrait of the Supreme Leader. Two men, in well-cut suits, got up as he walked in and nodded respectfully. They knew exactly who he was, but that did not exempt Karim Zamani from the security protocols. Jacket off, passed through the scanner, then a thorough body search and finally his mobile phone taken from him. Zamani made no objections: he had personally insisted on these measures. No electronic device was to be allowed into the building, absolutely nothing that might be prone to hacking and eavesdropping by those scheming bastards in America's National Security Agency. Memories of the damage done to Iran's nuclear industry by their Stuxnet virus were still fresh. The waves of paranoia it had set off had yet to subside. Hence today's meeting of the Dayere was being held under absolute secrecy – in fact, even the group's existence was known only to a very few. Its members assumed that it had been quietly sanctioned by the Office of the Supreme Leader. Karim Zamani knew that not to have been the case.

Upstairs in the meeting room on the second floor the heating was on and the windows were grey with condensation. The eight men – no women – sat expectantly around the table. No notes were to be taken, no recordings made. The eight began with a prayer for divine guidance in their mission, delivered by one of their number, a black-turbaned mullah, and also for divine justice to be meted out on those who stood in their way. The next to speak was a man who, like most of them, wore a dark suit over a white, collarless shirt. Wire-framed glasses and no tie. Ever since the Islamic Revolution of '79, ties had been frowned on as symbols of Western imperialism. He was blessed with one of the more creative and innovative brains in the intelligence wing of the IRGC, a division that by 2018 had almost completely eclipsed Iran's official Ministry of Intelligence and Security, the Ettela'at.

'Let us start,' he began, in an accent they all recognized as coming from the holy city of Mashad, home to the most sacred Shia shrine in Iran, 'with an assessment of what went wrong in Armenia.' There were nods and frowns of disapproval around the table, but Zamani was watching him closely. He had already privately earmarked this man for a special role. If their plans were ever discovered, and they were forced to explain themselves to the Supreme Leader's office, Zamani had more than enough on him to let him take the fall.

'The decision to monitor the Armenian border crossing proved a wise one,' the man from Mashad continued. 'We thank you, Karim-*jaan*, for your foresight and planning.'

Zamani tipped his head in modest acknowledgement.

'We believe that disaster was only narrowly averted, thanks to our surveillance team. The traitor who crossed illegally had high-level clearance at Parchin. He could have compromised everything. But, as you know, we . . . dealt with the situation. It is our assessment that no information has escaped these borders.'

'How can you be so certain?' an older man asked. He was sitting towards the back of the room, with thinning hair, a faded suit, and permanently surprised eyebrows. Zamani knew him well. He had been his mentor when he'd first graduated into the Revolutionary Guards Corps.

'Because if anything had leaked out,' replied the man from Mashad, 'you can be certain that those UN nuclear inspectors would be crawling all over us by now. And they are not.' He adjusted his glasses and threw him a glance that seemed to say, 'No more interruptions.'

'And yet we now have unfinished business here,' he resumed. 'Our Armenian friends tell us they had nothing to do with the martyrdom of our men at Geghard Monastery and I believe them. So who killed him? Whoever it was, he has slipped through their hands, like rice through open fingers. Karim-*jaan*?'

Zamani's turn to speak. He stood up and, as he always did on these occasions, smoothed the creases from his tunic before he spoke. 'I think we are all agreed, are we not, that the man who did this is dangerous?' It was a rhetorical question and he didn't wait for an answer. 'He is a danger to our project and a danger to us – yes, all of us, here in this room. We must assume he was sent by a Western agency – CIA, Mossad, MI6, the French, we don't know yet. But we must find him.'

Zamani could see the questioning look in their eyes. Why were they wasting precious time talking about going after this one individual when there was urgent work down in the tunnel at Parchin to discuss?

'My brothers,' Zamani continued, 'this is not about vengeance for our martyrs, it's not even about justice. We have to know what is in his head. We need to find out what *they* know. So . . . I am pleased to tell you that progress is already under way in identifying him. Our agents in Yerevan are making checks at all the hotels, examining the registers. Once we have a name, our people at the airport will find a face, a passport number, a description. Let me assure you now, here in this room, in this blessed city of Qom that is so dear to our hearts, that wherever he is hiding in the world, we will find this . . . this *kosskesh*, this pimp! And when we do he will dearly regret the choices he has made.'

Chapter 23

Goring Hotel, London

LUKE CARLTON WAS on his best behaviour. Jumping smartly out of the taxi as they pulled up at 15 Beeston Place, SW1, holding open the door, then offering his arm as he helped Elise's mother up the steps from the pavement. It was always this way when he was around her. Luke had warmed to Helen Mayhew right from the first heart-in-mouth moment, that Saturday morning two years ago, the day when Elise had brought him home to Buckinghamshire to meet The Parents. Luke had brought chocolates, good ones, and flowers, addressing her respectfully as 'Mrs Mayhew' and offering to help with the washing-up after lunch. Elise teased him afterwards that he was behaving like an obedient spaniel, but in the months that followed Luke, orphaned at the age of ten, had come to see Helen as the mother he had never had.

Now the three were sitting on sofas in the Edwardian dining room at the Goring Hotel, their faces lit by the subdued light of green-shaded lamps. Coming here for afternoon tea at the discreet, upmarket establishment, just a stone's throw from Buckingham Palace, had been an annual pre-Christmas indulgence that Elise and her mother had shared since the year she'd graduated from Durham.

'So, I gather the trip to Armenia was a bit disappointing?' Helen flashed him the sweetest of smiles as she poured the tea.

Just a bit. You could say it was a total bloody car crash. But Luke just smiled at the question and turned to Elise for help.

'A lot of the galleries turned out to be closed,' she lied, 'so we came back earlier than expected.' Luke watched her admiringly as she spoke. She was wearing a soft white cashmere poncho, which he'd bought her on a ski trip to Courmayeur, and a small gold pendant around her neck. Such an angelic creature, such perfect poise, he noted, and so easily the lie tripped off her tongue. Luke was impressed.

'I see.' Helen turned to him. 'And now you're here to stay for a while, I hope? No more trips in the pipeline so close to Christmas? My daughter does miss you when you're away, you know.' She patted his knee affectionately.

'Nothing.' Even as he said it Luke knew full well that his phone could ring in the next minute, he'd get his marching orders from Vauxhall and be on a flight that night to somewhere he could never reveal to either her or Elise.

'Good,' said Helen. 'That's what I like to hear. Family is everything, you know, and you're a part of ours, Luke. Now, let me go and find out what's happened to our sandwiches. Oh, here they come.'

A uniformed young man appeared at their table and gave a deferential nod to Elise's mother. She spoke quietly into his ear, as if confiding some great secret. Minutes later he returned with a bottle, its green glass surface glistening with beads of condensation. He peeled back the gold foil, gently popping the cork into a white napkin, then filled their glasses with an ice-cold Bollinger.

Luke wondered what they should be celebrating. Their escape from Armenia? The impending Christmas season? That he was still in a job after failing to debrief a doomed agent in time, leaving a trail of dead bodies behind him? It really didn't matter. What counted for him was that this was a wonderful interlude of calm, a luxurious moment of escape from all the pressures around them. He looked at Elise's mother, serene and dignified in her pearls and country tweeds, and raised a glass towards her. 'To you, Helen, and thank you.'

'And to both of you,' she replied. She took a long sip, winced and placed a hand on her abdomen.

Elise leaned forward, concerned. 'Mummy? Are you all right?'

The colour seemed to drain from Helen Mayhew's cheeks. Then whatever it was passed and she was back to her normal self. 'I'm fine, darling. I don't know what that was.' She giggled. 'Probably just wind. Right, come on now, drink up both of you. Nothing worse than warm champagne.'

Luke sensed Elise drawing subtly closer to him on the sofa. Beneath the table he could feel her hand, warm and soft, resting on his knee as she closed the space between them. There would come a time, he was absolutely certain, when he was somewhere dark and dangerous and he would treasure this moment, drag it up from his memory banks, turn it over in his mind and savour it.

Chapter 24

MI6 Headquarters, Vauxhall Cross

THE POST-ACTION REPORT from Poland Station lay on the table, like a piece of damning evidence, staring up at everyone in the room. Graham Leach picked it up, riffled through its pages, frowning, and stopped at a passage in the conclusion that he had already marked and began to read out loud.

' "Carlton's obvious physical stamina and personal survival skills do not mask the fact that his mission was essentially a failure. He reached Black Run too late to carry out the debrief before the agent was murdered and the intelligence was lost to us. It is therefore my conclusion that an officer with a more in-depth knowledge of the region might have reached the target sooner and completed the mission with none of the three murders taking place." '

MI6's Head of Iran and Caucasus replaced the file on the table and swept his glasses off his face. 'So, Luke, anything you'd like to add?'

Luke looked quickly round the room before he spoke. In the military, a meeting like this was known as 'an interview without coffee'. Aside from him and Leach, three others were present. There was the ubiquitous Angela Scott, his line manager, whose last words to him before he had left for Armenia had been

93

'Don't sweat it, Luke. It's just a debrief.' There was the rather unwelcome figure of John Friend, a Service lawyer he recognized from Legal Affairs. Christ, those people had practically a whole floor to themselves, these days, and seeing him right now did not bode well. And then there was a small, neat woman he didn't know, wearing a white *hijab*, and a dark blue suit over a white blouse.

'Well, yes,' Luke replied, looking Leach straight in the eyes and holding his gaze. 'I would like to comment. As I said in the initial debrief on that stopover in Warsaw, I could not have got to the monastery any sooner. The moment I got the message with the RV location I was in a cab and on my way. In fact I was there early . . .' He trailed off because he could see Leach was holding up his hand for silence. *So let me guess. It's a foregone conclusion. I'm to be fired and this lady in the headscarf has been sent over from HR to sign off on the end of my career here.*

'I hear you,' said Leach. 'I've read the report, I've talked to our embassy in Yerevan and . . .' He paused.

'And?' *Come on, don't drag this out. Let's get it over with.*

'. . . I'm satisfied,' continued Leach, 'that you did everything you could. In fact', he leaned forward in his chair towards Luke, 'I would probably have done exactly the same in your position.'

Luke relaxed, just slightly, but he was damned if he was going to show it. MI6 might be his employer but he still trusted nobody, inside or outside this building.

'You're probably wondering what all these people are doing here.' Leach swept an arm round the room. 'Well, John Friend is from Legal, as I think you know. He's here to sign off on the next operation. I wanted him in on the ground floor of what we're planning. And Jasmine is on loan from GCHQ. She's helping us get the most out of the SIGINT intercepts we get from Cheltenham.'

Luke tipped his head towards her and the lawyer and turned back to Leach. 'So what are you planning?' he asked.

It was Jasmine who answered, speaking with just a trace of an accent. 'Hello, Luke,' she began, as if they had met before, which he was certain they hadn't. 'You know, of course, that we've been watching Karim Zamani in Iran for some time now. Black Run saw him in the tunnels at Parchin only last week before he was . . . Well, you know the rest. Anyway, Targeting think there may be an opportunity, an opening, we can exploit.'

Luke watched her as she spoke, listening intently. She had pronounced angular features and a thin, aquiline nose. Her eyes seemed to sparkle as she addressed him, yet he detected seriousness behind them. *You don't say? This lady is either Arab or Iranian and she's working for the biggest government eavesdropping station in Europe, listening in on her former countrymen's conversations and tagging the bad guys for surveillance. Of course she's bloody serious.*

'We've learned that Zamani's wife is about to take a trip outside Iran,' Jasmine continued. 'To Abu Dhabi. She's taking her daughter Tannaz with her, to visit an art fair in the Emirates.'

Leach cleared his throat. 'We want you to get in front of her,' he said bluntly. 'Remember, she's a serious party girl.'

'Meaning?'

'Meaning she's into a Western lifestyle and can't stand the people her father works for, the Revolutionary Guards. She's ripe for recruitment, Luke. If we can get her onboard it'll give us unparallel access into what Zamani's up to.'

Luke thought for a moment. He was used to winging it and taking snap decisions, but this wasn't the military: it was intelligence work and to him it felt very, very rushed. 'I can see the end-state we're aiming for here,' he said, 'but I've got to say this feels a bit hasty. I mean, I only went on the agent-handling course a short while ago and you pulled me off that, remember?'

Leach smiled. 'It is rushed. I won't deny that. But we don't have the luxury of time. The situation in the Gulf is getting extremely tense and we've got the National Security Council screaming at us for better optics on Iran. We're pulling out all the stops here, Luke.'

'How soon are we talking?'

Leach and Angela exchanged glances. 'You fly tonight. You're booked on the overnight Etihad flight to Abu Dhabi. Jasmine will give you the full target profile and everything you need to know about Tannaz. You'll be met off your flight so don't worry about that bit.'

All this time, Luke noticed, the Service lawyer had sat there quietly without saying a word. Luke remembered John Friend from his Colombia mission two years back. The man's heart might have been in the right place but he had been a royal pain in the arse. Please, God, don't tell me I'm being saddled with him again on this one.

'John!' Luke addressed him briskly, so briskly that the lawyer started and dropped the pen he was holding. 'What's your part in all this? Are you coming to hold my hand again?'

'Me? Heavens, no, you're on your own on this one. I'm just here to sign off on this at the ground floor, so to speak. It's the way C likes things done, these days, dotting the *is* and crossing the *t*s. Nobody wants another Gibson Inquiry, do they?' He laughed weakly, then busied himself with his notes.

As the room cleared and Luke moved to where Jasmine was sitting, bringing up a page on her data tablet to begin her briefing, a thought struck him. This is your last bloody chance, Carlton. You messed up on the agent-handling course, you came back from Armenia in mild disgrace and with a triple body count. That makes this trip to Abu Dhabi your last-chance saloon. One more fuck-up, and you'll be out. End of.

Chapter 25

Abu Dhabi

BLINDING SUNLIGHT AND cloudless blue skies. Luke squinted as he peered through the plane's smudged window at the sunbaked tarmac. Not yet eight o'clock and already the heat of the Gulf made everything appear bleached white. Blending in with all the disembarking passengers, he strode up the sloping air bridge to the terminal, his eyelids still sticky with sleep. Just a single piece of hand luggage, a holdall slung over his left shoulder containing everything he would need. 'Never check anything into the hold' had been his mantra for as long as he could remember. Low profile, incognito, under the radar: that was how he liked to operate – just an inconspicuous British art dealer come to visit an art fair and conduct a little gentle networking. True, he was still coming to terms with the absurd cover name they had given him. 'Brendan Hall'. One day, he vowed, he would track down the bastard at Vauxhall Cross who had come up with it.

'Excuse, please, Mr Hall?'

They were still in the air bridge when he spotted a tall Emirati official in spotless white national dress and black camel-rope headband, holding up a sign with his cover name handwritten in felt tip. Luke looked around him to check whether anyone was paying attention. They weren't.

'Yes, that's me,' he said quietly to the man from Government Protocol, and followed him through a glass door into Abu Dhabi airport's futuristic terminal. Luke had been there before, years ago, on an SBS job, training Emirati Special Forces. They had spent most of their time sweating it out in the desert and mountains but, still, he could do without any of them recognizing him now. Somehow he didn't think they would buy the art-dealer story.

'Juice, sir?' Inside the VIP lounge a Filipina waitress came up to offer him a chilled rolled face towel and a choice of mango or carrot juice. Luke chose mango and drank it in one gulp. The lounge was decked out with soft cushions and Islamic patterns on the walls, interspersed with a giant portrait of the founding ruler of the modern UAE, Sheikh Zayed bin Sultan Al-Nahyan. Over in the corner a trio of jaded British business types had formed a circle round their matching Samsonite luggage. A very thin Indian waiter busied himself with straightening the already straight copies of that day's newspapers as they lay on glass tables.

Luke's passport had been whisked from him to be processed, sparing him the tedium of Immigration. Rubbing the sleep from his eyes after the overnight flight, he picked up a copy of a local English-language paper. On page four of that day's *Gulf News* there was an article about the exhibition: 'Manarat Art Gallery Draws Thousands' ran the headline. Was that a deliberate pun? He looked up, checking that no one was watching, then neatly tore out the page with the article, quickly folded it and slipped it into his jacket pocket. 'Brendan Hall' had better know everything there was to be known about this art fair.

The trio of businessmen got up and left, passports in hand, luggage trailing behind them on wheels. Luke was alone. He took out his smartphone, keeping it offline and on flight mode in case there were scanners in the vicinity. He scrolled through Photos until he came to the image he was after: Tannaz Zamani. His target. In another life, on covert night raids into mudwalled Afghan compounds with the SBS, a 'target' meant exactly that: some local warlord considered to be a serious enough threat that he had to be removed from the battlefield, often permanently. But

Tannaz was an intelligence target and that was a different proposition. He would need charm and guile, picking his way through a verbal minefield to avoid revealing who he was and what he was after.

What did he see when he looked into that face on the screen? A beautiful twenty-something Iranian university student, with a privileged lifestyle? Yes, there was a hint of a smile on her face, as if she just knew that, somehow, normal rules would never apply to her. And, given her father's position in the Revolutionary Guards, she was probably right. But what lay behind those dark, intense, almond eyes? What made her tick? Was it just boys, fashion, drugs and sex? That was certainly the inference he had taken from her personal intelligence profile, worked up by a joint team of targeting officers from MI6 and GCHQ. Surely there was more to her than that.

'Mr Hall!' A policeman was standing over him, dressed in a blue-grey uniform with a maroon beret and gold badge. 'Please, this your passport.' Luke took it from him as he got up, then grabbed his holdall and followed him out to the car park. The moment he stepped outside he felt the heat of the Gulf wash over him, like a warm bath, willing him to relax. A long black limousine with tinted rear windows and UAE Government Protocol number plates was waiting, the rear door held open for him by a uniformed driver. Luke swung himself in, pulled the door shut and sank onto the cream rear seat.

'Good journey?'

A man in the front passenger seat was twisting himself round to face Luke and holding out his hand. 'Faisal Rizki. I run Dubai Station.' Short dark curly hair, an easy smile and a stain on his shirt collar, Luke noted. He had a slightly crumpled look about him, which Luke put down to his new-found status as a father.

'Brendan Hall,' Luke replied – got to keep living the cover, even with the home team. 'Congratulations,' he added.

Rizki raised an eyebrow, then laughed. 'Oh, right, yes, fatherhood. It's a mixed blessing, I can tell you. Right now all I want to do is sleep into next week!' He patted the car's upholstery. 'Look,

I'm sorry about all this. I know you'd have preferred something a bit more discreet but our Emirati friends insisted.'

'Not a problem,' Luke said, 'but no one told me this was going to be a combined op.'

'It isn't. They just like to know what we're up to on their turf. They'll drop us off at your hotel and that's it. Here comes the driver. We'll talk more later.'

For forty-five minutes they drove in silence through a landscape of windblown sand and lines of pink oleander, whitewashed villas and towering construction cranes. Then Rizki turned to him once more. 'Okay, this is your hotel coming up right here.' Through the tinted rear windows Luke looked up at an enormous portico entrance, built in the Moorish style of North Africa, with water cascading from fountains and desert plants sprouting from well-tended beds. The wheels of their Mercedes had barely finished turning before the car doors were whisked open by liveried attendants wearing white gloves.

'Welcome to the St Regis,' they intoned in unison, and Luke almost had to fight to carry his bag, which he always insisted on doing. Rizki came round to join him as they moved into the shade of the hotel's portico and the limousine purred away. Luke got his first proper view of MI6's Dubai Station Chief, the man who had recruited and developed Black Run and whose shoes he was now being expected to fill. Rizki was shorter than him, but stockily built. He wore his sleeves rolled up, revealing a tangle of black hair across his forearms and a large gold signet ring.

'Once you've checked in, ask them to show you down to the beach terrace,' he said quietly, as they approached the reception desk. 'It's called Turquoise Bar or something like that. I'll meet you there and brief you. Oh, and you'll probably want to lose the jacket,' he said, with a smile. 'Makes you look like you've just stepped off a plane from London.'

Fifteen minutes later Luke was heading along a sandy path towards the beach. He made way for two Western girls in bikinis coming the other way, singing along together from shared iPhone earbuds. He had shed his London winter clothes in favour of chinos, loafers, a checked shirt, and a pair of sunglasses that Elise had made him buy. It was a contrived holiday look, yet still he felt overdressed and out of place.

He found Rizki sitting on the beach terrace in a rattan chair, facing out to sea, sipping what looked like iced coffee.

'Feels wrong, doesn't it?' he said amicably, as Luke took a seat next to him. 'You know, us being fully dressed and talking shop in a place like this.' They looked towards the beach where a family were running into the waves, holding hands, laughing and screaming. 'But there's a reason we're in this hotel.'

'I'd guessed as much,' said Luke, beckoning to a waiter to order himself an iced coffee. 'So is this where . . . ?'

'It is. You won't see them down here at the beach, though. They're careful, Tannaz and her mother, Forouz. They may be out of Iran but this is still the Middle East and they'll be on their guard.'

'Keeping to their rooms?'

'They checked in last night,' Rizki continued, 'and the only place they've been so far is the coffee shop. But that's about to change.' He looked at his watch. 'In just under two hours' time, at twelve noon, the exhibition opens at the Manaret Gallery. It's only five minutes' drive away, thirty-four exhibitors' stands but only one of them is Iranian, which makes our job a little easier. Here.' He produced a thin, glossy brochure from a portfolio on his lap. 'Take a look at this.'

'The Faridoon Gallery,' Luke read from the cover. 'Tehran, Paris, London . . .' He leafed through it. 'Looks pretty flash,' he said.

'Yes, there's money there, all right,' replied Rizki. 'In fact there's so much we've had to wade in to stop some rather over-enthusiastic gentlemen from HM Customs and Excise poking their noses into it. Zamani's wife is friends with the gallery owner – they went to the same art academy in Tehran in the nineties.'

'Okay,' said Luke. 'Let's cut to the chase. How do we get me in front of Tannaz?'

'We've been working on that. We've got someone inside the

gallery you're going to. I'll airdrop his photo into your phone in a moment. He'll introduce you, casually, to Tannaz and her mother when they're on site. After that, it's over to you and your charms. How good's your Farsi?'

'Very basic.'

'Well, they speak perfect English but if you can manage a few phrases it will go a long, long way. Trust me.' Rizki glanced around to make sure no one was watching. 'But, first, I need to show you something.' He slipped his hand into the portfolio on his lap once more and took out a sheaf of photographs contained in a clear plastic folder. 'You might want to take a look at these, but I should warn you, they're not pretty.' He handed the folder to Luke. 'This is Tannaz's father's handiwork . . . Take your time,' he added.

Until that moment Luke had been enjoying himself. The morning sun was sparkling on the waters of the Gulf, the iced coffee was slipping down a treat and he found he was quickly warming to Faisal Rizki. Abu Dhabi was Easy Street compared to Armenia. But now, as he took in the full horror of the photographs, Luke was reminded of what he was there to do and why it mattered.

'Christ . . .' he murmured, as he turned to the second photograph, then the third.

He had seen plenty of dead bodies in his time, mostly in Afghanistan and Iraq, but these were in a different league altogether. The men had been tortured to death. There were burn marks, jagged incisions, missing teeth, bulging eyes, empty eye sockets, and the raw chafing weals made by a constriction placed around the neck. They had not died easy deaths. For a moment, the images brought back all the horror he had experienced in his own adult life: the Taliban bullet that had severed his finger, the deranged cruelty of a Colombian 'chop house', where he had nearly been dismembered by half-drunk narco-thugs, and then, more recent, indelible, Black Run's slashed throat in that cold, bleak Armenian monastery. He pushed away the remains of his iced coffee.

'You know the most disgusting thing about these photos?' he said, when he had finally come to the last.

'What's that?'

'Their quality. These are hi-res, Faisal. Somebody took their time over them. It's almost as if they enjoyed their work.'

'Oh, I'm sure they did. These were smuggled out of the political wing at Evin Prison, on the outskirts of Tehran. All done on Zamani's orders. Seems he's intent on making something of a name for himself.'

'Right. But you're not seriously suggesting I show these to his daughter, Tannaz? She'll run a mile.'

'Take a closer look at the last one,' Rizki said. He was looking out to sea now. The happy cries of children could be heard above the clamour of gulls and waves. Luke turned back to the final photograph in the pile. And there he was, Karim Zamani, standing upright and proud next to the bloodied and battered corpse of one of his victims.

'Jesus . . .' Luke felt nauseous just looking at him and what he was capable of doing. 'The man is a monster.'

'You could say that,' Rizki replied. 'And when the moment comes, and you get in front of Tannaz, you might find that image quite persuasive.'

Chapter 26

Abu Dhabi

LUKE PAID THE driver and took his place in the growing queue outside the Manarat Gallery. It was just past midday and the December sun was scorching his forehead. But it still beat wading through an icy stream in Armenia, pursued by slavering dogs and trigger-happy policemen. The people around him seemed to be a microcosm of expat society in the Emirates: a British family, pink and freckled, was immediately in front. 'Sean, put that back now!' the mother commanded as her errant five-year-old tried to run off with a traffic cone. Beyond them a large family of Sikhs, colourfully dressed, was impeccably behaved. There were well-fed Egyptian families and a quiet couple from Syria, all under the bored gaze of Emirati policemen. The Manaret Gallery was indeed drawing a diverse and well-heeled crowd.

Inside, a steward directed visitors to the exhibition floor plan on a far wall. Luke followed the crowd, pushing his way gently through to where he could scan the list of exhibitors. Quatro Fine Art . . . Leila Hammoudi . . . There it was, the Faridoon Gallery, Hall C6. No rush, take your time, just saunter over when you're ready. Luke felt certain that Brendan Hall, contemporary art dealer from fashionable Bloomsbury, would probably not be a man in a hurry.

From force of habit, his eyes swept the room for security cameras. This was supposedly friendly territory, the UAE an ally of Britain, but you never knew just who was watching those camera feeds and what sort of company they were keeping. Luke made a mental note of the positions of all four CCTV cameras and steered a careful course around them. Not easy, when there must have been at least a thousand people milling around the exhibition, their voices echoing off the walls of the exhibitors' stands in a dozen different languages.

Luke took refuge some way off in a stand from Jeddah. He stood facing a massive collage of black-and-white photographs of the Old City, measuring at least four metres by four metres, expensively mounted and largely ignored. Out of the corner of his eye he could see the Faridoon Gallery, partly obscured by a throng of visitors. He watched it discreetly, while feigning interest in the pictures of Old Jeddah, then walked slowly towards it.

'Mr Brendan?' A young man detached himself from a group in conversation and approached Luke with a welcoming smile. Dark blue suit, polished black leather shoes, crisp white shirt. He fitted the description of the man Rizki said would meet him, but he couldn't be certain until they'd gone through the validation phrases. 'Hi,' the man said cheerfully as they shook hands. 'I'm Alireza. Welcome to the Faridoon.' He steered Luke past a large metallic sculpture mounted on a pedestal. 'You must be the first British visitor we've had today,' he continued.

Words spoken so casually, so off the cuff, it almost sounded like he meant them. But this, Luke knew, was the confirmation of his identity, and he needed to get the response right first time or the conversation would end there and then. 'They don't know what they're missing,' he replied, enunciating the words carefully, but not too slowly. 'This gallery is, how do you say it in Farsi? *Khayli ba haala* – so cool!'

Alireza laughed convincingly. 'Please, have a seat,' he said, pointing at a chair next to a small round table in the corner, 'while I get you our brochure.'

The Faridoon Gallery was busy: people were arriving in groups and greeting each other affectionately. It seemed to Luke to be something of a social hub for Iranians living in Abu Dhabi. Even with his limited knowledge of the Persian language he recognized the noisy chatter around him as Farsi, not Arabic. It sounded somehow softer, gentler, without the guttural tones of Gulf Arabic. From his seat in the corner, he had a good look at the melee of faces. The clientele was mostly women, all strikingly good-looking and wearing a lot of jewellery, with large, designer sunglasses pushed up high onto their immaculate hair. He noticed some had unusually straight noses, a sign of the extraordinary popularity of cosmetic surgery in modern Iran.

So which two were Tannaz and her mother? He thought he had memorized their faces well enough but now he wasn't so sure. Hell, they could be any of these women. And what if they weren't here? What if they'd gone shopping? The thought prompted a sudden pang of regret. Christmas was just days away and he should be with Elise, not sitting in an Abu Dhabi art gallery, waiting to meet two women who had no idea who he was, and probably little interest in him anyway.

Alireza returned with a brochure. It was the same as the one Faisal Rizki had produced earlier that morning. Luke thanked him as he watched the young man hover around a tall, dark-haired woman in a jacket, designer jeans and leather boots. She had her back to Luke and was deep in conversation with four or five others, but the moment they moved on Luke saw Alireza seize his chance. He touched her arm, whispered something in her ear and led her to Luke, who stood as she approached.

'This is Madame Sara Faridoon.' Luke smiled as Alireza made the fawning introductions. 'We are in her gallery. Sara, let me introduce you to Brendan Hall, a dealer from London.'

'From London?' She raised a sculpted eyebrow. 'You've come so far. I hope it's not just for our little exhibition here?' She waved a languid, exquisitely manicured hand around the gallery.

Millions, he thought, as he gave her his best smile. The stuff in here will be worth millions. '*Khosh bakhtam*,' he replied. 'Pleased to meet you.' It was a phrase he had taught himself on the plane over and now it was having exactly the desired effect. The gallery owner's face lit up like a lamp and she immediately addressed him in a stream of Farsi.

Luke held up his hands in apology. 'I'm afraid that's about the limit of my Farsi, sorry. But I'm keen to learn more. In fact, I'm an open book when it comes to modern Persian art. I'm happy to be educated!' Too forward, he wondered, even as he said it. But apparently not.

'In that case,' replied Sara Faridoon, 'we must do our best to help you!' She considered him for a moment, her head cocked to one side. 'Tell me, Mr . . . ?'

'Please call me Brendan.'

'Do you like Persian food, Brendan?'

'Love it,' he lied. If this was going to be an invitation to anything like the stuff he'd had to eat while visiting tribal leaders in Kandahar, it would be nothing short of an ordeal.

'Excellent.' She clapped her hands together, her bracelets jangling. 'Then why don't you join us this evening for dinner? I'm having a little get-together in honour of my friend Forouz and her daughter Tannaz. They're over here from Tehran and you can ask them all about Persian art.'

Bingo. Luke kept his face impassive but his heart rate had just picked up a gear. This was it. He'd made it to first base.

'I'd be delighted,' he replied. 'Which restaurant?'

Sara touched his arm, as if anointing him into her inner circle. 'Eight o'clock at the embassy. The Iranian Embassy. And do be sure to bring your passport. They can be very strict about security.'

Chapter 27

'I SHOULD PROBABLY tell you all,' said Nigel Batstone, addressing the weekly Foreign and Commonwealth Office Iran departmental meeting in King Charles Street, 'that I've had a visit from our friends across the river.' The Director of the Middle East and North Africa Department, known as MENA, tipped his head in a south-westerly direction towards Vauxhall Cross. 'More of a representation, if you will. I won't go into the finer details but suffice it to say they're having profound reservations about our cosying up to the Iranians.'

'Don't we all?' murmured someone else at the table.

Batstone ignored the remark. 'Let's just say,' he continued, 'their concerns are more technical than political. More to do with . . . compliance. That is to say, compliance with the terms of the nuclear deal, the Joint Comprehensive Plan of Action.'

'Has this been shared with Number Ten and the NSC?' asked the woman next to him. Sheila Babcock had been the Deputy Head of Mission at the British Embassy in Tehran until the place was ransacked in 2011.

'I'm sure SIS are sharing it with anyone who'll listen,' said Batstone, 'but I believe our job is to focus more on the political angle. I think we're all agreed that the transition from Presidents

Ahmedinejad to Rouhani in 2013 was a positive step, a decisive move towards normalization of relations with the rest of the world. Now we need to encourage the Iranians to keep moving down that path.'

'I have to say,' asserted Sheila Babcock, taking off her glasses and placing them on the table in front of her, 'that their human-rights record is still absolutely abysmal. If anything, it's getting worse. They executed at least two hundred people last year, most of them in secret. Some are comparing it to the worst of the purges in the first years after the Islamic Revolution.'

'I hear you,' replied Batstone, evenly. He gave her what he hoped was a conciliatory smile and noticed she didn't return it. 'I accept that their record on human rights is . . . How shall I put it? Sub-optimal? But I can assure you we have raised those concerns with the Iranians at ministerial level. But, Sheila, we are living in a world of realpolitik, if you'll pardon the vernacular. Let's not forget that our friends on the other side of the Gulf, the Saudis, have also racked up a pretty hefty number of executions this year and we're not letting that get in the way of business as usual!' He looked quickly around the table. He was eager to press on.

'But what about the Americans?' asked an older man, sporting a florid grey moustache. 'Everything that comes out of the White House, these days, seems to be an absolute gift to the hardliners in Iran.'

Batstone thought this man must be the only person left in the FCO to have visited Iran under the Shah and, frankly, he didn't have a lot of time for his opinions. It was surely time for him to retire. 'Gordon,' he replied testily, 'our job, in this department, is to work towards the best possible relations with the moderates in the Iranian political system. *Pour encourager les autres.*'

'Excuse me?' The man with the grey moustache again.

'It's French, Gordon. Presumably you did learn French at school? It means "to encourage the others".' Batstone shook his head sadly. What had happened to all the linguists in this place since he joined?

'Right, moving on,' he said briskly, rubbing his hands together as if he had just come in from the cold. 'There has been some discussion, as you are all aware, that with the current tension in the Gulf, now would be a good time for the Foreign Secretary to pay a visit to Tehran. This would be the highest-level representation from the UK since the Iranian elections. We've reached out to certain moderate figures in the Foreign Ministry and I'm pleased to say we've had a positive response.'

He noticed Sheila Babcock shaking her head almost imperceptibly. He would have to have a straight talk with her after this. If there was one thing Nigel Batstone insisted on it was departmental unity of purpose.

'Therefore,' he continued, 'in an effort to help defuse the current tensions, I will, this afternoon, be putting my signature to the visit.' He drew himself up to his full height and ever so slightly puffed out his chest as he spoke. 'As Director of the Middle East and North Africa Department I'm going to recommend our Foreign Secretary visits Iran at the first available opportunity in the new year.' He paused for emphasis. 'This will set the pattern for future relations and put them squarely on a solid footing.'

Chapter 28

Abu Dhabi

IT WAS JUST past seven p.m. and an old man, wearing a long and tattered *shalwar kameez* that might once have been a gentle shade of blue, pushed his trolley slowly past the Ministry of Higher Education on Abu Dhabi's Karamah Street. No one paid any attention to the Pakistani sweeper. After all, more than a million of his countrymen had made the UAE their home, faithfully sending home their monthly pay cheques to support an extended family in Punjab, Sindh or the tribal territories that ran along the Afghan border. No one noticed as he paused to peer inside his cart and touched his ear with his right hand. And there was no one around to hear when he spoke into the wireless micro audio transmitter sewn into the lapel of his shirt.

'Shaheen Three. In position. I have eyes on.'

'The old man', a graduate of Leeds Metropolitan University, had yet to reach his fortieth birthday.

Less than a mile away, just off Abu Dhabi's Corniche Road, the VHF antenna on the roof of the British Embassy picked up his transmission, and bounced it onwards, encrypted, to a window-less room deep within a green-and-sandstone-coloured building 3,400 miles away. There, a terse voice replied: 'Okay, make a second pass across the entrance gate in fifteen minutes and report.'

In an alley off Karamah Street, Luke Carlton sat in the back of a taxi, meter ticking. He, too, wore an earpiece and was waiting for the all-clear from Vauxhall to proceed. Things had moved fast since he'd received Sara's invitation to dinner at the embassy. On hearing the news, MI6's Dubai Station Chief had been incredulous.

'What? The Iranian Embassy? Here in Abu Dhabi? Bloody hell!' There'd been a pause on the encrypted line before Faisal Rizki continued: 'Are you absolutely sure that's what she said?'

'Positive.' Luke had called him from the car park outside the Manarat Gallery, where he was just another art lover among the hundreds thronging the exhibition that afternoon.

'I must admit,' Rizki had said, 'I hadn't seen that one coming. So you accepted, I hope?'

'Obviously.'

'Good . . . good.' Luke could almost hear him working up a plan in his head. The other man had already returned home to his villa in Dubai, probably just finished a stint of nappy duty with his newborn. 'Right, we're going to have to alert Security section back in London,' he had told Luke. 'Need to go over your cover story one more time, make sure your Facebook history and Twitter feed back it all up. The Iranians are not stupid. They'll be going over it with a fine-toothed comb. Let's just hope they're not using any biometrics on the door. That could cause you problems further down the line. We'll get someone down there to check if there's any unusual activity.'

'Anything else I should know?' Luke had asked.

There had been a long pause, and in the background Luke had heard a baby crying.

'Well, yes . . .' Rizki had said eventually.

Luke had thought he sounded distracted, which was hardly surprising. Officially, Rizki was on paternity leave but he clearly had too much invested in this operation to sit by and let it flow over his patch.

'Luke, I hope you're ready for this? I mean, the Iranian Embassy is sovereign territory. You're effectively setting foot inside the Islamic Republic of Iran here. You're going in. You'd better be a hundred per cent watertight.'

'Got it,' Luke had replied, with a confidence he hadn't entirely felt. And now, a few hours later, sitting in the back of a taxi, he still wasn't sure. But, hey, what was the worst that could happen? Get a finger blown off by a bullet? Done that in Afghanistan. Have a hole drilled in his foot? Had that done to him by those narco bastards in Colombia. Get bundled onto an Iranair cargo flight to Tehran and spend the next ten years in Evin jail? That didn't quite fit with his career plan.

Luke's earpiece crackled into life and he sat up, now on full alert. 'Control. You're clear to go in. Good luck.'

Luke reached into the pocket of his linen jacket and pulled out a wad of faded green ten-dirham notes and handed them to the driver. He clambered out of the taxi. As he did, he reached up and removed the earpiece. Dropping it, he crushed it underfoot and kicked the remains into the gutter.

He was within two hundred metres of the embassy now, an impressive white-walled building with blue windows and traditional stacked wind towers – *badgheers*, they called them, here in the Gulf. He had found that out on Wikipedia. Don't march in there like you're on parade, Luke reminded himself. You're a civvy now, an art dealer, so act the part.

Situated just across a busy intersection from the New Zealand Embassy, the Iranian Embassy was surrounded by mature trees and a high wall. The sun had been down for more than an hour by the time Luke walked up to its gates, and the warmth of the mild Gulf winter's day had given way to a chilly breeze. Luke buttoned his jacket and approached the man on the gate, a slight figure in glasses, wearing baggy trousers and scuffed shoes. No sign of a weapon, just a clipboard held in his left hand.

'*Salaamu aleikum*,' Luke greeted him. 'Brendan Hall. I'm here for the dinner tonight?' The man grunted and peered down at his list. For several seconds neither man spoke. The guard looked up once at Luke, squinting from beneath thick, bushy eyebrows, then went back to scanning his list. Luke began to whistle softly, then trailed off. He had never been much good at whistling.

'Burrendin?' said the guard.

'Yes, that's right. Brendan Hall.'

'Give passport.' Luke handed it over. The face was his but the name was not.

'Phone? Mobile phone? Put here,' the guard instructed. Luke pulled out a Samsung and handed it over. Were anyone inside the Iranian Embassy to check, they would find its log to reveal a number of calls made to various art galleries in London, New York and the Middle East, one to a hotel in Dubai and another to a British Airways ticket-sales desk. 'Brendan Hall' had been going about his normal business. Luke Carlton had never used it.

The man with the clipboard motioned for him to wait while he checked a car coming in. Tinted windows, clearly somebody important: the guard stood stiffly to attention as the gate slid back and the limousine drove through. He pointed Luke towards an X-ray scanner, which he went through without a beep. He was in. No biometric iris scan, no fingerprint check, no pat-down. He felt his shoulders relax: he had just passed the most dangerous moment . . . because inside his linen jacket were three ordinary-looking biros, all in a row in their pocket. All three could write perfectly well but the middle one could do rather more than that. Hidden inside the cap was a Minbel, a passive Bluetooth receptor, designed to hoover up every mobile number within five metres and store it digitally. It was something Vauxhall had insisted on. Getting an MI6 intelligence officer inside a key Iranian embassy like this one was not an opportunity they would pass up.

Luke's relief was short-lived. A large man in a dark green suit was approaching. Regulation four days' stubble, no tie and a fierce expression beneath knitted eyebrows. Luke judged him immediately to be from embassy security, and had an unpleasant flashback to the two heavies he'd confronted in the mountains above the Geghard Monastery less than a month ago. This man had the same powerful wrestler's build, and now Luke wasn't on neutral turf: he was on theirs. What had Rizki said to him that afternoon? 'You're on their ground now. If they want to lift you, they can.'

'This way,' the man said, taking Luke firmly by the arm.

Christ, don't tell me they've made me already? Still smiling as he let himself be led away from the entrance gate, Luke ran through a mental checklist of all the things that might possibly have given him away. Short of being betrayed by Faisal Rizki, he could not think of a single one.

The man in the green suit stopped in front of a door. 'Party?' His dour, default expression dissolved into a grin. 'You come for art party, yes? Please . . .' He strode towards the door and opened it for Luke, revealing a large, well-lit reception room adorned with chandeliers and a life-size portrait of Iran's Supreme Leader, Ayatollah Khamenei, hanging on the wall. There must have been at least a hundred guests, who seemed all to be talking at once, the hubbub rolling around Luke. The security guard spoke briefly into his lapel mic, then shook Luke's hand and left.

For a moment Luke stood stock-still in the doorway, over-whelmed with relief. So the Iranians hadn't made him after all. But now he had another problem. Naively, perhaps, he had envis-aged 'dinner party' to mean a dozen people sitting round a table, when it would have been easy to strike up a conversation with Zamani's daughter, Tannaz. But now he found himself swim-ming alone in a sea of unfamiliar faces. Was he really the only Westerner in the room? He could see waiters in starched white shirts and bow ties scurrying back and forth with trays of can-apés while a trio of musicians played traditional Iranian flute music. It seemed everyone knew someone here except him: they were all immersed in their own private conversations, but as for him? What were his chances now of finding Tannaz, let alone recruiting her? Luke, frankly, felt lost.

'Brendan! So glad you made it!' He whirled round to see Sara Faridoon sweeping towards him. She was enveloped in an embroi-dered crimson silk dress, full length, with elaborate brocade at the neck and sleeves, gold dangling from her ear lobes. Luke took all of this in at a glance, that, and the young man trailing at her side wearing a suit with sharp, pointed lapels. 'This is Behzad, our cultural attaché here in Abu Dhabi.' He offered Luke a limp handshake, his attention already elsewhere, and Luke found he had taken an instant dislike to him.

'So,' he ventured, 'I hear great things about Iranian culture.' Not the most dynamic of openings but Luke felt he had to make an effort.

'Great things,' Behzad repeated quietly, looking somewhere into the middle distance. 'Great things.' With that, he excused himself and wandered off.

'Come,' said Sara, oblivious to the snub, 'let me introduce you to my friends from the art world.'

Luke was only too happy to follow in her wake, breathing in her perfume, fascinated by this woman, who seemed to move so easily between two different worlds: the West and the Islamic Republic. He decided to adopt an expression of what he hoped was boyish innocence. True, it didn't quite go with the scar on his cheek, his missing middle finger and his weathered complexion from all those days serving in the heat and ice of Afghanistan's extreme climate. Luke had been a fighting man nearly all his adult life, and twelve years in the forces had left their mark. But Vauxhall had been nothing if not thorough: they had schooled him to come up with an answer for every question. The missing finger? A nasty accident on my gap year – Peru, since you ask. That scar on my cheek? Oh, that was my brother messing about with a penknife when we were kids.

A tray of drinks was being offered to him. Watermelon and pomegranate juice, with a sprig of something green thrown on the top. Luke had never felt more in need of a cold beer in his life but he took the proffered glass and nodded gratefully. Sara was steering him towards an Iranian woman he guessed to be in her late forties. A strong, confident woman with an air of authority about her. Luke recognized her immediately from her photograph.

'Now you can try out your Farsi on my friend here,' teased

Sara, a hand on each of their shoulders. 'This is Forouz, just arrived from Tehran. Forouz-*jaan*, this is Mr Hall from London. He wants to learn all about Iranian art.'

Forouz's dark eyes widened flirtatiously, as if this suggestion were the most daring and exciting thing she had ever heard. Luke put it down to a well-practised cocktail-party trick to flatter her guests.

'So tell me, Mr Hall . . .' Forouz Zamani considered him for a moment '. . . what kind of art excites you?'

'Excites me?'

'Interests you. I'm sorry, it is my English. I meant, do you have a favourite Iranian artist?'

OK, Carlton. You're up. This is the opening gambit. Stage one of the Pitch. Time to deploy what you learned on that bloody agent-handling course down on the south coast. Guile, charm, patience, all of that. So think hard: what was the name of that artist they briefed you about at Vauxhall Cross? Reza someone. Reza who?

'Well, yes, I do have one,' he replied. 'I've had my eye on a Reza—' Luke broke into a contrived cough.

She bought it. 'Ah! You like Reza Derakshani!' She clenched her hands together in mock triumph, her long, manicured fingers heavy with jewels. 'Then you have excellent taste! Like my daughter, she is also a fan. Here she is now. Tannaz-*jaan*, meet Mr Hall. From London.'

Christ . . . They don't teach you how not to overreact when you're introduced to somebody so drop-dead beautiful. That photograph in her Service profile didn't do her justice. Tannaz Zamani was smaller, slimmer than Elise, and her dark hair was swept up high in the style of Audrey Hepburn in *Breakfast at Tiffany's*. She had her mother's eyes, flashing beneath long, curved lashes, while her unblemished skin bore just the faintest tan – skiing in the Elburz Mountains? – and she wore no discernible make-up. That they were inside the Iranian Embassy would perhaps account for her rather conservative dress, covering almost everything but her hands and ankles. Still, Luke caught himself glancing at the curves of her body as it moved beneath that dress.

117

'A pleasure,' she said, holding out a delicate hand. He detected a hint of jasmine as she leaned in to catch his name a second time.

Out of respect Luke turned quickly to address her mother – they were, after all, on Iranian sovereign territory – but Forouz Zamani was already off and away, talking to someone else. A middle-aged couple squeezed past them, forcing Tannaz to move nearer to Luke. She was close now, so close he could detect something other than her perfume, something pheromonal. It was her personal scent, and he found it intoxicating.

Get a grip of yourself, Carlton. You're on duty, operational. You're inside the Iranian Embassy. Hostile territory. Your target is right in front of you and you're busy fantasizing about what's beneath her dress? And you have a gorgeous girlfriend of your own back home? Sort yourself out, man, and focus on the job.

Tannaz was saying something to him now, interrupting the subconscious bollocking Luke was giving himself inside his head. 'I'm sorry, I didn't catch that?'

'I said, are you living here in the Emirates?' Her English was perfect, with a slight transatlantic twang.

'No. We – I live in London. I'm here for the exhibition.'

'Ah.' She turned her head away, as if suddenly remembering something. 'I love London. You know King's Road?'

'I do.'

'Love that place. It's like my second home. Baba – my father – doesn't approve!' Those eyes twinkled mischievously.

'Why not?' Luke asked. 'What does he do, your dad?' *He's a senior officer in the Revolutionary Guards Corps. That would be why I'm here.*

'Oh, he's in the government, sort of. A lot of these people here are his people.' She gestured towards the reception room. It was emptying now as they were being directed next door for dinner. 'Well, some of them are his people. You can always spot them – they're the ones checking everybody else out! My country is a complicated place, Mr Hall, but you mustn't judge us too harshly.'

'Please, call me—' He caught himself just in time. 'Call me Brendan.'

'Yes. Brendan. Well, maybe we will meet up in London. You can take me to dinner and I can tell you about Persian art.'

Wow. That was forward. Things were moving faster than he had anticipated. Perhaps a little too fast.

'Here.' She opened her handbag, took out a pen and a tiny mauve notebook. She wrote something down, tore off the page and gave it to Luke. 'My number. We can use Telegram. My name will come up as Aesthetica.' It was not so much a suggestion as an invitation. He remembered another time long ago: a rainy Friday night on Union Street in Plymouth with his mates from the Corps, messing about in the street outside some club called Jesters, while a girl with tired eyes and smudged lipstick pressed her phone number into his hand.

'I'll certainly do that,' Luke replied. Tannaz looked hurriedly round the room. They were the last to go in to dinner. Soon there would be interminable speeches in Farsi, none of which he would understand.

And then it happened. Quite unexpectedly. Taking him completely by surprise. It was just after she had handed him her number and he was turning to accompany her into the dining room. She stood on tiptoe, smiling, her lips moist, and planted a kiss on his lips. Then she was gone and he was alone, staring down at the piece of paper in his hand with her number on it, thinking, What the hell just happened there?

Chapter 29

Buckinghamshire

THEY DROVE IN silence, Elise at the wheel, her mother beside her, staring straight ahead at the darkened road, her lips pursed. Their headlights swept across high hedges on either side and glistened off the surface of the tarmac.

'Slow down here!' snapped Helen Mayhew, as they approached a corner.

'I *was* slowing down!' protested Elise. She shook her head as she drove. That wasn't like her mother at all – in fact, she couldn't remember seeing her like this since she'd been a teenager and they used to fight practically every day. It must be the stress, of course, and the waiting for results. The pain her mother had felt in her abdomen that afternoon in the Goring Hotel, the day Luke had left on his trip, had come back. That, and a sudden, inexplicable loss of appetite. At Elise's insistence she had gone straight to see her GP and he had sent her for a blood test. Elise had come to pick her up from the hospital's Outpatients Department.

'I can't bear hospitals,' said Helen, in a calmer tone.

'We all dislike them, Mummy, but they're just doing their job. Anyway, what did your GP say?'

'He said it's probably nothing but . . .'

'But what?'

'But he wants to make sure.'

'Make sure about what?' Elise threw a quick glance at her mother as she slowed for a T-junction.

Helen didn't answer straight away. She looked out of her window at the wet, darkened hedgerows flashing past, then turned back to Elise. 'He wants to make sure it's not liver cancer. That's all.'

Chapter 30

'I DON'T LIKE it. It doesn't smell right.' Graham Leach's brow was furrowed, as if he were faced with a final, unfathomable clue to a *Times* cryptic crossword. The Head of Iran and Caucasus had called this meeting to take place as soon as Luke could get himself back to Vauxhall Cross from Abu Dhabi.

He had excused himself early from the Iranian Embassy dinner, feigning a headache, then caught the red-eye back to London, landing at Heathrow at some godawful time of the morning. He had taken the tube to Victoria, then a taxi south of the river in driving rain, and now here he was, sitting at a table on the fourth floor. Luke had fired off an initial Flash Report of his encounter with Tannaz the night before, sent from his encrypted phone, which had been printed out and distributed to everyone in the room.

'With no disrespect to you, Luke,' continued Leach, 'you're a good-looking chap and all that, but, come on, nobody works that fast. I think it's fishy. You're saying she kissed you? *Inside* the Iranian Embassy? That makes no sense to me, even for a wild child like Tannaz. I mean, weren't there any cameras on the wall, for God's sake? Didn't she know the risk that entailed?'

'There were no cameras in that room. I checked,' Luke replied.

122

'At least, none that I could see. And she checked too. I saw her do it just before she made her move.'

There was a short silence in the room.

'I say we let it play.' This was from Angela Scott. She had her hair tied back tightly this morning, with a green ribbon, and he noticed she was wearing just a hint of blusher, which added colour to her usually pale complexion. In the relatively short time Luke had known her at MI6 she had always watched his back, like a godmother, stood up for him when others had said he was too impetuous for the job, and had done her best to spare him the worst of the bureaucratic bullshit that was creeping like a fungus into everyone's workload.

She turned to address him. 'What's your feeling?'

Luke was in two minds. Making the initial contact with Tannaz had been easier than he'd expected, thanks to all the work put in behind the scenes by Dubai Station. His cover story had held up and he had got himself inside the Iranian Embassy. The Service now had Tannaz's mobile-phone number, effectively a direct line into Karim Zamani's family, as well as a host of other numbers culled from the embassy party using that concealed Bluetooth receptor. All these could now be 'exploited' by the tech wizards over at GCHQ in Cheltenham and fed into a shared database with MI6. But Tannaz? That was a different matter. If she had done as she had anywhere other than in the Iranian Embassy, under the very noses of the people she purported to dislike, her behaviour would have been absolutely in keeping with her profile. But somehow he smelt trouble. A honey-trap by the Iranians? Unlikely. The Russians, Israelis and several other countries' agencies might go in for such games but that wasn't Tehran's style. Still, something wasn't right.

'I think it's risky,' he said.

'Go on,' said Angela, gently. 'In what way?'

'I'm not sure. It all seemed rather forced. Just a bit too obvious. As if someone had put her up to it, you know?'

Leach, still frowning, looked up and nodded in agreement.

'How much do you all know about this girl, Tannaz Zamani?'

asked the woman next to Luke. Her jet-black hair was starting to go grey, and rather severe thick-rimmed spectacles rested half-way down the bridge of her nose. Luke had met her for the first time today when she had introduced herself. This was Trish Fryer, Mission Controller for the Middle East, and she had a formidable reputation. 'I'm sure everyone's up to speed on her IRGC father,' she continued, 'but what do we really know about her?' It was a rhetorical question. Trish Fryer knew a great deal about Tannaz Zamani and her family.

'Because, let me tell you,' she continued, 'this girl is a wild one. At least by Tehran standards. She's the apple of her father's eye and she's a rebel at the same time. Parties, boyfriends, underground rock concerts. There's a couple of Instagram postings I'd like to share with you.'

Trish passed round a pair of photographs blown up to A4 size. One showed Tannaz, daughter of a senior officer in the Revolutionary Guards, lounging in a Jacuzzi while wearing the skimpiest of bikinis, a bottle of Smirnoff in one hand, cigarette in the other, her arm draped around a boy of about the same age. Behind her, just out of focus, a couple were locked in an intimate embrace. The other photo showed her sprawled on the floor at some house party. Her head was tossed back, her cleavage on display, and she was wearing what appeared to be scarlet hot pants. This was the girl, Luke reminded himself, who, less than twenty-four hours earlier, had sauntered up to him at that embassy party in an all-enveloping black dress and whose number was now burning a hole in his phone.

Leach held the photos at arm's length. 'She posted these from Iran?' he queried. 'I didn't think that was possible.'

'No, they were uploaded from an account in Germany. GCHQ tracked them down with FaceUp.'

'Sorry?' Luke interjected. 'FaceUp?'

'Facial recognition software,' Trish replied. 'It's fast but it still took them most of a day to come up with the match.'

'What's your point?' asked Leach.

'My point is,' said Trish Fryer, removing her thick-rimmed

spectacles and regarding Leach with thoughtful, pale blue eyes, 'Tannaz is exploitable. She's got no time for the fun-detector morality brigade her father represents. We know she can't stand them.'

Luke watched her as she spoke. She'd been a lifelong smoker, he guessed, by the rich tone of her voice and the tiny vertical lines on her upper lip. Probably gave it up not long ago after a scare.

'So *if* we can recruit her,' Trish Fryer continued, 'we could find ourselves in a very good place indeed. She could develop into one of our best agents inside Iran since we lost Black Run.'

Just the mention of the murdered agent sent a frisson round the room. His death had left the Service with a gaping hole in intelligence-gathering on what Iran's nuclear scientists might be up to at Parchin. For Luke, it was something more visceral, personal even: the fleeting memory of a brave man he had never had the chance to meet alive. Even if nobody was going to say it to his face, Luke knew that Black Run was his failure. He owned it.

'Look, I hate to break up this conversation,' said a Scots voice at the other end of the table. It was Dr Ken Paterson, Head of Counter-proliferation. Luke remembered being told he was a scientist by trade and, yes, he certainly came across differently from the others. This wasn't a man who liked to deal in half-completed jigsaw puzzles and vague uncertainties.

'Can I just point out the urgency of the situation we're facing here?' he said, without waiting for anyone to reply. 'Let's remind ourselves of the facts, shall we? The hardliners don't like the nuclear deal, right? That much we know. Add to that what Black Run thought he saw down in the tunnel at Parchin and what have we got? Eh?' He stared around the room. To Luke he appeared a touch manic. But maybe you needed someone like Paterson in a world where North Korea was able to build itself a hydrogen bomb without the world knowing.

'I'll tell you what you've got!' Paterson was riled, his voice raised. Luke was close enough to him to see the beads of perspiration appearing on his pink forehead. 'You've got a fucking nuclear warhead being built down there and Karim Zamani is right behind it.' Paterson sat back, having delivered his piece.

Eventually Leach broke the silence. 'Ken, we're all completely with you on the urgency of this,' he said, 'but I'm just not entirely convinced that a twenty-two-year-old Tehran socialite is our best route for getting inside his head.'

'No?' retorted Trish Fryer. 'Even when that person is his daughter? Then who else d'you suggest? Because we can forget about his wife, Forouz. She and Zamani are hardly speaking to each other and their son is barely into his teens. Tannaz is our only option, Graham.'

He pushed his chair back from the table, and Luke saw him exchanging a momentary glance with Angela. She gave him the faintest of nods, then Leach looked straight at Luke as he spoke. 'Very well. I think that settles it. Luke, unless you have any objections, we'd like you to take this one on. We need to go all out now to bring Tannaz Zamani onboard. Any idea when you can next get in front of her?'

'She's coming to London next week,' Luke replied. He looked at Trish Fryer. 'But I expect you knew that already, since Cheltenham are feeding you the contents of her messages. She texted me this morning.' Damn. He hadn't meant it to come across like that: he just couldn't help feeling uncomfortable that his comms were being monitored by his own side. He'd have to get used to it.

'Cheltenham are fast,' Trish replied, with a smile, 'but not that fast. I wasn't aware of this new development. But it's good.'

'Right, then.' Leach rubbed his hands together. 'Let's get cracking. Trish, can I leave it to you to get Agent Handling in on this and work up a plan?'

'They're already on it,' she said.

The meeting broke up.

Chapter 31

Bluebird Restaurant, King's Road, London

IN A DARK blue suit over a black woollen polo neck, with a seat at the bar and a drink on order, Luke was ready, in position and ahead of time. The Bluebird Restaurant in Chelsea would not have been his first choice for the rendezvous, for the simple reason that he sometimes liked to go there with Elise and her friends. He preferred not to mix business with pleasure and this was strictly business, masquerading as pleasure. But Agent Handling had selected the venue after careful consideration, so Bluebird it was. He would meet Tannaz for drinks upstairs, then move from the bar to a discreet table in the corner behind the industrial-look red-painted girders and the climbing plants sprouting up like beanstalks from sculpted pots.

'Your Bluebird Winter Punch, sir.' The barman set the glass in front of him with a flourish. 'I have your card behind the bar.'

'Thanks.' Vodka, amaretto, lemon juice, cranberry juice and a slice of fresh fig. A bit of a poncy drink, his SBS mates would have told him, and it certainly wasn't cheap but, sod it, MI6 were picking up the tab tonight.

Luke took a sip while keeping one eye on where people were coming in and handing over their coats, then turning right into the bar. He had an uncontrollable urge to scratch his chest where the wire had been taped to his skin. The listener was stationed just twenty metres away in the disabled loo, the door locked and a pair of borrowed crutches propped against the wall in case anyone came knocking. Luke avoided looking over his right shoulder where a young couple were seemingly deep in conversation. The 'watchers' from Vauxhall: they would be observing every movement, every gesture, every flick of the hair, going over it all with him afterwards as they played back the recording, seeking out a joint decision on whether she was genuine or if this was a set-up. The Service was taking no chances.

Tannaz was late. Nothing surprising there. He imagined she was still on Tehran time. Luke scrolled idly through the messages on his phone, hoping for something from Elise. Nothing. Things had not gone well when he had tried to explain what he was doing here tonight. True, the timing hadn't helped: Elise had been distracted lately, worried about her mother. He wouldn't normally have shared anything about his work with her, it was against Service protocol, but the Bluebird? He imagined her walking in with her friends, seeing him sitting at the bar with this girl, turning on her heel and walking straight out. He had told her the barest of details.

'So, let me get this straight,' Elise had shot back. 'You're telling me you're going on a date? At the Bluebird?'

'No! Well, it's not a date exactly, it's work. I'm letting you know because I don't want to keep anything from you.' Luke had realized, even as he said it, that this sounded so lame. ''Lise, I'm as uncomfortable about this as you are but—'

'Then just say no.' She had cut him off in mid-sentence. 'Tell them you've already got a girlfriend and you don't need to go on a date, thank you very much. Unless, of course, that's not the case any more.'

'No! God, no! That's not what I'm saying at all. Look, I can't go into why I've got to meet this girl so you're just going to have to trust me.'

Elise had fallen silent. 'I do trust you,' she had said at last. 'It

128

just sounds odd, that's all.' Then she had gone off into the other room to deal with the laundry.

How had it come to this? he wondered, as he sat alone at the bar, people drinking, laughing and flirting at either side of him. Hell, planning and leading a night raid with Special Forces in Kandahar Province had been easier than this. What had he become? Some kind of sex-bait for an Iranian party girl who might or might not end up supplying information for the Secret Intelligence Service? His career seemed to be veering off into uncharted territory.

He was aware of her even before he looked up from his phone. Maybe it was her perfume, that sweet hint of jasmine, or maybe it was because he caught sight of her reflection on the surface of the bar. Tannaz was suddenly in front of him, petite, dark, beautiful. She smiled as he stood up, her lips glistening with freshly applied gloss. He leaned forward to kiss her on both cheeks. She was wearing a low-cut black dress and a simple gold pendant round her neck.

'What can I get you?' he asked. It sounded ridiculously formal for a girl barely out of her teens but he needed to play the game. Whatever it was Tannaz saw in him, well, he needed her to keep believing it. Suave, debonair English art dealer? Yup, he could do that. Protective father figure? At a pinch, yes. Tall, blond sex-god? Maybe not.

'You choose,' she said, settling herself on the stool next to him. He had a sudden flashback to his first date with Elise. What was it she had ordered for them that night? Mojitos. Luke waved over the barman and ordered a Spiced Apple Mojito.

'So . . . good flight?' he asked her. Seriously? Had he really just said that? Was it the best he could do? A first-class degree in international relations from Edinburgh, twelve years as a Royal Marines officer, four with the SBS, followed by some of the best training in espionage that the world had to offer and he was reduced to such banal small-talk? She flashed him a look and nodded slowly, reaching for her drink. He had to up his conversation.

He thought about challenging her to a mind game but, no, he needed to get to know her first.

For the next twenty minutes they talked art and museums, with Luke swiftly reaching the conclusion that her artistic interests were dwarfed by her enthusiasm for going on trips out of Iran, preferably to cities in the US and Europe. That was fine, he could work with it. They moved to their table, and when the chilled bottle of Gavi de Gavi arrived in a silver ice bucket, he changed tack.

'Tell me about your life in Iran,' he prompted. 'Friends, boyfriends . . . girlfriends. I've heard about those parties in north Tehran.' He smiled. 'Are they really that wild?'

Tannaz laughed and ran the fingers of both hands through her silky black hair.

'Depends which ones you go to,' she replied. 'They can be a lot of fun, yes, sure. Maybe I'll invite you next time you're over.'

Luke sat back, feigning surprise. 'Next time? I haven't been to Iran once yet!' That, at least, was true.

'Oh, my God, you're shitting me!' It was the first time he had heard her swear. He noticed her second glass of wine was nearly empty. 'Well, you should come,' she gushed. 'You'd be amazed. People think Iran's all black cloaks and ayatollahs but that's just the way the media here portrays us. You know we have a history going back three thousand years?'

'But not a lot of freedom, these days,' he ventured.

There. Strike one. If recruiting Tannaz as an agent for MI6 was like climbing the north face of the Eiger, then Luke had just swung his pick into the ice wall on the lowest slopes. She laughed again and drained her glass. Damn, this girl could drink.

'No, you're right there,' she said, 'but it helps to have connections.'

'In what way?' He knew exactly what she meant. That was why he was there.

'My father . . .' Tannaz hesitated. 'I shouldn't really be telling you this but, have you heard of something called the IRGC? The Iranian Revolutionary Guards Corps?'

'Um, no,' he lied. 'What's that?'

'Never mind. He works for them. Believe me, you really don't want to cross them.'

'Wow. I'll remember that,' said Luke. He reached out his arm and gently stroked the back of her hand. 'It must be hard being you, Tannaz. I mean, d'you ever feel conflicted? Like, your dad works for this hardcore IRGC thing and you seem to enjoy the freedom you get here in the West. How do you reconcile the two?' *Too much? Too fast?* He would know soon enough.

But Tannaz wasn't really listening. She gave a slight shrug of her shoulders and shifted closer to him, resting her perfect face on her palm. The drinks were kicking in now and he could tell she was done with this conversation. Her lips were pouting at him, her right hand was resting on his inner thigh, and her left was reaching round the back of his neck, pulling him towards her. She brushed her lips against his, then moved them across his cheek to whisper into his ear, 'I'm staying close by, in Cadogan Gardens. Mama's out until late with friends. Why don't you come and join me for a nightcap?'

Shit. This was one situation they definitely hadn't trained him for. Her hand was still resting on his thigh and her invitation hung in the air. Hesitate any longer and he'd lose the chance to make a pitch. And then he felt it, the familiar silent buzz of his mobile going off in his jacket pocket. That must be the Service, listening from two tables away to what was about to go down and springing to his rescue. Thanks, guys, appreciate it. Gently, he extricated himself from Tannaz's embrace and twisted round as he looked to see who was calling.

Oh, Jesus, it was Elise and she was Facetiming him in-vision. He pressed cancel, stood up and, mouthing an apology to Tannaz, moved out of earshot before ringing Elise back.

''Lise! Everything okay?'

'No, it bloody isn't. Mum's had the test back . . . It's confirmed. She . . . she's got liver cancer. Luke, I need you back here right now.'

Chapter 32

Shahid Beheshti airbase, Iran

IN A SECURE and secluded corner of the airbase, set far apart from the aircraft hangars, the runways and the administration blocks, a rather specialized training area was surrounded by signs that read '*Vared Nostavid.* Keep Out.'

There were three. Each was dressed in a Western suit and each was bound upright to a wooden post with cords of thick twine, tied over and over. Escape was never going to be an option for the men, arrested for subversion weeks ago on this very base, then tried, found guilty and handed the ultimate sentence. Over their heads were draped black hoods, of the sort worn by an executioner. Except these men were not the executioners: they were the condemned. Behind them stood a crude, life-size dummy, a shop-window mannequin of a man in a coat with glasses and a hat, a caricature of an old-fashioned European spy.

Karim Zamani stood some distance off, gathered with a small group of officers on a raised observation platform. He raised his right hand and paused, holding it still, then suddenly dropped it in an emphatic, chopping motion. From behind an anonymous-looking concrete building came the sound of a whistle. Seconds later there was the roar of an engine, the screech of brakes, and half a dozen black-clad figures emerged. Each wore a headband

and carried a pistol. Chanting in unison, they moved quickly past the observation stand and stopped just short of the bound prisoners.

On a given command they took aim and fired, just once. So tightly were the condemned men bound to the stakes that when the bullets slammed into them, their bodies jolted briefly but stayed upright. Only their heads had moved, lolling lifelessly forward onto their chests. Two of the gunmen were already moving forward, checking pulses – they wanted no survivors – while another pair made a dash for the mannequin in the coat and glasses. In a single movement one looped a gag over its mouth and covered its head with a hood as the other grasped the figure under the armpits and dragged it backwards towards a waiting 4x4. Twenty-two seconds later, the mannequin had been loaded aboard and the vehicle departed at speed with another screech of tyres.

There was a quiet ripple of applause from the officers observing. Karim Zamani nodded in approval. 'An excellent rehearsal,' he remarked, to no one in particular.

Chapter 33

IF THERE WAS one thing Luke hated more than anything else, it was being faced with a problem he couldn't solve. For years he had been trained to confront near-impossible situations and seek out unusual solutions. But this thing was bigger than Elise and him, and he hated that.

'Did they say . . . ?' He looked at her, sitting on the sofa in their Battersea flat, her eyes filled with tears. He hoped she didn't need him to finish that awful sentence.

'How long she's got?' She finished the question off for him. 'Yes, they did. Three or four months at most. It's a tumour, Luke. A fucking tumour!' Elise never swore but now her shoulders were quivering uncontrollably as he held her tight in his arms. He loved her, and he couldn't bear to see her like this. 'They say it must have been growing for the last six months,' she sobbed into his shoulder.

'Well, can't they cut it out?' The direct, military approach.

'Apparently it's got too big . . .' She shook her head.

'Cancer's a bastard,' he said. Hardly a consoling phrase but he couldn't think of what else to say. Losing his own parents, both of them, in a car crash in Colombia when he was just a boy had, he knew, hardened him, sometimes in ways he didn't like. Now everything in Luke's psyche made him want to find a practical solution: a treatment, a cure, a course of action, something, anything. But with all that clearly beyond his reach he was struggling to find the right words to comfort Elise. And what could you say to someone who's just been told they're going to lose their mother in the next few months? It certainly pushed the Iran operation to the back of his mind, made it seem almost irrelevant. Almost.

'Okay, this is what we're going to do right now,' he said, getting to his feet. 'I'm going to make you a cup of camomile tea, then we're going to snuggle up under that rug over there and we're going to watch something on Netflix that might help take our minds off things. Fancy an episode of *Peepshow*? A bit of Mitchell and Webb?'

'Thanks, babes.' She spoke in little more than a whisper but when she took his hand she held it with a strength that surprised him. 'No more travelling now, Luke, please. Not until this is over.'

Chapter 34

Vauxhall Cross

'DON'T. JUST DON'T, all right?' Luke walked into the windowless room on the ground floor of MI6 headquarters with a coffee cup in one hand, the other shielding his face in mock embarrassment. After all the sadness and emotion of the previous evening he felt strangely relieved to be back at work.

'Nice going,' said Trish Fryer, Middle East Controller, patting him lightly on the shoulder.

'Good job,' said someone from Targeting.

'You are da man!' said Graham Leach.

Luke stopped dead in his tracks and looked at him. Had Leach really just said that? Please, for the love of God, never, ever, use that expression again. Angela caught the look on Luke's face and shook her head in sympathy.

Over by the far wall someone from Tech was sorting out the audio-visuals, making sure the recording from last night's concealed chest-mic was fully synced up with the footage from the handbag camera the watchers had placed on their table. Leach was in an ebullient mood.

'We could always,' he said, with a smirk, 'just fast-forward straight to the bit at the end. That chest-mic is ace, you know, it picks up every little whisper.'

'Yeah, all right, all right,' said Luke. This was more like the sort of locker-room banter he'd been subjected to back at SBS head-quarters in Poole. He didn't expect it up here in the rarefied atmosphere of Her Majesty's Secret Intelligence Service. He also didn't feel like sharing the news of Elise's mother's diagnosis with anyone here. 'I take it you've already listened to the tape?' he asked them.

'Only the highlights, so to speak,' said Leach, still smirking.

'Look,' interrupted Angela, 'I hate to break up this boys' chit-chat but we're about to initiate a highly sensitive operation here. It's quite possible that in a matter of days Luke will be inserting himself into an extremely dangerous environment. Can we have a little focus, please?'

'Yes, of course,' said Leach, serious now. 'It looks like Tech have got the audio synced. Let's take a seat and have a listen.' The screen on the wall showed a paused image of Tannaz taking a sip of her wine and giving Luke a coy look over the rim of her glass, her dark eyes sparkling. 'Trish? Your thoughts?'

'She's legit. I'd stake my pension on it.'

'Luke? You still have misgivings?'

Well, yes. I'm getting serious come-on vibes from this girl but, guys, if you don't mind, I'm in love with Elise. It was probably time to say something. 'You do know I'm pretty serious about Elise?' They all looked at him, waiting for the rest of the sentence. 'I mean, you've met her, right? Well, you have, Angela. So . . . I just need to get this out there, that I'm not some kind of James Bond gigolo who goes crash-banging and shagging his way around the world. I'm in it for the long haul with Elise. So I'm, er, sorry if that upsets your plans.' There. Cards on the table. And not before time – he wanted to make it clear to these people that he wasn't some kind of cock-for-hire.

Leach was already on his feet. Still grinning from ear to ear, he strolled round to refill Luke's coffee cup. 'Luke, Luke, Luke,' he soothed. 'There is a difference between charm and sleaze.' He was pacing the room now, one of the smallest in the building, and he could take only three steps before he had to walk back to where he'd started. 'But the point is this. Tannaz Zamani is the daughter of Karim Zamani, codename Echo Sierra. He's one of the most elusive, fanatical and therefore most dangerous of all the senior players in the IRGC. We need to get inside his head and we haven't a lot of time. The way things are going in the Gulf right now we could be looking at war within weeks. Personally, I don't believe this visit by the Foreign Secretary is going to make a damned bit of difference. So, the bottom line, Luke, is we need Tannaz Zamani brought over to our side fast and passing on to us whatever her father is up to. Do you think you can do it?'

Luke took a deep breath. All eyes were on him now. As a captain in the Royal Marines, and later in the SBS, he had been used to saying, 'Yes, can do, we'll make it work.' But this felt different. There was a heap of extra baggage attached to it. 'I'll give it a go, yes,' he replied at last.

'No, Luke, I'm afraid we need more than that.' The banter was gone now. An invisible tension had seeped into that cramped ground-floor meeting room. 'I'm going to ask you again,' said Leach. 'Can you do it? Can you recruit this target for us? If we give you all the back-up you need?'

This time Luke didn't hesitate. 'Yes,' he said flatly.

'Good,' replied Leach, and there was almost palpable relief in the room, 'because if you'd said no, I'm hard pushed to think of anyone else who could stir up that kind of chemistry. You're a natural at this.'

Christ, don't make me change my mind, thought Luke.

'So,' concluded Leach, rubbing his hands together, 'this is what's going to happen. We're going to get you into Iran – as Brendan Hall, obviously. Agent Cover will be going over your legend to make absolutely dead sure every single aspect holds water. And I mean everything: Facebook, LinkedIn, Twitter, the lot. There'll be someone ready to answer the phone every hour of every working day at your art dealership. You've even written a couple of articles for trade journals. With me so far?'

Luke nodded, saying nothing.

'Oh, and talking of phones,' Leach continued, 'Angela, can we make sure he gets one of those new waterproof ones? We can't have a repeat of what happened in Armenia.' Angela jotted a note as Leach resumed: 'Then you're going to make contact with Tannaz,' he said, 'work on her, and when you judge the moment is right, you make your pitch, establish a secure means of comms and get yourself out. Are we clear?'

'We're clear,' Luke said.

'Good. And from now on we don't refer to her as Tannaz. We use her designated codename, Elixir.'

'Got it.'

Chapter 35

Cambridgeshire, England

THERE WERE RELATIVELY few passengers on the 08.11 the following morning, as it headed north out of London's King's Cross station. And fewer still took any notice when exactly forty-three minutes later the train pulled into Huntingdon in Cambridgeshire and a middle-aged man in a beige cashmere coat stepped off. He was flanked by a thin woman with short, spiky hair and an eager-looking young man in a pinstripe suit. From the platform they passed quickly through the station and out into the car park where a dark blue BMW G30 5-series was waiting for them, engine running, beside a Military Police Land Rover. The trio from London climbed into the saloon car and the two-vehicle convoy moved off immediately, driving through the quiet country lanes of the Fens.

A short while later it arrived at the wire-mesh perimeter of a large military base, where the entrance was guarded by a red-brick sentry house and a steel barrier. A 1950s-era Canberra bomber, still in its camouflage livery, was mounted in permanent display on a grassy bank nearby. A large sign in front of it read simply: 'RAF Wyton'.

As the convoy slowed to a halt, a guard emerged. Despite the cold, she wore her shirtsleeves rolled up, exposing vast tattooed forearms. She peered in through the passenger window of the BMW. On seeing who was inside she checked a list on a clipboard she held, then straightened up, stood to attention, and signalled for the barrier to be raised, the convoy waved through.

Inside the base the convoy continued straight ahead, then turned left, parking outside a vast, futuristic structure that resembled an international space station. The elegant curves of its white roof sloped to manicured lawns where a row of flags led up to the entrance hall. US, British, Canadian, Australian, New Zealand: the flags of the Five Eyes nations, with perhaps the closest intelligence-sharing partnership in the world.

This was the Pathfinder Building. Named after the RAF's Pathfinder unit in the Second World War, it had in recent years become the very nerve centre of UK Defence Intelligence. The visitors from London stepped out of their vehicle and were escorted into the cavernous lobby. A reception committee was lined up to greet them: a senior officer from each of the three services, Army, Navy and Air Force, all in uniform, with a cluster of suited civil servants from GCHQ, MI6 and the Defence Intelligence Service. They were all wearing their personal ID cards suspended from a coloured lanyard that hung around their necks, denoting authorized access to the secure area. A Royal Navy commodore stepped forward to welcome them.

'Foreign Secretary ... welcome to Joint Forces Intelligence Group. On behalf of everyone here, welcome to the Fusion Centre. We'll just get your passes organized and we can go through when you're ready.'

The briefing lasted three and a half hours, with a short 'comfort break' in the middle. There was satellite imagery from the Image Intelligence – the IMINT – team, photographic reconnaissance, and strategic threat assessments. There were close-ups and biographies of all the most senior officers in Iran's air, sea and land forces, its specialized ballistic-missile force, its submarine force and the key players in the Iranian Revolutionary Guards Corps' ever-growing flotilla of small, below-the-radar missile attack boats and miniature submarines. A grizzled Royal Marines sergeant gave an account of the humiliating capture of Royal Navy sailors and marines in 2007 by the Iranian Navy. He was followed by a US Navy Commander, on secondment to RAF Wyton, who delivered an assessment of Iran's mine-laying capabilities in the Strait of Hormuz.

By the time the Foreign Secretary boarded the 14.33 back to London, having enjoyed a brief curry lunch with senior officers in the mess, he had become one of the best-briefed politicians in the world on the military, security and intelligence capabilities of the Islamic Republic of Iran.

Chapter 36

Buckinghamshire

LUKE RECKONED HE must have had a worse Christmas Day at some time in his life but he was hard pushed to remember one as miserable as this. They were staying with Elise's parents. Just the four of them, ensconced in the cosy, half-timbered family cottage, with its gently sloping garden and its adjacent paddock where the six-year-old Elise had learned to ride. There were festive sprigs of holly above the paintings, slender, tapering red candles on the dining table, and Classic FM was playing carols from King's College. A string of Christmas cards hung above the fire-place where chopped logs crackled and spat. Yet the shadow of Helen Mayhew's illness hung like a spectre over the scene.

Less than a month had passed since Luke had seen her but already her symptoms were showing. When Helen had greeted him at the front door on Christmas morning and hugged him he had felt her thinness. Her skin was papery and jaundiced, there was a tinge of yellow in her eyes and a curious swelling at her midriff.

'Turkey's in the Aga,' she had announced briskly, leading him into the low-ceilinged kitchen, adding, 'I hope you'll do the carving.'

John, Elise's father, had busied himself with the drinks,

opening more bottles than were necessary and making an elaborate ceremony of mixing a simple gin and tonic for his wife. Luke could see that his face was set in a fixed grimace, his attempt at stoicism in the face of the news that had descended on his family. Elise barely left her mother's side.

When the turkey was ready Luke duly did the carving. In deference to Helen's condition he gave her a smaller portion than usual, but she barely touched it, just chasing it around her plate with her fork as she kept the conversation going. Twice he saw her wince, and some time after they had all sat down she excused herself and went next door. They all heard it then, the unmistakable sound of retching coming from beyond the thin wooden door of the loo. After lunch they played charades, just as they had last year, but it was a joyless exercise and when it came to Helen she said. 'You take my turn, Luke. I'll sit this one out, if you don't mind.' By four in the afternoon, she had retired to bed, propped up on pillows with Radio 3 on the little transistor beside her.

Luke spent the next few hours chopping logs outside, happy to be doing something active, wielding the axe even though it was dark. It gave him the space he needed to think. How was he going to juggle the next few weeks? The Iran crisis wasn't going away – if anything, it looked to be getting worse. MI6 were bound to make some unpredictable demands of him, calling him up at short notice and packing him off to destinations unknown, and all when Elise needed him here with her. So what were his options? Take compassionate leave? So soon into his new career? Just when he was getting started as an agent runner and a live operation was under way? No, that was hardly an option. He lowered the axe, leaning on the handle as he got his breath back. He had to face it. He didn't have an option. He'd have to tough this one out. He had signed over his soul to the Secret Intelligence Service in a Faustian pact. Luke Carlton had committed himself.

He and Elise stayed that night in the guest bedroom, where the low murmur of her parents' voices still reached them across the corridor. Luke propped himself up on one elbow and looked at her. He could see the tears welling in her eyes as she stared up at the ceiling, unblinking.

'She hasn't got long, Luke,' Elise said quietly.

'I'm so sorry, 'Lise. What did they say at the hospital?'

'Six months at most. She just wants to see her garden in spring.'

Chapter 37

Tehran

FLOWERS. EVERYWHERE. THAT was the first thing Luke noticed in Arrivals. Rows and rows of them, mostly roses, arranged beneath portraits of Iran's revolutionary leadership, and people clutching bunches, like mascots. Bleary-eyed and sleep-deprived after a six-hour overnight flight from London, he had joined the queue for Immigration at IKIA – Imam Khomeini International Airport. Perhaps it was the lack of sleep, perhaps it was being lulled into a false sense of security by the reassuring inflight service on the BA153 from London, with its apologetic announcement as the bar closed once they crossed into Iranian airspace, but Luke felt remarkably relaxed. And he shouldn't. Because this was big – no, it was huge. He was going into Iran, on his own, undercover.

The call had come through on Boxing Day, just as they were packing up to head back to London. He had taken it outside, in the rain, standing next to the woodshed. Would he be so good as to come into Vauxhall Cross the next day, the twenty-seventh? No details had been given but Luke had recognized it for what it was: an order couched as a polite request. And there they all were the next morning, in casual, holiday clothes, Graham Leach, Trish Fryer, Angela Scott and some well-built suit from Security Section.

Leach had cut straight to the point. 'We're sending you in, Luke. The mission is on. The Chief has signed off on it.' There had followed a week of preparation, of going over his cover story again and again, under hostile questioning this time by a pair of military interrogators sent from Chicksands, home of the British Army's Intelligence Corps. What was Brendan Hall, art dealer from Bloomsbury, doing in Tehran? Who did he know? Why was he here at this time? Then the Security people had spent three whole days with him, going over his newly contrived social-media profile, his backstory, making sure it checked out, testing him on why he had posted certain pictures two years ago, where his friends liked to go on holiday, which movies he enjoyed, even which year he had captained his school cricket team. And finally there was his new waterproof Service phone, an ordinary-looking smartphone configured with a virtual private network connection that would route all his calls via Akrotiri, in Cyprus. None of the calls he made while in Iran should show up as emanating from inside that country. They were long days for Luke and those working with him, cocooned in the sandstone-coloured monolith on the banks of the Thames, his head crammed with information, while the rest of London took the week off.

Elise had been less than thrilled. Halfway through his second day away she had rung him to tell him she was heading back to her parents in Buckinghamshire. 'It's the Christmas bloody holidays, Luke. At least, it is for normal people. I know this job of yours is important, I get that. But this is taking the piss. I'll see you back here on New Year's Eve.' He had only just made it up to Buckinghamshire in time for that one, too. Drinks in a local pub where everyone seemed to know Elise, and he'd had the definite feeling he was an outsider. It had taken several hours and several drinks before she had given him a proper kiss. And then, ten days later, his Iranian visa had come through and now here he was, standing beneath a large blue sign marked 'A' for Arrivals.

'This your first visit?' Luke turned round to see who was asking. It was a British businessman behind him as they approached the Immigration booth.

147

'It is.' Luke kept his voice low. The last thing he wanted was to attract anyone's attention, and he certainly didn't feel like striking up a conversation.

'Ah, then you're in for a pleasant surprise,' said the man, pressing forward as the queue moved up. 'The driving's atrocious but apart from that Iran's all right. It's changing fast. I'm sure you won't have any problems. Here, let me give you my card. I'm staying at the Parsian Azadi if you want to drop by.'

Luke thanked the man, then turned to the sour-looking official in his glass booth. He made a point of giving him his passport with his right hand, keeping his left out of sight in case the man might decide to question why a finger was missing. He seemed too old to Luke to be doing that job, as if he should really have been lecturing in sociology at Tehran University, rather than stamping passports and asking questions of strangers.

'Burrendin Holl?' The man peered at him through the glass, his pen poised over a form. Luke forced a smile and nodded. His heart was beating faster now: if anyone had clocked who he really was at that embassy dinner in Abu Dhabi, this was when the walls were going to crash down on top of him. He could almost feel someone watching him right now through that pane of glass behind the official, undoubtedly a two-way mirror, and that someone would be IRGC intelligence, waiting to pick up anyone who flashed up on their database as a Person of Interest. This was a watershed moment and he knew it. In the next thirty seconds Luke was about to find out if his cover had held up or if he was about to spend the next ten years in the solitary wing of Evin Prison.

'Purpose of visit?'

'Business.'

The man peered at him, glanced down at his visa for the briefest of moments, then stamped his passport, handed it back to him and waved him on. And that was it. He was in. Relief surged through him, but he kept walking, showing nothing. Landside of the airport, and Luke could see yet more flowers. Everyone waiting in Arrivals seemed to have a bunch in their hand as tearful reunions erupted all around him. He felt conspicuous, an outsider with no one to meet and greet him. Even that British businessman was being escorted out to a waiting car by someone carrying his bags.

Luke pushed his way through the crowd and followed the signs to the plate-glass exit and the taxi rank outside. The cold air hit him the moment he left the terminal, that and the acrid tang of pollution. His breath misting in the early-morning chill, he joined the queue of families, solitary businessmen and the occasional bespectacled cleric in brown cloak and white headdress.

When it was finally his turn he climbed into the back seat of a yellow Toyota Camry, dumped his bag next to him and handed the driver a card with an address. As they pulled away from the terminal Luke tugged instinctively at the seatbelt but it dangled, limp and dysfunctional, from a hook by the door. He gave up trying and instead took out his phone, tapped on the Telegram icon and scrolled down to a contact listed simply as 'Aesthetica'. He typed in three words: *Arrived in Tehran*.

Driving along the traffic-choked six-lane highway through the drab southern suburbs of Tehran, Luke gazed out at a wintry scene of bare trees and rows of white, flat-roofed buildings interspersed with giant hoardings, some commercial, some religious. He caught his first sight of the snow-capped Elburz Mountains, and the majestic, conical, 5,600-metre peak of Mount Damavand that towered over the capital.

The Hotel Shahrestan was small and discreet, tucked away in a quiet residential street in a nondescript district, its grey exterior barely marking it out as a hotel. Luke's reservation had been made for him in the name of a fictional art dealership in London, his room on the first floor taken for a week. Dog-tired now, he paid off the driver, checked in at Reception, carried his bag upstairs, let himself into the room and flopped onto the bed. Setting the alarm on his phone, he closed his eyes and slept. Three hours later, he was woken by electronic beeping and reached over to check for messages. There was only one on his Telegram app and it was from 'Aesthetica'.

Welcome to my city! it read. *Meet me at Café Rameez, 2 p.m.*

Chapter 38

LOW LIGHTING, TILES on the floor and bare brick walls hung with framed, black-and-white photographs of Iranian musicians, past and present, Café Rameez was understated Tehran chic. It was just a short walk from the Tehran Museum of Contemporary Art. Luke had known about the place before he'd boarded his flight at Heathrow. Using phone and internet intercepts, the GCHQ analysts in Cheltenham had mapped out for him a detailed picture of Tannaz Zamani's daily movements around the Iranian capital. They knew where she lived, which faculty of Tehran University she studied at, and where she went to socialize. Café Rameez was one of her favourite haunts, a popular meeting place for the university crowd. The Gasht-e-Ershad, the morality police, had largely left it in peace – their last raid had been more than a year ago – but Luke was all too aware they could still have watchers in place and, as a Westerner, he would be noticed the moment he walked through the door. He had to remember everything he had learned during those weeks of counter-surveillance training down at the Base if he was to stay inconspicuous.

Luke got there early. He liked to scope out a place well before the appointed hour – choose a spot where he could sit with his back to a wall and keep an eye on the entrance without needing to look around. Somewhere close to an alternative exit point, in case he needed to bug out in a hurry. He pushed open the door and took in the scene with one glance. The interior was dimly lit and students crowded round the tables, talking, arguing, laughing, while a pall of tobacco smoke coiled towards the ceiling and condensation fogged the inside of the windows. There was a lot of noise, which suited him fine. He found a seat at the back and dumped his purchases on the table: a coffee-table book and a set of postcards. If anyone was watching, they would see from the logo on the plastic bag that he had just been to the Museum of Contemporary Art down the road. And he had. The two hours he had spent inside its walls had been absolutely mind-blowing, a visual banquet of masterpieces ranging from Renoir to Jackson Pollock and even portraits by Andy Warhol of Mick Jagger and Marilyn Monroe. In Iran? Seriously? He hadn't expected that.

Luke looked at his watch. Nearly one thirty – he had half an hour or so before Tannaz turned up and his growling stomach reminded him that he hadn't eaten anything in hours. Waving over a young waiter in designer jeans and T-shirt, he ordered a bowl of Ash-e-reshteh, a thick winter soup of Persian noodles and vegetables, with a glass of tea on the side. It was what everyone seemed to be having.

'Enjoy,' the waiter told him, with a smile, as he set it down in front of him, speaking in a strong American accent. As Luke ate, he watched the café and his training took over, quartering the room and noting the clientele. To his half-left there was a bulky man in a black leather jacket sitting alone. A watcher? Maybe. He'd need to keep an eye on him. Straight ahead, a table of three young women, headscarves pushed well back over their hair, their exquisitely shaped eyebrows raised in expressions of constant surprise. A little too much Botox. To their right, a large round table, all students, all male, and another similar one behind that. No one was taking any notice of him. His eyes switched back to the man in the leather jacket. He had just been joined by an elderly woman in a tightly wrapped headscarf, probably his mother, and she wasn't happy. They seemed to be having quite an argument. Luke relaxed just a little.

But then, almost immediately, the fear kicked in. Not so much the fear of discovery, which would always be there, loitering just beneath the surface. No, it was the fear of failure that stalked him now. Try as he might, he could not forget how he'd screwed up in training. The hidden alarm button, those two heavies crashing through the door. He shuddered at the memory. And now here he was, out in the field. In Iran. This was for real. What if his pitch to Tannaz failed? So much seemed to be resting on him succeeding. The Armenia trip had been a disaster, and he knew he could not afford to balls this one up. Yet the people at Vauxhall Cross were asking a hell of a lot of him. Getting to know Tannaz, winning her trust, building up to the moment when he could make the Pitch and try to bring her onside – it should be taking months, years maybe. Instead, with all the tension mounting in the Gulf, he was expected to compress the whole process into just a week. A thought occurred to him: was it because he was so new to the Service that he was in some way expendable? A low-cost commodity to be burned and abandoned if things went south? He dismissed it.

A quarter past two, and the lunchtime crowd was thinning out. Luke had almost finished his bowl of noodle soup when a slightly built student slipped into Café Rameez. She went largely unnoticed, just another modestly dressed woman going about her business in the capital. Luke looked up and his eyes took in a woman in a headscarf and a long green raincoat. She wore dark glasses, despite the dullness of the day outside, and no lipstick. It took him a moment to recognize her. Could this really be the same girl who had shimmied up to him at the Bluebird in a tight, low-cut black dress?

'Hello, Tannaz,' he said quietly, pulling out a chair for her. And now she was close to him, he was reminded of just how gorgeous this girl was, her natural beauty all the more pronounced without make-up. Seeing her again, right here, on her home turf in Tehran, made something stir inside him, something that made him feel instantly guilty.

'Don't kiss me,' she said abruptly, casting a precautionary glance to left and right before she sat down.

Luke sat back theatrically in his chair, feigning shock. 'I wouldn't dream of it,' he replied.

'Sorry,' she said, adjusting her headscarf and tucking a wisp of hair into place. 'I just wasn't sure how much you know about how we do things here. You wouldn't believe what some people think is okay when it's not. A German couple was fined and deported only last week for kissing beneath a poster of the Supreme Leader.' She glanced down at the remains of his soup. 'It's good, isn't it? Hey, don't stop for me – I've already eaten.'

'Well, let's get you something to drink, at least?'

She was ahead of him, already signalling to the young man in the T-shirt, who came over to greet her, then returned with her favourite: a glass of watermelon and pomegranate juice. Tannaz took a sip before placing her hands on the table, one resting on the other. She leaned forward slightly and regarded him for a long moment, a smile playing around her lips. 'So, Mr Art Dealer . . . I can't believe you're actually here, in my city.'

Luke gave a modest shrug of the shoulders.

'Why not?' he said, tapping the bag from the Museum of Contemporary Art. 'I have to say, I'm massively impressed by what I've seen so far.'

'Oh, that,' she replied dismissively, taking another sip of her juice and glancing briefly around to see if she recognized anyone at the other tables. 'You should hear what my father has to say about that place. "Decadent imperialist baubles that should be sent straight back to the West!" '

'And is that what you think too?' He kept his tone light but his question was serious.

Tannaz put down her drink and gave him a withering look. 'What the fuck do *you* think? Do I look like a girl who'd fall for that sort of outdated crap?'

Maybe it was because of where they were, in a Tehran café in the beating heart of the Islamic Republic, but Luke was taken aback at the vehemence of her answer. 'No, no, obviously not,' he backtracked. 'In fact, I really don't know how you cope with your father's views.'

'So you said, the last time we met, in the Bluebird restaurant.' She narrowed her eyes at him. 'The time you ran out on me.'

'Hey, hey, hey, that's not fair, Tannaz. I didn't run out on you. I had to go and deal with a sick relative, as I told you.' Not entirely untrue, but best to move on quickly. 'So, will it ever change here, d'you think?'

She looked down and stirred the thick residue of fruit at the bottom of her glass with the straw. 'It depends . . . There are some people, like my father, I suppose, who want to keep Iran isolated, like an island. Or a big prison. But change is happening. We have more freedoms now and at least we have elections.'

Luke took a last mouthful of soup before answering. It had gone cold but he needed a moment to think, given the path he was about to take. 'Don't you ever wish,' he said slowly, 'that you could, you know, help speed up that change? Like, help to open up Iran to the rest of the world? Take it to a better place. In your lifetime.'

Tannaz gave him a quizzical look. 'How do you mean?' she said.

Careful here. One step at a time. Luke paused before answering, looking first around the café. He noticed that the boy in the T-shirt had been replaced by an older man in a white apron. He was shuffling around with a teapot, refilling people's glasses without waiting to be asked, and standing by the door a very young girl in a headscarf, maybe just ten years old, was selling flowers, but no one was paying him or Tannaz any attention.

'Well,' he said, 'it seems pretty black and white to me. There are the good guys, your lot, people who want to give Iranians a bit more freedom to breathe. Modernize the economy and all that. And then there are the regressives, those who seem to be permanently stuck in a revolutionary mindset, the clock stopped in 1979.'

Tannaz laughed and pushed away her glass, resting her hands on the table once more. 'Yes, this is true,' she conceded.

154

Luke studied her for a moment. She seemed relaxed and at ease. This was her home environment and she obviously liked this café. It was time to turn it up a notch. 'So, listen, Tannaz,' he said, as casually as he could, looking down at his hands and intertwining his fingers, 'I have a friend back home. He works in human rights – a group called Citizens Concern. I hope you don't mind but he's done a little digging. You told me your dad was with "those people", the processionists, you know, the hardliners.'

Tannaz looked up sharply. She wasn't laughing any more. She was listening very intently. 'You've been checking up on my dad?'

'Not me. My friend.' Luke was struggling now to keep his tone light. 'I just happened to mention your dad's name to him.' He gave her what he hoped was a reassuring smile but the colour had drained from her face.

Tannaz looked furious. 'But how is that possible?' she said. 'I never told you his name.'

Chapter 39

Tehran

EVERYTHING SEEMED TO have frozen between them. All around, plates clattered and glasses clinked, other people's conversations rose and fell, but Luke and Tannaz just looked at each other. For Luke, in that one moment, Café Rameez threatened to become a very dangerous place indeed. He knew he needed to retrieve the situation or things could spin badly out of control and he'd be in deep trouble. Tannaz Zamani, far from being a prospective informant, could just as easily turn into the catalyst for his arrest and trial. 'No, you're right. You didn't,' he told her amiably.

'Excuse me?' Her tone was harsh, abrasive, as if responding to a stinging insult.

'You're right. You didn't tell me your father's name. But you did say he was in the Revolutionary Guards. This human-rights friend of mine in London, he spends his whole life tracking people down, mostly prisoners of conscience, that kind of thing. I suppose he must have done some sort of cross-check on senior Revolutionary Guards officers who have a daughter called Tannaz. I honestly don't know.' Luke shrugged his shoulders in nonchalant dismissal. It was a weak explanation and he knew it, but he was clutching at straws. Tannaz was frowning at him, so there was still suspicion, but at least her jawline had relaxed a little.

'So what about my father, then?'

'I hate to say this, Tannaz, but he's done some bad things, really bad things.'

Her reaction took him by surprise: she tossed her hair back and laughed sarcastically. 'And you're telling *me* this? You think we don't know what he does, working for those people? You think we enjoy living this double life, Mama and me? Of course we don't. I somehow doubt your friend in London can tell me anything I don't already know about him.'

For a second Luke was tempted to show her, right there and then, to bring out the photographs he had cached on his phone. But he thought better of it. Not here, in this café – it was way too public. 'Listen,' he said, 'is there somewhere more private we can go? I mean, don't get me wrong, this place Café Rameez is great but—'

'You want somewhere more private?' she repeated, cutting him off. 'I think you had your chance for that when we were in the Bluebird and you walked out.' She looked away, feigning boredom.

'Yes, I did, and I'm sorry.' God, was she ever going to get over that and forgive him?

Abruptly Tannaz got up. 'Okay, come on. Follow me.'

The park was freezing, the colours all brown and grey, and there were few people about. They walked quickly, leaving behind them the rush and hum of the Tehran traffic, until they reached a bench beside a stone water fountain and she motioned for them to sit. 'This had better be quick,' she said, pulling her coat around her slender shoulders. 'What did you want to tell me?'

'I'm really sorry to be the one to do this to you, Tannaz.' Luke already had the phone in his hand and was thumbing in the code to unlock his cache of photos. 'But I'm not sure you know just what your father's been doing to people.' He selected the first photo on his phone and passed it to her. 'Please, take a look at this.'

'I don't want to.'

'I'm sure you don't,' he replied. 'Neither did the family of the man in that photo when they came to collect the body. But I'm asking you, Tannaz, if you give a damn about humanity, about your own people, your country, you'll want to know what your father and his people are doing to them.' He paused but Tannaz was silent, her face giving nothing away. 'Or is it all just about parties and fun for you?'

'Fuck you! What do you know what I care about?' she spat. It had struck a raw nerve.

'Then go ahead and take a look,' he challenged her.

Tannaz snatched the phone from him. She began to scroll through the cache of images and Luke studied her face as her expression changed. By the time she got to the last photograph, the one of her father standing proudly above a battered human corpse, shirtless and bleeding, she clapped her hand over her mouth as if to silence a scream. When she turned at last to look at Luke, tears were streaming down her cheeks.

Chapter 40

Tehran

GEOFFREY CHAPLIN STRODE confidently into the VIP lounge of
Imam Khomeini International Airport, wearing a fixed smile as
the cameras flashed to left and right. It was, he knew, a momentous event. Weeks of preparation had gone into this, the first visit
to Iran by a British Foreign Secretary since Philip Hammond
had reopened the British Embassy in 2015, four years after it had
been ransacked by a mob. And now a figure he recognized was
waiting to receive him at the head of the Iranian government
delegation.

Dark suit, white shirt buttoned to the top and no tie, Dr Erfan
Askari, Iran's newly appointed Foreign Minister, looked exactly
like his photo in the file, prepared by the UK's Joint Forces Intelligence Group. His words of welcome were spoken softly and
without emotion. 'Foreign Secretary, *khosh amadid*. Welcome to
the Islamic Republic of Iran.'

They were upstairs in the VIP terminal beneath the giant twin
portraits of the Ayatollah Khomeini and his successor as Iran's
Supreme Leader, Ayatollah Ali Khamenei. Official photog-
raphers in checked shirts and baggy black trousers hovered
nervously in the wings, snatching pictures as the two ministers
shook hands, then darting around in search of better angles.

Chaplin, flanked by his aides and his Principal Protection Officer, kept smiling as a female interpreter stepped forward, her hair only partly covered by a dark blue headscarf. She introduced herself as Zahra, then made the formal introductions as he moved down the line, shaking hands and bowing slightly to each official. He counted six in total, all men, all dressed in suits except the one at the end, who wore military service dress with a rack of medals and, incongruously, given that they were indoors, sunglasses with mirrored lenses.

He tried to recall the correct phrase he had been told to say in Farsi, something about being honoured to be there. 'The Iranians will appreciate it,' the FCO linguists had suggested back in London. 'It'll help to break the ice, that sort of thing.' But it eluded him now. Heaven knew he'd had enough on his plate before setting off on this trip: Brexit, the Lebanese crisis, and then on the phone almost every day to his US counterpart, talking through the current tension in the Gulf. And Chaplin knew full well there were those in the White House who thought this ministerial visit was pointless, that it was well past time for talking with this regime in Tehran. Even the briefing from the famously cautious Foreign and Commonwealth Office had been explicit. He had read it again on the flight over and could almost remember it word for word:

[UK OFFICIAL]

It should be noted there are elements within the Iranian powerbase that will not *welcome this government-to-government rapprochement with the United Kingdom. It must be assumed that hardcore members of the clergy, the judiciary and Iranian Revolutionary Guards Corps (IRGC) will view this visit as running contrary to the principles of the Islamic Revolution of 1979 and detrimental to the security of the Islamic Republic.*

'This way, please.' The interpreter was inviting him to take a seat on a white leather sofa next to a small, lacquered wooden table. She was young, he noticed, not much more than twenty-five, and pretty, her manner demure yet observant. He bet she must have fought off a lot of competition to get this job.

Chaplin eased himself onto the sofa. There was just enough room for him, his private secretary and his two advisers while the Iranian officials took their places on chairs in front of them. He threw a discreet glance over his shoulder to check where his security people were. His three Close Protection Officers, from the Metropolitan Police Royal and Specialist Protection Command, remained standing, the flaps of their jackets hanging loosely over their hip holsters, which housed their Glock 19 semi-automatic pistols. My goodness, what a fuss there had been getting those into the country. The Iranians had refused permission at first, until it had looked as if the whole trip would be cancelled, but Whitehall had held its nerve and the host country had relented. 'A special exception' was made, for the sake of goodwill.

He looked up as a pair of waiters detached themselves from the wall behind a counter and hovered over them, bearing a tray of glasses filled with a reddish-brown liquid. He was thirsty, he realized, but not that thirsty. In fact the Foreign Secretary didn't like the look of that liquid one bit. There were cubes of ice bobbing around in there – he had been warned about that – and a whole lot of tiny orange pips floating on top.

'*Khakshir*,' explained Zahra. 'It is our welcome drink. Made with turmeric and saffron. It reduces fever. And also tension,' she added, with just a hint of irony. For a few seconds they sat in awkward silence, the two delegations facing each other as they sipped their drinks. Chaplin raised his glass in a mock toast, touched the liquid to his lips and swallowed, but without imbibing. It was a habit he had acquired on the job after attending endless diplomatic cocktail parties.

The Iranian Foreign Minister was addressing him in Farsi. Waiting patiently for the translation, he noticed that the man seemed to be moving his lips while keeping the rest of his face perfectly still. Yet there was a twinkle in those eyes, behind the

161

spectacles, and a clear intelligence. Dr Askari's CV, he remembered, had mentioned a master's in philosophy.

'His Excellency the Minister thanks you for your visit,' said Zahra, translating once he had finished. 'He hopes that you will forgive the humble quality of this arrivals hall, which pales into insignificance compared to what you have in Europe.'

What? thought Chaplain. This place is palatial. One of his advisers leaned over to him and explained in hushed tones: 'It's called *ta'arof*,' he said. 'It's Iranian modesty, a part of their culture. People tell you things they think you want to hear.'

'I see.' Chaplin looked across at the Foreign Minister. Did this mean he wasn't to take this man at his word? How did business ever get done in this country if that were the case? It was all very confusing but now Zahra was translating again. 'The Minister hopes that past misunderstandings can be put behind us . . .' she said '. . . and that we can look forward to a long and mutually beneficial partnership in the Persian Gulf region.'

Persian Gulf? 'Arabian Gulf' was the term preferred by the FCO and most of Whitehall, a phrase he knew the Iranians detested since they always considered the Gulf to be a Persian lake. He ignored it and nodded in polite appreciation, raising his glass once more, its murky contents still undrunk. He was about to deliver a formal reply but it seemed his Iranian opposite number still had more to say.

'His Excellency expects that you would like to rest now after your long journey,' Zahra translated. She was pressing the palms of her hands together as she spoke, as if in supplication. 'Our cars are waiting outside to take you, when you are ready, to your embassy compound on Ferdowsi Avenue. Tonight there is the banquet at Sa'adabad Palace and tomorrow morning the Minister looks forward to receiving you and your delegation in his office at the Foreign Ministry. Also . . .' the interpreter hardly drew breath as she said this '. . . His Excellency very much looks forward to accompanying you after that to the great city of Isfahan in the afternoon. We believe that this has already been recorded in your programme.'

It definitely had not. This was completely unexpected and Chaplin found it hard to hide his surprise. He twisted round on the sofa to make eye contact with Sara Vallance, his special adviser – or SPAD, in Whitehall parlance. He raised a questioning eyebrow. Her shoulders lifted almost imperceptibly in response, a polite shrug but her expression was blank. No, an excursion to Isfahan had not been on anyone's programme. Craig Dunne, the team's Principal Protection Officer, had been standing just behind the Foreign Secretary and bent down to whisper in his minister's ear. Dunne, Chaplin knew, had more than seventeen years' experience in the Met, the last eight of which had been in close protection of VIPs. Caution obviously ran in the man's veins. As succinctly as he could, he pointed out the risks inherent in an unforeseen change of plan. They'd have no time to carry out a proper recce of the routes or hotels, and that was just the beginning. Chaplin understood there were bound to be variables involved, but the clock was ticking and the invitation was still hanging in the air. He was damned if he was going to mess up the whole trip before it had started by giving offence.

'Please tell the Minister,' he said to Zahra, with elaborate courtesy, 'that we would be honoured to join him in Isfahan tomorrow.'

They filed out, making small-talk as they passed the sentries on the door, and went down in the chrome-plated lift to the waiting convoy of black government Mercedes, escorted at both ends by security minivans with sliding doors and balaclavaed marksmen crouched inside. 'For your safety,' Zahra explained to Geoffrey Chaplin. 'But you have nothing to fear here. Everywhere in Iran is quite safe.'

Craig Dunne took his place in the front passenger seat of Chaplin's limousine, his hand resting lightly on the holster beneath his jacket. The Foreign Secretary settled himself into the seat behind, Sara Vallance beside him, the thick leather armrest between them. He noticed that the driver had put all the windows up and locked the doors. But even sealed into their comfortable car they heard it. A rising cacophony of angry chants that grew louder as the cavalcade moved on. When the convoy swung left onto the Tehran–Qom Highway the demonstrators came clearly into view. Crowds of young men were pressing against the barricades, confronting the line of baton-carrying, green-uniformed policemen who faced them. The chanting had become one continuous repetitive roar.

'*Marg bar Ingilistan! Marg bar Ingilistan!*'

'What are they shouting?' Chaplin asked the driver, as their car edged past. When he didn't answer, Chaplin tried again.

'It is not important,' the driver replied, his knuckles white as he gripped the steering wheel. 'These are not educated people. Please, take no notice.'

Chaplin could see that he was embarrassed but he persisted. 'But what are they saying?' he said, peering forward in his seat. 'They do seem very worked up.'

'They are saying . . .' the driver hesitated, then finished his sentence in a rush '. . . they are saying,"Death to England."'

'Oh. I see.' The Foreign Secretary peered anxiously through the car's windows. He had never seen such a parade of hostile, contemptuous faces – it certainly put Prime Minister's Questions into the shade. There were men with headbands tied round their foreheads with slogans in Farsi, shaking their fists at the convoy. Briefly, some of them managed to break through the barrier to slam their hands on the roof of the car, making a terrible din. Chaplin looked up into the face of one, a heavily built man with a vivid scar running down his left cheek, his eyes shining with what seemed almost demonic fury. A second later he vanished from view, hauled back into line by the police as the convoy swept on, flanked by the police motorcycle outriders, heading north into the vast, sprawling, traffic-choked metropolis that was the Iranian capital.

'This isn't good,' said Dunne, from the front seat, his hand now inside his jacket. 'This does not look good at all.'

Chapter 41

Buckinghamshire

EVER SINCE SHE was a child, Elise Mayhew had always found something strangely comforting about the sound of car wheels on gravel. It spoke of a car pulling into the driveway of her parents' place, of familiarity, of safety – the sound of coming home. Except that now, on this winter afternoon, it wasn't home and it wasn't her parents' driveway she was turning into: it was the swept and tidy forecourt of the North Bucks Hospice, where they had moved her mother just two days earlier.

Just for some rest and professional care, Elise told herself, just for a few days, and then she'll be coming home. The lie helped her keep the tears at bay, to stay strong for when she walked into her mother's room, all bright and breezy with a bouquet wrapped in pink tissue paper. Who knew? Maybe there would be some improvement in her condition. But one look at her father's face, as he sat at the bedside, shoulders hunched, glasses perched on the end of his nose, half-empty box of Kleenex by his side, said otherwise. It was a look of resignation, as if all the lights in his world were going out, one by one.

'The tumour's grown too big to operate.' It was her mother who spoke, telling it how it was, just as she always had. Helen Mayhew had never been one to beat around the bush. But Elise could see the illness was taking its toll. Her mother's eyes were still clear and blue, but her skin was pale, drawn, almost like parchment. Elise rushed forward and hugged her as she lay propped up on several pillows.

'Well,' Helen said, after they had embraced, 'that's what the specialists here are telling me and we've got to assume they know what they're talking about, haven't we?' She gave a wan smile and reached out to grip her husband's hand. He had yet to utter a word. 'Still,' she continued brightly, 'the doctors here are lovely and the nurses couldn't be nicer. There's a lovely girl from Rwanda. Oh, and I'm not in any pain, in case you're wondering. They have a team here, the Pally-something-or-other, that takes care of all that.'

'Palliative Care?' said Elise.

'That's the one.' She turned to look at her husband and squeezed his hand. 'Darling, would you be an angel and see if you can rustle up some Rich Tea biscuits? I've got a sudden craving for them.'

'Of course.' Elise's father got up, nodded to Elise, kissed his wife's forehead and shuffled out, closing the door softly behind him.

He looks old, Elise thought, prematurely stooped and old, so very different from the man she had known only a few months ago, before all of this had happened.

'He's taken it pretty badly,' her mother remarked, when they were alone. 'You'll have to keep an eye on him, you know.'

Elise nodded as she held her mother's hands. For a while neither of them spoke. When Helen broke the silence, it was to ask Elise to pass her a book that was just out of reach. 'I've been reading this,' she said, turning it over in her hand as if seeing it for the first time. Elise inclined her head so she could read the title. It was called *A Time of Light* by Elizabeth R. Johnson. Elise had never heard of her, but if it was about dying she wasn't at all keen on her mother reading it. The stark cover depicted a solitary candle flickering in a darkened room. It looked utterly morbid.

'It's about a man who knows he hasn't got much time left,' said Helen.

166

'Mummy, please . . .' Even as she spoke, Elise thought how wonderfully strong and clear her mother's voice was, despite all the medication she must be getting.

'No. Let me finish.' She was still very much in command even at this eleventh hour in her life. 'He has all these things he wants to tell his family. But he just doesn't know how to. I've almost got to the end of the book and I have an awful feeling I know how it's going to end.'

Elise wasn't sure but she thought she'd detected a break in her mother's voice, a chink in the indomitable armour she'd known all her life. 'It sounds unspeakably grim,' she remarked.

'Well, I suppose you could call it that,' her mother conceded, with a smile. 'But, darling, it's got me thinking. There are things I've wanted to say to you and your father for some time and now I don't see any point in holding back. He and I have had quite a chat, these past few days. Got a lot off our chests.'

'That's something.' Elise wasn't too sure where her mother was going with this.

'He's a good man, Elise.' Helen's hand was cupped over Elise's, her grip still warm and firm.

'Who? Daddy?'

'No. I was referring to Luke. You've been together a while now, haven't you? What's it been? Eighteen months? Two years?'

Elise put a hand in front of her face and closed her eyes in exasperation. 'Mummy, if you're going to give me the big speech about marriage I—'

Her mother stopped her. 'No. Not today. That can be for another time. No, I wanted to ask you how you feel about what Luke does. For a living.'

'Well, I know he's very happy at the Foreign Office,' said Elise, defensively.

Her mother turned her laser gaze onto her and mustered a withering look. 'Darling, I wasn't born yesterday. I've been around the block long enough. I've known for some time what he does. He's an SIS intelligence officer. He works for MI6.'

Elise was shocked. 'You knew?' she asked. 'How?'

Helen took a sip from some nutrition drink that a nurse had placed on her bedside table and grimaced. 'I stepped out with a spy, long before I met your father,' she said. 'It got quite serious, actually.'

Elise leaned forward, fascinated. 'You mean you dated him? Mummy! You never told me this!'

'I suppose I kept it to myself. Well, his name was Bernard. At one point I even thought about marrying him.'

Elise clapped her hand over her mouth. 'You're kidding!'

'No, I'm not "kidding", as you put it. But then something happened. His friends came to see me one evening. I suppose nowadays people would call it an intervention. They told me I needed to know that he was gay – and, of course, in those days that was a complete no-no in government service. It meant the end of your career.'

'So, hang on, why was he dating you?' Elise asked, just as the answer occurred to her.

'As cover.' She looked sad for a moment, and Elise realized that at the time this discovery had probably hurt her mother more than she cared to admit. 'Apparently he just wanted to look "respectable" and carry on doing whatever he was doing.' She waved a hand dismissively, as if consigning the whole episode to history. 'Of course, it sounds ridiculous in this day and age.'

Why is she telling me all this? Elise wondered.

'Anyway . . .' Her mother shifted her position on the pillows and winced once more '. . . the point I'm trying to make, darling, is that Luke is . . . Luke is a good man. You should hang on to him.'

'I intend to,' said Elise. 'Is that it?' She didn't feel ready for a lecture right now.

'Not quite. Just remember, spies lie for a living. It's what they do. So listen, and I'm not saying this will ever be the case, but if you ever think he's deceiving you, hiding something that you have a right to know, well, you make jolly sure you confront him. There has to be total trust between you two. You can't have him bringing his double life into the bedroom, if you know what I mean.'

168

'Mummy!' Elise was not at all sure what to make of this conversation.

But Helen had not quite finished. 'Let's not fool ourselves here, sweetheart. I haven't got much time left. I may not be around if that time ever comes, God forbid. Now . . .' she cleared her throat, all businesslike again '. . . make sure you look after your father, won't you? He's going to need a lot of support.'

As if on cue, the door opened and Elise's father came in holding a plate of biscuits. 'Rich Tea. That was what you wanted, wasn't it?' He placed them on the bedside table and Elise noticed a slight tremor in his hand.

They talked on for a while, as the light drained away from the grey winter afternoon outside, and the corridor beyond the door echoed to the hushed comings and goings of carers and visitors. Elise had rarely felt so low. Where was Luke when she needed him? Off on another bloody mission. She needed him here, right now, at this awful moment in her life.

'Can you excuse me for a moment?' She stepped into the corridor, making way for a man in light green pyjamas clutching a Zimmer frame and trailing an IV drip on a rolling stand. She knew she wasn't supposed to call Luke when he was on a live op except in emergencies. Well, this bloody well was an emergency, wasn't it? An emotional emergency. She dialled his number and waited.

And, what a surprise, his phone was switched off again.

Chapter 42

Isfahan

'THE IMAM MOSQUE is a UNESCO World Heritage Site,' declared Zahra, proudly, addressing her words to the British delegation as they squinted into the sun. Her words were impressive, the location was impressive, but Geoffrey Chaplin, Britain's Foreign Secretary, was struggling to pay attention. He had slept badly last night, despite being safe and secure behind the lofty red-brick walls of the British Embassy compound in Tehran. The situation in Lebanon, already perilous, was showing no signs of improvement, and twice in the night he had had to take a call from London. There was even talk of having to evacuate all UK nationals, and now the PM wanted him to stop off in Beirut on his way home. He had had a devil of a time trying to explain that one to Gillian, his wife, on a secure line from Tehran.

A very early morning of delicate talks at the Foreign Ministry, a 200-mile flight south, and now here they were in Isfahan, the British diplomatic delegation all standing in a huddle, dwarfed by the magnificence of the vast courtyard. Chaplin held up his hand to shield his eyes from the sun and took in the vaulted domes, the honeycombed niches, and the walls decorated with countless dazzling blue tiles, inscribed with intricate calligraphy. Yes, it truly was impressive – in fact, it probably outdid what he could remember of the Taj Mahal, but, God, he was tired. A flock of pigeons wheeled in formation above them, sunbeams lancing down between their wings. The shadow of a minaret fell across the pale yellow stone at their feet, and Zahra pressed on with her facts and figures.

'Built by Shah Abbas in your calendar year of 1611,' she told them, 'it is said that this mosque was constructed using eighteen million bricks and four hundred and seventy-five thousand tiles.' Her blue *roosari* – her headscarf - was draped just a fraction more loosely around her today and Chaplin couldn't help noticing she was wearing a hint of lip gloss.

'You see,' she continued, 'our Persian culture goes back thousands of years, not like our Arab neighbours across the Gulf.' That must have been a dig at the Saudis: Iran's relations there were at rock bottom. Zahra was about to continue, but Dr Askari interrupted her in Farsi.

'His Excellency the Minister would like to show you something', she translated. 'Please, come this way.' Dr Erfan Askari gently took the elbow of his British counterpart and guided him towards a black square mark on the ground, in the shadow of a dome. He stopped, held up a finger for silence, then clapped his hands once. The sound bounced off the walls, echoing exactly seven times.

'It was designed,' Zahra explained, 'so that whoever spoke from this spot could be heard by everyone around. Perhaps you would like to try it.' She was looking directly at Geoffrey Chaplin. 'You just stamp your foot here, like this. We had the French minister here just two months ago,' she added pointedly, 'and he made a big noise!'

'I'm sure he did,' murmured Chaplin. Despite the current standoff with the US in the Gulf, a French company had recently won the contract for a major construction project in Tabriz, undercutting its British rival by a considerable margin.

Chaplin was wearing a pair of polished tan brogues from a gentlemen's outfitter in St James's, his concession to dressing down for the occasion, and it made an incongruous sight, the shirtsleeved Whitehall warrior bringing his expensively heeled foot crashing down on a 400-year-old Persian tile. 'By Jove, you're right,' he declared. 'That's quite some echo.'

At one thirty, 'lunch' was announced and it was a feast, held in a converted caravanserai just off the *maidan*, the main square, Persian food served at its absolute best. First came trays of rose-coloured pistachios, passed round to take the edge off their appetites, then steaming dishes of *fesanjoun*, a lamb stew infused with walnut and pomegranate, served with *must-o-moosir*, wild shallot mixed with soft cheese, then assorted salads and mountainous trays of Tajik rice. Glasses of *doogh* were placed in front of everyone, a yoghurt drink flavoured with dried mint, and followed by bowls of rice pudding sprinkled with slices of almond harvested from the orchards at the foothills of the Elburz. After all his years in Westminster, Geoffrey Chaplin was no stranger to large lunches, but this meal left him fit to burst. And he remembered the old adage: there is no such thing as a free lunch. Here it comes, he thought, as Dr Askari rose from his chair, cleared his throat and began to deliver a prepared speech in Farsi.

'What you have seen today in this glorious city of Isfahan,' he began, 'is only the tiniest fraction of our three-thousand-year-old culture. The tiniest fraction!' He held up his hand and put his thumb and forefinger together until they almost touched. 'I will tell you something now,' he went on, lowering his voice as if about to impart a great secret, then pausing to let Zahra translate. 'You will not find culture like this on the other side of the Persian Gulf. No, sir!' His eyes rested briefly on Geoffrey Chaplin, who shifted uncomfortably. Britain had recently delivered the latest batch of British-built Typhoon jets to Saudi Arabia, a deal worth several billion pounds. Was he about to hear a second swipe at the Saudis in under an hour?

'Will you see beautiful blue tiles like these on a building in Riyadh?' asked Dr Askari, rhetorically. 'I don't think so. Will you see ancient friezes like the ones we have at Takht-e-Jamshid? I think not.'

Chaplin leaned over to the Political Secretary from the embassy. 'What's he talking about?' he whispered.

'Takht-e-Jamshid,' replied the diplomat, 'is Persian for the ruins at Persepolis. It's true, they are quite something.'

'Ours is an ancient civilization,' continued the Iranian Foreign Minister, 'older than that of the Romans, even. We Persians invented the game of chess. Yes! And what do our neighbours have across the water? Oil. That is all.' He flipped his palms upwards, like a conjuror waiting for applause. 'And when that runs out? Nothing. They will go back to tending their camels and their goats in the desert. Their skyscrapers will crumble into dust, their highways will crack in the heat, and their deserts will fill up with the cars they can no longer afford to drive. That, my friends, is what will become of our Arab neighbours.'

Geoffrey Chaplin stifled a yawn and fanned his face with a napkin. He had been told to expect a speech like this, and now the pace of the trip was starting to catch up with him. He excused himself and went in search of the bathroom. When he returned he saw that Dr Askari had, mercifully, sat down. Twenty minutes later the party gathered outside for a proposed tour of Isfahan's Grand Bazaar.

In the last twenty-four hours it had been hastily agreed that this would be a discreet, low-profile event. No cordons, no flashing lights, no overt security presence. The Iranian protocol people had first suggested, then insisted, that for the visiting British Foreign Secretary to gain a full appreciation of a fully functioning Persian bazaar in action they would move around it as a very small party, like everyday tourists. Their security detail would be reduced to a minimum, just two armed British Close Protection Officers and three more from Iranian government security officials. This way, it was assured, they would attract the minimum of attention.

That morning, there had been a fairly heated debate on the way to the airport between Chaplin and Sara Vallance on the one hand and Craig Dunne on the other. This whole Isfahan excursion, Dunne had advised them, was a breach of normal security protocols. His job, they had to remember, was to keep the Foreign Secretary safe, and without being able to recce the route in advance he couldn't guarantee to do that.

'I hear you,' Chaplin had told him, 'and I have the utmost respect for how you do your job, Craig. But I have mine to do, too, and if we say no to the Iranians on this one it could bugger up the whole trip, if you'll excuse my French.'

So now here they were, walking into the great covered bazaar of Isfahan, and Chaplin's attention had suddenly perked up. Moving from the broad open expanse of the Naqsh-e-Jahan Square into the labyrinthine half-light of the covered market was like passing from day to night. Beneath its massive, vaulted ceilings an Aladdin's Cave of treasures awaited him, a world of carpets, ceramics, brasswork and ornate lanterns. Everything, he noticed, was infused with a soft glow, as if he were viewing the entire experience through rose-tinted spectacles, which, in a way, he was. This would be something to tell Gillian about when he got home – perhaps he could even bring her back a souvenir.

Dr Askari and Zahra walked alongside him, one on each side, pointing out objects of interest, pausing to pick up the occasional artefact and pass it to their guest. When they came to a stall selling elaborate silverwork Dr Askari stopped and spoke to the owner. It was as if he had read the Foreign Secretary's mind because a moment later he handed him a heavy silver ornament, a bust of a winged Persian horse. 'A gift for your wife,' he announced, in suspiciously flawless English.

Chaplin, somewhat flustered as he realized he had nothing to give in return, fumbled for his glasses, then examined the horse, turning it over in his hands. 'It's um, it's quite exquisite,' he told them, then handed it straight to his SPAD to carry.

He could see Craig Dunne standing just a few feet away, speaking into his Motorola PTT short-range radio, the acoustic tube earpiece dangling from his right ear. He had stationed one officer up ahead and one behind at the entrance to the bazaar. 'If you see anything you don't like,' he was telling his team, 'inform me immediately. And keep an eye out for exit routes. We need to keep everyone moving.'

'Shall we?' said Zahra, steering them towards a narrow alley-way where Chaplin could see hessian sacks piled high with dates, dried apricots and pistachios. As they moved deeper into the narrow confines of the bazaar, walking just two abreast now, the walls seemed to close in on their party, squeezing them through passageways where lacquered clocks competed against wall decorations carved with elaborate octagonal Islamic patterns. Curious, smiling faces loomed out of the shadows, passing them briefly, and were gone. And Geoffrey Chaplin realized to his surprise that he was thoroughly enjoying himself. He even tried his hand at exchanging a few words in broken Farsi with a cloth merchant.

It was when they reached the spice market, a stall on the corner selling bags of saffron, that they heard it. A deep-throated angry chanting, rising and falling, coming at them down the alleyway, like a rolling wave. Sara Vallance grabbed Chaplin's arm and looked up at him in alarm. Chaplin glanced from her to his hosts. He could see the concern on their faces. The roar of voices was the same that they had encountered on the road out of Tehran airport. Chaplin recognized the words.

'Marg bar Ingilistan! Marg bar Ingilistan!'

Chaplin whirled round. Craig Dunne was already beside him, his jacket open, looking this way and that as he searched for the best way out. He reached up to his earpiece, straining to hear what was being said above the noise in the bazaar. Moments later he turned to Chaplin and Sara Vallance. 'We need to move! Right now! That was one of my officers up ahead. Says there are masses of protesters heading this way. Sounds like somebody's tipped them off you're here.'

Zahra, the interpreter, rushed up to them and tugged at Chaplin's sleeve, pointing at an alleyway behind them and to the left. Shopkeepers were frantically bringing down the metal shutters on their displays and some were already rushing past them.

'Come! Please come, Minister, we must go this way quickly!'

she said breathlessly. Chaplin could see the fear in her eyes and started to follow her but Craig Dunne had other ideas.

'It could be a set-up,' he hissed, in Chaplin's ear. 'We'll go this way instead. Follow me.' He led them down a second passageway, narrow yet almost deserted, but they hadn't gone twenty metres before they stopped in their tracks. A solid stream of people was coming towards them. They didn't look to Chaplin like protesters, more like shoppers and merchants, and they were abandoning their stalls and rushing down the passageway in a stampede of panic, trying to escape whatever was behind them. The trio of Britons was forced to flatten themselves against the walls to avoid being trampled and now, from somewhere close, came more chanting, so much closer now.

Suddenly there was the loud report of a firearm going off, followed immediately by screams. The noise sent a stab of fear through Chaplin and he flinched as a small fragment of the vaulted ceiling fell to the floor beside them, then a shower of masonry. Stumbling and tripping over bags of abandoned shopping, the group tried to turn back towards the ceramics bazaar. Craig Dunne kept looking round for their Iranian escort and, for a second, he thought he saw them, shepherding away their Foreign Minister before their heads disappeared in the crowd.

'For God's sake!' Chaplin shouted at him, his voice rising in panic. 'Get us out of here, will you!'

'I'm trying!' he shouted back. Dunne had his weapon drawn now, the Glock 19 cocked with the safety on, as he kept scanning for an exit. Sara Vallance was right behind him, the headscarf she had modestly put on to conform with her hosts had come loose and was now hanging halfway down her shoulder.

'Oh, God!' she screamed. 'Here they are!'

Chaplin turned to see a wall of black-clad figures coming towards them, their heads wrapped in yellow headbands inscribed in Farsi, black-and-white scarves draped around their necks. With a jolt, he saw that one was brandishing a pistol. He was a huge, bearded figure, and in the split second he caught sight of him, Chaplin thought he looked exactly like the man who had lunged at their car as they'd left Tehran airport. Someone was shouting in English and he realized it was Dunne.

'Over here!' His Principal Protection Officer was gesturing frantically at a gap between market stalls. Sara Vallance was already squeezing through it, her headscarf now lost and trampled somewhere underfoot. Chaplin's heart was thumping – he was unused to sudden physical exercise and knew he was slow. Dunne reached out and grabbed his arm, pulling him through the gap. Looking around him, Dunne pointed at a dark recess beneath a trestle table, the nearest hiding place he could see. 'Get down! Low! Lower!' he hissed. 'Cover your faces.'

They sank to the floor, flattening their bodies against the cold flagstones as booted feet trampled past in a blur of black. Thank God, thought Chaplin. But then he heard a triumphant shout, followed by a roaring cheer, and suddenly the crowd was back. Their hiding place had been discovered.

The mob came pouring through the market stalls. Dunne was already getting to his feet, both hands on the Glock that he now held steady in front of him. If the first young men to reach him had any fear they didn't show it. Ignoring the policeman's gun, they surged on top of the three Britons, overwhelming them in seconds. Dunne managed to fire once, a warning shot above their heads. It was a futile gesture. Arms reached out and, in a blur of limbs, the weapon was knocked out of his hand. Chaplin looked on in horror as Dunne was forced to the ground, his face pressed onto the rough stone floor. He could hear a woman screaming. It was Sara, his special adviser, her hands clamped over her face in terror at what she was witnessing. Now a man stood over Dunne, legs slightly apart, black shirtsleeves rolled up. In his hands he held a pistol and was aiming it, execution-style, at the Close Protection Officer's head.

'No!' shouted Chaplin, and in that same instant he saw the pistol buck with the recoil as the shot reverberated all around the bazaar. Craig Dunne's body slumped. Numb with shock,

Chaplin stared. This couldn't be happening. He turned to see another man knock Sara Vallance unconscious, then felt himself being dragged to his feet and a cloth clamped over his face.

Not far away, inside a windowless van parked in a side-street, a man in a grey tracksuit punched a message into his phone and sent it, using an encrypted app. It was a single word, one of millions criss-crossing cyberspace at that moment, and it made its way to an upstairs room in a nondescript building in Qom. The word was 'Shalamcheh' and the man who received it knew exactly what it meant.

It meant it had begun.

Chapter 43

Tehran

THE MOTORBIKE WAS parked in a side-street off Ferdowsi Avenue, engine idling. Two figures sat astride it, both in black leather jackets and helmets with tinted visors. The man in front revved the bike with a gloved hand, ready to go. Behind him, the pillion rider tensed, waiting. Then the earpiece inside his helmet crackled into life. It was the word they had been waiting for: '*Shalamcheh.*' He tapped the rider in front twice on the left shoulder and held on tight as they accelerated down the street.

They drove fast, weaving and swerving through the backed-up traffic along Jomhouri Avenue, ignoring the angry hoots of motorists as they cut across them. At the junction with Ferdowsi Avenue, between the National Bank headquarters and a fast-food outlet, the bike swung left and hugged the red-brick walls of the British Embassy. Seconds before they reached the blue metal entrance gates, topped with spikes and flanked by a bronze lion rampant, the motorbike passenger reached down and grabbed a broken half-brick. He could see them clearly now, the two Iranian government guards posted outside the gates, armed with German Heckler & Koch MP5s. He had to time this just right. Make the move too soon – or too late – and he'd end up dead. They couldn't afford a mistake and they had trained hard for this. Zamani had seen to that.

As they drew level with the embassy gates, he lobbed the brick onto the pavement between the two guards. Alerted by the roar of the bike, one swung round, bringing his weapon up to his shoulder and taking aim, but he was too late, his target had gone, vanished into the maelstrom of Tehran's traffic. The other rushed forward to retrieve the brick.

Reg Weston saw the whole thing unfold on his CCTV monitor. As the embassy's Regional Security Officer, he liked to keep a close eye on what was happening outside the compound gates. He, for one, would never forget what had happened in 2011 when a mob had breached the walls and ransacked the embassy. A former British Army bomb-disposal specialist, with many proud years of service in the Royal Engineers, his first thought now was that someone had hurled an improvised explosive device, an IED, at the embassy. He raced across the forecourt, through the security building and out onto Ferdowsi Avenue.

'Don't touch it!' he yelled. He saw the guard holding what seemed to be a fragment of brick. 'Move back!' He walked slowly, carefully, to where the projectile lay. As he walked he reached into his pocket and pulled out the pair of purple forensic gloves he always carried for just such a contingency. His initial fears seemed to be unfounded. He couldn't see any wires protruding, no obvious detonator. It looked like an ordinary brick, after all. Just a random piece of masonry used for a casual act of anti-Western vandalism.

He squatted down, cursing quietly as his knees cracked, and picked up the brick between the tips of his fingers, turning it over carefully. And that was when he saw the envelope taped to its underside. Scrawled on it in black ink were the words 'TO BRITISH GOVERMENT'. The embassy guards were standing over him now and one was holding out his hand for him to pass it over. But Reg Weston, late of 33 Engineer Regt (EOD), was having none of that, no, sir. He peeled the envelope away from the brick, stuffed it inside his jacket pocket, then stood up facing the guards. 'This,' he announced, patting his pocket, 'comes with me.' And with that he strode back inside the embassy.

The Ambassador was still down in Isfahan, escorting the Foreign Secretary on his up-country trip, which by recent accounts seemed to be going rather well. So Reg Weston reckoned the right thing to do was to take the envelope straight to Clare James, the Deputy Head of Mission, or DHM. He was almost inside the main Chancery building when he heard the shout from within.

'Christ! *No!*'

He covered the remaining distance at a sprint, flung open the door to the Chancery and found the DHM sitting bolt upright behind her desk, one hand clamped to her forehead, the other holding the phone. She was still on the line but she broke off to give him the catastrophic news. 'There's been an – an incident at the bazaar, in Isfahan.' She was struggling to find the words to describe the colossal magnitude of what had just taken place. 'The Foreign Secretary's been taken. Kidnapped! By armed men. He's been driven off and the Iranians are going all out to locate him now. His SPAD's been injured, she's concussed, but she'll be okay. But, oh, God, Reg, I've got some terrible news. Craig Dunne, his Protection Officer? I think you knew him?'

Weston sat down heavily in a padded armchair and nodded. He already knew from the tone of her voice what was coming.

'He's – he's been killed. Doing his job. Trying to protect the Foreign Secretary. I'm going to have to notify his next of kin. Whitehall will go ballistic.'

Reg Weston didn't answer at first. He looked away from her to the grandiose painting on the wall behind her, some imperial grandee with a sheathed sword and plumed hat, a nineteenth-century relic from the Great Game, a throwback to the days when Britain and Russia were vying for control of the trade routes to India. Well, there's not much of a game about this, he thought. This is bloody serious. He had known Craig Dunne for years, met him as an instructor on a training course at Hendon. And now he was gone. Dead. Killed in the line of duty. It was a lot to take in. And then he remembered the envelope, just as the DHM was putting down the phone to the team in Isfahan.

'We've had an incident here ourselves, just now,' he told her.

181

'Two blokes on a bike just went past and threw a brick at Gate Security. They got away but I've retrieved this. It was taped to the brick.' He pulled out the envelope from his jacket pocket and handed it to her.

'You'd better open it,' she told him. 'Here, use this.' She passed him a silver letter-opener from her desk, engraved with the letters ER.

Reg Weston held up the envelope to the light, making one final check that it didn't contain something nasty. Then he slit it open and gingerly removed a single sheet of paper, holding it by one corner. It would have to be sent to the forensic labs at Fort Halstead and dusted for prints later. The page was a handwritten note, in Farsi, a language that had so far eluded him. He held the letter in front of the Deputy Ambassador. Clare James put on her spectacles and leaned forward to read the message. Reg Weston watched her as she mouthed the words in Farsi, her brow furrowing.

When she had finished she sat back and turned to him. Her jaw was set firm, her eyes narrowed. Weston had never seen her look like that: she seemed almost feral.

'So what does it say?' he prompted her.

'It's an ultimatum, Reg. It's a frigging ultimatum.' Her voice was very low and quiet. 'They've given us a deadline.'

'What deadline? Who's they?'

'The people who've taken the Foreign Secretary. They're holding him and they're threatening to kill him if there's a rescue mission.'

'But what's the deadline?' he reminded her. She seemed distracted, which was hardly surprising. All hell was about to break loose.

'They've given us a time limit. Just forty-two hours to withdraw all Western military forces from the Gulf or . . .'

'Or what?' Again, he probably knew the answer even as he spoke.

'Or they'll murder the Foreign Secretary on the morning of the third day. Live on camera.'

Chapter 44

Tehran

THREE MISSED CALLS, all from Vauxhall Cross. In the hum and din of Tehran traffic Luke hadn't noticed his phone ringing as he made his way back to his first-floor room at the Hotel Shahrestan. His mind was busy working out how best to 'play' Tannaz, now he'd shown her the photos. She'd been shocked, no doubt about it. He'd got the reaction he'd hoped for. But shocked enough to inform on her father? No, he definitely needed more time.

So if this call was some deskbound reports officer in London pestering him to come up with fresh material on Zamani he'd tell them where to get off. Luke would do this his way, on his terms and his timetable. He dialled Vauxhall Cross. The phone was answered on the second ring. It was his immediate boss, Angela.

'Have you heard what's happened?' Her voice sounded unusually brittle.

'No? What?' Luke was at the far end of the corridor outside his room. If he kept his voice down, he reckoned it was probably the safest place to make a call, just in case someone was listening in on his room.

'The Foreign Secretary's been kidnapped. In Isfahan.'

'What? When? Who's got him?'

'About . . . twenty-five minutes ago. We don't know who's

behind it yet. The host country's denying all blame. As you'd expect. Oh, and the kidnappers have issued an ultimatum. Forty-two hours for Western forces to leave the Gulf.' She let out a long sigh.

'Jesus . . .' Luke was still struggling to digest this news. 'Forty-two hours? That's a strange number, what's that about?'

'It takes us to oh nine hundred local the day after tomorrow,' she replied. 'Maybe they're timing it for maximum news effect. We just don't know.'

'So how did this happen?' Luke pressed. 'What about his CP team? Didn't he have a bodyguard with him?'

'He did. And he's dead. Listen, we don't have time to go into that now. We need you to focus one hundred per cent on finding the Foreign Secretary.' From the urgency in her voice he could only guess at the pressure now piling onto the Service. 'Do whatever it takes, spend whatever you have to,' she continued. 'Just find out where he's being held and who's got him. We'll do the rest. You'll have all the back-up you need.'

That's what you said when you sent me to Armenia, Luke thought, but he didn't say it.

'Can you use Elixir?' Angela continued.

'I'll try. She's seen the photos now. It's made an impression. But she's not ready yet. I'll need more time.' He detected another sigh down the line.

'We don't have it, Luke. I can't tell you how serious this is. Things are on a knife-edge here. We don't know how Washington's going to react. This could be just the provocation the White House is looking for.'

'For what?'

'Do I have to spell it out? The hawks in DC have been angling for something like this for months. Now Iran has just handed it to them on a plate. So you'd better get out there and find Chaplin for us. Before it's too late.'

'Or what?' Luke persisted.

'Before the Foreign Secretary is murdered and this turns into Gulf War Three. With ballistic missiles.' She hung up.

Chapter 45

Whitehall, London

IN THE INNER office at Number 10 they had been going over the final preparations for Prime Minister's Questions. Once again, the weekly Wednesday session in Parliament looked set to be dominated by questions over Brexit, trade deals, the single European market, immigration and the NHS. It was all there in the notes for the PM. Specific instructions had been left for no interruptions and all calls were to be held. But this call was an exception. It came from Sir Charles Bennett, the National Security Adviser. He could have walked across from the Cabinet Office, only a few corridors away, but what he had to say couldn't wait and he asked to be put straight through to the PM.

There were only three people in the room when that call came through, just three people in 10 Downing Street who now knew the full extent of what had taken place in a country three thousand miles away. There was the PM, his Chief of Staff and his principal speechwriter.

In the shocked silence that followed it was the Chief of Staff who was the first to speak. 'We'll have to cancel PMQs,' she said, already pulling out her phone. 'I'll get onto the Speaker's Office straight away.' She began scrolling through her contacts, searching for the number, but the PM held up his hand to stop her.

Cancelling Prime Minister's Questions was a rare and drastic step. The last time it had happened had been in 2009 when David Cameron's son had died. Cancelling them now would immediately set the hares racing when the news from Iran was not yet out.

'No,' said the PM, emphatically. 'We will end the session in Parliament at twelve thirty sharp, not a minute later. I will chair COBRA in the Cabinet Office immediately afterwards. Make sure we get everybody who needs to be there. And I want to speak to our Ambassador directly. Get him on the line, will you?'

COBRA – short for 'Cabinet Office Briefing Room' – was the government's crisis response team, convened in times of national emergency. It had assembled in record time, just fifty-seven minutes after the call came through to Number 10. From Vauxhall Cross came Sir Adam Keeling, Chief of SIS, and his Director of Counter-terrorism, Sid Khan. From New Scotland Yard came the Metropolitan Police Commissioner, and from the MoD the Director of Special Forces. Others, like Jane Haslett from the FCO, had less far to travel. Some, like the Chief of Defence Staff, Sir Jeremy Buckshaw, had only to make their way across on foot from MoD Main Building, or use the secret underground passage beneath Whitehall to reach Building 70. Others were dropped off by car. Only the Director General of GCHQ, the government listening station in Cheltenham, was unable to cover the distance from Gloucestershire in time. Instead, he'd sent a deputy from their little-known office in St James's.

In the hushed underground conference room concealed beneath the pavements and government offices of Whitehall, the meeting began bang on time with a grim announcement from the PM.

'As most of you are aware, the unthinkable has happened. Just under two hours ago Geoffrey Chaplin, our Foreign Secretary, was taken hostage by armed men in the city of Isfahan while on a ministerial visit to Iran. His Close Protection Officer, Craig Dunne, was murdered while trying to prevent his abduction. We've informed his next of kin. Now, I've spoken to Mervyn

Davies, our Ambassador to Iran – he's on his way back from Isfahan – and his view is that the Iranian government was not behind this. But, of course, we still hold them entirely responsible. We have also received what amounts to a ransom note, an ultimatum if you will, with an impossible demand. The sender is calling for all Western forces to be withdrawn from the Gulf within forty-two hours, which is clearly a non-starter.'

'I'm sorry to interrupt, Prime Minister.' It was Sir Jeremy Buckshaw, the Chief of Defence Staff, who spoke, a veteran of many COBRA meetings but none as serious as this. The operational medals emblazoned across his chest stood testimony to his experience in Bosnia, Kosovo, Sierre Leone, Iraq and Afghanistan. 'Has Washington been told?'

'Thank you, CDS. The Ambassador in DC is briefing the White House as we speak. So . . .' A pause to let everyone in the room digest what they had just heard. No one moved a muscle. 'As Mervyn is still in transit back to Tehran I'm going to ask Clare James, his deputy, to give us her assessment of the situation.'

All eyes turned to the video display screen at the far end of the room where a worried face swam into focus. Just visible behind her, a pale green wall was hung with antique gilt-framed prints, all softly lit. It was an oddly calming backdrop, completely at odds with the reality of what had just taken place. Clare James's disembodied voice erupted from the speakers, a little too loud, as she launched straight in, without preamble.

'We are working flat out with the host nation,' she told the COBRA meeting, 'to establish the whereabouts of the Foreign Secretary. I've just got off the phone to Dr Askari, Iran's Foreign Minister, and he's given me personal assurance that his government had nothing to do with this. I should add—'

'Do you believe him, Clare?' interrupted the PM.

'I'm sorry? Could you repeat that?' The video picture quivered on the screen then froze, treating the room to an image of the Deputy Head of Mission with her mouth half open in midsentence, her eyes tight shut as she collected her thoughts. Then it came back onstream.

187

'Do we believe Dr Askari? Can we take him at his word?' The PM was frowning, his fingers drumming impatiently on the table, as if he had already made up his mind. 'Because if we don't think he's telling the truth, if the Iranian government turns out to be behind this, well, it's effectively an act of war, isn't it?' He was looking directly at the Chief of Defence Staff as he said this but he knew that his next conversation was probably going to have to be with the Attorney General. No one in the room was an expert on the legal ramifications of a British Foreign Secretary getting kidnapped overseas.

'Yes . . .' came the answer, from deep within the embassy compound in Tehran, the voice sounding somewhat hesitant. 'I do believe Dr Askari is being sincere.' Then she added: 'This is a national embarrassment for the Iranians. At least, it will be as soon as it breaks. We've agreed a news blackout on it for now to give them a chance to find him – Geoffrey, that is. Meanwhile there's this.' She held up a piece of typewritten paper towards the camera – she was wearing a pair of forensic gloves. The paper was too blurred for anyone to read. 'It was delivered to our embassy here just after three this afternoon by two men on a motorbike. They haven't been found yet. I'll translate it for you.' She put on her glasses, then began to read out loud: ' "To the British government. We have your minister. He is safe for now. We have one simple demand for his release. All imperialist Western armed forces must commit to vacate Persian Gulf waters. Today is Day One. You have until 0900 on Day Three, Iran time. If you do not comply then we regret your minister will be killed and his death will be broadcast." '

Clare James removed her spectacles and looked straight into the camera again, her pale face looming just a little too close to the lens. 'So it's an ultimatum. Just forty-two hours to pull out of the Gulf. It's totally absurd. Whoever's behind this knows full well we're not going to comply. So it's a stunt, they're testing us, but I think we have to assume they're serious. Serious, that is, about carrying out their threat . . .'

Her words hung for a moment in the room. Almost everyone

there that afternoon had met Geoffrey Chaplin at some time in their career. 'A likeable chap', 'A safe pair of hands', 'Not one to rock the boat'. People rarely had anything bad – or exciting – to say about him. So the idea of the Foreign Secretary now being bundled away by armed men in a distant country was just too hard to contemplate.

It was the PM who broke the silence, addressing the COBRA meeting in a deadpan voice. 'Right. I would like to know two things. Who is behind this? And what can we bring to bear, right now, to effect his release, unharmed?' He turned towards the video screen. 'Clare, are you still hearing us there?'

'I am, Prime Minister.' A two-second delay, then a nod.

'I'm getting a team of Met detectives over to you today, from the Hostage and Crisis Negotiation Unit. I don't want to hear any nonsense from Tehran about not letting them in. Full access, d'you understand? See that they get it.'

Another nod from Clare James on the video screen.

A sharp cough and everyone turned their attention to the Secret Intelligence Service Chief, who sat two chairs down from the PM on the left. 'I'd like to add something, if I may.' Quietly effective, Sir Adam Keeling had risen through the ranks of MI6, establishing himself as a Soviet expert during the Cold War, later moving with the times to focus instead on what Whitehall liked to call 'international terrorism', meaning the jihadist threat from Al-Qaeda and ISIS. Trying to keep tabs on Iran's covert nuclear activities and cultivate agents inside that country had also been a priority in his service for years. 'There is a strong possibility there's a link here to the hardliners in the IRGC, the Revolutionary Guards. They've been looking for ways to embarrass their own government since before the last elections. They're even more determined now. They want the reforms put on hold and they want Iran to return to international isolation. They're the only ones with the brass to do something like this. It's got their stamp all over it.'

'Hold on, that's a pretty strong statement, if you don't mind my saying.' The National Security Adviser swept his glasses off his face and gave Keeling a fixed smile, devoid of all warmth. 'Would you care to share some of the evidence for this conclusion?'

'Not in this room, right now, no, I'm afraid I wouldn't,' he replied, returning him an equally frosty smile. 'I'm quite sure you'll understand my reasons.' There was a grunt from the National Security Adviser. It was clear he was far from satisfied.

'Right now,' cut in the PM, 'we need to stay focused on one thing alone. And that's finding Geoffrey.' He turned to the Chief of Defence Staff. 'Sir Jeremy, I want a hostage-rescue team put on standby. I don't care if the Iranians say they can handle it. This is our problem, we own it, and we need to move extremely fast.'

Chapter 46

South Tehran suburbs

GEOFFREY CHAPLIN COULDN'T move. He was in pain, he was in shock, and he was terrified. Britain's Secretary of State for Foreign and Commonwealth Affairs lay helpless on the hard metal floor of a moving van, slumped in the spot where they had dragged and deposited him earlier. He was gagged, blindfolded, his hands bound behind his back with plasticuffs. After years of moving through life in a protected ministerial bubble, he was now completely defenceless.

The shock of capture, back there in the Isfahan bazaar, was still raw. While he tried hard not to, he couldn't help replaying those last terrifying minutes over and over in his head. What had become of his team? Oh, God. Craig Dunne was dead. He had watched it happen with his own eyes, that man standing over him with the pistol, execution-style. And Sara? He remembered seeing her struck, but then what? Was she a captive too? Bound, gagged and humiliated like him, being driven away by masked men in the back of some lurching van?

The one thing he wasn't thinking of was escape. Geoffrey Chaplin had no military experience. Instead, years of parliamentary lunches and endless sedentary meetings in Westminster had left him decidedly overweight and out of shape. On the cusp of his sixty-second birthday, he had already been told by his doctor that he needed to reduce his cholesterol and take more exercise. He also needed a stronger pair of glasses. Geoffrey Chaplin was in no position to put up a fight or make a run for it. He knew his best chance of getting through this in one piece was to cooperate and do exactly as his abductors demanded. There would be others, surely, working frantically on his release.

And now he desperately needed to pee. He grunted as loudly as he could through the cloth gag around his mouth but, with all the noise and movement, nobody heard him. They seemed to be travelling at speed, turning sharply to left and right, accelerating then braking abruptly. Every turn meant more pain, his head banging into something hard and metallic, the plasticuffs biting into the chafed flesh of his wrists. And he felt car-sick. He wondered what would happen if he threw up into his gag. Would he end up choking on his own vomit? What a dreadful way to go – and what a pitiful end that would be to his thirty-two-year political career.

A sudden screech of brakes and he felt himself sliding briefly, helplessly across the metal floor of the van, then crashing into some other hard object. They had stopped. Oh, God, what now? Was this about to be his execution? Who were these people, for Christ's sake? He could hear the van's rear door being yanked open, letting in a flood of daylight that he sensed from behind his blindfold. It must still be late afternoon, then. Chaplin could hear several voices all talking at once in hushed tones. Then hands were grabbing him and he was being half pulled, half lifted out of the back of the van. They were trying to make him stand, he could feel arms holding him roughly on either side but at first his legs gave way and he fell in a heap at their feet. When they pulled him up and made him try again, something happened. His blindfold slipped, only a fraction. They had wrapped it round his glasses and now the gap was just enough for him to catch a glimpse of the men who held him. Police uniforms. Good God, they were wearing Iranian police uniforms! He was no expert but they looked identical to those worn by the very people who had been chaperoning him around Tehran only yes-terday. So was this an Iranian government operation after all? It couldn't be, could it? But then he remembered the hostage crisis back in 2007, when five Britons had been seized in Baghdad. True, that was Iraq, not Iran, but the kidnappers had belonged to a fanatical Shia militia group trained in Iran and, as he remem-bered from the reports at the time, they had worn stolen Iraqi police uniforms.

'Toilet,' he mumbled through his gag.

'No toilet,' came the answer, and now he was being steered towards another vehicle – he could hear its engine running. Switching vehicles? That would make sense, buying his abduc-tors more time. More time? Heavens, why hadn't he been rescued already? What was taking them so long, for God's sake? Chaplin fought to control the rising panic that was welling inside him. Suddenly he could feel rough hands grabbing his own behind his back. There was a click and his wrists were free of the plasti-cuffs, blood coming back into his hands. So he was being released. Well, good. I should think so. About time. He'd expect a full apol-ogy from the Iranians after this. And a detailed report from his own side once he got back to London. But no one was removing the gag, or the blindfold. And now someone was tugging at his clothes and there was a man saying something to him, just behind his ear.

'Take off your clothes,' said a menacing voice, in English. A wave of panic swept over him as his mind leaped to the unthink-able. He hugged his jacket tightly around him and hunched his shoulders. He was damned if he was undressing for anybody.

'No,' he told them firmly, through the gag, but it came out so distorted it sounded like a grunt. The next thing he knew some-one was kicking his legs out from under him and he was flat on the ground. It took them less than thirty seconds to strip him of his jacket and shirt. His shoes took a little longer, the precious polished brown brogues, from the shop in Jermyn Street, that Gillian had given him. Next to go were his socks and finally he could feel them unbuckling his belt and pulling off his trousers as his arms were held back. So this is it, he thought, this is how it happens. Still blindfolded and unable to see what was coming next, he flinched as a man's hand reached down between his legs and briefly cupped his genitals before feeling all around the seam of his underpants. He said something to the others in Farsi, then felt a garment being pulled up over his legs and his arms being pushed through holes. It was a boiler suit, and it smelt of diesel. The moment it was on him they stood him up and led him over to the other vehicle.

'Toilet!' he protested again, through his gag. 'I need the damn toilet.' But no one paid any attention as he was pushed through onto the floor of another van and the doors slammed shut behind him. And that was when he realized it. These people were serious. They knew what they were doing. There was a reason they had made him change clothes back there, and it wasn't about humiliating a visiting British minister. They must have guessed he'd have a tracking device on him. By now they must have found it, his Track24 Pocket Buddy, the personal GPS satellite locator device that the FCO Security people had insisted was Velcroed into the inside of his left sock. Which meant that right now, someone back in Tehran or London ought to be able to see where he was on a map. So why hadn't he been rescued? For the second time he asked himself what was taking them so long. Every minute that passed, now that he'd been separated from his tracker, meant his chances of being found were reducing.

As the van moved off he felt his gag being untied and someone was trying to push something into his mouth. He turned his head away, then realized it was a straw.

'Drink,' said a voice, and he did as he was told. Chaplin hadn't drunk anything since the banquet in Isfahan and his throat was parched. It tasted like warm, flat Coca-Cola but he drank it anyway. And now, of course, he was desperate to pee. It was when the vehicle gave a particularly violent jolt that he couldn't help himself, and he let it go. Slowly, the hot, wet sensation spread from his groin down his legs and he could smell the familiar acrid tang of ammonia. He heard a low ripple of laughter from the people around him. Their captive had just humiliated himself. Slumped in the back of a van, being driven across Iran by armed men, Geoffrey Chaplin was cramped, blindfolded and soaked in his own urine. Like the ominous signs of an approaching storm, he felt something he hadn't known in a very long time: the beginnings of despair.

Chapter 47

'OH, CHRIST!' THE Prime Minister held the tablet at arm's length as if he really didn't want to read its contents. The COBRA meeting had been about to break up when a Number 10 aide had dashed breathlessly in and handed it to him. The PM now held it up for everyone in the room to see before examining it more closely.

'The story's got out,' he said grimly. 'It's already in the public domain.' Lurid colours danced across the screen and a banner headline screamed: 'Chaplin Kidnapped!' It was a *Mail*Online exclusive and there were subheadings like 'War with Iran'. Beneath a large file photograph of the Foreign Secretary, there was a map of Iran and then a smaller photo of Craig Dunne, his murdered bodyguard.

'A tearful relative of Mr Dunne contacted the *Daily Mail* to tell them he had died a hero,' read the paragraph beneath that. 'But she blamed the Foreign Office for putting him in harm's way.' The PM stopped reading and addressed the room, face stern, brow furrowed. 'This crisis is now in the public eye,' he told them. 'Everything we do to resolve it is going to be picked over by the media. Foreign Office Counter-terrorism will take the lead, which means all enquiries are to go through their news desk. I do not want to hear of anyone else blabbing to the press. Is that clear?' There were nods up and down the table.

'Right. Meeting adjourned until the same time tomorrow.'

As the intelligence chiefs, ministers, diplomats, senior police, senior servicemen and -women who had gathered around the table in that COBRA meeting got up to leave, they were stopped at the door by an apologetic Cabinet Office official. 'There are satellite TV trucks outside on Whitehall,' he told them, 'and the media are at the steps outside with cameras. You'll have to leave by the rear entrance.'

Everyone was crowding round the lifts on their phones. One call being made that afternoon was from the Director of Special Forces to a well-guarded military base in Dorset. It went straight through to a sparse, functional room in Poole, the office of Lieutenant Colonel Chip Nuttall, Commanding Officer of the Special Boat Service. The standby squadron for crisis operations and hostage situations such as this rotated between the SBS and their more famous cousins, the SAS. Right now, Poole was the standby squadron.

'You've seen the news?'

'Just heard it,' Nuttall replied.

'Good. You're on four hours' notice-to-move.'

Chapter 48

Qom, Iran

JUST AS THE COBRA meeting was ending in Whitehall, in an upstairs room of a nondescript building in the holy city of Qom, Karim Zamani allowed himself a rare smile. It was, he knew, far too early to celebrate. And yet, as he looked around the table at the five men he trusted most, his loyal co-conspirators, he couldn't help but feel a sense of triumph. Battle had been joined, the first shots fired, literally, in the Circle's strategic plan. The seizure of 'the goods' in Isfahan bazaar had gone precisely to plan. He looked at his watch. Where would the van containing its precious human cargo be? Somewhere just south of Isfahan, he estimated. The device had been prepared the previous week on his orders, transported at night in an industrial supplies delivery van, then manoeuvred, with some difficulty, he had been told, into its current resting place. The ultimatum had been delivered, as planned, to the embassy of the Little Satan on Ferdowsi Avenue, and the crisis he had hoped to initiate for his government was developing nicely. Zamani ran his hand over his neatly trimmed stubble before he spoke.

'We have every reason to offer prayers of thanks for this day,' he told the assembled company, spreading his hands before him on the table, then continuing, with a frown, 'But we must not be complacent. No, my brothers, that would be a mistake.' His eyebrows knitted together as he looked from one face to another. 'There are still many pitfalls ahead and much that could go wrong.' They nodded. 'And we must be vigilant! Yes! The Zionists and the Americans will be trying their best to uncover our secrets and we must not let them. My brother Hoshyar.' He turned to the man on his left: black leather jacket, worn thin at the elbows, a large, bearded face and a forehead that was deeply lined. 'I believe you have an update for us on the operation in Armenia?'

'I do, Karim-*jaan*. Our sources in Yerevan have made many enquiries and worked tirelessly to discover who could have killed our men in that monastery.' He looked at Zamani, who gestured for him to continue.

'And?'

'And they found a taxi driver who drove a foreigner, an Englishman, from his hotel up to the monastery on that same morning. There were no other visitors from Europe that day, only one man from Japan.'

'Go on,' Zamani said.

'They located his hotel where he was registered under the name of "Brendan Hall". He had a woman with him. Maybe his wife, maybe his cover, we don't know. And we have obtained a photograph of him from his passport copy at hotel reception.'

'This is excellent work,' Zamani replied. 'Your people are to be congratulated, Hoshyar-*jaan*. And do we know if this Brendan Hall has tried to enter the Islamic Republic?'

'That is being checked. An instruction has gone out to border police and Immigration. If he has entered Iran we will find him.'

Karim Zamani nodded approvingly. 'Good,' he concluded. 'Please make this a priority. And if this Zionist-imperialist agent has dared to come to our country, bring him to me when you find him. You know where I will be.'

Chapter 49

Tehran

THINK. THINK HARD. I've got just one asset in this country, Luke said to himself, and that's Tannaz Zamani. So how do I turn this to work to my advantage? And all with the clock ticking and Vauxhall breathing down my neck for updates.

He sat on the bed in his room and ran his fingers through his hair. The photos he had shown her on the park bench earlier that day had cut deep. Tannaz was vulnerable right now, but that didn't mean she'd be prepared to help him. What would it take to make her turn against her father, to betray him?

He remembered the words the instructors had used, over and over, on the agent-running course at the Base. 'Your job is to make contact with the person chosen by Targeting, recruit them, then act on the information they supply. You'll need to use your personal intellectual charm, your emotional intelligence, to build up a source and develop them.' Did he, Luke, have any 'personal intellectual charm'? God knew. That hadn't exactly been part of the job spec when he was serving in the Corps or going out on night raids into Taliban territory with the SBS in Afghanistan. But he certainly needed it now, in spades. A plan began to form in his head, a proposition that just might work. He needed to see Tannaz again, as soon as possible. But would she be prepared to see *him*, given their last meeting had ended in tears? He took out his phone, scrolled through his Telegram contacts till he found 'Aesthetica' and sent her a quick text message. She didn't answer at first, and when she did, her message was curt and business-like. *Can't meet now. Suggest we meet Café Rameez 6 p.m.*

Damn. That was still more than an hour away. Frustrated and impatient, he lay on his bed, switched on the TV and tuned in to the BBC World Service. The Chaplin abduction was all over the news, that and the murder in Isfahan bazaar of Craig Dunne, the Protection Officer. There followed commentary and punditry from various ex-ambassadors and Iran 'experts'. Luke listened for a while, then used his phone to read whatever he could find online.

'All US Options on the Table' read the headline on CNN.com. It quoted an unnamed Pentagon official as saying, ominously: 'The US is ready to play its part to support its ally Britain to bring this crisis to an end in a decisive and effective manner.' Al-Jazeera English, the Qatar-based satellite TV station, was already running a logo on its main portal that said: 'Gulf Crisis Day 1'. It reprinted an official statement from IRNA, Iran's state news agency:

> The government of the Islamic Republic of Iran deplores this despicable act. It condemns kidnapping in all its forms. The Supreme Leader has expressed his confidence that state security agencies will succeed in bringing a swift end to this situation without interference from external powers.

There was no mention of the ultimatum handed in to the British Embassy but it concluded: 'Those responsible for this Zionist-inspired plot will surely be hunted down and punished.'

Logging off, he got up and reached for his jacket, pocketing his phone and his room key, then glanced round the room before heading out to meet Tannaz. At the last minute he stuffed some packets of peanuts and sweets in his pockets, just in case. In the hotel lobby the young receptionist came out from behind his desk and stopped him with an excited wave of the hand. 'Have you heard the news, Mr Hall? Very bad things. And now they are saying we must watch out for spies in our country. What do you think will happen? How will America react?'

'God knows,' Luke replied. 'But who do *you* think is behind this kidnapping?'

'But it's the Israelis, of course! And the CIA,' he replied, without hesitation. 'They are doing this to bring shame on Iran and make problem with other countries.'

Luke smiled but said nothing. Pushing open the door, he stepped out into the cold Tehran night and flagged down a cab to Café Rameez. He managed to get the same table as before – at the back, up against the wall, and with a clear view of the entrance – and waited for Tannaz. A TV set was mounted on one of the walls, volume turned up, and nearly everyone in the café was glued to it. It was all in Farsi but Luke could follow the gist of it from the pictures on the screen. Iranian Air Force Mig-29s and Sukhoi fighter jets were shown flying over the Gulf in formation; there were flotillas of high-speed gunboats, then radar installations scanning the skies in perpetual vigilance. People in the café were talking animatedly, some nodding approvingly. Others, perhaps old enough to remember the devastation left by eight years of war with Iraq, looked deeply concerned.

The screen cut abruptly to the owlish features of a man pictured beside a diminutive Union flag. With a shock, Luke recognized him as Geoffrey Chaplin, the Foreign Secretary. He wished he could understand the commentary but then the image changed to a shot of the Israeli flag, with a large question mark superimposed over it. Finally, he watched a clip of the US President addressing a large audience of men and women in uniform in some cavernous hall decked out with Stars and Stripes flags. He was pumping his fist up and down, shouting something, and he did not look happy.

The café door swung open, letting in a blast of icy air, and Tannaz swept in, the tails of her coat trailing behind her. She hurried over to Luke's table, her face a mask of worry. Luke waved her towards a chair next to him but at first she seemed almost reluctant to join him. He put it down to the national state of nervousness now gripping the country. 'No more nasty photos, I promise,' he reassured her, but she dismissed this with a shake of her head.

'Brendan!' she hissed, taking her seat while checking no one was watching them. Luke winced inwardly – he still hated his cover name. 'You don't know what's happened, do you?' she said.

'Well, yes,' he replied. 'Our Foreign Secretary's been taken. In Isfahan today. In fact, I wanted to talk to you about it.'

'No! That's not it.' Tannaz's eyes were darting around the café now. She was a bundle of nerves. He couldn't remember ever seeing her like that. 'Oh, my God, you don't know, do you? It was on the radio, just now.'

'What was?' Luke's face was calm, in sharp contrast to hers.

'The police and the Revolutionary Guards are looking for you! They named you in person! They're charging you under *moharebeh*!'

'What? What's that?'

'*Moharebeh* means "making war against God". It allows them to arrest whoever they want. They're saying you might be connected to this kidnapping on the news today.' Tannaz's eyes were wide open and staring at him. 'Brendan, what are you really doing in Iran? Who *are* you exactly?'

'Tannaz, this is crazy!' He lowered his voice to a whisper. 'Honestly, do I look like a troublemaker to you?' Fuck. This was serious. This changed everything. He'd need to alert Vauxhall.

'Is it? Is it really so crazy?' Tannaz hadn't even bothered to remove her scarf – she looked ready to get up and walk out again at any moment. 'Maybe you really are a British spy and you've been lying to me all this time,' she replied. She looked both sad and worried. Luke glanced round at the clientele. People had gathered in huddles, noisily discussing the news they'd just watched. As possibly the only non-Iranian in the café, he felt distinctly self-conscious.

'Oh, come on, Tannaz. You don't believe this crap, do you? I'm being framed! It's obvious. Surely you can see that. Look, I've been right here in Tehran, all day, and the Foreign Secretary got kidnapped in Isfahan. This makes no sense at all. None.'

Tannaz considered him, her head cocked slightly to one side, as if judging him. And right there, in that moment, Luke knew he was horribly exposed. Everything, his mission, his freedom, perhaps his life, lay in the hands of the twenty-two-year-old Tehran University student who happened to have a dad in the IRGC. This was not a good position to be in.

'All right,' she said at last, giving him a calculating look, then glancing quickly round the café once more. 'We need to get you out of here. And fast. You don't have much time left, mister.'

Chapter 50

Musandam peninsula, Oman

SCORCHED AND BLEACHED by a relentless sun, the massive mountains of Oman's Musandam peninsula rise up sheer from the glittering waters of the Gulf. Formed at the end of the Cretaceous period, the sedimentary rock formations lie piled one on top of another, resembling a block of flats collapsed by an earthquake. At some of their highest points, the mountains afford a commanding view across the strategic Strait of Hormuz towards the coast of Iran. In one place, the two countries' territories are just twenty miles apart across the channel. Winding up through this austere, shadeless, rust-coloured landscape, a narrow road twists and turns past the rough stone shelters of hardy goatherds and long-gone hermits.

The road is not accessible to the general public because what lies up there is classified 'Secret' by the Omani government. Beyond the barrier and the sentry post, the road leads up to a well-guarded and highly secretive establishment: the Musandam listening post. With permission from Oman's Sandhurst-trained ruler, the Sultan, the base is staffed by Western Signals Intelligence – SIGINT – operators, trawling daily through the wealth of data gleaned from underwater cables, listening into phone calls, emails and internet traffic emanating from across the water in the Islamic

Republic of Iran. Their reports are fed directly into the UK and US intelligence agencies: GCHQ and the NSA respectively.

At 1732 hours Oman time, thirty minutes ahead of Iran time, the team of monitors up at Musandam were at full stretch. It had already been a frantically busy day. Iran's military and security apparatus was in a state of near-nationwide panic following the Chaplin abduction, its commanders convinced they were about to be attacked by the US, Israel or both. In the Musandam listening post the empty coffee cups and drained plastic bottles of Masafi mineral water stood testament to long hours of constant scanning, listening, recording and filing of encrypted reports back to Cheltenham and NSA HQ at Fort Meade, Maryland.

US Airforce Sergeant Todd Bergensen took off his spectacles and rubbed his eyes. With his talent for making sense out of streams of numbers and data, he had always known he was destined for a lifetime of staring at screens, which suited him just fine. He drained the last of his lukewarm coffee and tossed the cup into the bin beside him. Then something caught his eye. It was just the briefest of messages, something that, on its own, would not have attracted the slightest attention. It contained no trigger-words, nothing that would set off any alarm bells in Washington or London. No, it was the sender's number that was significant. It was from a known senior operative in the IRGC's Quds force, the covert action wing of the Revolutionary Guards, a man on the watchlist databases of several Western intelligence agencies. It was the first time this number had surfaced in weeks and it was being used to send a message from Qom to an unknown recipient in the Iranian port of Bandar Abbas.

The algorithms in Todd Bergensen's system had already made a connection. The alert icon was blinking red, on and off, in the top right-hand corner of his screen. He pushed back his swivel chair, got up and hurried to the adjacent room. The door was open, but he still tapped politely on the glass window anyway. 'Ma'am, you'd better come take a look at this,' he said.

'Be with you in one,' she replied, holding up her index finger without looking up. She had her headphones on and was busy writing something on a pad.

The analyst was insistent. 'Ma'am, we might have some actionable intel here. I think you need to see it now.'

She swept off her headphones, shook out her hair, then followed him next door without a word. They stood leaning over his console, peering at the words of the text, which had been instantly and automatically translated for them using Parstext, a program preloaded into their monitoring system along with similar ones for Arabic, Urdu and Baluchi.

'I'm correct, aren't I, ma'am?' Todd asked. 'This is significant, right?'

'Are you kidding?' his team leader replied. 'Damn right it's significant. This could be a major piece of the jigsaw right now. Good work, Todd.' She peered at the message again. *Praise be to God*, it read. *The goods have been sent.*

'Okay, then,' she said, pointing both index fingers straight at him, like drawn pistols. 'We need the number of whoever received that message. We need to geo-locate his exact location and we need to pass all of this data ASAP to Cheltenham and Fort Meade. I'll warn them it's coming in.' She turned on her heels, then paused in the doorway and looked directly at the analyst. There was a strident edge to her voice. 'Don't waste a moment here, Todd. Do whatever it takes. I'm counting on you.'

Chapter 51

THE SHAME AND humiliation he felt at having been unable to control his bladder had given way to something else. Geoffrey Chaplin, father of two, Her Majesty's Foreign Secretary, was starting to shiver uncontrollably. He was cold, soaked from the waist down, and he stank. He stank of the rank, ammonial smell you only got under bridges in certain cities or round the back of the suburban pubs he vaguely remembered from when he was a teenager. As far as he could tell, this vehicle, the mobile prison they had loaded him into, with his captors, had no heating as well as no suspension.

With every hour that passed, his captors seemed to grow less nervous, he could hear it in the pitch of their voices as they started to come down off high alert. When they stopped again, after several hours' driving, someone behind him pulled him up into a sitting position, then fumbled at the back of his head. The next thing he knew both the gag and the blindfold had been removed and Geoffrey Chaplin got his first proper view of his surroundings and of the people holding him prisoner. Neither filled him with a great deal of hope.

A heavily built man in a faded green jacket of the sort worn by

American GIs in the Vietnam war was seated directly opposite him. He had a scar running down his left cheek and looked familiar. Yes, he was sure now: this was the same man who'd loomed over him in the bazaar at Isfahan. He shuddered as he remembered that moment. It must have been only hours ago, yet it felt like a lifetime. The man's large face was framed by his beard and his eyes seemed almost disproportionately small compared to the rest of him. He held a pistol casually in his lap and regarded the British minister with an impassive gaze, as if inspecting a commodity in a shop. Good God, thought Chaplin. Is that what I am to these people? A commodity? Well, let's hope this is resolved quickly because I'm not sure I'm up to it. He looked round the interior of the van, not that he could make out very much in the semi-darkness. Another figure was seated behind him, probably the one who had untied his blindfold, and there were more people in the front – they seemed to be getting out.

'Foods,' said the man behind him. 'Lunch.'

What? Lunch? It was dark outside – that much he could see. God knew what the time was, but it must be late in the evening, maybe even past midnight. Chaplin moved his head a fraction so he could look out through the driver's window. He half expected a reprimand, but nobody seemed bothered. These people obviously felt completely in control, which, again, was probably not a good sign. He could see garish coloured lights beyond the window and saw they had parked beside an all-night fast-food stall. After a while two men climbed back into the van and passed cardboard cartons of biryani rice, plastic forks and some paper napkins. Chaplin's hands were still tied behind his back, a needless precaution in his view, taken after they had put him into the change of clothes. Nobody moved to untie him: instead they fed him like an invalid, or a very small child, prodding him every few seconds to open his mouth until the carton was empty. His abductors tossed the empty containers out of the window and started the engine.

Grimacing as the vehicle lurched back onto the road once

more, Britain's Foreign Secretary tried hard not to think of his family. By now, surely, they must have heard what had happened. And they would be worrying terribly. Alone, cold and afraid, being driven at speed across Iran through the night, he felt a solitary tear roll down his ruddy, spider-veined cheek.

Chapter 52

Café Rameez, Tehran

MOVING CAREFULLY SO he did not attract attention, avoiding all eye contact with the other customers, Luke followed Tannaz out of the café. It could take only one unlucky glance, he reckoned, for a sharp-eyed observer to connect the tall, rangy Westerner with 'the English spy' now being sought on national radio. Luke had put on his beige baseball cap, which he'd packed at the last minute, and also a grey woollen scarf that Elise had insisted he take. Not exactly a foolproof disguise but at least it wouldn't look out of place on a cold winter evening in Tehran. Behind him, he could hear a fiery speech blaring from the TV set mounted on the wall. It sounded like a rabble-rousing sermon and he was grateful for it. Everyone's eyes were focused on the screen and nobody noticed them as they slipped out of Café Rameez into the night.

The first thing Luke saw was a line of black-clad security men, some on motorbikes, gathered round a junction some way down the road to their right. Tannaz saw them, too, and turned left, walking quickly away from the café, leading him through the throng of pedestrians. 'We have to get you off the street,' she whispered, the moment they stopped to cross the road. 'Follow me.' Her petite figure wove, with practised ease, between the people they passed, and twice he nearly lost sight of her. When she turned left into a side-street the crowd had thinned. He followed her down the alleyway, past some dustbins, where cats scattered at her approach. Without warning, Tannaz stopped abruptly, turned on her heels to face him and grabbed him roughly by the collar, pulling his face close to hers.

'Just what the fuck are you doing in my country?' she demanded. 'I mean, what is going on here? Hmm? First you show me those pictures of my dad with what you say are tortured prisoners – and I don't even know if they're real or fake – then I hear you being named on national radio as a spy!' Even in the dark he could see her beautiful eyes blazing with anger. 'I don't need this shit, Brendan,' she continued. 'I thought you were just a nice English art dealer when I met you in Abu Dhabi. But you're not, are you? You're something else. So how about you tell me the truth before I walk back onto that street and call a policeman?'

Luke was taken aback by the ferocity of her reaction. He had always known there would be risks in recruiting her. He'd said as much when the decision to go ahead was taken in that room back at Vauxhall Cross. But he hadn't expected it to turn out like this. How the hell had Iranian intelligence put their finger on him so quickly? Had he been careless somewhere down the line? Had the MI6 security team missed something on his social-media footprint? Had someone betrayed him? All these thoughts flashed through his mind in that darkened alleyway, but this was no time for contemplation. Tannaz was waiting for his response and he had better come up with something pretty damned convincing. Tell her too little and she wouldn't believe him, tell her too much and it would all be over in a wail of sirens.

'Okay, okay.' He sighed, lowering his head and closing his eyes for a moment. Looking up, he held her gaze. 'You're right, Tannaz. I owe you an apology. I do. *And* an explanation.' She had backed off slightly and her arms were tightly folded across her chest, her head tilted to one side, as if challenging him to convince her.

'So, yes,' he began, looking her straight in the eye. 'I'm a little more than an art dealer and, yes, I'm sorry for lying to you about that.'

'So. You are a spy,' she said flatly. 'I knew it.' Tannaz turned her head towards the empty street, then faced him again. He sensed she was trying to decide what to do with this information.

'That bit isn't true,' he replied. 'But I do some work on the side for that human-rights organization, Citizens Concern, I mentioned. They approached me,' he continued seamlessly, one lie merging into another, 'when they heard I was coming to Iran.'

'To do what?' she interrupted, tilting up her chin, her arms still folded. 'To make friends with me so you could spy on my dad?'

Whoa, she'd seen right through him and it hadn't taken her long.

'God, no. Quite the opposite, Tannaz. They wanted me to warn you about him. About what he really does to people here, in your country. Look, do you have any idea what he does when he goes to work every day?'

Tannaz opened her mouth to speak but at that exact moment Luke's mobile buzzed in his pocket. The office. It had to be. He put up his hand, as if to keep her in place. 'Don't go away, Tannaz. I have to take this call.' He half turned his body away from her as he pressed the green light on his phone.

It was Angela, at Vauxhall, and she sounded more stressed than ever. 'We might have a lead on Chaplin,' she said, without preamble, 'and we need you to follow it up immediately.'

'Hang on, Angela, there's been a development here I need to tell you about.'

'In a moment. Listen, we've had a comms intercept and there's enough to suggest Zamani's involved in the abduction. Seventy per cent certainty. You need to get yourself to where he's going.'

Luke threw a quick glance at Tannaz and forced a smile. She had one hand resting on her hip now. Not a good sign. He took the phone momentarily away from his ear to whisper loudly to her, 'It's Citizens Concern, in London.' He resumed the call. 'So where is he heading?'

'Bandar Abbas. It's a port. On the Gulf coast. How fast can you get there?'

'Angela, listen. I've been blown here. There was a bloody announcement about me on national radio just half an hour ago and my picture's all over the television. I'm going to need to extract.'

'Oh, Jesus, that's not good.' A pause. 'Where are you now? Are you safe?'

'Hardly. I'm in a back-street in Tehran with Elixir. The moment I go back on the main street I risk being picked up. I'm telling you, this place is on maximum alert since the abduction and they're looking for scapegoats.' It was a last resort but he had to ask: 'Can the embassy help?'

Angela paused. He could hear her speaking to someone in the room behind her but couldn't make out the words. When she came back, her tone was apologetic. 'I'm sorry, Luke, that's not going to be possible, not this time. Everyone there's being followed and the intelligence people would pick you up in a heartbeat. They're shadowing every vehicle in and out. And you don't have diplomatic cover, remember? Look, try to use Elixir if you can. Get yourself to Bandar Abbas and report in once you're on your way.' Another pause, and he heard the emotion in her voice. 'I'm sorry it has to be like this, Luke, but if anyone can do this job it's you. Good luck.' The call ended, he put away the phone. He took a deep breath and turned back towards Tannaz.

'So,' he began, 'I have a massive favour to ask.'

Chapter 53

Vauxhall Cross

THE MOMENT ANGELA Scott ended her call to Luke she left her office, walked quickly to the central lift bank and went up two floors to see Graham Leach. The Head of Iran and Caucasus was on the phone but he waved her to a chair. She remained standing, waiting for him to finish his call.

'That was Damian over at the Joint Intelligence Org,' he explained, when he put the phone down. 'They keep asking for answers we haven't got yet. Anyway,' he said amicably, 'what can I do for you?'

'It's Luke,' she said. 'His cover's been blown. The Iranians have made him. He's up Shit Creek.'

'Oh, God. Seriously? Wait, don't tell me they have him?' Leach was half out of his chair. Angela was close enough now to see the deep worry lines on his forehead.

'Not yet, no, but he'll have to go into hiding. I've told him to get himself to Bandar Abbas. I think it'll be a miracle if he gets that far. Graham, can't we do something for him? Can't we get him out?'

Leach sat down again and put his hands up to his face. For a moment she thought he was about to cry. Instead he rubbed his eyes with the tips of his fingers, then put his hands back on his desk and addressed her question. 'In a word, no. We simply don't have the means. That whole country's in lockdown. We lost a large part of our optics when they killed Black Run in Armenia. I'm afraid he's on his own, Angela.'

'Well, how the hell did this happen?' she demanded, her voice rising. 'I thought Security had worked up a watertight cover story for him. Weren't they supposed to have every angle covered?'

Leach made a calming motion with his hands. 'Steady on, Angela, let's not get carried away here. Yes, there'll be an internal inquiry to find out what went wrong but the fact is these IRGC intelligence people in Iran are bloody good at what they do. They are a serious challenge for us, and you know that. In the meantime . . .' he spread his hands and gave a slight shrug '. . . Luke is still our only active asset in-country. If he can get himself into deep cover this could still work for us. He's a resourceful chap, your man Luke. He's impressed a lot of people here already.'

Angela shook her head slowly in disbelief. Professionally, personally, emotionally, she felt sick. She had been instrumental in helping to send Luke to Iran. When HR had asked her if he was fully ready for the mission, she had put her signature to the internal memo. And now he was being left to swing in the wind. 'My God, Graham, you don't get it, do you? You're telling me about Luke Carlton impressing the directors when the reality is there's every chance we've just sent him on a one-way mission to his death.'

Chapter 54

Tehran

IT WAS AN agonizing wait, standing alone in the back-street. Standing in the shadow of the great Elburz Mountains, and at over a thousand metres above sea level, Tehran winters could be harsh and now it was growing colder by the minute. Luke stamped his feet and blew on his hands in an effort to keep warm, while he weighed up the odds of whether he was about to be betrayed and whether he should now make a run for it. Once again, he felt himself trapped, like a cornered rat. A wanted man on borrowed time, he had decided he had no other choice but to ask Tannaz for help. It had not been an easy conversation. Her earlier hostility had subsided but she had remained guarded, suspicious, her tone almost businesslike.

'So tell me why,' she had put it to him bluntly, 'they are calling you a foreign spy if all you do is art and human rights? Please, answer me that.'

'I have no idea, Tannaz, but just look around you. This whole country is on red alert. The kidnapping thing has sent the authorities into a tail-spin and—'

'A what?'

'A tail-spin. A panic. Look, this is a major crisis for them. Think about it, they invite a British minister here and what happens? He gets abducted from right under their noses in Isfahan. It's hugely embarrassing so they're looking for someone to blame. And that would be me. As I say, I have no idea why but I'm clearly being made the scapegoat here. So, in short, Tannaz, I need your help . . . Please, I'm asking you.'

She had regarded him for a long time, saying nothing, while Luke could only guess at what must be going through her mind. Then she had done something he wasn't expecting. She had reached up and touched his cheek, gently, with her manicured hand. 'Okay, I will help you, but understand we can never meet again after this. Is that clear?'

'Absolutely.'

'Good. Now we need to get you out of sight. I have a friend with an empty house in Kajan. It's not far from Tehran so maybe—'

Luke had cut her off mid-sentence. 'Bandar Abbas. I need to get to Bandar Abbas on the coast. If I can get there, I can get a boat out of the country.'

Tannaz had let out a short, sarcastic laugh.

'Bandar Abbas! Are you kidding, mister? Do you have any idea how far that is? It's the other end of the country! You can't fly, you can't take the train or the bus – you'd never get past the checkpoints. You'd need to drive and that would take you twenty-four hours, at least. No, forget Bandar Abbas.'

But Luke wasn't giving up without a fight. 'Come on, Tannaz, there must be someone you know with a car, someone who wants to get the hell out of Tehran and all this tension.'

'What – and drive a wanted "foreign spy" halfway across the country? I don't think so.'

'Tell you what,' he had suggested, grasping at straws now, 'do you know anyone with a relative in jail? A political prisoner, not a common criminal.'

'Yes, of course. Why?'

'Well, here's my suggestion . . .' Luke had paused then, as he caught sight of a figure turning off the main boulevard and start-ing to walk towards them. Then the man had appeared to change his mind and wandered off, back into the stream of pedestrians. 'If you can arrange a lift for me to Bandar Abbas,' he'd continued, 'I can get Citizens Concern to profile their imprisoned relative as a high-priority case. They can feature him – or her – as their Prisoner of the Month. It'll get them the international attention they need.'

'You can do this?'

'I can.'

'Prove it.'

'All right,' Luke had responded. 'Ahmet Yildirim. Turkish journalist and social commentator. Sentenced to ten years in prison. We got him out early last year.' Even now, after all those intensive, last-minute coaching sessions, it still amazed Luke how easily the lies came into his head, then tripped off his tongue. 'Evelina Karilova. Arrested in Azerbaijan on suspicion of insulting the President. Again, we got her out after a campaign. Then there's Soltana Makirova—'

'Yes, all right, you've made your point,' Tannaz had interrupted him. 'So maybe, yes, there is someone I know. His name is Farzad – we call him Farz. His brother is an artist, a good one. He was picked up six months ago here in Tehran.' In the dim light from the streetlamp behind them he could see the sadness in her face. 'They accused him of "undermining national security". This is rubbish – he's done nothing wrong and we've had no news for weeks.'

'I'm sorry, that sounds grim,' Luke had said, thinking: He sounds ideal. 'Does he have a car?'

'I will try to ask him now,' she'd said. 'I'm not promising.' Tannaz hadn't seemed so certain. She had taken out her phone, dialled a number and immediately got into an animated conversation in Farsi. Unable to follow a word, Luke had watched as she argued and gesticulated with her free hand. And then, just like that, the call was over.

'It's fixed. Stay right here and don't move from this spot. Farz will come and collect you in less than one hour.' Then she had looked around at the empty side-street, cupped his face in both hands, stroking his cheeks with her thumbs. 'I hope it works out for you, Brendan, I really do. And please stay safe.' Then she was gone, leaving him alone and uncertain in the alleyway.

And that had been just over two hours ago. There had been no sign of either Farz or Tannaz. It was now seriously cold. His breath plumed as he endeavoured to keep warm in his hiding place behind a communal dustbin. He thought abut his room back at the Shahrestan but that was a non-starter. Iranian security would be all over that place by now, carting off his belongings in plastic evidence bags, taking in the receptionist for intensive questioning. They would find nothing to incriminate him in there. Luke was confident about that. Yet absurdly, given the danger he was in, it annoyed him that he had left his phone charger in the room. A 46 per cent charge was not going to last him all the way to Bandar Abbas.

He was suddenly alert, as he detected sound and movement at the entrance to the alleyway. Something was turning into his street. Luke had already checked it for exits: there were none. He had gambled everything on Tannaz, throwing himself on her mercy. Now he was about to find out if he had made the worst decision of his life. If the vehicle was a van with blacked-out windows, he was definitely fucked.

The grey Peugeot Pars 405 made a horrendous noise as it drove down the alleyway towards him. There were a clanking and grinding as if the very engine itself were in pain. Luke breathed out. Whatever or whoever this was, it wasn't police or security. As it drew closer Luke could see a crack across its windscreen and the engine seemed to be in some distress. He stepped out into its path and the car lurched to a stop. An arm reached across and wound down the window on the passenger side. A voice behind the wheel spoke with an American accent: 'Jump in the back, my friend. I'm Farz.' He hadn't bothered to ask who Luke was – it must have been obvious: there couldn't have been many other six-foot-tall Westerners hanging around an empty Tehran back-street at nine o'clock at night.

The driver twisted round and held out a hand. The face was young, open, and framed by a mop of shoulder-length hair.

A faded red bandanna was wrapped around his forehead, pirate-style, and he was wearing ripped jeans and a faded beige top. The whole car reeked of the sweet, unmistakable smell of marijuana, and the dashboard was a jumble of old cassette tapes, some spewing out their brown ribbon contents.

Luke didn't want to sound ungrateful but he had to ask: 'Is this going to make it to Bandar Abbas?'

'This?' Farz gave the steering wheel an affectionate pat as he laboriously executed a three-point turn in the narrow alleyway. 'Who knows? Guess we'll find out. But you, my friend, need to keep your head down. There's a blanket in the back there beside you. I heard it on the radio – there's a lot of people looking for you right now.'

Chapter 55

Muharraq airport, Bahrain

IN A DISCREET corner of Bahrain's Muharraq airport, out of sight of the main terminal, an RAF Sentinel surveillance plane took off over the shallow waters of the Gulf. Climbing up to cruising altitude, it positioned itself high above the seas that separate Iran from the UAE and Oman, then deployed its multimode look-down radar to scan up to three hundred nautical miles into Iranian airspace. Onboard, sitting in a line strung out along the fuselage and facing their screens, the comms data analysts worked quietly and methodically. They had a single purpose: to exploit every last byte of intelligence from the data picked up by the listening station on Musandam. By hoovering up every call, every text message, every email associated with the number identified in Bandar Abbas, they were tasked with pinpointing the location of those holding the Foreign Secretary hostage.

Back at Vauxhall Cross, a 'fusion cell' had been set up on the ground floor. This joint team of comms data exploitation experts from MI6 and GCHQ had already matched up one phone number to the commander of an IRGC missile battery on Hormuz Island in the Gulf. Now whole conversations were opening up as numbers dropped into place for both ends of previously encrypted conversations. 'Jog-back intelligence' was being gleaned retro-actively by revisiting earlier interceptions.

Trish Fryer, Middle East Controller, was directing the team. A veteran of countless clandestine operations, she had organized everyone into eight-hour shifts, working round the clock. She divided her own time between hovering next to those working up the data, giving them advice and suggestions, and writing the latest report to be presented at the next COBRA meeting. But something was niggling her. Something didn't make sense.

'We're missing a piece of the puzzle here. A piece we need,' she had told her team at the afternoon briefing. 'We've only seen that one message from Zamani, then he's gone dark on us. So what do we conclude from that?' She scanned the rows of faces until a young analyst put up his hand.

'That he knows he's being monitored, ma'am?'

'Yes,' said Trish, slowly. 'Possibly. Or . . . or . . .' She was hoping someone would complete the sentence but they didn't. 'Or that he's communicating by another means. So I want you to find it. I want to know where Karim Zamani is, what he's doing and what he's saying to whom. We need that piece of the jigsaw urgently.' The team sat there expecting more but she was done.

'Well, come on, get going,' she said sharply. 'That number's not going to find itself. We're facing a bloody ultimatum here in case you'd all forgotten!'

Chapter 56

Tehran

LED ZEPPELIN. SANTANA. Procul Harum. Luke felt as if he were trapped in a 1970s timewarp. Cramped and contorted in the narrow floor space behind the front seats of Farz's battered old Peugeot, he realized this was the second time in two months he'd found himself in this position. He was listening to 'Stairway To Heaven' as they ground through the interminable night-time suburbs of Tehran. Head down under the blanket, he could see nothing of the world outside but he could hear Farz's incessant rummaging for cassettes beneath the dashboard, then the occasional click of his lighter as he lit yet another cigarette. Cassettes? Who used those nowadays?

'You like "Black Magic Woman"?' asked Farz, from his seat up front.

'What?'

'Santana. "Black Magic Woman". You like that song?'

Luke grunted noncommittally from his hiding place. He didn't give a stuff what music Farz played as long as he managed to get him out of town. 'Stay low, eat everything.' That was what the instructors had told him, back on the Joint Services survival course all those years ago. And now look where he was: being

224

driven across Iran in the back of a clapped-out boneshaker by some retro hippie. This was not a good situation.

Then he felt a gentle bump and the car stopped. So too did the music. The front door opened, and Luke tensed beneath his blanket as he heard voices. Jesus. Was this a checkpoint? A roadblock? A police barrier? Why hadn't Farz warned him it was coming? Then came the rush of cold night air as the back door opened abruptly behind his head. He braced himself for the grab around the collar before they dragged him, prone and helpless, out of the back of the Peugeot and into an anonymous official vehicle.

It was just Farz, still smoking, still chilled.

'Mechanic,' he explained, in a hushed voice. 'Engine's bad. My friend will fix it.'

Luke remained where he was, concealed under the blanket, as the noises of tinkering and scraping came from beneath the bonnet. They seemed to go on for ever.

Back on the road and Farz had just put on a Bob Dylan album. *'Che bahaal!'* he remarked. 'How cool is this!'

'Amazing,' said Luke, from the back. 'But where are we exactly?'

'Eslamshahr. It's a suburb. You know, normally, right, I'd take Persian Gulf Highway down to Bandar Abbas. But the Basij militia are running checkpoints everywhere now. I've got them all here on my screen.' Farz picked up his phone and passed it back to Luke. Given the antiquity of Farz's music system Luke was surprised to see it was a smartphone and there, dotted around a moving map, were half a dozen tiny icons of black beards.

'It's an app we use called Gershad,' explained Farz. 'It stands for Gasht-e-Ershad, the morality police. They're using them for security checks on us now, given the situation.'

Luke handed back the phone. This was Iranian popular counter-surveillance in action. He was impressed.

'So,' continued Farz, shifting in his seat as he peered ahead down the road, 'I'm gonna play it safe for both our sakes. We're gonna take Route Sixty-five. Nobody uses that way. A lot of twists and turns, my friend, a lot of twists and bumps, so better hold on tight.'

Hold on tight? He couldn't be wedged in any tighter if he tried.

It was another four hours before they stopped for a comfort break. Four hours in which he had dozed fitfully between prolonged bouts of thinking about Elise and her mother, Helen. He thought about calling her but didn't think he could conduct a conversation all crunched up as he was on the floor of a car. The moment this mission was over, he decided, he would take some leave and spend as much time with both of them as he could.

When they stopped at a deserted roadside halt Luke could barely feel his legs. Something, he wasn't even sure what, was digging into his ribs while his skull felt like it had been knocked repeatedly against a solid object, which it had in the form of the floor. Slowly, painfully, he extricated himself from his hiding place and stretched himself in the dark. A bitterly cold wind buffeted him in the face, whipping up unseen flurries of dust that swirled around his legs. 'Where is this place?' he called to Farz above the wind.

'Mouteh. It's a wildlife reserve. We used to come here as kids.'

From somewhere down in the darkened valley below came the bark of sleepless dogs. It was a desolate place. 'But no one comes here now,' Farz added, moving closer so he didn't have to shout above the wind. 'I'm gonna park over there by those trees so we can catch some sleep before it gets light.' He pointed to a clump of pines lit up by the car's headlights. 'In the morning I'll tell you about my brother Darius – he's in jail. Tannaz tells me you can get him out?'

'We can certainly try,' Luke lied. He felt bad, deceiving the poor guy into thinking there was hope for his brother. Focus on the mission, he reminded himself. Whatever gets you down to Bandar Abbas and close to Zamani is what matters, remember that. The end justifies the means.

Luke had started to walk towards the trees when he felt his phone vibrating in his pocket. It was Elise, calling him while he was on a mission, which they had agreed was a no-no, except in emergencies.

"Lise,' he answered warily, turning his back against the wind and shielding the phone with his hand. 'Are you okay? How's your mum doing?'

There was a long pause before she answered. 'Luke . . . I have some news.' Her voice sounded unfamiliar, strained and distant. Oh, God, he already knew what was coming.

'Mum died.' Another pause, and when she next spoke, he could hear the crack in her voice. 'She passed away an hour ago. She was asking after you . . . Luke, I need you back here. Please, I'm begging you, finish whatever you're doing and come home now. I mean it.'

Luke lifted his eyes to the sky and saw, for the first time, what a clear, starlit night it was. He could hear Farz parking beneath the trees, the wind scything through their boughs and grit skittering around his feet. What could he possibly tell Elise? That he was now a hunted man – on the run and unable to hop on a plane and fly back to her? That Britain's Secret Intelligence Service had pinned its hopes on his being able to find a fanatical IRGC commander and his captive before it was too late? That he already had enough on his plate without this news? Of course he couldn't. But Helen Mayhew, Elise's mother, whom he'd come to think of as a surrogate parent, was dead. So stop being a selfish bastard, Carlton, and show some compassion. This must be Elise's darkest hour. She'll be going through hell right now. Get a grip and do the right thing.

'Luke? Are you still there?' Her voice was pleading, imploring.

'Yes.'

'Well?'

'I'm so, so sorry, 'Lise, but I just can't right now.'

Luke hung up and walked slowly towards the parked car beneath the trees. He felt empty inside, hollowed out, soulless. What had he become? Just what the hell had he turned into?

227

Chapter 57

Bandar Abbas, Iran

KARIM ZAMANI LOOKED at his watch for the third time in an hour: 06.30. He was on a tight schedule, the timings worked out with precision well in advance. After chairing the meeting of the Circle in Qom, he had headed straight for the military airport on the outskirts of town and caught an evening flight to the coast. Using his IRGC credentials, he had commandeered a Harbin Y-12 utility turboprop plane of the IRGC Air Force and flown down to Bandar Abbas. He had correctly assessed that, with Iran on full alert, it would not look out of place for someone in his position to go down to the Gulf coast to check on the nation's maritime defences. He would report in at the local Revolutionary Guards base while his own commander, a white-haired veteran of the Iran–Iraq war, a man close to retirement, stayed in Tehran.

After some earlier unpleasant exchanges the older man had chosen to give Zamani a large degree of autonomy in how he carried out his duties. Those exchanges had not ended well for his commander, a pious man of little intellect, outwitted by the sheer venal cunning of a man twenty years his junior. Karim Zamani had known from an early age exactly how to play the system in post-revolutionary Iran.

So today, on the morning after Chaplin's abduction, Karim

Zamani had risen early from his bed in the officers' quarters at the IRGC base. Out of the window, a hazy sun was lifting above the desert to the east, illuminating the tops of the buildings and waking the pigeons, which took off in formation. The events of the previous day in Isfahan had gone exactly to plan, but there was still much to do, much to supervise, and much that could go wrong.

He breakfasted alone, savouring the simplicity of the meal of flatbread, olives, honey and black tea. He dabbed his mouth with a napkin, then went outside to meet the local Revolutionary Guards Deputy Commander, Brigadier General Hamid Dariush. They headed straight to Shahid Bahonar naval base, the largest and most important of a dozen IRGC naval bases dotted around Iran's Persian Gulf coast. In recent years the Revolutionary Guards Navy had effectively supplanted the conventional Iranian Navy, despised by hardliners as a relic from the time of the Shah and his Imperial Navy. All along Iran's Gulf coast, IRGC Navy units had taken over, with their hard-to-intercept Seraj-1, Bavar-2 and Zolfaghar fast-attack craft, armed with heavy machine-guns, rocket-propelled grenades and Nasr-1 cruise missiles. The conventional Iranian Navy had been pushed southwards into the Gulf of Oman, but even there the IRGC Navy was starting to dominate. After all, the IRGC, as guardians of the Islamic Revolution, were the most trusted by the Supreme Leader. Hard lessons had been learned from the Iran–Iraq war of 1980–88, and Iran had invested heavily in naval technology. Its latest attack boats, some of them reverse-engineered from Western designs, were capable of 'swarming' towards an enemy vessel in large numbers and at speeds of well over 65 knots. With the current tension in the Gulf, this was a scenario that kept the US Navy's 5th Fleet Commanders awake at night. And brought a smile to the face of Karim Zamani.

At the Shahid Bahonar naval base the two officers drove past the accommodation blocks and onto the edge of the parade ground. There, beneath a fluttering white, green and red flag, Karim Zamani stood side by side with the Brigadier General as the senior officer addressed the morning parade. It was a rousing speech, with the country now practically on a war footing.

'Our enemies may seek to harm us,' he told them, 'but we will match them blow for blow. We are working day and night for the security of the Islamic Republic. If we see even the smallest misstep from our enemies, our roaring missiles will fall on their heads. And we will find and punish the malicious spies who have sought to shame this great country with this treacherous and cowardly act of kidnapping!'

Impassive and silent behind aviator sunglasses, which concealed most of his face, Zamani listened and nodded his agreement.

'But we must be prepared!' the Brigadier General continued, his eyes blazing. 'We must stay strong. And vigilant. Look to your defences. Seek out these counter-revolutionaries and foreign agents wherever they are. Do not drop your guard for one minute!'

There followed loud applause before Zamani excused himself to visit the bathroom. In the privacy of a locked cubicle, he checked his phone. There was a single cryptic text message and he knew exactly who it was from. *Praise be to God*, it said. *Everything is in place.*

Chapter 58

'ONCE WE CAN pinpoint the location of the hostage,' declared Sir Jeremy Buckshaw, the Chief of Defence Staff, 'there will be only two practical options available to us.' He was addressing the Defence Secretary, a new and relatively untested addition to the Cabinet. 'And if you'll allow me, Secretary of State, I'll outline them both now.'

It was the second COBRA meeting that day and diplomacy was being worked to the bone in the international effort to locate Geoffrey Chaplin. There was, however, a grim predictability about the situation and a consensus in the room that military rescue was looking increasingly likely.

'Option one,' continued Britain's most senior serving military officer, 'we parachute in a team from offshore. High altitude, high opening. It's fast – we could theoretically launch within twenty-four hours – and the Americans would help us jam their radar.' There were nods of agreement and optimistic murmurings from many of the civil servants round the table. However, the more experienced men and women in that room knew a 'but' was coming.

'But the odds of success are not good,' he continued. 'I'd put them at less than fifty per cent. The Iranians would know something was up the moment their radar was jammed, and might even launch a pre-emptive missile strike on the US 5th Fleet in Bahrain, or our ships, or both. Then there's the met piece to factor in.'

'Excuse me?' The Home Secretary had a well-known aversion to jargon.

'Ah. My apologies. I was referring to the metereological state – the weather. It's unpredictable at this time of year. We won't have much of a window to get it right. So, no, I am not a fan of that option.'

Those round the table who had appeared to welcome the first option now looked rather foolish.

'And that leaves option two. A covert insertion by SSN—'

'I'm sorry?' interrupted the Home Secretary again. 'Did you say "a covert insertion by the SS"?' He looked round the room for support in the face of yet more baffling military jargon.

'I do apologize,' replied Buckshaw. 'An SSN is a nuclear submarine. We currently have one in the Gulf of Oman. And covert—'

'Yes, I know what "covert" means!' the Home Secretary snapped.

There was a rare moment of levity in the room as smiles were quietly smothered.

'So this will be primarily a dark blue operation,' Buckshaw continued.

'Oh, for God's sake!' exclaimed the exasperated Home Secretary. 'It's a what?'

'Dark blue – it's maritime. The Royal Navy has primacy on this one. So I'm going to let my oppo here take you through the plan. ACOS?'

The man sitting next to him stood up and introduced himself to the room. 'For those of you who don't know me, I'm Rear Admiral John Bleake and I'm ACOS Submarines. That's Assistant Chief of Staff. I'm responsible for all our underwater operations. My staff have spent this afternoon working with the Director of Special Forces. I know that time is short so I'll give you the plan in outline. We already have an SBS assault team inbound to theatre. They could be dropped by night into the Gulf of Oman where they'll be picked up by *Astute*.' He nodded towards the Home Secretary. 'She's our submarine on-station in theatre. She would then proceed, submerged, through the Strait of Hormuz to get as close as tactically possible to the Iranian coast off Bandar Abbas. Once we have the hostage's exact location the troop will be in a position to insert below the surface by SDV – a Swimmer Delivery Vehicle – until just off the beach. Once the op is completed they'll be extracted by the same means.'

There was a stunned silence. So this was really happening. Everyone in the COBRA meeting had been security-cleared to UK Level Secret but it was the first time they had all been privy to what this covert operation might actually involve.

'I thought *Astute* was still down in Diego Garcia,' somebody from the MoD whispered.

'Apparently not,' replied someone else. 'Subs move in mysterious ways.'

'Just one point, if I may,' this from the Defence Secretary. Unlike the senior military men present he retained a boyish youthfulness, his brow still unfurrowed by the cares of office. Yet now he stared hard at the Chief of Defence Staff. When this meeting ended he would have to phone the PM and give the plan his recommendation, or not. His career, still on the ascendant, would now depend on him taking the right decision. 'If I remember my geography,' he said, 'the Strait of Hormuz is only about twenty-five miles wide between Oman and Iran. How are we going to get our sub through that gap without it being picked up by the Iranians?'

'That's a fair question, Secretary of State. It's actually just twenty miles at its narrowest point,' the Rear Admiral corrected him, 'and the shipping lanes are only two miles wide in each direction. But, yes, we are working up a plan for that as we speak.'

'Which is?' The Defence Secretary was now tapping his pen nervously on the table and casting wary glances at a woman seated four chairs down on his right. The Attorney General.

Whatever plan was agreed in this room today, he would have to get her to sign it off for compliance with international law. That, he knew, would be the first question the PM fired at him.

'We go in,' replied the naval officer, 'right underneath a VLCC.' He could already see the Home Secretary's eyes rolling towards the ceiling in exasperation so he was quick to follow up with a translation. 'A VLCC is a very large crude carrier. What people used to call an oil tanker. The Strait of Hormuz is the world's primary oil chokepoint with a daily average of fifteen tankers passing through it in each direction.'

'Ingenious,' muttered the Home Secretary, approvingly.

'All right, but hang on,' said the Defence Secretary, 'how will you know which one to latch on to? Couldn't it simply turn left and dock in Dubai?'

'PJHQ – Permanent Joint Headquarters – are looking at exactly that issue now,' said the Navy man. 'They're going through a list of all the pre-registered transits and they'll be selecting one that'll be hugging the Iranian coast. One that suits our purpose.'

'Attorney General?' All eyes in the room switched to the small, neatly dressed woman, hair tied back in a tight bun. She had a well-earned reputation for asking difficult questions, and the room held its breath as she cleared her throat.

'Well,' she began, very quietly, 'I obviously need to see if it complies with UNCLOS, the UN Convention on Laws of the Sea.' She spoke slowly, apparently weighing each word, as if it would need to stand up in court – with notes being taken verbatim, that probably wasn't far from the truth. 'It's the international treaty that makes the first twelve miles offshore part of the sovereign territorial waters of the littoral state.'

'So I take it,' the Defence Secretary said, turning to the Rear Admiral, 'that our sub would pass through closer to the Omani side than the Iranian one. Do we even need to notify the Omanis?'

A formidable multi-tasker, the Attorney General was already scrolling through several pages of condensed text on her laptop. She looked up. 'It is not possible,' she said, in a flat monotone, 'for any vessel to enter the Arabian Gulf without either being in Omani or Iranian territorial waters. Submarines cannot remain submerged and still exercise innocent passage. To remain submerged without permission is a very serious breach of UNCLOS principles.'

'Right,' said the Defence Secretary, briskly, 'but that's just a guideline, isn't it? We don't have to comply with their recommendations, do we?'

The Attorney General removed her glasses and laid them on the table before her as if they were an item of evidence. They were thin-framed and functional, rather like their owner. She looked straight at the minister as he sat, shifting uncomfortably in his seat at the head of the table. 'If a British submarine enters the Strait of Hormuz beneath a VLCC tanker, then under the Traffic Separation Scheme the boat would be entirely in Omani territorial waters. Whether you choose to inform the Omanis of this is up to you. But it's my job to inform you that, technically, what you plan to do is illegal.'

Chapter 59

Bandar Abbas, Iran

GEOFFREY CHAPLIN STANK. It was the reek of body odour waft-
ing up from his armpits, a smell he hadn't known since those
days of cold showers and early-morning runs at an unforgiving
Scottish boarding school. Was it really possible that a little over
twenty-four hours ago he had been washing his hands with
scented soap in a spotless basin at the British Ambassador's resi-
dence in Tehran? Now look at him. After only a few hours in
captivity the British Foreign Secretary knew he must make a
pathetic sight for those guarding him. When all the trappings of
power and office were stripped away from him, all the red boxes,
the ministerial briefs, the chauffeur-driven limousines, the special advisers and the VIP departure lounges, this was all that
was left. A man of late middle age who had lost control of his
destiny.

At least it felt warmer wherever they were now. The overnight
journey in the van had been horrific and had seemed interminable. But now it had stopped and he couldn't tell where. Geoffrey
Chaplin knew his way intimately around the Palace of Westminster, the corridors of the Cabinet Office and the shortcut from
there through the passageway to Number 10. But he had only the
vaguest sense of how Iran appeared on a map. It bordered on two

236

seas, he remembered that much. There was one in the north, the Caspian, where the caviar came from, and then there was what the Americans called 'the Persian Gulf' down in the south where it would be warmer. That must be where he was now. Which meant what? That they were going to take him out to sea and dump him? Why keep him alive to do that? Whoever had seized him, and these people still hadn't told him what their demands were, he doubted they would be from ISIS. This was Iran, a predominately Shia country, a nation implacably opposed to the Sunni fanatics of ISIS. That, at least, gave Chaplin some crumb of comfort.

Now the back doors of the van were being opened, the light was almost blinding him, and a large figure was climbing in. Chaplin caught only the briefest glimpse of a broad, unshaven face and close-cropped hair before the blindfold went back on. He could feel it being tied tightly at the back of his head. More discussions in Farsi, then hands grabbed his arms and they manoeuvred him roughly out of the vehicle. The moment he stood outside, in the fresh air, he sensed the change, even from behind his blindfold. For a start, he could smell the sea, that unmistakable hint of brine, and hear gulls screeching from all directions. As they pushed him along, stumbling awkwardly at times, he heard the sound of water slapping against the side of boats. There was something else too, something he remembered from sailing off the Norfolk coast with his family: it was the familiar thump of inflatable fenders striking the wall of a jetty, cushioning the side of a boat as the swell rocked it from side to side. Geoffrey Chaplin could only guess what was happening: they were moving him offshore, taking him somewhere remote where he would be harder to find. In his deepening despair, he felt his chances of rescue receding by the hour.

Chapter 60

ANGELA SCOTT SANK into the soft leather upholstery of the black Jaguar XF executive limousine and adjusted the hem of her skirt so it covered her knees. Sir Adam Keeling, Chief of the Secret Intelligence Service, took his place beside her in the back and tightened the knot of his tie. Quietly, almost imperceptibly, the chauffeur nudged the car out from beneath the Vauxhall Cross HQ, through the sliding metal gates in the wall, then into the traffic moving eastwards along Albert Embankment. This was only the second time in her career that Angela had been invited to share a ride with the Chief but the moment held little pleasure for her, or for him. It was now the morning after Chaplin's abduction, both of them had been working through half the night and were heading for a COBRA crisis meeting in the Cabinet Office where questions would be asked to which they had no satisfactory answers.

'Any word from Carlton?' enquired the Chief. He turned his face away from the window as they overtook a large yellow bus taking tourists on a journey of exploration up the Thames, a snapshot of a very different world from theirs.

'No. His phone's switched off,' she replied. 'Probably trying to conserve battery.'

'When was his last transmission?' Keeling looked at her, one eyebrow raised, but there was no hostility in his question: he just liked to know all the facts.

'Last night,' Angela said. 'Just after six p.m. our time. That's when I got the text saying he'd found a way to get himself to Bandar Abbas.' She glanced at her watch. 'I'm expecting to hear from him soon.' Was now the time to bring up what was on her mind? It was unlikely to do her career any good, but there was no time like the present. She cleared her throat.

'Chief,' she began, 'is there really nothing more we can do to help get him out of Iran?'

'Get him *out* of Iran?' repeated Keeling, both eyebrows now raised. 'Angela, do you have any idea how much work it's taken to get Carlton *into* that country? This isn't just our operation, remember. It's a tri-service operation that needed sign-off from Number Ten. We've got the Americans breathing down our necks wanting to ramp the whole thing up – they've got a second carrier battle group steaming towards the Gulf, and their finger's on the trigger.' His voice was stern now, and it carried a hint of disapproval. 'Since we lost Black Run in Armenia we no longer have optics on the Iranian nuclear programme, and meanwhile there's an ultimatum ticking on the life of our Foreign Secretary. I don't need to remind you this is top priority and the Service has miraculously – with your help, Angela – managed to get a man into Iran. Luke Carlton is our best hope of getting eyes on the hostage. So, no, in a word, we're not about to pull him out now, just when we need him most.' The Chief looked away to his left, as they crossed Lambeth Bridge onto Millbank. He was clearly riled by her suggestion. 'I'm quite sure Carlton is more than capable of looking after himself, Angela. That's precisely why we took him on.'

She could, she thought, tell the Chief about the treatment Luke could expect if he was picked up by the Basij militia or any other arm of Iranian state security. She had read up on exactly what happened to those accused of spying and she rather wished she hadn't. She could remind him of how this would look if it ever came up in Parliament or if the press found out that the Service had effectively abandoned its case officer to his fate. But Angela Scott held her tongue. She had already crossed swords with enough people from senior management to know she would never make it to the SIS Main Board of Directors. This was not a battle she could win.

They were coming onto Parliament Square now, passing a motley collection of protesters holding up banners that read 'No More War' and 'Hands off the Gulf'.

'I'm sorry,' she said in a conciliatory tone. 'I didn't mean to be unhelpful.'

'That's all right, Angela. Your concern is commendable.' For one awful moment she thought the Chief was about to pat her on the knee, but if he was, he clearly thought better of it.

They sat in silence until the driver turned to them, his earpiece still in place. 'We'll take the back route if you don't mind, Chief. There are TV crews all over the Whitehall entrance.'

'Very wise,' Keeling observed.

Their car swept past the raised barrier at the police guard post where Horse Guards Road met the discreet rear entrance to Downing Street, the little-known route into the Cabinet Office for those who preferred not to be seen.

'Time to get to work,' said Keeling.

Chapter 61

THE PM WAS in the chair, the heads of all three intelligence agencies present, along with the National Security Adviser, the Chief of Defence Staff, the Metropolitan Police Commissioner, and Jane Haslett, Head of the Diplomatic Service. Geoffrey Chaplin, himself a familiar presence at previous COBRA meetings, had now been missing for just over eighteen hours.

Angela Scott took her place next to Sir Adam Keeling. On her other side sat a grizzled detective from the Met's Hostage and Crisis Negotiation Unit. She remembered him from the Iraq hostage crisis of 2007 when four of the five kidnapped Britons had been murdered. Hostage-taking in the Middle East was a particularly grim business, and since on principle Britain didn't pay ransoms to terrorists, Whitehall's track record of getting them out alive was distinctly mixed.

The PM called the meeting to order and addressed the Chief of Defence Staff. 'Sir Jeremy. Bring us up to speed, will you?'

Sir Jeremy Buckshaw stood up and removed his spectacles. They were gold-framed and seemed out of place on the bull-chested, no-nonsense figure, with his impressive rows of operational medals. 'Thank you, Prime Minister. So, things are moving fast down in the Gulf. The US Navy's 5th Fleet, headquartered in Bahrain, is at full operational readiness. Their second carrier group is due to arrive on-station within twenty-four hours. The USS *George H.W. Bush* has been launching CAPS off the deck – launching combat air patrols – right up to the edge of Iran's maritime border. There was a near-miss overnight that you probably heard about. Three Iranian missile boats got to within three hundred metres of a US destroyer in the Strait of Hormuz and only backed off when they were fired on.'

Angela was only half listening. She knew that any minute now the PM would turn to her Chief to ask him for an intelligence update. She also knew that he was going to hand over the question to her. She went over her notes for the third time that morning as the Chief of Defence Staff rounded off his briefing.

'Turning to our own forces,' he continued, 'we've deployed a squadron of Typhoons to Minhad airbase in the UAE in support of the Americans. We have all four Royal Navy minesweepers out on patrol around Hormuz in case the Iranians mine the strait. And we've forward-deployed the SBS standby squadron from Poole.'

'Excellent,' commented the PM. 'And where is that squadron now, precisely?'

'It's currently in the Gulf region,' the General replied cryptically. Even with everyone in the COBRA meeting having been security-cleared, he had decided this was not a piece of information that needed to be widely shared. The PM appeared to get the message and didn't press him.

'Jane?' He turned to the Head of the Diplomatic Service. 'What have you got from your side?'

Jane Haslett got to her feet as the Defence Chief sat down. Angela regarded her from across the table with curiosity. The FCO mandarin had chosen today of all days to wear a cherry-pink jacket with an outsize silver brooch pinned to the lapel. It was the sort of outfit, Angela mused, that one might wear to a Buckingham Palace garden party, not a Whitehall crisis meeting.

'I spoke to Iran's Foreign Minister just under an hour ago,' Jane told the room. 'He remains adamant that his government has nothing to do with Geoffrey's abduction. He's offered us his

242

"sincere and profound apologies" for what's happened.' At this there were a few sarcastic scoffs. 'But I have to say that the rhetoric coming out of other parts of the establishment there is getting pretty bellicose. You may have seen,' she continued, 'the speech from the Supreme Leader.' She picked up a page of text and read it out loud. 'He's saying, "Iran will not allow the sanctity of its territory to be defiled by the forces or agents of foreign powers."' She put down the paper and looked at the PM. 'Which I would take as a direct warning to us – and the Americans, for that matter – not to attempt a rescue mission of our own.'

There was a grunt from the National Security Adviser. 'Well, he would say that, wouldn't he? But as far as we can see, the Iranians have made bugger-all progress – excuse my French – in locating Geoffrey. They don't even seem to know who's taken him. Discounting, of course, all the usual guff about Israeli agents and what-not.'

The PM nodded, apparently in agreement, and looked down the table towards where Angela and the MI6 Chief were sitting. 'Sir Adam? I realize you're somewhat constrained in what you can say at this stage but tell us what you can, will you?'

Angela mentally braced herself as she watched her boss push back his chair and address the room.

'What we are seeing from our sources,' he began, 'is a nation-wide crackdown by the Iranian authorities. They're using the episode as an excuse to round up anyone they don't like and sling them into jail. We suspect hundreds have been arrested so far since the kidnapping.'

'Right,' said the PM. 'Interesting. But where does that get us in locating our Foreign Secretary?'

There were some subtly exchanged glances around the table. As Chief of the Secret Intelligence Service, Sir Adam Keeling was a revered and respected figure in Whitehall, but there were still some in the room who quietly resented his unfettered access to the PM.

'I'm going to let Angela give you the latest from our side of the river,' he replied smoothly. 'Angela?'

Angela Scott gave the Chief her sweetest smile as he passed her the baton. 'The early lead we got,' she began, 'came from an intercept that indicated a possible border crossing by the hostage group at a place on Iran's western border with Iraq, a place called Shalamcheh.' Everyone in the room was very still, listening intently. 'That lead turned out to be false. However, with input from our colleagues at Cheltenham,' and here she nodded respectfully to the GCHQ Director, 'as well as our US partners, we have been able to narrow down the location of the hostage group to a coastal city on the Gulf called Bandar Abbas. We have also identified one of the key figures we believe is involved in Geoffrey's abduction. He's a senior officer in the Revolutionary Guards Corps.'

'So, let me get this right,' interrupted the National Security Adviser. 'You're saying we know where he is and who's holding him? Well, what the hell's stopping us? Let's steam in and get him! I don't recall the Americans asking Pakistan's permission to go after Bin Laden.'

Angela looked to her Chief for help. This one was, in the vernacular of Whitehall, well above her pay grade. Keeling got to his feet and stood in support. 'It's not quite that simple,' he said, with a forced smile. 'Bandar Abbas has a population of nearly half a million people. It covers a considerable area and it's home to a lot of Iran's defence and security infrastructure. Any one of those bases could be holding him, or he could be held by non-state actors in a private house. We still don't know.'

'Or offshore,' added Angela.

'Indeed,' said the MI6 Chief. 'Or offshore on any of the islands, though we think that's less likely. Transferring him would carry an added risk for his kidnappers. Now . . .' his tone deepened, as if everything that had been said in the room up until now was of far less importance '. . . the Service and its partners are focusing on getting all the personal comms data we can on this key figure. Once we have that we expect to be able to pinpoint his location, and the hostage's. Then we're in business.'

'Timescale?' asked the PM.

'How long is a piece of string?' answered Keeling. 'I can't tell you yet, sorry. I'm sure you'll all appreciate this situation is pretty fluid, to put it mildly.'

He paused and glanced at Angela. She seemed to be staring at her phone. Keeling frowned but she passed it to him without a word. It was a message – from Luke Carlton. He was a few hours away from Bandar Abbas.

Chapter 62

Bandar Abbas, Iran

THE HOUSE WAS simple and unobtrusive: one storey, white-washed walls, the paint flaking and peeling in the damp air, low, flat roof, and a scrubby, neglected garden at the front. Luke would have preferred to arrive under cover of darkness, but the journey from Tehran had taken so long, with its detours, delays and emergency lie-ups, that it was nearly midday by the time Farz nosed the Peugeot 405 down a rutted mud back-street and parked in the shade.

They had stopped en route for a couple of hours, no more, in that bleak and windswept wildlife reserve. Farz had put his seat back as far as it would go, pulled a beanie hat over his eyes and gone straight out like a light. But Luke couldn't sleep. He was on permanent alert – at one point convinced he'd seen shapes heading in the direction of their car. He'd quietly opened the passenger door, rolled silently onto the ground, and gone to investigate. But there had been no one there: no one had seen them, and no one had come for them.

When Farz had woken, he had lit a cigarette, walked off to relieve himself, then checked his Gershad app for checkpoints ahead. Satisfied, he had put the car into gear and set off. They had driven south, skirting the cities of Isfahan and Shiraz, and sticking always to the minor roads. Farz, despite having had so little sleep, had been in a talkative mood and it hadn't been long before the subject of his brother Darius had come up.

'Nothing,' he had said, just as the first rays of the morning sun began to light up the landscape, a sight denied to Luke in his hiding place. 'We've heard nothing for five weeks now. Every week my father goes to the gates of Evin Prison to ask after him and each time they tell him to come back the next week.'

'So what did he do?' Luke had asked.

'Nothing! I'm telling you, man. Just one stupid picture they didn't like. So Darius is an artist, right? He paints for a living. Nothing wrong with that.'

'Right,' offered Luke.

'Wrong. They said one of his paintings had disrespected the mullahs. This is bullshit, man. My bro doesn't even know about that stuff, he does commissions. He only just gets by. And now he's in jail. I'm telling you, it sucks.'

The car had slowed to a stop to allow a flock of sheep to cross the road. Luke had heard the jangle of their neck bells and the cry of the shepherd urging his animals along.

'But, hey,' Farz had continued brightly, 'tell me about this campaign you guys are gonna run for him. That's sounding good.' For the next few kilometres Luke had spun and deceived, weaving a web of lies about how his mythical human-rights group would hold 'a Darius day' in support of the imprisoned artist and maybe even present a petition to Number 10 Downing Street. And Luke had hated himself as he said all of this. He had let down Elise, and now he was offering false hope to someone good enough to help him. One day, he knew, this would catch up with him, but for now he had other things to worry about.

The police jeep had pulled out into the road in front of them without warning. The first Luke had known about it was when Farz had slammed on the brakes and muttered quietly, 'Oh, shit, not good. You gotta stay down and keep quiet.'

Someone had come up to Farz's window, Luke had heard questions being asked. Then there had been a pause and the sound of a cigarette being lit. More questions, as Luke had pressed his face into the rank black carpet at the bottom of the car. Had he covered every inch of his body sufficiently with the blanket? Had it disguised his bulk or was his outline going to be bone obvious to anyone looking in through the window? The minutes passed, he'd heard the boot being opened and closed and then had come the sweetest sound to his ears: the revving of the engine as Farz had driven off. The danger had passed.

'Dumb cops,' Farz had said, once they were clear. 'They didn't even know what they were looking for. Guess they just wanted my cigarettes.'

Luke had stayed down for the rest of the journey so had missed the breathtaking landscape of Hormuzgan Province in the south of the country. On reflection, it had been a small price to pay for remaining a free man. Luke had warmed to Farz during the journey and now they had arrived at the house his family owned in the Bandar Abbas back-street.

Luke approved of the precautions he was taking. Leaving his passenger in the back of the car, Farz had crossed the street and let himself into the house to check it was safe for him to come in. Only when he was certain no one was looking had he returned to fetch Luke, allowing him just the briefest glimpse of where they were before shepherding him inside the door.

Luke adjusted his eyes to the semi-darkness within and saw they were in a small kitchen-cum-living room where cushions and rugs lay scattered across the floor and washing-up was piled in the sink. He detected the sweet, unmistakable tang of hashish in the air. A door opened, he presumed to a bedroom, and a thin, dishevelled figure emerged, wearing a Bob Marley T-shirt and loose-fitting pants tied with a drawstring. He was young – Luke put him in his mid-twenties – and he had clearly been sleeping when they arrived. He rubbed the sleep out of his eyes, embraced Farz, then held out a hand to Luke, who shook it.

'I'm Mort,' he said. Then he recoiled. 'Oh, my God,' he exclaimed. 'You're missing a finger! What happened to you, man?'

Luke smiled. He was used to this, although most people he

met tried harder to disguise their surprise. 'Car crash,' he lied. 'Long time ago. Can I use your toilet?'

'Sure. Help yourself, man. It's through there.'

It was a footprint loo with a bucket of water, a dripping tap, a hose and no toilet paper. Luke slid his trousers down to his ankles and squatted over the filthy hole in the floor. Left hand, he reminded himself. Always use your left hand in these situations. And then he heard it. The loud knock on the front door in the living room. An urgent exchange in Farsi between Farz and Mort, then more knocking, more insistent. Luke was scrambling to wash and pull up his trousers when he heard a female voice. He waited, then slowly, cautiously, pushed open the door into the living room.

A woman was standing in the middle of the room. She was small, petite even, her face hidden behind enormous sunglasses, which she removed. She looked directly at him and Luke was staring straight into the eyes of Tannaz Zamani.

Chapter 63

KARIM ZAMANI RAN the tips of his fingers along the smooth black nose cone of the Sunburn missile and smiled approvingly. This glorious weapon, this instrument of death, this agent of America's humiliation: it felt good to see it up close, to sense its raw destructive power. With its NATO designation of SS-N-22, the super-fast Russian-made anti-ship missile was one of the most powerful weapons in Iran's armoury. It had a speed of Mach 3 at altitude, allowing it to reach any one of the US Navy's 5th Fleet destroyers out in the Gulf in just two minutes or less. That was why this particular battery was concealed deep in the caves, high up in the Zagros Mountains that dominated Iran's Persian Gulf coast.

Since arriving at the port of Bandar Abbas, Zamani had spent a busy morning inspecting his country's coastal defences. With every military unit in the Islamic Republic on full alert, there was much to go over and he had packed a lot into just a few hours. From the parade ground at the Shahid Bahonar naval base, he had been taken on an escorted tour of the submarine dock. There he had posed proudly for an official photograph alongside a near-silent Kilo-class diesel-electric submarine as it was readied for operations. He knew that Iran's other two Russian-built subs

250

were already at sea, lurking beneath the waves close to the ship-ping chokepoint of the strategic Strait of Hormuz.

Karim Zamani had stood on the concrete dock, shielding his eyes from the slanting rays of the morning sun and listening intently as the submarine commander explained the capabilities of his boat's Hoot torpedoes. They travelled four times faster than a conventional torpedo, he told Zamani, making the Hoot, or 'Whale', the fastest in the world. Genuinely interested, Zamani had asked how this was possible, and the commander, originally an engineer, had replied that the Hoot used something called 'supercavitation', a technology devised by the Russians that vaporized the water around the torpedo, propelling it forward at 100 metres a second.

'I look forward to the blessed day,' Zamani had announced to the group of Revolutionary Guard Navy officers gathered round him, 'when we will see this weapon go into action against the side of a billion-dollar US warship!' That had brought cheers and laughter before they had moved on to examine some of the fast attack patrol boats, each armed with torpedoes and mines.

Karim Zamani's brother officers in the Revolutionary Guards Navy had devised the swarm strategy, aimed at overwhelming a superior naval force by sheer weight of numbers. Iran, they knew, could not hope to match the sophistication and firepower of the US Navy's giant carrier battle groups so instead they had gone into mass production of small fast attack boats like the Seraj-1. Even a giant 90,000-ton aircraft-carrier would find it a challenge to beat off a concerted attack by a flotilla of thirty such vessels, all encroaching at speeds of more than 70 knots. Some were designed to be packed with explosives and remotely controlled. The lesson of the Aden harbour attack on USS *Cole* in 2000 had not gone unnoticed in Iran. Al-Qaeda that day had rammed a tiny speed-boat loaded with at least 300 kilos of C4 explosive into the side of a state-of-the-art US guided missile destroyer, killing seventeen sailors and crippling the billion-dollar warship.

Karim Zamani was not given to displays of emotion, but what he had seen that morning had lifted his spirits and brought him an overriding sense of peace. When the tour of inspection was over, he warmly embraced all those present, then returned to the officers' mess for a late lunch of *chello kebab* and rice. When that was over he thanked the Brigadier General for his hospitality and assured him that his report to their superiors would be most favourable. There was no need, he added, to escort him back to the airport because he, Zamani, would be making some private visits to relatives before returning to the capital and his pressing duties at this time of crisis.

But Karim Zamani had other intentions. Everything he had done in the last few hours – the tour, the photographs, the speeches – was for show. His real work was about to begin.

In his sparsely furnished officer's quarters he changed out of his Revolutionary Guards uniform, folding it away into a holdall. He put on a pair of loose grey trousers, old trainers, a white T-shirt under a beige jacket and finally a black baseball cap pulled down over his eyes. He walked calmly out of the accommodation block and along the neatly planted rosebed that lined the road. Stopping at the guardhouse, he signed himself out and strolled to a roadside bus shelter. Minutes later, a Paykan car pulled up. The driver avoided eye contact and kept looking straight ahead. It was as if the man might be afraid of him. Well, thought Zamani, that is how it should be. *'Baya bareem,'* he told him quietly. 'Let's go.'

He sat in silence in the back seat, tugging distractedly at his beard as they drove through Bandar Abbas. They were heading for a little-known jetty, just to the west of the main port. Outwardly impassive, Zamani was going through everything in his mind. He smiled to himself. It was all coming together as he'd planned. The two 'items' due for delivery had arrived safely at their destinations, and before this day was out he would, God willing, see them both with his own eyes. The national state of alert was having its desired effect. His country's own soft, spineless, and foolishly elected government was chasing its tail as it tried to explain to the world how a British minister could be kidnapped on its soil without its involvement. The bellicose words coming out of Washington were helping to fan the winds of resistance as the people's militias mobilized and kept up their vigilance against Western-backed counter-revolutionaries.

He had only one concern, one irritation, one dark cloud to spoil that perfect vista. His family. Karim Zamani would never admit it, even to himself, but however brilliant a career might be unfolding before him in the Revolutionary Guards, he was a failure at home. What had it been now? Eighteen months? Two years? He had lost track of how much time since he and Forouz had been even remotely intimate with each other. Her life now seemed quite separate from his. They had so little in common that at times he seriously doubted her commitment to the Islamic Revolution. There had been cross words during their last conversation and it had ended abruptly. And then there was Tannaz. What had become of his darling daughter, this child of the Revolution, who used to march around the kitchen with a wooden spoon for a rifle and a patriotic song on her lips? Corrupted. That was the only word for it. Tannaz had been corrupted by blasphemous Western values and now risked destroying her virtue.

As the car drove up onto the jetty Karim Zamani resolved he would deal with her at the right time. When this was over, when the dust had settled, and a new and glorious future had unfolded for the Islamic Republic, he would exert his authority at home. There would be no more of these frivolous shopping trips and pointless art excursions to Abu Dhabi with her mother. No, it was time to return to traditional values and his word – yes, his word alone – would be law within their four walls.

The speedboat was waiting for him at the dock. Even from behind his car window Zamani could see it was so new it still had plastic sheeting covering the seats. He noted the powerful black Yamaha 200 h.p. outboard engine at the stern and the deeply tanned pilot sitting at the wheel. He thanked his driver politely, then flashed his ID to the pilot as he clambered aboard. How often had he rehearsed this journey in his head? How long had he prepared himself for the events that were about to unfold? Karim Zamani felt a rising tide of excitement, the intoxicating thrill of being on the cusp of momentous change. Great things were about to happen in his country, historic things, and he felt supremely honoured to have been chosen by God to play his part in them.

They cast off without a word: the pilot already had his orders and knew exactly where he was taking his passenger. As Zamani settled himself on a cushioned bench at the back, the man gunned the engine into a throaty roar and they sped out into the calm blue waters of the Gulf. Squinting against the afternoon sun, Zamani could just make out the approaching mud-coloured mountains of Qeshm Island to the south. He pulled his cap down tight on his brow, and for a few minutes he closed his eyes and allowed himself to enjoy the sensation of speed and movement. He had earned it, hadn't he, with all of the meticulous planning and, so far, no mistakes? He could, he reflected, have taken the regular speedboat taxi or even the car ferry from the mainland across to the port of Qeshm. But that would have been too risky. At this late and delicate stage in the Circle's operation, he preferred to be seen by as few people as possible. The pilot took them westwards, looping around a headland on Qeshm Island, then to a dilapidated jetty next to a seemingly deserted village.

'Bandar-e-Laft?' he asked the pilot. He needed to be sure he had brought him to the right port. The man nodded as he threw a rope around a corroded cleat and secured the boat. It was three p.m., that dead hour of the afternoon in the Gulf when most people were resting indoors after a late lunch.

Zamani stepped out of the speedboat onto the jetty, then made his way along the wooden boardwalk past a beached row of empty dhows. He spotted the pick-up truck idling just beyond a pile of nets. These days, with his exalted rank and status in the Revolutionary Guards, Karim Zamani was more used to travelling in comfort, chauffeured around Tehran in the back of a limousine. But, as he often reminded himself, his had been a simple upbringing in a dusty village.

They drove for nearly an hour across the flat, lunar landscape of Qeshm Island. Mudwalled fortresses would shimmer into focus on the horizon behind palm groves quivering in the heat haze, but then, when Zamani looked closer, they would turn out to be mud and rock, nothing more. It was a barren land, scorched by the sun, and fatigue was catching up with him now. At times he dared not close his eyes in case plans started to unravel while he slept. He glanced down from his vantage-point in the truck's cab as they passed through a village where women squatted by the roadside, offering trays of dates for sale. They were wearing colourful bangles round their ankles and the distinctive shiny gold, hawklike masks of Qeshm Island. To Zamani, it was as if he were visiting a different and rather primitive country, but he didn't let the outdated ways of the Qeshm islanders concern him. This place suited him – and the Circle – for a very specific purpose.

They followed the road as it wound through a mangrove swamp – the trees laden with herons – until they came to a small side road, signposted in Farsi, and, curiously, in English as Salt Cave Road. It pointed inland, towards a range of low, dun-coloured hills. Ahead, a no-entry sign had been placed in the middle of the dusty track and a chain of 'stingers', their vicious spikes sharp enough to shred the tyres of any unsuspecting vehicle, had been stretched across its surface. Excellent. Zamani's orders had been followed to the letter. Beyond that a dark blue van, marked 'Border Security', waited, and nearby stood two uniformed guards, each cradling an assault rifle. Everything was as it should be. The Namakdan Salt Caves had become strictly off-limits to the public.

Chapter 64

Wahiba Sands, Oman

TEN-YEAR-OLD MAZIN AL-WAHIBI stopped in his tracks on the crest of a dune and stared at what was unfolding before his eyes, down in the valley below. A large aircraft, painted in brown and black, had just descended out of the clear blue sky at an impossibly steep angle, its four propeller engines roaring as it taxied on the hard-packed sand of the valley floor. Within seconds it had rolled to a stop, its engines still turning. Clouds of dust and sand billowed into the air as the tail ramp went down. From his vantage-point on the dune, Mazin saw two lines of men stream out of the back. They seemed to be carrying guns and had large packs on their backs. He'd no idea that it had a name, but Mazin Al-Wahibi had just witnessed a TALO – a tactical air landing operation.

Like all the Bedu who live in the searing heat of the Wahiba Sands, Mazin had grown up quickly amid its mountainous dunes. He was eight years old when his father taught him how to drive the family's ancient pick-up truck and he began to run short errands into the nearest village. By the age of nine, he was entrusted with guarding the family's precious herd of sheep and goats, almost their entire worldly wealth, across the rippling dunes of this Omani desert. On his daily foraging trips, watching

256

over the two dozen animals as they nibbled and chewed at the sparse vegetation that grew wherever there was water, he had often seen soldiers training. They were always Omani soldiers, from the Sultan of Oman's armed forces, men from his own country's national army with their distinctive green and khaki *shimagh* headdresses. He would wave at them and they would wave cheerfully back. But these men today were different. They were bigger, broader, and they moved more quickly, with a sense of purpose.

Mazin squatted on his dune, twirling the stick he always carried. He watched as the men the aeroplane had brought now busied themselves putting up tents and nets that made dappled patterns on the sand. And then they seemed to be running to and fro, shouting in a language he didn't understand. Their guns were making loud bangs but nobody was falling down so Mazin assumed they could not be firing real bullets, only pretend ones.

He sighed. The sun was setting and it was time to go. He called happily as he rounded up his animals. This was definitely something to tell his family when he got back to the corrugated-iron and chicken-wire encampment that was their home. Mazin Al-Wahibi didn't know it but he was the only person in Oman to have watched the UK's highly secretive Special Boat Service assault team carry out their final rehearsals for a covert hostage-rescue mission.

Chapter 65

Qeshm Island, Iran

LONG SHADOWS WERE reaching out from the sandstone cliffs behind him as Karim Zamani jumped down from the pick-up truck. As the door slammed, the two men at the checkpoint raised their weapons, muzzles pointing straight at his chest. This he approved of. *'Kuh be kuh nemi-rasad,'* he called to them. 'A mountain never meets a mountain.'

'Adam be âdam mi-rasad,' they replied in unison, lowering their assault rifles. 'But a man can always meet a man.' The challenge completed, he walked towards them and the three men embraced.

'How long has it been?' he asked them, offering a packet of Winston International cigarettes.

They thanked him. 'Eight, maybe nine hours since they came through,' one answered.

'Khayli khubeh,' replied Zamani. 'Excellent. And no one else?'

'No one.'

Karim Zamani didn't want to linger out in the open. Acutely conscious of the West's aerial and geospatial surveillance, he was keen to avoid being singled out by one of its drones or spy planes. His driver had kept the pick-up truck's engine running and now he hurried back to the relative safety of the cab. As they drove on, deeper inland, Zamani felt a mounting excitement. He was

258

nearing the end of his journey. Looking out at the darkening landscape, this was a barren, deserted place, which was exactly why the Circle had chosen it. Here the desert floor appeared white and brittle, like the sugary glaze on the cakes his grandfather used to bring them when he was growing up. It was salt. He remembered that from the reconnaissance team's detailed report. And that meant they were getting close.

The cave entrance was so well concealed behind a scree of fallen boulders that at first Zamani failed to spot it. As the truck pulled up and he dismounted, three men stepped out from the shadows. Each carried an MPT-9 sub-machine-gun levelled at him and the driver. And there was something else: a tiny red dot danced across his chest, then held still. A laser sight. Again the challenge was offered and the response accepted before the men lowered their weapons and came forward to greet him. Moments later, a fourth man appeared, hefting a Russian-designed Nakhjir sniper rifle. Congratulating them all on their vigilance, Zamani sought to put the sentries at their ease.

'Asbaab bazi haro bezar kenar!' he quipped. 'Put the toys away!' In the gathering darkness he went up to two of the men and gave them their orders. They would be the ones to guide him into the cave. Words were murmured into a walkie-talkie, a crackled response received, and Zamani was led towards the entrance.

There were no lights to show the way, not even a hurricane lamp, just the weak red beam from a military-issue torch held by the man in front. The cave's mouth was barely three metres high and Karim Zamani felt as if he were entering the lair of some great dormant beast. The moment thrilled and excited him. This was everything that he and the Circle had worked for. It was down here, in this remote and hidden cave, where no one would come looking for it until it was much too late. And now he, Karim Zamani, selfless and loyal guardian of the Islamic Revolution, was about to see it with his own eyes.

They moved slowly, carefully picking their way along the damp, slippery surface, Zamani staying close behind the guard with the torch. The beam picked out glistening white stalactites that dripped in jagged columns from the ceiling. Crystals crunched like gravel beneath their feet as the cavern grew narrower, the ceiling closed in, the temperature fell and the atmosphere became ever-more oppressive and claustrophobic.

It was another twenty minutes before they saw the lights and shadows moving, like ghosts, across the wall of the cavern in front of them. Zamani pushed ahead. Waiting for him was the man he hoped to see – instantly recognizable from the livid scar that ran down the side of his face.

'Ali-*jaan*.' The two men embraced and held each other for a long moment, saying nothing, only patting each other's backs. Others now gathered round, eager to greet him, but Zamani held up his hand for silence and looked questioningly at the man with the scar.

He nodded. 'If you are ready?'

'I am,' Zamani replied, and followed him deeper into the cavern.

In the subterranean beauty of the Namakdan Salt Caves the cage looked curiously out of place. Situated in a smaller cave to one side, its door was secured by a heavy padlock and chain, while a pair of armed guards stood at either side of it. Zamani stepped forward to take a closer look, his fingers closing around the cold, damp bars. He couldn't help but smile. At the base of the cage there was a thin, soiled mattress, and lying on it, half propped up on his elbow, was a man. To Zamani, he was a pathetic sight, dejected, dishevelled, lying there in his own filth. And Zamani felt no pity, only a sense of enormous satisfaction.

Karim Zamani cleared his throat and spat on the cave floor. It was time to introduce himself to his guest. He spoke in slow, halting English. 'Welcome . . . Mr Foreign Secretary. My name is Karim Zamani and this . . .' he paused to wave his arm expansively around the cave, a parody of lavish hospitality '. . . is your new home.'

Chapter 66

Bandar Abbas, Iran

HE HARDLY RECOGNIZED Tannaz. The girl who had left him in a Tehran side-street the day before had been cool, sardonic, self-confident. Now she stood before him, her headscarf discarded on a cushion at her feet, tears pouring down her cheeks and her shoulders heaving with each sob. She looked broken. Hesitating for only a second, Luke went to fold her into a hug. Farz and Mort looked at each other, clearly embarrassed and unsure what to do. But as her sobs subsided, Tannaz disentangled herself from Luke and slumped onto one of the cushions. Luke squatted in front of her.

'Tannaz,' he whispered. She looked up at him – her make-up had run – and he saw a deep sadness in her eyes. It took him by surprise but he realized then that he cared about this girl. Of course it wasn't like with Elise – that was different. No, this was something else. For all her bravado, her confidence, he sensed vulnerability in Tannaz, and he wanted to help her. He was aware that this was deeply unprofessional. What was it they had said to him back on the agent-handling course in Hampshire? 'One of the hardest things you'll find in this job is knowing how to keep a distance from your agent. Form a bond, by all means, establish mutual trust, but never, ever get emotionally attached to them.'

Luke leaned forward, put his hand over hers and held it there.

'It's good to see you again, Tannaz,' he said quietly. She raised her eyes to his briefly, then looked down at her feet. 'D'you want to tell me why you're here?'

She didn't answer at first. Instead she reached for a napkin, then gratefully took the cup of rose-petal tea that Mort had brought her.

'To be honest,' Luke continued, 'I kind of thought we'd said goodbye back in Tehran. That was your choice, not mine. So . . .' He stopped as she held up her hand, then took a sip of her tea.

When Tannaz spoke her voice was so quiet he had to move closer to catch her words. 'You were right.' Her jaw was set tight and she was nodding slowly. 'You were right about everything. I should have listened.' Something had clearly happened to her, he could see that. He was desperate to find out what it was and, shamefully, he recognized a part of him was already whispering in his head: *Play this to your advantage, Luke. You can work it into the mission.*

There was no park for them to stroll out into, no cosmopolitan café in which to hide. They were in a private house in a quiet corner of Bandar Abbas, a bustling port on Iran's Gulf coast, and there was nowhere else for them to go. Whatever she had to say would have to be said there, in front of Farz and Mort. The two men sat down in a corner, giving her space, leaning their backs against the wall, both looking at her expectantly.

'It was Mama who told me,' she began, staring at her feet, her hands clasped tightly together.

'Told you what?' Luke prompted.

'Sorry? What?' Tannaz looked up at him abruptly, as if noticing him for the first time.

'What did your mum tell you, Tannaz?'

'They spoke last night,' she replied, 'on the phone, my father and her. A big argument. So loud I could hear it from the next room so I came in to be with her.' Tannaz had stopped again, busy with her thoughts. 'When it ended Mama told me it was over, her and him. She's leaving him today. She's taking my brother, Parviz. They're leaving the country, but she hasn't told my father. Oh, my God . . .' She buried her head in her hands. 'There's something else. Something I'm ashamed to tell you.'

Luke sensed Farz and Mort edging closer. Whatever Tannaz had to say, they wanted to hear it.

'My father . . . my father . . .' Tannaz shook her head as if the truth were too painful to tell. 'My father is involved. He has a part in the kidnapping of the British man!' she blurted.

He made a show of recoiling in shock, while the surprise on the faces of Farz and Mort was real. Tannaz was confirming exactly what Vauxhall Cross had suspected. Luke replayed Angela's words in his mind: *We've had a comms intercept . . . enough to suggest Zamani's involved in the abduction. Seventy per cent certainty . . . need to get yourself to where he's going.*

'Christ, Tannaz,' he said. 'I'm so sorry. Are you absolutely sure?'

'Mama told me. She confronted him on the phone. She said he seemed very happy about this whole crisis we are in right now. So she asked him what good it could possibly do for the country. And do you know what my father replied? He said, "Soon you will see," and then he said, "*Tanha khoda mi taeva dar bareh ye man gheza vat konad.*"'

Immediately Farz and Mort nodded knowingly while Luke had to wait for her to translate.

'It means "Only God can judge." And that's when she knew! She's known him all these years, remember. He cannot hide things from her. The truth was plain for her to see and she made up her mind to leave.'

'But you're here, Tannaz? In Bandar Abbas.' His question was left hanging in the air.

'Yes. I took the plane. I got the eleven-fifteen flight from Tehran on Aseman.'

'What I meant,' said Luke, 'was why are you here and not with your mother?'

Tannaz didn't answer straight away. Instead she got to her feet. 'Give me a moment,' she said and disappeared into another room. The door closed. Farz and Mort burst into a heated discussion, leaving Luke to consider his next move. He looked at his watch. *Exploit the situation*, the voice in his head repeated. *Find a way to leverage off this. You don't have much time left.*

Tannaz reappeared minutes later, her make-up reapplied, her hair brushed. She looked fresh and reinvigorated. She smiled briefly before speaking to her two friends. They looked puzzled, but nodded and disappeared out of the house.

'I've asked them to give us some privacy for an hour or so,' she said. The familiar self-assurance was back as she patted the cushion next to her. 'Come, sit with me.'

Luke did as she suggested but inwardly he tensed, wary of what might come next. He still didn't really know her, and the possibilities raced through his mind as he sat and turned to face her. Yet still he didn't see it coming.

'We want asylum. In Britain,' announced Tannaz. 'For all three of us. My mother, my brother and me.' She looked at him intently, the sadness gone from her eyes, replaced by a burning determination. 'You can fix it, yes?'

Luke rubbed the bald stump of his missing finger. He suddenly felt very tired. How much sleep had he had in the last twenty-four hours? Almost none. 'Let me get this right,' he said. 'You came down here to Bandar Abbas to ask me this face to face?'

'Yes.'

Still the intent gaze. Luke exhaled. This, he realized, was a watershed moment. Get it right and Tannaz could help him pin down the exact whereabouts of Zamani and the captive Geoffrey Chaplin.

'All right,' he said. 'I can speak to people in London. I can give it a go.' Before he could say another word Tannaz put her hands behind his head, pulling him towards her. She kissed him full on the lips, just as she had done at their first strange encounter in Abu Dhabi all those weeks ago. He felt her tongue probing his, her hands running down his back and pulling him closer still. Luke didn't resist.

As they broke away, he continued kissing her neck, working his way up until his lips brushed her ear. 'You do know, Tannaz,' he whispered, 'that I'm going to need you to help me in return?'

Her eyes were closed, her hands round his hips now. 'Anything,' she murmured. 'Anything you ask.'

Chapter 67

AT JUST PAST two o'clock in the afternoon, London time, the weak winter light was already fading and motorists on the A4125 had switched on their sidelights. Just beyond the dank, dripping woods that bordered the road outside London, Britain's Permanent Joint Headquarters had quietly gone into overdrive. Behind the chain-link fences, the surveillance cameras and the twenty-four-hour perimeter patrols, the Joint Ops planning teams were working round the clock, all minds focusing on the task ahead. How to deliver an assault team of fully laden Special Boat Service commandos, at night, onto a submarine that was 3,600 miles away, then deploy them, undetected, into Iran. The logistics were mind-boggling and, under a directive issued by the Chief of Defence Staff, a unit of Navy Command specialists had raced up from Portsmouth to advise.

With a large-scale map of the Gulf projected onto the wall behind him, Rear Admiral John Bleake was bringing his team up to speed. The briefing room was packed, naval officers mostly but also a scattering of Royal Marines, sporting the distinctive black-and-red dagger flash on their left shoulders. There was an almost palpable tension in the room as he addressed them.

'*Astute* will stay deep outside the strait,' he said, his voice calm but authoritative. Removing a laser pointer from a pocket, he aimed it at the map, circling a small patch of open sea with the green dot. 'The pick-up point will be here.' He indicated a patch of open sea marked 'Gulf of Oman', midway between the Omani port of Sohar and the Iranian naval base at Jask; the Navy referred to it as 'the GOO'.

'You'll note that the GOO is deep in the centre, but the approach to the strait is a chokepoint. The merchant vessel that *Astute* will conceal herself under will have to reduce speed as she nears the strait. So *Astute* will be aiming to come up beneath her just . . . about . . . here.' Bleake shone his laser on the map once more, indicating a point to the east of the Musandam peninsula, which jutted out into the sea.

'Now, on to the type of ship in question. Tankers.' He turned to his ops officer. The young man standing behind him handed him a sheet of A4 paper. It was a printout of all the merchant tankers currently on course for the Strait of Hormuz. Three had question marks beside them. One was circled in red. Bleake ran his eyes down it, then looked up and surveyed the room.

'The *Ocean Star*,' he told the assembled company. 'That's the one we've chosen. She's a Suez-Max tanker, registered in Panama, two hundred and eighty-three metres from bow to stern, with a deadweight of a hundred and eight thousand tons.' Several of those present were busy scribbling notes, the younger officers typing the details straight into iPads, which would remain securely locked away on the base.

'Where is she right now, sir?' asked a Royal Navy Lieutenant Commander in the second row.

'Ops?' The Rear Admiral turned again to the ops officer.

'She's currently in transit from Suez to the Arabian Gulf, heading up the Omani coast from Salalah,' replied the younger man, a note of urgency in his voice as he addressed, first, the admiral, then the rest of the room. 'She's making her way up the coast of Oman, heading for Kharg Island to pick up a cargo of Iranian crude. That puts her inside Iranian territorial waters, which gets us round that little problem.'

'Thank you, John.' Admiral Bleake resumed his briefing, 'Now. I know you're all security-cleared up to Strap Level so I can tell you there's another reason why we've selected the *Ocean Star.*' He already had their full attention but now several officers leaned forward. 'Like a lot of merchant vessels transiting the Somali Basin, these days, she's got an armed protection team onboard. Nothing unusual in that. But the team leader happens to be a former Royal Marine. Let's just say he's being most cooperative.' There were some knowing grins around the room.

'Nice one,' muttered someone at the back.

'Right. That brings us to depth,' continued Bleake. 'I have to say that, given the shallow waters of the Gulf, this is going to be tight. *Ocean Star* has a twenty-one-metre draught, but she's in ballast so that figure will be closer to nineteen metres. We need to factor in a twenty-metre safety margin for *Astute* – that's twenty metres from the top of her fin up to *Ocean Star*'s keel. Excuse me.' He stopped abruptly and whipped out a handkerchief, catching his sneeze just in time.

'Our submarine,' said Bleake, 'is fifteen metres from fin to keel and then we need a twenty-metre gap beneath her to seabed. So, come on, the mathematicians among you, what does that give us as a minimum depth?'

'Sixty-nine metres?' called a thick-set bearded man in the front row.

'Wrong!' said Bleake, tapping his laser pointer impatiently against the palm of his hand. 'Anyone? You're supposed to be the brightest brains in the military!'

'Seventy-four metres,' said several officers at once.

'Correct,' replied the Admiral. He turned back to the chart on the wall. 'And this is the stretch that's going to keep us all awake at night.' He indicated the left of the two parallel channels bending round the tip of the Musandam peninsula towards the Gulf. 'Squeezing through that, at night, is going to take some serious *cojones* on the part of *Astute*'s captain. Fortunately I rode Ben Wallis pretty hard on his Perisher course, and if anyone's up to the job, he is. Okay. Questions?'

A hand went up. 'Timings, sir?' asked a Royal Marine.

'TBC. We're just waiting for sign-off from the PM, then it's all systems go. Hold on.' The ops officer had coughed quietly to get his attention. Admiral Bleake held up his hand as he was passed a printed signal. It was from the MoD in Whitehall and he read it out to the room: ' "Operation Shearwater approved. Proceed." Ladies and gentlemen, we're on. It's time to prove you're worth the expensive training Her Majesty's given you.'

Chapter 68

ON THE OTHER side of the Strait of Hormuz, and almost due south of Bandar Abbas, a light wind was blowing across the hard-packed desert sand as the last of the daylight ebbed away. In two lines, weighed down by their meticulously packed square-rig 'chutes, their eclectic mix of chosen personal weapons, and their customized equipment, the SBS assault team and the reserve troop filed out to the waiting C130 Hercules transport plane. The breeze ruffled the camouflage netting they were leaving behind and flung a tumble of dried vegetation across the sand, sending it spinning off across the desert floor into the gathering gloom of the Omani night. The operation was on.

A fraction over eight hundred kilometres to the west, inside the British naval base of HMS *Juffair* in Bahrain, Lieutenant Colonel Chip Nuttall took a swig from his can of lukewarm Diet Coke, adjusted his headset and settled in front of a monitor. As the Commanding Officer of the UK's Special Boat Service and the man sending those troops into action, he knew he would be getting precious little sleep until the operation was over. Nuttall and his staff had already spent a fraught day juggling timings, grid references, pick-up points, wind speeds, moonstates, payloads, intercept updates and drone feeds. There were risks and contingencies to be planned for, and a framework agreed with HQ for the 'go/no go' criteria. At times the CO had felt like an old-fashioned telephone-exchange operator as he ended one call to his troop commander in the Wahiba Sands only to be patched through immediately to another at Northwood. Or Special Forces Headquarters. Or Poole. Or Portsmouth. As if it were not enough having to plan a complex air, sea and land insertion into hostile territory, he was having to spend much of his time appearing by video conference call in COBRA. The government's crisis committee was being convened for hours on end, and Nuttall was summoned to the camera nearly every hour.

Pulled in every direction, he relied on the team around him. He had hand-picked the command team that had come out to Bahrain with him. Most of the men, but not all, had proved themselves on earlier covert operations, events that the British public would not hear about for another thirty years. In the brief moments when he wasn't on the radio to Oman or on a conference call to the UK, Nuttall was receiving constant updates from his team on the wider political perspective. He needed to know if the Third World War was about to erupt around the operators he was sending in.

The most recent report they had handed him was unsettling. Persuading the White House to back off and let the UK resolve this in its own way had not been easy. There were certain political figures on the US National Security Council, the report read, who were itching to make this an 'America First' operation. It was time, some voices were saying, 'to teach those ayatollahs a lesson'. Emotive expressions like 'playing with fire' and 'payback time' were being bandied about in the corridors of power at 1600 Pennsylvania Avenue, NW Washington, DC. There was an emerging school of thought doing the rounds in the US capital that, after successive defence cuts and underinvestment by the British government, the plucky little island that had produced Winston Churchill no longer had what it took to mount an operation so complex. It would be just a matter of time, they said, before Uncle Sam had to step in and show the Brits how to do it right.

Chip Nuttall read that last brief and filed it vertically – in the waste-bin beside his desk. He had no time for speculation: he dealt in facts. And he knew that none of this would be of any concern to the sixteen men now filing into the gaping underbelly of the C130 Hercules. As they trudged up the metal ramp, black swim fins attached to their belts, diver's knives strapped to their calves, automatic carbines hanging vertically beside their right legs, he knew their minds were elsewhere. Some men's thoughts would be turning to their families and whether they had put all their affairs in order, should the unthinkable happen and they did not return. All would be aware of the death of a US Navy SEAL commando on a Special Ops raid into Yemen in 2017. They would be trying hard not to think about it, but every man onboard that C130 understood that this mission might be his last.

Up front, in the relative comfort of the plane's cockpit, the assault team Commander settled back in the jump seat, positioned just behind the pilot and co-pilot. Captain Chris Barkwell was only thirty-one, yet had considerable operational experience under his belt, with stints in Afghanistan, Iraq and a few of the more dangerous corners of West Africa. Kitted out with a headset and mic, he studied the laminated military map of Oman and its adjacent coast that was open across his knees.

As the flight crew made their final pre-flight checks, the co-pilot reached round behind him and passed Barkwell a plastic cup of orange juice. 'We'll be taking off into the wind to the south-east,' he told him, speaking loudly into his mic as the noise level built up from the four Allison turboprop engines. 'Wind speed here is nine knots but I'll get you an update when we near the drop zone.'

'Cheers.' Barkwell drained the cup and crushed it into the trash box behind the co-pilot's seat.

'We'll be skirting just east of the Saudi border, then passing Muscat on our right-hand side,' the co-pilot added. 'We should have comms with *Astute* once we're airborne.'

'That'd be a bonus!' shouted Barkwell. The engines were almost at full thrust now. 'I wasn't planning on us dropping into an empty ocean.'

Behind him, facing each other along the length of the C130's fuselage, the troopers were strapped into their canvas bucket seats, helmets and protective goggles on. Seemingly oblivious to the roar of the engines, they were checking and rechecking their kit, rehearsing the drills for a smooth exit from the plane. Some had their eyes shut, wide awake but offering a silent prayer, while others knocked gloved fists together, the final salute before a mission.

Darkness had settled over the rippling sands of the Wahiba desert when the C130 Hercules accelerated across the valley floor. This time there was no one to observe it as it lifted off into the night sky over Oman, climbing steeply before turning due north. As they crossed the edge of the Empty Quarter, the plane was briefly buffeted by a patch of clear-air turbulence, then the desert was behind them and they were crossing the Omani coastline. In the cockpit, Barkwell looked up from the map on his knees. The plane had already begun its descent in the dark.

When the red warning light came on, it was as if a jolt of electricity had passed through the plane. Ten minutes to the drop zone and the men began checking pockets, clips and fastenings, securing their weapons, attaching the static-line jump cords with snap hooks to the anchor-line cable that ran the length of the fuselage at head height. Each trooper then hooked his Bergen rucksack – with its thirty kilos of ammunition, rations, radio, batteries, field first-aid kit – to the front of his parachute harness. Each man wore round his neck what the Royal Navy called a 'dongle and trongle' – a life-saving device that emitted a traceable pulse of sound as soon as it hit the water.

In the C130's interior the jumpmaster made his way down the line of waiting men, checking each individual, tugging on straps, giving shoulders an encouraging squeeze. Two minutes to go: the ramp of the great plane jawed open and the night air swirled in. The jumpmaster checked the last man and the message was passed down the line – each trooper tapping the man in front on the shoulder, giving the okay. The stick – those selected to make the jump – were ushered forward to the plane's tailgate. The roar of the engines was deafening.

Then the light turned green, the jumpmaster yelled, 'Go!' and the troop piled out in a single plummeting stream. Barkwell had been the first to make the leap into darkness. The force of the slipstream slammed into him, easing off as his square-rig 'chute deployed. The rest of his team followed, guided down by the luminous green strip on the back of his helmet. They'd exited the aircraft at just under 250 metres above sea level, and moments later the warm waters of the Gulf of Oman seemed to be rushing up to meet them.

Fifteen metres over the water and their training kicked in. Each operator hit the quick-release catches on his harness to send his bergen, connected by just a simple nylon cord, into the water. Seconds later, they each executed a Capewell manoeuvre, releasing just one side of their harness so allowing the wind to drag the canopies off and away behind them. However hard and often they trained for this moment, the impact always came as a shock. Barkwell held his breath as he was briefly submerged beneath the waves. Resurfacing, he wrestled to put on the fins he'd worn strapped to his chest, then began to swim, dragging his pack behind him.

Ahead, he could just make out the silhouette of the rigid inflatable boat that had been launched from *Astute*, and was now homing in on the short-range pulses emitted from the dongles he and his team were wearing. And beyond the black inflatable, water pouring off her sides, was the massive 97-metre hull of the submarine. Treading water, the SBS officer watched as the sub's recovery crew helped his troop onboard. Then it was his turn. Hands reached out to haul him from the sea, and minutes later, he and his men were safely inside the submarine. Above them, hatches were pulled shut and *Astute* began her descent beneath the waves. The first phase of Operation Shearwater was complete: the Royal Navy nuclear submarine could now continue its passage north-westwards, unseen and unnoticed among the myriad vessels passing through the Strait of Hormuz.

Chapter 69

LUKE ROLLED OFF the bed and reached down for his shirt. He felt doubly dirty. He had never intended this to happen, but it had, and now he hated himself for what he had just done. *How low can you go, Carlton? Elise has lost her mother, Britain's lost her Foreign Secretary, and what are you doing? Writhing around naked in a windowless room in Bandar Abbas with a girl you're supposed to be tapping for information. Nice going, arsehole, you've let everybody down.*

Tannaz had her back to him. She was sitting on the edge of the bed without a stitch on, fixing her hair. He took a last look at the smooth contours of her back and those dimples in her caramel skin just above her perfect hips. Would he ever see her like this again? *Absolutely not. This is never going to be repeated.* When he spoke he hardly recognized his own voice. It was flat and formal, as if he were overcompensating for the intensity of what they had just shared. 'Will you excuse me, Tannaz? I need to make a quick phone call. About your asylum request . . . Hey, is everything okay?'

She nodded, a hair-tie clamped between her teeth. 'Yes, I will leave you in a moment. Farzad and Mort will be back soon. I will make tea.'

He waited for her to close the door, then took out his phone and coded in to Vauxhall Cross. He had managed to fire off a

274

quick text to Angela earlier, to let her know he'd reached the out-skirts of Bandar Abbas, but there had been no response. With everything kicking off, she'd have been caught up in endless Whitehall crisis meetings. He pressed the dial button and this time his boss answered immediately.

'Thank God,' Angela said, 'I was about to call you. Just got out of a COBRA. It's mayhem here.'

Somewhere in the background he could hear a printer whir-ring into life, the mundane machinery of office espionage, printing out some numbered and classified report. She waited until it stopped. 'Are you somewhere safe?'

He detected a slight delay on the line as her words were rerouted through the VPN network, scrambled into binary ones and zeros as their encrypted conversation criss-crossed the globe. 'For now, yes,' he replied. 'I need to keep my head down, though. Listen, I have some news.'

But her voice cut across his, the delay on the line throwing their conversation out of sync. 'So here's where we are,' Angela said. 'The Iranians are stalling on us. They won't let in the hos-tage negotiators from the Met – that team hasn't even left Heathrow and I doubt they ever will. So we're taking matters into our own hands, if you catch my drift.'

Luke knew exactly what she meant. He could just picture the scene in North Camp, down at the SBS base in Poole, when the orders came through for the Special Forces standby squadron to prepare for action. The issuing of special-to-task kit from the stores, the drawing-out of weapons and ammo from the armoury, the loading of equipment onto trailers under tarpaulins, then the road move to the airfield at Brize Norton. 'How close to that are we?' he asked.

'The team are already in-theatre,' she replied. 'You don't need to know where. But there's a problem. They can't go in until we get the exact location of the hostage. And once we do they'll need someone to guide them in to the target. That would be you, Luke. But only if you can get there in time . . .'

It sounded like a challenge, which was probably exactly what

Angela intended. She was playing him, willing him to use every last resource to get himself up close to the target before it was too late. Luke felt his pulse quicken and looked at his watch. Chaplin had been missing for barely twenty-four hours. Things were moving very fast.

'Angela, listen. I have something from my end. I've got a second source on Zamani. It's Elixir. Her mother says he's involved. He's right at the heart of this. And I think I can get us his private mobile number.'

'You can?' She sounded suddenly upbeat. 'Well, this is what half of Cheltenham's been working on. Go for it.'

There was a sudden clatter from the room next door and the sound of voices. Farz and Mort had returned.

'I've got to go,' Luke said, 'but I'm going to need something in exchange.' He didn't wait for her to ask what it was, just went straight in. 'I need UK asylum for Elixir and her family. She's with me now, in the next-door room. Her family are leaving him and Iran. Come on, Angela, this is an open goal.' He waited for the pause on the line to elapse.

Then her voice came back. 'Luke, you do know it's not that simple, don't you? Home Office Immigration would have to get involved and—'

'Fuck the Home Office,' he cut in angrily. He wasn't in the mood for this. 'It *is* that simple, Angela, and you know it. Just make the call. We need that number, right? Well, she's got it. So let's make a trade and do the right thing by her.' This time the delay on the line was longer than usual.

'Angela? Are you still there?'

'I am. Okay, just get us that number as quick as you can and then we'll talk about it, all right? Stay safe, Luke.' Angela hung up.

There was a gentle knock on the bedroom door and Tannaz let herself in. She set down a steaming cup of rose-petal tea on the table next to him. As she did so she caressed the back of his neck with her other hand and he felt a frisson. *You're not letting yourself get involved with this girl, are you?* Yes. He was. And Luke had yet to work out what the hell he was going to do about it.

Chapter 70

LUKE TOOK THE piece of paper from her as casually as he could, but his heart was pounding. It was just a dozen digits scribbled on a torn-off scrap of notepaper, one man's mobile-phone number, the private contact details for a father, a husband, a family man in the Islamic Republic of Iran. And yet this, he knew, was intelligence gold dust. Could it save the life of Britain's Foreign Secretary? Christ, it might even help stop a war that seemed poised to consume both sides of the Gulf. God alone knew, but big stakes were at play here. He just couldn't reveal any of this to Tannaz. Not yet.

'Well?' she said, raising one perfectly sculpted eyebrow as she regarded him.

He smiled, noticing that her face was still slightly flushed. 'Thank you.'

'*Bisho'ur!*' She slapped him on the knee. 'Idiot! I'm not asking you to thank me. I want you to tell me what they said about giving asylum. This is my family we're talking here, Brendan! My family and my life.'

'Right. Yes, sorry.' Luke had gone over this conversation in his head. He could, of course, be totally honest and tell her it was highly unlikely that London would agree to asylum. Or he could spin it out, ask her for more information about her father. But what could she tell him that they didn't already know? Luke made an executive decision. He would tell her exactly what worked for him, nothing more.

'It's looking good,' he said. 'But you have to realize they've got a lot on their hands right now, with the kidnapping.' He was expecting her to protest.

Instead she nodded thoughtfully. 'I want to help,' Tannaz said.

'You already have. Let me get this number over to Citizens Concern in London,' Luke said, as he started to text it to Angela at Vauxhall Cross.

'No,' Tannaz replied, putting her hand back on his knee. 'I want to help *you*. You're helping me and my family so I must help you in return. That's how we do things here in Iran.'

Luke stopped in mid-text, put down the phone and waved his hand around the room. 'Tannaz, look at where we are,' he said, 'I'm somewhere safe and off the streets, and that's thanks to you. So, trust me, I really appreciate this.'

'I know you do. But you can't stay here. This is too dangerous for them.' She gestured towards the living room. 'For Farz and for Mort. Where do you go now?'

Her directness was refreshing but he didn't know the answer to that question. He needed to get Zamani's number punched into his phone and over to Vauxhall Cross so they could triangulate his location, then give Luke the coordinates. He just didn't expect what came next.

'I invite you,' Tannaz said.

'You invite me?'

'Yes. I invite you to come with me. I'm going to look for him. For my father.'

There was a sudden burst of laughter from next door.

'Hold on – your father? You know where he is?'

'No. But when I find him I'm going to tell him what I think of these stupid games he's playing and tell him to stop. I know he will listen to me.'

Luke held her hands while he silently assessed this new

development. *Use Elixir to get close to her father.* Those had been his orders all along. The parameters had changed but her suggestion still fitted with his original mission. Tannaz could get him close enough to guide in the hostage-rescue team, but not so close that he was caught. 'How do you plan to find him?' he asked.

'Easy.' She pulled away and reached for her phone. 'I'm going to call him on that number I just gave you.'

Chapter 71

Namakdan Salt Caves, Qeshm Island

GEOFFREY CHAPLIN WAS lying on his side, eyes closed, resting on the thin damp mattress, when the visitor appeared outside his cage. To keep his spirits up, he had been playing out a rescue scenario in his head. He was remembering the training exercise he'd had to undergo in Hereford soon after his appointment as Foreign Secretary.

'We've all had to do it,' the PM had told him cheerfully, 'even the Cambridges have been through it.' They had whisked him off down the M4, ministerial briefs on his lap, as they drove westwards until they reached Stirling Lines, home of the SAS and the legendary Killing House. It had looked deceptively ordinary, Chaplin recalled, a two-storey grey building with four rooms on each floor. But the briefing had made clear what this was about: rubber-coated walls to absorb the bullets that would be fired perilously close to him, movable partitions and CCTV cameras to record every move, every second of his discomfort.

Chaplin had once been a cadet in his university Officers' Training Corps but that was the sum total of his military experience. Nothing, absolutely nothing, had prepared him for the blind terror he had experienced as big men in gas-masks and anonymous black uniforms had blasted their way into the room where he'd sat, rigid with fear, on a wooden chair. There had been a split-second pause, then the man closest to him had fired two rounds into the dummy propped next to him. Chaplin was sure he had felt the impact as the bullets slammed into the fibreglass effigy of a terrorist hostage-taker. The Killing House had a deadly purpose: to teach VIPs what would happen if they were ever taken hostage, and to hone the skills of the men coming after their kidnappers. Chaplin was glad he'd been through it. Now he thought, Just hurry up and come and get me. And make sure you put a bullet through the chest of every one of these people, whoever they are.

But his reverie had been cut short, and now he looked at the man standing outside the cage. He didn't cut a particularly impressive figure. He was dressed scruffily in a pair of old trainers, baggy grey trousers, a beige jacket and a black baseball cap pulled down over his eyes. Yet the people around him were behaving deferentially towards him. He must be someone of authority. It was hard to tell in this country, where everyone he'd met seemed to have several days' stubble and no one wore a tie. Well, if this was a senior figure, he was jolly well going to demand his release, perhaps even suggest some sort of bargain. Chaplin was about to speak but the man got in first.

'Welcome . . . Mr Foreign Secretary,' he began. So they knew who they were holding. Chaplin wasn't sure if that was a good thing or not. 'My name is Karim Zamani and this . . .' the man continued, in hesitant English, '. . . is your new home.'

Chaplin's indignation rose. This was nothing like any home he'd ever experienced. It was his turn to speak. 'This is *not* my home and I don't know who you are.' His voice cracked. It must be the damp and the cold down here. He coughed and continued: 'But whatever it is you want I'm certain we can work something out. I demand to see a representative of the International Red Cross.'

'*Che goft?*' said the man, turning to someone next to him. 'What did he say?'

Zamani laughed when he heard the translation, which Chaplin

found both insulting and troubling. Now the man was speaking again. 'We have doctor for you,' he was saying.

'I don't need a damn doctor!' Chaplin retorted. 'I need you to release me. Immediately.'

But the man didn't seem to be listening. Chaplin watched warily from his mattress as a guard produced a key from his belt and undid the padlock on his cage. Was the man coming in? Was he being released? No. The man stepped aside and another individual appeared, someone he hadn't seen before.

'This man is doctor,' Zamani said. He indicated an elderly man with a white moustache, round glasses and baggy brown trousers. He didn't look like any doctor Chaplin had ever seen but nothing surprised him in this country. And what was that he was carrying in his right hand? It looked like a freezer bag, the sort of thing he and Gillian used to take on picnics in the summer to keep the drinks cool when the children were growing up. Except this one was white and had a red cross stencilled on the side. Geoffrey Chaplin gave an involuntary shiver. He was beginning to feel uneasy. Something wasn't right about this.

He pushed himself upright as the elderly man squeezed into the cage. He was accompanied by two guards, one of whom was carrying a flimsy metal chair. The other lunged for Chaplin, grabbed his arms and hauled him onto the seat.

'Christ!' the British politician protested. 'I can do this myself, you know. You don't have to manhandle me like that.' But he could see they weren't listening. The 'doctor' stood meekly by and one of the guards produced a length of nylon rope. Alarmed, Chaplin tried to stand but was roughly pushed down. His arms pinned to his sides, he felt the rope being expertly tied around his upper torso, then his legs. This was too much.

'What the hell are you doing?' he shouted, but no one paid any attention. He was now completely immobilized. As the rope cut into his arms and legs, he decided it was best to reason with his captors. 'You don't need to do this!' he told them, desperation creeping into his voice as the fear took over. 'I'm not going to run away from here, am I?' Zamani, in the beige jacket, was standing impassively outside the cage, watching. There was something about his manner that spoke of ruthlessness, and his eyes were cold. Chaplin's heart was pounding now. Something very bad was about to happen, he could tell.

What happened next was very sudden. His head was pulled back and he was about to cry out in protest but a strip of grimy cloth was tied tightly around his mouth. He could feel the knot at the base of his skull. Chaplin watched, wide-eyed, as the doctor approached and knelt at his feet. He was fiddling with the white box he had brought with him, then he glanced nervously over his shoulder at Zamani. It was almost as if he were seeking his approval. Straightening, his face just inches from Chaplin's, he stared intently at a small glass phial that he now held up to the feeble light from the nearby hurricane lamp. He was checking its contents. In his other hand he held a hypodermic syringe. He inserted the needle into the phial, drawing out the colourless fluid. Chaplin tensed. They were going to inject him. But with what? A truth drug? He watched as the elderly doctor flicked the syringe and compressed the plunger slightly. A small spurt of liquid landed on his hand, which he wiped on his shirt. Chaplin looked at the old man's face. By God, he thought, I hope he knows what he's doing.

It was as if the doctor had read his mind because he made a soothing sound and patted Chaplin's left arm as though to reassure him. Then he stopped, closed his eyes and uttered what sounded like a prayer. From the periphery of his vision, Chaplin could see the two guards smirking and then, without any warning, came the stinging pain of a needle going in. Chaplin grunted from behind his gag, tasting a foul combination of salt and oil, as he watched in horror. The doctor was emptying the contents of the syringe into his hand. Beyond, he could just make out the man in the beige jacket, his expression unreadable.

The doctor withdrew the needle, and replaced it in his white box. Chaplin wiggled his fingers. He didn't feel any different, although his hand was a little numb. Again, the doctor's face loomed up to his. He could see the man's eyes peering at him through his round spectacles as if he were a specimen. What was he doing, for goodness' sake? Checking he was still alive? The doctor turned to the two guards behind him and nodded. Stepping closer, one produced a small black sack. It was a hood, Chaplin realized, as it was forced over his head and his world went dark. This wasn't what he'd expected and the fear was back. Chaplin was bound, gagged and sightless beneath his hood. And his left hand felt strange, very strange, as though it had been anaesthetized, but only partially. Christ, he thought, that's just what they've done: they've tried to give me some sort of anaesthetic. But why in the hand, of all places? And then a searing red-hot pain lanced through him as he felt something slicing into his finger.

Chaplin's scream, muffled by the gag, came out as a stifled groan. The cutting stopped. The pain eased momentarily, leaving Chaplin gasping. Suddenly he felt a pressure on his finger. It was as if it were on fire. His body convulsed as shards of agony tore through it. He thought his brain might be about to explode. Between the pain and the confusion, he realized what the men had done. They had just cut off his finger.

And then Geoffrey Chaplin, Secretary of State for Foreign and Commonwealth Affairs, blacked out.

Chapter 72

Bandar Abbas, Iran

'WAIT!' LUKE'S ARM shot out and he grabbed Tannaz's wrist. She gasped, dropping her phone, and cried out.

'*Aya divaneh hasti?* Are you crazy? What are you doing?'

He let go immediately, embarrassed at the force of his reaction. 'I'm sorry, Tannaz, but you were about to call your father.'

'And?' Her eyes blazed. 'He's *my* father and you don't get to tell me who I can call!'

'Of course not,' Luke said soothingly. 'I didn't mean it like that. But just stop and think for a moment. If you call him now he's not going to let you near him, is he? In fact, he'll probably send someone here to take you back to Tehran. D'you want that?' Her shoulders relaxed. He hoped she saw the logic in his argument. 'Better we find him by another way,' he added. 'Then you can confront him face to face.'

'How d'you mean "by another way"?'

Luke shrugged. 'I'll talk to Citizens Concern in London. They've got some great tech people on their team.'

Tannaz's eyes narrowed, just as they had when she'd confronted him in that side-street in Tehran. He wondered how long he could keep up this flimsy cover story. She wasn't stupid – in fact, she seemed to be ahead of him half the time.

'Just give me a few minutes,' he told her, 'and then I'll come and join you and the others.' Luke watched her leave. From next door came the smell of cooking and he felt his stomach contract in response. He suddenly realized how little he had eaten since leaving Tehran. But that had to wait. He looked at the scrap of paper with Zamani's number and smiled. This was it. He keyed it into his phone and pressed 'send'. He waited. It took under a minute for a response to come through. *Received, Stand by.*

Another wait, longer this time, more laughter from the kitchen and the clatter of plates. It must have been the familiar sound of domesticity that made him think of Elise. To say he'd treated her badly was an understatement. He knew he should call her now while he had the chance. Yes, that was the right thing to do. But to tell her what? Anything less than 'I'm coming straight home' was bound to end in an argument and he didn't need that right now.

His phone buzzed.

'Bloody excellent work,' said a low voice. It was Trish Fryer, Mission Controller, Middle East, at Vauxhall Cross. 'This was exactly the missing piece we needed,' she said.

'Good to hear,' Luke replied, keeping his voice down. 'Let's see this thing through. D'you have his coordinates for me?'

'They'll be coming through on your phone in a minute. You'll need the Gama function to access the map. Go into Settings and make sure it's enabled. Look . . . um . . .' Trish stopped in mid-flow, suddenly sounding more hesitant. 'I'm going to level with you, Luke. This isn't perfect science. It looks like Zamani's on the move. We've only got two transmissions from that number you got for us. One was made from Bandar Abbas and the other from an island called Qeshm. We're sending you that one because it's the most recent.'

'How recent?'

'An hour ago.'

'That's good enough for me. Keep me posted.' Luke ended the call and looked around the room. He had nothing to take with him except his phone and his passport. Everything else he had brought with him to Iran – the washbag, razors, his change of underwear – would all have been lifted from his hotel room by now. He assumed they'd have been tagged and bagged and were now most likely sitting in some Intelligence Ministry evidence box in Tehran, awaiting his trial if they ever managed to catch him. He grunted to himself. They were welcome to them.

Pushing open the door to the main room, Luke found the three friends sitting on cushions around a large, circular dish. They were taking flaps of *nan* flatbread and scooping up a fiery-looking sauce from the communal bowl between them. 'Better be quick.' Tannaz grinned. 'It's nearly all gone.'

Farz shuffled up to make room for him and passed him a plate. Luke thanked him and took his place. He was acutely aware that the clock was ticking and that he didn't have time for this but he was hungry and the food was good. Once they'd finished, the two young men went into the kitchen to clear up, and he was able to speak to Tannaz.

'Qeshm Island,' he whispered. 'D'you know it? I – we – need to get there. Quickly.'

She looked up sharply. 'Why Qeshm? Is that where . . . ? Oh, okay, I get it.' Before he could stop her, she'd pushed open the kitchen door. 'Hey, Farz!' she called. 'How do we get to Qeshm from here?'

'Qeshm?' Farz repeated in surprise. 'What d'you wanna go there for?' He was still wearing the clothes he'd had on for last night's marathon drive down from Tehran. But now Mort turned to Luke, his expression far from friendly. He stopped what he was doing at the sink and spoke sharply to Farz in Farsi.

'Mort thinks it's dangerous to go to Qeshm,' Farz explained, for Luke's benefit.

'Why?'

Farz shrugged. 'You know, this whole security-alert thing. They'll be checking everyone's ID on the ferry over. You'll be picked up in no time.'

'There must be another way,' said Tannaz. 'What about a private boat?'

'Yeah, I guess so. You could go from Bandar Khamir,' replied Farz, but now Mort strode over to where Luke was standing.

'Look, man,' he began, 'I don't think you get the risk you're making us take just by being here in this house. The police are looking for you, right? That's ten years minimum in jail for us if they find you here. Ten years of my life gone, and you know what? I don't know you from shit. So . . .'

Farz put a restraining hand on his shoulder. 'Hey, c'mon, Mort,' he was still speaking in English, 'he's a guest, for God's sake. And he's going to run a campaign in London to get Darius released.'

But Mort shook him off. 'That's bullshit, man. Look at him.' He stood back, inviting the others to look at Luke. 'This guy doesn't work in human rights. I don't know what he does for a living but I'm telling you he's trouble.' He hadn't taken his eyes off Luke. 'Listen, mister, you've had your lift from Tehran, you've had your free meal in this house. It's time for you to go. Nothing personal but, please, I'm asking you nicely, just go away and leave us alone.'

Luke remained silent. He could see the shock on the faces of the others. Did they believe Mort's theory or were they just embarrassed? Either way, his time here was definitely up. He put up his hands. 'I don't blame you,' he said. 'You know what? I'd be the same. Don't worry, I'll be out of here as soon as it's dark.' He reached into his pocket. 'And I'd like to leave something for all the food and fuel.' He placed a folded hundred-dollar bill on the table beside the cushions.

Mort looked at him with undisguised contempt. 'We don't want your money, man.' He reached over and swept it off the table onto the floor. 'You think you can just buy us off, like some kind of imperial power? God, you people piss me off!' He went back to the sink, as if to wash his hands of the intruder who had come into his house.

It was Farz who broke the uneasy silence. 'Look, I'll drive you,' he said, glancing at Mort. 'I can take you both to Bandar Khamir. It's not far down the coast. I know the back-roads.'

Mort erupted into a heated stream of Farsi. Luke didn't need to understand a word: the meaning was obvious. 'Don't do it. Leave this foreigner to fend for himself.'

Tannaz, who had watched this exchange with mounting alarm, came and stood next to Luke. She looked worried. 'We must go now. We should leave at once.'

288

Chapter 73

MORT'S OUTBURST WAS a wake-up call. His heartfelt but angry words had shattered the genial atmosphere inside the back-street house. The trouble was that he was right, and they all knew it, including Luke. His presence there was a danger to all of them. For Tannaz, who had grown up under the protective umbrella of her father's Revolutionary Guards connections, the confrontation would have been an uncomfortable reminder that her safety net was about to be whipped away.

Luke stood just behind her as she waited in the open doorway. Farz had gone to bring the car round to the worn white steps at the front of the house. Inside, he heard Mort busying himself at the sink. He had nothing more to say. Outside in the street there were people about, mostly women, many heavily veiled. In stark contrast to the cosmopolitan women in the capital, they seemed to favour a more conservative, traditional dress – baggy floral pantaloons, bare ankles adorned with anklets, occasionally hawklike masks of black and gold. Tannaz, too, had noticed the change.

'My God,' Luke heard the disdain in her voice, 'how do they put up with wearing that thing? It looks so uncomfortable.'

They were interrupted by the rattle of a car engine that had seen better days, and there was Farz in the Peugeot. He waved at them to hurry. Tannaz appeared to hesitate, glancing back into the house. 'Come on,' Luke urged. He took her arm and led her towards the car. Even with a baseball cap pulled down over his eyes, he knew his height, his hair and complexion made him stand out. All it would take was one sharp-eyed local to spot him and call the police. They clambered into the battered Peugeot 405 as Farz emptied the last incriminating roaches and flakes of hash out of the window. Tannaz sat next to him in the front, headscarf modestly in place, while Luke stayed low on the back seat, ready to sink to the floor, if need be. He took a last look back at the house and did not like what he saw. Mort had come to the front door to watch them leave, his expression one of concentrated disapproval. Luke saw him raise his hand in a half-hearted farewell before he turned and shut the door on them.

'I'm really sorry you had to hear all that,' said Farz, catching Luke's eye in his rear-view mirror as they lurched off down the narrow, sandy alleyway. 'But you've got to excuse Mort. He has some personal issues.' He slowed to let a dog lope past, limping as it crossed the street in front of them. 'You see, they took his brother away a few years back, and when he came out of prison, well, he was never the same.'

'Who?' Luke asked. 'Mort or the brother?'

'Both.'

A brief but uncomfortable silence followed. Luke could only guess what the others were thinking, but Farz had a brother in prison too. Was he going to end up angry and bitter like Mort?

They drove west, through dimly lit streets, then a suburban bazaar with garish, neon-lit shops, their wares piled on the pavement, and men sitting around on white plastic chairs smoking waterpipes. It seemed a far cry from the state of emergency Luke had left in Tehran, but round a corner they had to pull over for a convoy of military trucks. After that Luke kept his head down. With no view to distract him his thoughts turned again to something he really didn't want to address: Elise. He'd betrayed her. Would he – should he – come clean and tell her about Tannaz?

290

And her mother. They'd been so close. He assumed they must be making plans for the funeral. It was probably only days away and Elise would expect him to be by her side as the coffin was lowered into the ground. It was the least she could expect from him. Would he make it back in time? Right now, the odds were not looking good.

It was a relief when Farz broke the silence. Luke dragged his attention back to the here and now. They were nearing the fishing village of Bandar Khamir, and Tannaz had started to thank him when Farz brought the car to a stop.

'Wait here while I check it out,' he said. 'I'm gonna find you a boat, then come straight back.'

Farz had pulled up behind an overflowing bin in a quiet, residential street lined with low, sandstone-coloured houses. Luke heard the car door open and close and the crunch of Farz's retreating footsteps. A group of cats skittered and yowled among the rubbish that had spilled onto the ground and an overpowering smell of rot tainted the evening air. Minutes passed. Neither the smell nor the cats bothered Luke, but hanging around in the back seat of a car waiting to be collected, like luggage, did. Sitting up and peering into the darkened, empty street, he was on hyperalert. Mort's behaviour back at the house had spooked him and now he felt like a sitting duck. It was decision time.

'Something's wrong here,' he told Tannaz. 'We need to move. Grab your bag and follow me.' Checking the coast was clear, he pushed open the door and got out, but Tannaz seemed to be taking her time.

'We don't have time for this!' he hissed, yanking open the passenger door.

Catching the urgency in his voice, she scrambled out and together they hurried down a narrow alleyway, past shuttered windows and darkened doorways. The place looked deserted. They were a hundred metres or so from where they'd left the car when Luke spotted a gap between two houses and a flight of crumbling steps leading up. 'This way,' he whispered, and grabbed Tannaz's hand, but she pulled back.

'What about Farz?' she pleaded. 'We should wait for him.'

Luke grunted and looked back to where her friend's car sat empty, bathed in a yellow halo of light from a single streetlamp. 'Farz has done all he can,' he replied. 'The longer he's with me, the more of a risk he's taking.' Tannaz didn't seem convinced by this but he gave her no time to argue. Taking her hand, he made for the steps, emerging onto a flat roof. They were alone but a rising tide of voices was flowing up and over from the other side. It sounded like an argument.

Crouching low, Luke and Tannaz edged their way to where they could look down without being seen. Suddenly she let out a gasp and clamped her hand to her mouth.

'Shit!' Luke hissed, pulling Tannaz down and away from the roof edge. Below them a crowd had gathered, forming a circle. And in the middle of that circle were a dozen dark-green-uniformed policemen. They had their guns drawn and two were shouting excitedly into walkie-talkies while two others roughly frisked the shambolic figure that stood at the very centre.

It was Farz and he was absolutely terrified.

Chapter 74

Gulf of Oman

PLUCKED FROM THE waters of the Gulf of Oman by the nuclear-powered *Astute*, Barkwell and his SBS assault team climbed down from the engine-room hatch and shed their wetsuits. It was a drill they had rehearsed many times. Space was always at a premium on submarines and the sixteen operators were now crammed uncomfortably close together in the after escape platform, situated between the vessel's nuclear reactor and its main machinery spaces. Royal Navy ratings in functional dark blue overalls busied around them, then moved aside as an officer came in, blue shirt, gold-and-black epaulettes indicating the rank of a Lieutenant Commander, her blonde hair tied back. There were a few surprised looks on the faces of the SBS men. She was used to that and dealt with it immediately.

'Welcome aboard, gentlemen,' she told them. 'I'm Lieutenant Commander Jess Pearson and, yes, you've guessed correctly, I'm a woman. It might shock you to hear we've had women on Royal Navy submarines since 2014.' She paused, as if challenging anyone to come back with an ill-advised comment. No one said a word. 'Right. We've got about an eight-hour passage ahead of us so please make yourselves at home. I'll take you forward now. We'll get you some food and give you a safety brief, then take you to your accommodation. It's not exactly the Ritz down here. We've put you in the bomb shop, next to the torpedoes, so no lighting up, if you don't mind. In fact, the whole boat is no smoking.' Her look was severe but her eyes were smiling as she turned to the troop commander. 'Captain Barkwell, if you'd like to follow me afterwards we've got a bunk for you to kip down in, when the Duty Weapons Officer isn't in it.'

There were a few nudged elbows at that and murmurs from the troop of 'It's all right for some,' but most of the men knew their commander would be spending much of the passage working up plans and going over every possible contingency.

Once he'd seen his men settled in, Barkwell followed the submariner to the control room. A keen long-distance runner, he couldn't understand how anyone would want to spend their lives cooped up in such a place. A spaghetti of pipes ran along the ceiling while every last inch of workspace was crammed with screens and complex electronic equipment. An orange glow came from a large bulb in a corner and there was a strange smell that he put down to some cleaning product. The whole place was a mystery to him.

She led Barkwell to where two officers were poring over an electronic chart of the Strait of Hormuz shipping lanes. They straightened as he approached, and the taller of the two held out his hand. 'Commander Ben Wallis. Glad you made it aboard okay. No injuries?'

'None, thank you, sir.' Barkwell passed a hand through his already thinning hair, still wet and glossy from the parachute drop into the sea.

'Good. Let me bring you up to speed. There's good news and bad news. The Iranians have stepped up their patrols in this area. They're on a state of high alert. They seem to suspect something's coming their way. Can't think why.'

Barkwell caught the faintest twinkle in the naval officer's eye. 'What have they deployed, sir?' he asked.

'Everything. They're putting up helicopters, maritime patrol aircraft, small craft, larger vessels, the lot.' Wallis gave him an even stare. 'We should be able to handle it on the insertion phase but the extraction could be a bit lively. Here.' Wallis beckoned him to the chart. 'Let me show you how it's looking. Excuse me, Vasco.'

Barkwell had to think for a moment, then remembered: 'Vasco', in Royal Navy jargon, was any navigating officer, after the sixteenth-century Portuguese explorer Vasco da Gama. Now he gave Barkwell a cursory nod and made space for him at the charts.

Wallis squeezed between them and jabbed his finger at a point midway between the coasts of Oman and Iran. 'This is us here, right now, in international waters, where we picked you up from the drop zone. We've got about a hundred and eighty-five nautical miles to run from here to just off Qeshm Island where you'll egress and go ashore. The first hundred and twenty are in open ocean so I can plan on a speed of approach of sixteen knots or more. That should take us eight hours. With me so far?' He looked up from the chart to check he still had the SBS man's full attention.

Barkwell nodded. He was listening intently but a voice in the back of his head was shouting: 'Eight hours? Christ. Can't this thing go any faster? Chaplin could be dead by the time we get there!'

'Now,' said Wallis, waving his hand over the narrow Strait of Hormuz, 'this is where it gets tasty. You're aware of the tanker plan, yes?'

'I am, sir.'

'Good. Well, the *Ocean Star* is currently travelling four miles to the east of us, on a parallel course. Just before she reaches the narrowest part of the strait – just here – we'll be positioning ourselves under her, like a pilot fish with a shark, if you will. We'll stay under her for the next forty-five miles, or about three hours, to take us past the Musandam peninsula. That should get us through the area of intensive Iranian surveillance – radar, sonar, aerial, the works.'

'And if her crew find out we're hitching a ride beneath her?' said Barkwell.

Commander Wallis gave him a mirthless grin. 'They won't,' he said. 'Trust me. I've done this before.' He pointed once more at the chart, hovering over the narrow expanse of blue water between the tip of the Omani coast and the shoreline of Iran's Qeshm Island.

'This,' he went on, 'is where we'll do the creep-in for the final twenty miles. It's our period of maximum risk once we're out from under the tanker so we'll only be doing around four knots. And that's where you'll exit my boat and make the final approach.'

'I'll be giving your team plenty of notice,' interjected Lieutenant Commander Pearson. She had maintained a respectful silence during the briefing but she, too, was following every word.

'Appreciate it, ma'am,' said Barkwell, then turned back to Wallis. 'Did I hear you say there was some good news, sir?'

'You did. We've got you *Chalfont*, the latest swimmer delivery vehicle, for your final approach inshore. We picked her up in Duqm harbour in Oman and had her fitted onto the hull only yesterday. You might have seen her sitting aft of the fin when you came aboard.'

Barkwell shook his head. He'd been too busy getting his team recovered from the sea in the dark to notice anything else. 'That's good news,' he observed, but frowned under Wallis's seemingly critical gaze.

'You look concerned,' said the submariner.

'Sorry. No. Look, this is all brilliant. I've just got some worries over the variables once we get ashore. That's all.'

'Ah. That's understandable.' Not his problem.

An hour later, in his bunk, Barkwell lay awake thinking, and worrying. One thing was glaringly absent in all this: a covert operator already on land to guide them in. Bloody MI6 spooks, this was supposed to be their job. Those johnnies at Vauxhall Cross had proved to be all talk and no trousers.

Chapter 75

Bandar Khamir, Iran

MORT. IT HAD to have been Mort. The scheming bastard. There could be no other explanation. No one else had known their plans. And, for whatever screwed-up reason, he had chosen to betray not only him and Tannaz but his 'friend' Farz. And Farz was in a bad place right now. Luke had crawled forward to the edge of the roof. There he was, surrounded by armed police. His hands were behind his head as one police officer shone a torch into his face and another patted him down. What they found wouldn't make any difference. Farz was doomed. Once the interrogations began they'd get the whole story out of him: Luke, Tannaz, the journey from Tehran. Helping a foreign spy evade capture? They would hang him. Luke felt sick at the thought.

What made it worse was that he could do nothing to help. And he knew he couldn't afford to spend time thinking about it. They had a few minutes, no more, in which to get away. The police would find the car, then fan out and find them. There were no hiding places for two fugitives in the tiny fishing village. He looked back at Tannaz. Her hand was still over her mouth and she shook with fear. Luke scrambled over to her.

'Tannaz!' he hissed. 'Listen to me. We've got to go!' He rose, grabbed her hand and hauled her to her feet. 'Now!'

Keeping low, they raced back to the steps and went down them two at a time. At the bottom, they halted to catch their breath. The sandy street was empty in both directions, and no light came from the dark windows. Luke was checking the coast was clear when he felt Tannaz grab his arm. 'This way,' she said.

Luke fought the temptation to run as they made their way down a narrow lane. He braced himself as a figure loomed out of the darkness, but it was just a stooped old woman. As she shuffled past them, he noticed a pile of discarded clothes that had been left outside a door. He bent over and picked up an old blue shawl. He handed it to Tannaz.

'You need to change your appearance,' he told her. 'We both do. They'll have got descriptions from Mort. This should at least give you a chance if we get separated.' She paused and looked at the tatty shawl – in Tehran she wouldn't have been seen dead in it – then threw it over her head and shoulders.

'It had better not have fleas,' she said. She had guts, Luke gave her that, but fleas, he thought, were the least of their problems right now.

At the end of the lane, he stopped and turned back, listening for sounds of pursuit. In the distance there came the long, mournful wail of a police siren, growing fainter. He and Tannaz looked at each other in silence. That would be Farz, off to the cells. Then a thought struck him, and he held out his hand to the girl. 'Tannaz, give me your phone.' It sounded harsher than he'd intended.

'What? Why?' There was a quaver in her voice. Luke's entire working life had been spent confronting jeopardy so he could only guess at how utterly terrifying this must be for a pampered city girl. She looked at him, eyes glinting from under the shawl.

'Tannaz, please, trust me.'

Grudgingly, she passed him her smartphone, encased in a lurid gold cover.

'Sorry about this.' He let it fall, then stamped on it twice until it crunched and splintered.

'What the fuck?' she hissed. 'Are you crazy?' She lashed out at him, too late to stop him. 'Why would you do that?'

Luke caught her arm easily. 'Tracking,' he explained. 'They'll have your number by now. They'll be using it to find your location – our location.'

'Come on,' she said, holding out her hand. 'Now you give me yours.'

Luke shook his head. 'Sorry, Tannaz, it doesn't work like that—'

'Don't patronize me!'

'I'm sorry, that's not how I meant it. My phone doesn't have an Iranian number. It's not on their network so they can't trace it.'

They could ill afford this, he thought. They were being hunted down by Iranian police and security and what were they doing? Standing bickering in a back-street while the net closed around them. They needed to put some distance between themselves and this place. Luke bent to pick up the fragments of phone and threw them into a nearby pile of rubbish. It might buy them a few more minutes at most.

The alley opened out onto a metalled road. There was no sign of anyone about. According to a battered sign, bathed in the murky yellow light of a single sodium lamp, this was 'Route 96'. Seconds passed. The place was silent. Luke was about to step out but pulled back into the shadows as headlights swept round a corner towards them, accompanied by the grinding roar of a heavy vehicle. A lorry full of soldiers rumbled past. Were they looking for them? Luke couldn't be sure but he bet the chances were high. He could hear the lorry slowing and stopping further down the road. Letting off soldiers to search for them? Come on, Carlton, he told himself, get a grip. You've got to keep moving.

On the other side of the road there were no buildings, only darkness and silence. The village of Bandar Khamir had simply petered out. Crossing was their only option.

Luke sensed Tannaz just behind him. He turned and gave what he hoped was an encouraging look. 'When I say go, we run across, okay?' She nodded. He scanned the road in both directions. No traffic. But from the direction in which the lorry had gone, beams of light swept left and right. It was now or never.

Luke took Tannaz's hand and together they sprinted over. He half expected a shout or shots or both, but there was nothing, only soft ground underfoot and darkness all around them. They kept going, blindly, moving away from the road, leaving the village behind, until mud began to suck and claw at their feet. Luke had a sudden image of them caught in quicksand and stopped abruptly. There were new noises all around them now. Wet, gurgling sounds that came up from the mud, rustlings and, sure enough, the gentle slap of waves breaking on the shoreline ahead.

Luke's night vision had returned and his eyes had adjusted to the little ambient light there was. Early in his military career, even on the bleak, treeless slopes of Dartmoor, he had discovered there was no such thing as total darkness. He surveyed the ground at their feet where pale shapes skittered back and forth.

Tannaz let out a gasp and grabbed his hand. 'What *is* that?' she cried.

'They're crabs,' he reassured her.

'Crabs?' She sounded alarmed.

'Yes. I think we're on the edge of a swamp. Those look like mangroves over there. Which means the sea is close by.' Luke reached out and held her shoulders as if to steady her, then gently took her chin in his hand and raised her face towards his. 'So listen carefully, Tannaz, because you need to know this. They – the police, the security people, your father's people – are going to throw everything at us now. Helicopters, searchlights, infrared cameras . . . dogs.' At the mention of dogs he felt her shudder.

'I hate dogs,' she whispered.

German shepherds, he thought, that's what they'll send after us. 'So here's the thing.' He looked away for a moment. Should he say what he was about to? Yes, he should. It was the right thing to do. 'It's not too late for you, Tannaz. It's me they're after. You can turn back and give yourself up. Tell them I forced you to do this. Take your chances. Use your dad's connections. Because this way . . .' he pointed ahead, towards the forbidding darkness of the swamp '. . . this way is going to be tough. I've got to find a boat and get across to Qeshm Island. God knows, I might even

300

have to swim part of the way. And there's no easy outcome at the end of this, you know that.'

'What's that?' she replied.

'What d'you mean "what's that"?' I've just laid it all out for you.' Luke tried to keep the irritation out of his voice. Was she deliberately playing dumb?

'No! Quiet!' she ordered. 'That sound.' And then Luke heard it too. The low thud of rotors. The unmistakable beat of an approaching helicopter.

Chapter 76

Onboard HMS Astute, *Strait of Hormuz*

CRAMPED AND RESTLESS, the SBS assault team lay on their bunks, endlessly stripping, oiling and reassembling their weapons. Hemmed in by the narrow confines of the submarine, they packed and repacked their bergens, between dozing fitfully or queuing for one of *Astute's* five showers. All of them, from Captain Barkwell downwards, loathed being cooped up on a sub.

In *Astute's* control room, amid the constant electronic hum, the command went out over the tannoy, crisp and clear: 'Action stations!' There was no melodrama, no hysteria, no fuss, just intense concentration as everyone shifted into a higher gear. Coming up in the dark from sixty metres depth, everyone aboard *Astute* knew they were entering a phase where the smallest miscalculation could prove catastrophic.

Just over a mile out from the tanker MV *Ocean Star,* the nuclear submarine came up to periscope depth to confirm visual identification. The crew of *Astute* needed to take in a final SATCOM message update before they submerged once more, to position the submarine beneath the unsuspecting merchant vessel. Commander Wallis frowned as he studied the perforated sheet of

302

paper in his hand. It was a printout of a message from Permanent Joint Headquarters at Northwood, beamed down via satellite. He looked up and called to a man standing with his back to him, his Executive Officer. 'Maritime Patrol Aircraft have declared a CERTSUB.'

The XO turned round and took the printout from him. A CERTSUB was the highest submarine-detection signal and it meant that somewhere out there a hostile sub was patrolling beneath these same waves.

'It's the *Tareq*, out of Bandar Abbas,' Wallis continued. 'One of Iran's Russian-built Kilo-class boats. She may be old and diesel-powered but she's horribly quiet. We'll have to keep on our toes.'

Every British submarine commander knew that the Iranian Navy had spent years developing their concealment skills. Taking full advantage of the topography at the entrance to the Gulf, they would sit, silent and undetected, just waiting for a big fat target to steam into range.

If *Astute*'s captain was anxious, he didn't show it. The moment Ben Wallis got confirmation of *Ocean Star*'s course and speed, he ordered the sub to be taken back down to sixty metres. Standing just behind his XO and flicking his eyes across the screens in the control room, he told him to increase speed to close the gap with the tanker ahead. Wallis watched approvingly as *Astute*'s sonar adjusted her position, drawing on its legendary processing power, equivalent to two thousand laptops. A rating appeared at his side to offer him a mug of tea but Wallis waved him away: he needed absolute focus for this, and expected the same from his crew. Now he ordered the submarine up to the initial transit depth, allowing a clear fifty metres between her hull and the seabed.

'Keep the speed level with *Ocean Star*'s,' he ordered.

The atmosphere in the control room was quiet but tense, the calm before the storm. They were now at the narrowest point of the Strait of Hormuz, where the Omani and Iranian coastlines crowded towards each other to create one of the world's most infamous maritime chokepoints. Block this off and you disrupt the entire world's energy supplies. Wallis knew this and so did everyone in Whitehall. But right now he had other concerns. Any minute now this leviathan of a tanker above him was going to change course to angle herself around the contours of the Musandam peninsula. He needed to anticipate this accurately so that the sub remained directly beneath her hull.

'Course zero four eight,' he called, then ordered an adjustment on the helm. 'One right, up one rev.'

For just over three hours *Astute* manoeuvred through the strait, her crew straining to keep her undetected by hostile eyes and ears. By now she was concealed inside the digital 'blob' of the much larger MV *Ocean Star* above her. But, like all merchant ships navigating through this congested waterway, the tanker was changing course at frequent intervals, moving in a 'dog-leg' pattern that required constant, nail-biting attention from Wallis and his crew. Each of them knew that if they allowed her to stray outside that digital bubble she would likely be detected within seconds by *Tareq* or an Iranian surveillance plane. The entire rescue mission could be compromised.

In the control room Wallis was at 'the plot', studying his charts. So far, the transit had gone without a hitch. They had successfully turned the corner into the entrance of the Gulf, leaving the Arabian Sea and the Indian Ocean behind them. *Astute* was exactly where she should be: midway between the northernmost tip of Oman and the nearest point on the Iranian coast, the coast of Qeshm Island. Churning through the shallow waters above them, the MV *Ocean Star* would be steaming on to Kharg Island to pick up her cargo of crude. It was time to disengage from her. Once more Commander Wallis took the boat to action stations and slowed her right down, allowing the merchant vessel to pull ahead, oblivious to the underwater parasite she had just concealed for the last forty-five miles. Then he brought *Astute* up to periscope depth.

Wallis correctly assessed that the sea immediately behind the tanker would have been 'swept' clear by her passage. He was not unduly worried when the Officer of the Watch alerted him to several nearby blips on the sonar screen. Commercial traffic was to be expected in the crowded waterway of the Strait of Hormuz. Visually and electronically, Wallis used the periscope to scan the horizon, taking his time, swivelling from one vessel's outline to the next.

No one in that control room had ever heard him swear. In fact, Commander Ben Wallis rarely raised his voice unless it was absolutely necessary. So what he said next was all the more shocking to those around him.

'Fuck me!' he exclaimed. 'It's the *Tareq*! She's right there, four hundred metres off our starboard bow, just sitting on the surface.' He turned to the Officer of the Watch, alarm written all over his face. 'Take us down to sixty metres now!'

Chapter 77

Strait of Hormuz

KAMRAN DARZI KEPT the throttle on low as he nosed the speed-boat out of the inlet, just south of the Namakdan Salt Caves. A professional cigarette smuggler by trade, he knew exactly how long he needed to wait before the next Iranian border patrol boat would pass. His father had been a smuggler before him and had schooled him well. How many hundreds of times had he made the lightning dash across the strait between Iran and the Omani port of Khasab? He had given up counting. And how many times had he been caught? Once. Just once in twenty-three years. A quick bribe paid into the right hands and it was resolved. A few crates of contraband cigarettes lost, but that was all. And that was ancient history now. So when the man with the IRGC connections had approached him that afternoon in the café on Imam Mousa Sadr Street he had had few qualms. It wasn't cigarettes this time, and they wouldn't tell him exactly what they wanted shipped across, but the money was good and he didn't need to ask questions.

Darzi gripped the boat's wheel and looked up at the moon as it slipped out from behind a cloud, then vanished once more. His teenage son was beside him, learning the trade just as he had, scanning the horizon intently with a set of powerful Russian night-vision goggles.

'*Ab saaf,*' said the boy. 'The coast is clear.'

With a subdued roar, Darzi opened up the engines. Two Johnson 250 h.p. outboards surged into life, thrusting the bow into the air as the boat accelerated towards its top speed of more than 50 knots.

Fifty-three minutes after leaving Qeshm Island they slowed the engines. In front of them the rugged, imposing silhouette of the Omani coastline rose out of the waters of the Gulf. It seemed as if everything had been arranged. A 4x4 jeep – with Dubai plates and UAE registration – was waiting. Waves lapped at the sides of the boat, rocking it gently in the shallows where a figure waited. An eager pair of hands reached up and took the package that Kamran Darzi passed over. The transaction complete, he pushed the throttle into reverse and took the boat out into open water. The handover had taken seconds. It was easy money for a few hours' work.

Six thousand four hundred metres above the Omani coast, the attention of the crew of the RAF Sentinel was focused on other things, like the encrypted radio transmissions coming out of Shahid Bahonar naval base. A nocturnal crossing by just another cigarette smuggler's boat was of no interest to them.

Oblivious to the plane above, the 4x4 pulled away from the jetty and sped along a rutted mountain back-road that avoided the official Oman–UAE border crossing. Heading westwards in the dark, headlights switched off, the Iranian expatriate in the driving seat kept one hand on the wheel while the other rested protectively on the package on the seat beside him. He had been told in no uncertain terms what would happen to him and his family should he fail to deliver its contents intact and on time. It was shortly before ten p.m. when he merged the jeep into the stream of traffic clogging the motorway that linked the emirate of Sharjah to neighbouring Dubai, just another 4x4 among the thousands that passed through daily.

He took his eye off the road for a moment to glance down at his watch: 22.04. Still time. Last pick-up at the FedEx World Service counter was at 22.30. He looked up, swerved, narrowly missing a white pick-up, then indicated left and turned off the motorway into Quds Street and Dubai Airport Free Zone. He parked up next to Terminal Two and hurried through the door of the FedEx office. It was 22.21 and an Indian expat in a grey uniform was posted by the door, waiting to close it. He took his place in the queue, anxiously keeping an eye on the clock as the woman at the front hunted through her bag for something.

When it came to his turn he handed over the package and paid in cash. He wrote 'Commercial Samples' on the shipping label, adding the words 'No Commercial Value'. He grinned to himself as he entered a made-up name and address as the sender. In the box marked 'Addressee' he was careful to get everything just right.

H.E. The British Ambassador
British Embassy
Al Seef Road
Bur Dubai
PO Box 65
Dubai

It was as he was filling in the various labels that he smelt something. He sniffed. Was it his imagination or could he detect something faintly acrid and medicinal? He dismissed it as paranoia but decided that he really did not want to know what was inside that package.

Chapter 78

Haraye Khamir Mangrove Forest, Iran

LUKE RECOGNIZED THE sound at once. And then he saw it. A Bell Huey helicopter, low in the night sky, heading straight for them, its searchlight sweeping left and right, probing into the darkness that hid them. There was no time to think, no time to plan, just immediate evasive action.

'Run!' Luke shouted. 'Get into the water!' he yelled at Tannaz above the approaching clatter of the helicopter blades. Infrared, he was thinking. Shit. If they've got infrared night-vision goggles we're going to stand out like Christmas trees. Hiding in the water was their only hope.

Together they stumbled and ran through the oozing mud, tripping on mangrove roots in the dark as the noise of the helicopter filled their ears. He heard Tannaz cry out in fear. The searchlight beam was swinging closer to them. Seeking them out. Luke urged her on, dragging her alongside him until their feet hit the sand of the shoreline and they hurtled headlong into the inky waters of the Gulf.

'Get down!' he urged her. Tannaz couldn't hear him, she was still standing half out of the water, staring up at the helicopter above them, transfixed by the cacophony from its rotor blades as it hovered along the shoreline. The down-draught from the rotors was whipping up the water, driving a wall of spray into their eyes. It felt like they were in the eye of a hurricane.

Luke reached up and pulled her down into the water. He began to kick out, swim away from the shore, Tannaz following him. But now the search beam was racing across the water towards them. If it didn't change course it would find them any second now.

'Dive!' he yelled, twisting his head round in the water to check she was still with him. Luke took a last gulp of air and plunged under the surface, just as the silver beam began to light up the surface above him. He held his breath for as long as he could, groping his way to the shallow seabed, reaching out to grab hold of submerged mangrove roots as the gust from the helicopter rocked the water. He prayed that Tannaz was doing the same.

Fifty-five seconds later he broke the surface, gasping for air, shaking the water out of his eyes. Tannaz was nowhere to be seen but, looking up, he was greeted by the sweetest sight he could have hoped for: the chopper's red tail-light receding into the night sky, its searchlight still sweeping to and fro. It had missed them.

'I'm over here!' He could hear Tannaz's voice, high and plaintive, from somewhere across the water. Struggling to his feet in the soft sand, he waded towards her. She was back on the shore where they had just come from, sitting on the mud, her knees drawn up to her chest. She was trembling with cold and fear. He sat down next to her and pulled her close to him, sharing his body warmth with her.

'What are we doing here?' she asked. 'This is crazy, just crazy!' She was shaking her head in despair.

I did try to warn you, Tannaz. But there was no point in telling her that. He – they – needed to stay focused. They were cold, wet and being hunted, like prey, and Luke understood only too well that it was at this point, when the odds seemed stacked against you, despair could set in. He remembered a survival exercise in Scotland to avoid capture by the hunter force of Paras. He had learned a lot about himself that day. Now he needed to sort himself out and remind himself of what this mission was about. Get

310

to Qeshm Island. Locate Zamani and his hostage. Guide in the rescue team. If he could just focus on that, everything else would fall into place – in theory. Luke examined his phone, turning it over in his hand. The digital display was blinking on and off, and he could see the battery was already running low, but at least they'd given him a waterproof model.

With the helicopter gone, the sounds of the swamp had returned, with all its invisible slitherings and scuttlings. He should probably warn her about snakes, but there was only so much he could heap on her at one time.

'It's not just us two facing a crisis,' he told her. 'These are crazy times for the whole country. So listen, Tannaz, this is what needs to happen now. We're going to work our way around this shore-line until we can find a boat to steal.'

'Steal a boat?' she questioned.

'Yes.'

Tannaz thought about this, then shrugged. 'Okay. And then?'

'Then we'll get across to Qeshm and find your dad. You'll go to him and plead with him to end this hostage crisis. That's our plan, right?'

She didn't answer.

'Tannaz? That's the plan, okay? Because if we don't get to him before the deadline expires, the hostage could die and that would be a disaster for Iran. It might result in a war and your country would be ruined.'

'I don't know,' she murmured, her voice tailing off. 'I just don't know how he will react. My father can be very cruel. That's why Mama is leaving him.' She looked up at him, as if suddenly remembering he was there. 'What do you think he will say to me?'

'I have no idea, but I do know we've got to keep going. The police and security people will keep looking for us, and when daylight comes they'll find our footprints so we don't have much time.' He helped her to her feet and brushed the mud off her shawl. 'Let's get moving.' He checked his diver's watch and bit his lip. Less than ten hours before the ultimatum ran out.

*

311

The going was slow but they were helped by the crescent moon that now rose above the horizon, casting enough of its cold light to guide them along the shore. Neither spoke.

It was Tannaz who spotted them. In the distance, the twinkling lights of a fishing village on the coast of Qeshm. Too far to swim, but at least they had something to aim for. It was another hour before they found what they were looking for: roped to a mangrove tree and bobbing gently in the water, a small open boat, its outboard motor tilted up out of the mud. Could you hotwire an outboard? Luke knew plenty of people he'd served with in the SBS who could. He wasn't one of them. His question proved academic. As he and Tannaz grabbed hold of the boat's gunwales and were about to climb in, a figure clutching a boat hook reared up and lurched towards them, yelling in Farsi. Luke was ready to fend off the attack that seemed to be coming, but the man they'd disturbed was elderly. He looked more frightened than threatening.

Tannaz answered the man, her voice low and soothing, and he lowered the boathook. She had reached into a pocket and pulled out a wad of sodden banknotes and was holding them out to him. Luke could see him thinking this one through as he hesitated. What could a young city girl and a Western man be doing, their clothes soaked, on the edge of this mangrove swamp in the middle of the night? Were they eloping? Indulging in immoral relations? Should he report them to the authorities? But his eyes kept flicking back to the banknotes, and Luke breathed a sigh of relief when he saw him take them from Tannaz and stuff them into his top pocket. They climbed into his boat.

After what they had just been through, the sound of an outboard coughing into life, then puttering them out into open water, was familiar and reassuring. They were still wet and cold, but at least they were on their way. The sea's surface caught the moonlight in a myriad tiny silver reflections and the occasional fish leaped clear of the water as they passed, returning with a gentle plop. The boat's engine was old and weak, and was chugging along at less than ten knots, but Luke had reason to be relieved.

They had escaped Bandar Abbas and were on their way to Qeshm. He settled back on a coil of rope and turned his face against the wind, rubbing the scarred stump of his missing finger. It always ached as the adrenalin began to ease off. Lulled by the gentle sound of the engine, he dozed off.

He awoke to the crunch of the boat sliding up onto sand and shingle.

'Jazireh-o-Qeshm,' the old man announced. They had arrived.

A cloud had passed over the moon but in the faint light Luke could see the outline of low buildings a few hundred yards along the shore. He moved to the front of the boat and jumped clear, landing with a crunch on the wet shingle.

'Wait here and I'll help you down,' he called to Tannaz, then went off to check that the shoreline was deserted. A stifled cry of pain greeted him when he got back. Tannaz had ignored his suggestion and jumped, landing awkwardly on her ankle. He rushed over to her and found her wincing in pain and gripping her leg. 'Tannaz! Let me see if you've broken anything.'

But she waved him away. *'Khaak bar saret,'* she moaned. 'God damn you.'

Luke ignored her protests and gently felt around her ankle. It wasn't broken but it was almost certainly sprained. She'd be unable to walk on it now. Behind them came the sound of the fisherman pushing off from the shore, then the putter of his outboard as he pulled away. In the silence, a dog barked in the distance. They were alone, marooned on the shore, with no means of transport, and they had just one dodgy phone with a dying battery between them. There were only a few hours left to hide before daylight. And one of them couldn't walk. Brilliant, Luke thought. We are completely fucked.

313

Chapter 79

British Embassy, Dubai

SHORTLY BEFORE MIDNIGHT a white van, emblazoned with the words 'FedEx Express' in English and Arabic, pulled up close to the well-guarded gates of the British Embassy in Dubai. Having checked the paperwork, the driver stepped down from his cab, walked to the sentry house next to the gate and tapped on the reinforced glass. One of the two Gurkha guards on duty recognized the man and waved him round to a side window. There he handed over the package. Neither large nor heavy but bulging slightly in the middle, the white envelope was wrapped in cellophane. It was addressed to the Ambassador and marked 'Urgent'. The junior Gurkha on night duty who signed for it followed the standard protocol: he passed it through the embassy's HI-SCAN 7555 high-resolution X-ray sensor, checking for any microscopic particles of explosive residue. When the LED display on the machine signalled 'Clear', he carried the package across the embassy's inner courtyard, past the well-watered lawns and flowering bougainvillaea, and inside the main building to the night duty officer.

John Holmes was a retired policeman: thirty-one years of service with the West Yorkshire Police, several on the homicide and major inquiry team, before he'd taken a nice retirement job at the embassy in Dubai. John reckoned he'd seen most things in his time. Not a lot, he told people, could shock him, these days. So when the guard handed him the parcel and he started to open it on the table in his office, his mind was on other things. It was coming up to his ex-wife's birthday and he really ought to get himself down to the gold souk and buy her something decent this time.

It was the moment the smell hit his nostrils that he knew something was wrong. Using a stainless-steel letter-opener, Holmes slit open the cellophane wrapper and immediately recoiled. Jesus, what was that? He stopped, went over to a drawer in the cupboard and pulled on a pair of blue forensic gloves. Ever so carefully, he teased out the paper padding inside the envelope. It was the front page of yesterday's edition of Iran's *Kayhan* newspaper. A small, laminated card, about the size of a business card, dropped onto the table. On it was printed:

Sevenoaks Library
Buckhurst Lane, Sevenoaks, TL13 1LQ
Member: G. Chaplin
Membership No.: 4365

And at the top right-hand corner a photograph left no doubt as to who the library card belonged to: the Right Honourable Geoffrey Chaplin, Secretary of State for Foreign and Commonwealth Affairs.

But there was something else inside the envelope and now Holmes reached in to pull it out. Blue cellophane had been wrapped around a small cylindrical object. He looked more closely at it. It appeared to be stained a deep red and felt slightly soft to the touch. With a rising sense of revulsion, John Holmes suddenly knew exactly what it was.

'Jesus Christ,' he said, to the empty room. 'They've hacked off his bloody finger!'

Chapter 80

IN LONDON THE lights were burning on the sixth floor at Vauxhall Cross. Angela Scott paused in front of the outer door to the Chief's office and checked her reflection in one of the framed glass photographs on the wall. The tired face of a forty-one-year-old career intelligence officer stared back at her, surreally superimposed onto an image of the Prince of Wales visiting MI6 headquarters.

As Luke Carlton's line manager, she was on point for the Iran op, so the buck stopped with her. Sending him on a live mission into Iran, a 'hostile nation', had always been a gamble but it was one she'd been willing to take. He had initiative – he had more than proved that in South America – and he clearly had balls of steel. So she had backed him, against the advice of some of her seniors, and been vindicated. Only today his getting them Zamani's private phone number had been hailed as nothing short of a triumph. GCHQ now had a fix on Zamani's location.

But something was wrong. Luke had missed both his last two check-in times. It was supposed to be a simple coded text message – the single word 'Iskander' – sent through the VPN network via Akrotiri. Just enough to let his controllers in London know he was okay and still on-mission. Protocol dictated she

316

shouldn't contact him for another hour. Case officers can make mistakes, they're only human, or they can be engaged in something so sensitive they can't make the call at the appointed time. But when the silence from Luke extended past the second hour a knot of worry began to grow and fester in the pit of Angela's stomach. This was unlike Luke. He would be well aware of the pressure mounting on the Service. COBRA, the National Security Council, Number 10 – they were all demanding to know when MI6's man on the ground would be ready to guide in the rescue team. So now Angela was going to have to confess to the Chief that her protégé had gone dark on them.

She lifted her hand to knock on the outer door but it swung open before she could. The Chief's PA was waiting for her. An intense, earnest young man, he now stood awkwardly in the doorway, waving her past him into the inner sanctum. 'You'll have to be quick,' he told her, as Angela brushed past with murmured thanks. 'C's about to head across the river.'

They stood in the Chief's office, at opposite ends of the gaudy Caucasian carpet, an unsolicited gift from some distant intelligence service in one of the former Soviet republics. Sir Adam Keeling already had his overcoat on and was hunting around for his glasses.

'Your man Carlton did well,' he told Angela briskly. 'That phone number came at exactly the right time. The wheels are turning now. So, I gather you've got an update for me?'

Angela swallowed hard. *Don't look nervous. Just give it to him straight.* 'I know it's not what you want to hear, Chief.' Keeling stopped searching for his glasses and frowned at her. 'But we've lost contact with Luke Carlton. He's missed the last two check-ins.'

She saw him take a pace backwards and, for one awful moment, she thought he was going to explode with anger. Hell, it was hardly her fault that Luke had gone silent – he'd have a good reason for it. She just couldn't produce it right now.

Keeling pursed his lips. She could see him thinking hard, and when he spoke, it was as if he were making a supreme effort to

317

control himself. 'I am quite certain,' he said slowly, 'that you'll make every effort to locate him. Luke is instrumental to this whole operation. Please, Angela, just find him and keep him focused on the endgame. Now, if you'll excuse me, I have to be in the Cabinet Office.'

For the first time in her career, Angela Scott found herself standing alone in the private office of the Chief of the Secret Intelligence Service. She looked up past the row of souvenir gifts arranged on the windowsill – the carved wooden seagull, the miniature Omani incense burner, the curved Bahraini dagger – all donated over the years by intelligence partners around the world. Her gaze went beyond them to a barge on the Thames far below. It was emerging from beneath the darkened arches of Vauxhall Bridge. As she watched it, she felt sick with worry. *Right now I have no idea if Luke is alive, dead or, quite conceivably, being carted off in chains for an Iranian interrogation. And I was the one who sent him.*

Chapter 81

HMS Juffair *Naval Base, Bahrain*

BLEARY-EYED, EXHAUSTED AND surrounded by the detritus of a team on high alert, Lieutenant Colonel Chip Nuttall, Commanding Officer, SBS, stared at the screen in front of him, his head held between his hands. A green blip on the monitor showed the location of HMS *Astute* as she made painfully slow progress through the Strait of Hormuz. To the north and to the east, a scattering of red blips indicated the known positions of Iranian naval vessels.

Like all of his team, Nuttall was running on caffeine and adrenalin. The bin beside his desk inside the Royal Navy base at Mina Salman port in Bahrain was overflowing with half-compacted pizza boxes. A camp bed had been set up in the room next door for impromptu catnaps that rarely lasted more than twenty minutes.

From the moment the assault team had boarded the C130 in Oman, he and his staff had monitored them without a break from their forward base in Bahrain. Nuttall had chosen Captain Barkwell for this job, and in turn allowed him to pick his own operators from the standby squadron at Poole. He would have liked a bit of back-up from the Special Forces support group at St Athan, but Number 10 had been adamant: this had to be covert, which meant it had to stay small and it had to be discreet.

'Boss.' A voice behind him distracted him from the screen. 'You've got a visitor.' Nodding his thanks, Nuttall rubbed a hand across his face and stood. A young marine was at the door, showing in a US officer. Nuttall recognized him straight away. Tall, tanned, massive shoulders, chiselled jaw, Josh Katz was his opposite number in Bahrain, Commander of the US Navy's SEAL special forces contingent. They had met years ago on a Special Warfare course at Coronado in San Diego and bonded immediately, trading too many tequila slammers on the last night and challenging each other to bouts of arm-wrestling while men thumped tables and called for more beer. Nuttall smiled. That seemed a lifetime ago now.

'Yo, Chip.' Katz strode up to him and gave him a bear hug, then stepped back to look him up and down. 'You look beat, man.'

'Thanks.'

'Listen, you haven't seen me here.' The American's voice was suddenly serious. 'Can we get us some privacy?'

'Of course,' Nuttall replied, pointing to the anteroom with the bunk bed. Closing the door behind him, he turned to Katz. 'Okay, you were never here. So what's up?'

'I'm serious,' said Katz, glancing towards the door. 'This conversation never took place. But I wanted to let you know, speaking as one pro operator to another, that something very big is going down very soon. Something that's gonna impact big-time on your op.'

'Meaning?'

'Orders from the top. You'll appreciate I can't give you any details. But certain people in DC have . . . How can I put it?' He paused, searching for the right words. 'Look, they've simply run out of patience with the Iranians on this one. It's the final straw. They think the Iranian government's up to its neck in this kidnapping of your minister and now they're just stalling you Brits.'

Chip Nuttall's expression didn't alter. London had warned him that the Americans were itching to have a go at Iran and he cut straight to the point. 'How long have we got?'

The American checked his watch.

'Twenty-four hours. Then we're going in. We're gonna hit them where it hurts. Hard. You might want to have your guys well clear by then.'

'Thanks,' said Nuttall. 'I appreciate the heads-up.'

'What heads-up?' said the SEAL Commander, and winked as he left the room.

Chapter 82

Onboard HMS Astute, *the Gulf*

COMMANDER BEN WALLIS sucked in his cheeks and blew out hard. It was the only outward sign he gave of just how nervous he was. Because he had the same question running through his mind as they all did in the submarine's control room. Had *Tareq* spotted them?

Astute had only come up to periscope depth for a matter of seconds before they'd seen her, just before midnight local time, sitting quietly on the surface, her Russian-built diesel engines almost inaudible to other vessels. The departing tanker, MV *Ocean Star*, would have masked the sound of *Astute*'s propellers as she headed west into the Gulf but a watchful sonar operator would pick her up.

'We'll know soon enough,' said Wallis, to the Officer of the Watch, as *Astute* continued her descent to depth. 'Keep a close eye on *Tareq* to see if she starts to shadow us. Warn the sound room to look out for aircraft on top. This could throw our timings out completely.' And that's putting it mildly, he thought. This could even end up aborting the entire mission. Right now, at this exact moment, the life of the Foreign Secretary and the risk of all-out war in the Gulf rested on whether the crew of an ageing Iranian sub had spotted them.

Wallis called over Lieutenant Commander Jess Pearson. 'Go and get Barkwell, will you? Ask him to come up here to the control room. We'd better let his team know what's going on.'

Wallis was hunched over a hydrographic chart of all the depths and shallows around the Strait of Hormuz when Barkwell was brought in. He could see the look of expectation on the young SBS assault team Commander's face. The submariner had an awful feeling Barkwell's team might have made a wasted journey out to the Gulf.

'What I had planned to do,' Wallis told him, showing him where they currently were on the chart, 'was to take us quietly into Iranian waters, nice and slow, let you and your team egress in the submersible, then move to a loiter position, either here or here, ready for the extraction.' He pointed to two shaded areas on the chart, coloured with a blue Chinagraph pen. 'Both carry their own risks,' Wallis continued. 'The northern loitering area is likely to be heavily patrolled by the IRGC Navy, in the air and on the surface. But the southern one here . . .' he pointed to an area just west of the Musandam peninsula '. . . that one has a lot of coastal traffic we'd need to avoid, especially the Marlboro run.'

'Marlboro run?' Barkwell raised an eyebrow.

Wallis allowed himself a momentary smile. 'It's the Iranian cigarette-smuggling route. Twice a day a whole fleet of extremely fast speedboats leaves the Iranian coast for Oman to pick up cartons of fags they flog back home in the Islamic Republic for a hefty profit. Both governments pretty much turn a blind eye to it.'

'I see. And now?' said Barkwell.

'And now we have a problem.' Wallis understood only too well how all this waiting around prior to the mission could be almost more exhausting than the op itself. 'We came a damn sight closer to one of the Iranian subs than I'd have liked just now. If *Tareq* – that's their boat – spotted us they'll likely start shadowing us. And if that's the case I can't take you in. I'm not risking my boat. The Iranians would have you out of the water, like goldfish in a pond, the moment you get close inshore.' Wallis gave Barkwell what he hoped was a sympathetic look. 'It's an unfortunate state of affairs, Captain, but I'm afraid the risk comes with the badge.'

'With respect, sir, we don't know if she's spotted us, do we?'

'That's true,' said Wallis. 'So we're going to move slowly away from the datum – that's the last position we know *Tareq* was in – then return to PD—'

'PD?'

Wallis didn't mind the interruption. He had been in the Navy so long he sometimes forgot that much of its jargon was a mystery, even to Royal Marines like Barkwell. 'Periscope depth. We'll need to check if any of *Tareq*'s radio messages have been intercepted. You won't be surprised to hear that both GCHQ and NSA are monitoring all the Iranian military channels right now. But if they tell us we've been detected, I'm afraid it's ENDEX for your team and that's you back to shore.' Wallis gave him a fatherly pat on the shoulder. He hoped it didn't come across as patronizing. He watched the young man take in this news in silence, exhaling slowly as its awful significance sank in. He was probably thinking about all that training, all those rehearsals in the Omani desert, the night-time parachute drop, the cramped underwater passage, only to see his mission aborted by an unlucky encounter with an Iranian sub in the wrong place at the wrong time.

'Then what are our chances, sir?' Barkwell said eventually.

'Of not having been spotted? I'd say about fifty:fifty. It's pitch-dark up there and we were still close enough to *Ocean Star* to mask our noise profile. That, at least, is in our favour. Just depends if the Iranians were awake and alert. As I say, we'll know soon enough if that sub starts to dive. I'd advise holding off speaking to your guys just yet. We'll give it an hour.'

Barkwell nodded thoughtfully. 'I'll do just that,' he said. 'But I'd appreciate it if they don't hear this from anyone else.'

'That's a given,' said Wallis. 'And now you'll have to excuse me. We're about to play Grandmother's Footsteps with the Iranian sub. That's us making minute course changes every few minutes to throw a pursuer off the scent.'

Wallis watched the SBS man return to his bunk. He didn't envy him. He was the only member of his team to know it could all be called off at any moment.

Exactly one hour and seven minutes after Wallis had ordered *Astute* to go deep, he sent for Barkwell again. He stood up from his charts as the captain came into the control room. 'I have some news for you,' he said. '*Tareq* has stayed put. It looks like she missed us. So that means—'

'We're on?' Barkwell finished the sentence for him, his face breaking into a broad grin.

'Exactly. You'll need to be ready for the egress in three and a half hours. I'm sure you'll use that time wisely.'

Chapter 83

Qeshm Island, Iran

FOR A MINUTE or so Luke and Tannaz lay in the dark, listening to the receding putter of the little boat as it headed back to the mainland. It was cold and uncomfortable on the wet sand, and Luke's mind was whirling. Things had been looking up: they'd made it to the island – but now this. Her breath was coming in short, spasmodic gasps, and although he knew she was trying to be brave, Tannaz was clearly in a lot of pain. Luke felt a stab of guilt. He had got her into this, hadn't he? If it wasn't for him, she would still be living a relatively carefree life as a student in Tehran, or at least be with her mother and brother safely across the border in Azerbaijan. Instead, she was washed up on a beach on some godforsaken island, helping a British spy she barely knew on a mission with a minimal chance of success.

And what of the motto he'd seen pinned to a wall on that agent-handling course? 'The safety and wellbeing of all our agents is of paramount importance to the Service.' It didn't look that way to him right now. He reached out to comfort her, and this time she didn't push him away.

When Tannaz spoke, her voice was faint, as if a light inside her had gone out. '*Cheh khaaky bar saram bereezam?*' she muttered to herself, and then, for his benefit, 'What the hell am I going to do?

326

How do I find my father now? And how can I call Mama without my phone? Which you broke, remember?' She sat up, gasping with pain and grabbing at her ankle. 'And what about Farz?' she continued, agitated now. 'He's in prison because of you!'

Was it despair he'd heard in her voice? Luke wasn't sure but he knew they needed to get going.

'Okay, I'll tell you exactly what we're going to do,' he replied. 'We're going to find some transport and head south, to where your father is. We'll wait there until first light, then you'll contact him and we'll take it from there.' *And that's the bit where I guide in the SBS team, they take out your father, free his hostage and leave fast. But you don't need to know that.*

Luke sensed Tannaz looking critically in his direction.

'Mister, are you crazy? What transport? There's nothing here, nothing on this stupid island, I'm telling you!' Now he heard bitterness in her tone, as if she were already aware she'd made a terrible mistake in coming with him. He knew he should leave her but he felt responsible for her and – being blunt – he still needed her help for what was to come.

'Listen, Tannaz. Your ankle is badly sprained and you can't walk, but I'm not sure I can carry you halfway across this island. We need a vehicle and I'm going to try to find one, so let's find you some shelter.' He grunted as he got to his feet, pointing up the beach to a line of bushes silhouetted in the moonlight. 'I'll be back in an hour. Tannaz . . .' Luke squatted so that his face was close to hers and gently lifted her chin. God, she was beautiful. 'It's going to be okay,' he told her. 'I promise.' He kissed her forehead as he scooped her up and carried her to the bushes. 'Now don't go talking to any strangers,' he said, as he turned away. She didn't laugh.

Keeping low and moving fast, Luke made a beeline for the houses he'd noticed when they'd first come ashore, nestling close to the water's edge. Someone here must have a car, surely. He covered the few hundred metres' distance in long, easy strides. The night sky was clear, giving him good visibility, but also making him easier to spot. A dog barking in the distance reminded him he would need to be as silent as a ghost. As he closed in on the village he considered his priorities. He knew he should check in with Angela at Vauxhall Cross. But he needed every bar of battery for Tannaz to call her father.

And then there was Elise. Kind, beautiful, trusting Elise, mourning her mother, needing him there, by her side – but he still didn't feel he could call her. What was wrong with him? He could take care of himself in the most hostile of environments yet in matters of the heart he just didn't seem able to do the right thing.

He pushed these thoughts away as there, straight ahead, was a single-storey house. No lights, no sound, but – hallelujah! – a vehicle. Edging closer, he cursed inwardly. It was a modern 4x4 – too flash, too recognizable and almost certainly fitted with an alarm. No, he needed something clapped out and inconspicuous. He moved on, treading softly, keeping to the shadows and feeling his way round each building. Then, across what looked like a patch of waste ground, he saw a white Nissan pick-up truck. Even in the dark, he could tell it had seen better days. Would it be locked? Luke doubted it – Qeshm Island didn't seem the sort of place where people locked their front doors, let alone their cars.

He hurried across the open ground and crept up to the driver's door. Gingerly, he tried the handle and pulled. It didn't budge. Shit! The clock was ticking and his options were running out. The longer he skulked about in this tiny village, even at this time of night, the greater the chance he'd be rumbled. He moved to the passenger side and – yes, a click, the door swung open, and he was in. He felt around the steering column, hoping the keys might have been left in the ignition. No chance. He'd have to hotwire it. If he could remember how. He'd done the course at Poole. Think, Carlton, think.

That was it. Find the steering column and remove the cover. Easier said than done – he cut his thumb as he tore off the cover – but he got there in the end. What came next? The wiring harness connector. How the hell was he going to find that in the dark? He glanced at his phone. The blinking on the digital display had stopped so now he used the screen's glow to separate three distinct bundles of wiring. Okay, the one with the battery cable.

Then what? He needed to pull this bundle out of its socket and strip away a few centimetres of insulation to expose the battery wires. Now, deep breath. If he'd got this right then one – the red – was the battery and the other was the ignition. Now he had to marry them up. He was on the point of joining the two wires together when he heard a noise on the other side of the car. Somebody was out there.

Carefully covering the light from his phone, Luke sank lower into the seat, then waited. All he could hear was his own breathing but then there it was again, a scratching outside and panting. Dogs. He stayed very still, frozen in one position. The slightest sound from him could set off a cacophony of barking that would wake the village and bring men running. Minutes ticked by, and then at last he saw them through the windscreen: three pied mongrels trotting away into the night. *Good riddance, you bastards, and don't come back.*

He gave it another minute, then clambered into the driver's seat and twisted the two wires together. Immediately the dash lights came on, needles swung around on dials and the radio crackled into life. Frantically, he searched for the off button and killed it. But he wasn't out of the woods yet. Now came the really hard part. Working by the light of his phone's screen, Luke stripped the insulation off the live starter wire and touched it to the battery wire. With a low growl, the engine came to life. He was up and running.

Chapter 84

Buckinghamshire

PILLOW PLUMPED, DUVET crumpled, Elise Mayhew was red-eyed and wide awake. It had been just over twenty-four hours since her mother had passed away. Just over twenty-four hours since she had called Luke, wherever the hell he was in the world, given him the grim news and asked him to come home. And what had he done? He had all but hung up on her. Un-bloody-forgivable. Luke hadn't said so but she guessed he must be caught up in the kidnap of the Foreign Secretary, which was all over the news. That was still no excuse. This was family and her mother had taken Luke in, like he was her own son. Now was the time for him to show his gratitude to her family, and Elise expected more of him, so much more. There was the funeral to organize, the church, the order of service, the notice in the paper, those difficult phone calls to be made – and, above all, there was her father to take care of. Bloody Luke Carlton wasn't there and she didn't think she could do it all on her own. But there was someone who could help. She reached over to the bedside table, picked up her phone, scrolled through the numbers and dialled.

'Hugo? . . . It's Elise.' She looked at her watch, it was just past eleven p.m. 'Hope I'm not disturbing you? Can you talk?'

Hugo Squires had always been good to her, and if there was

one person she could count on it was him. She had never told Luke but she and Hugo had shared a kiss once, while Luke was off on some mission in South America. It had never been mentioned between her and Hugo since, but she knew Luke disliked him and that was partly why she was calling him now. She could hear music in the background but Hugo's voice was like a healing hand on her shoulder.

'I'm so sorry about Helen,' he said. 'What a dreadful time for you . . . Yes, of course . . . Listen, I'll take the afternoon off tomorrow. It's not a problem at all. I'll come round and help you sort everything out. We'll get you through this.'

'Thank you so much, Hugo. What would I do without you?'

'Don't mention it. See you tomorrow.'

When Elise finished the call she lay there for some time, looking at the bedroom wall. She had grown up in this room, and in the yellow light of her bedside lamp she could just make out the Blu-tack stains on the wall where her Coldplay poster had once been. On impulse, she picked up the phone again and composed a text to Luke. She was still furious with him.

Funeral arranged, it read. *Hugo sorting everything. Don't bother coming back for it.*

Chapter 85

Namakdan Salt Caves, Qeshm Island

IN THE DARK, dank recesses of the Namakdan Salt Caves, Karim Zamani ordered the chairs to be fetched. They had been brought up earlier from a café in Bandar-e-Doulab. They were white, made of plastic, and there were just two. That was all he needed.

He coughed and patted his chest as he looked around the cave. The air was bad down here, deep inside this coastal mountain. He could feel it in his lungs and all across his chest. Karim Zamani, forty-four, senior commander in the Sepah, the IRGC, liked to think of himself as a soldier of the Islamic Revolution, someone who could be deployed anywhere, anytime, at a moment's notice. Had he not already proved himself in the Beka'a Valley? In Homs? In providing expert advice to his country's allies, the popular mobilization units in Iraq, as they retook the town of Tikrit from those godless barbarians, ISIS?

But the truth was, Zamani was a mountain man, a son of the great Elburz range that stood between Tehran and the shores of the Caspian Sea and he disliked the damp, cloying heat on the Gulf coast. His prisoner, too, seemed to be suffering the ill effects of the airless atmosphere in the caves. That, and the effects of the earlier 'procedure', he thought. Zamani chuckled to himself. Indeed, the British politician had developed a wet, rasping cough and it was already getting on his nerves. No matter: it would not be troubling either of them for much longer. The hour was fast approaching.

The steel cage in which the man was incarcerated was big enough – just – to accommodate two people sitting opposite one another, as they did now: the senior trusted officer in the IRGC, a man who had devoted all his adult life to the Revolution, and opposite him, within touching distance, his captive, the British Foreign Secretary, a man who looked ready for retirement. Behind Zamani, just beyond the cage, an interpreter stood poised with a notepad.

The IRGC man sat for some seconds staring at the slumped figure in front of him. And what a pathetic sight he was. Chaplin's hand was bound and bandaged where they had carried out the operation earlier. Already it was bloodstained and filthy. It had taken two of his guards to lift the man to his feet and sit him on the chair. Zamani had had to wait while they positioned his prisoner so he didn't just fall forward.

'I would like to talk to you,' Zamani said at last, and waited for this to be translated.

The Foreign Secretary's breath came in rasps. He raised his head and stared back at Zamani, his eyelids heavy with pain and exhaustion. He was trying to speak but there was something wrong with his mouth. It was dry and his lips were flecked with dried white spittle.

'What . . .' Chaplin was saying '. . . what is it you want with me?'

'*Che goft?* What's he saying?' Zamani smiled as he spoke, not just because he was witnessing Chaplin's obvious discomfort, which pleased him, but because the sight before him confirmed everything he had always thought about Britain, the Little Satan that always did America's bidding. The British were weak, that much was obvious. Could this man, this dishevelled wreck of a human being before him, really stand at the helm of Britain's foreign policy? Its supreme diplomat? Zamani laughed. Britain's glory was all behind it now. It was a declining power in the world and Chaplin was the living embodiment of its sad failures.

'You may think,' Zamani told him, 'that the new pact you have concluded with my government will allow you to reinsert yourself back into our country, give you access to our wealth, our people. Hmm?' He leaned forward and put his hand under Chaplin's chin, lifting it so their faces were on the same level. The man's flesh felt soft and weak to him. This was clearly someone who had never done a day's manual work in his life. 'But you are very wrong,' Zamani continued. 'You should have learned the lessons of 1953. Your stupid plots and your meddling in our affairs will always fail. You should know that. Our people are strong and you, my friend, are weak.'

Zamani grunted, as if to emphasize his last point. Chaplin certainly looked weak. His eyes were barely open and he seemed to have no answer to these words, which meant he clearly accepted they were true.

Zamani decided to leave another long pause before he continued. He was in no hurry: he was enjoying this. 'Would you like to see your family again?' he asked quietly, a concerned smile on his face.

'What?' Chaplin's voice was a faint rasp but Zamani detected a note of anger. That was good: he wanted to see a reaction. 'Of course I bloody would,' Chaplin replied. 'Don't you go bringing them into this.'

Zamani made a soothing, patting motion with his hand, then raised it in a signal to the guard behind him. He stepped forward and handed Zamani a sheaf of photographs through the bars. Zamani licked his lips, then smiled to himself as he leafed through them before selecting the one he wanted. Yes, this was perfect. He turned it around so that Chaplin could see it. It was a large glossy photograph of the minister's wife, Gillian – that was her name. She was smiling as she tended a bed of yellow roses – their garden in Suffolk. Zamani noted with some satisfaction the shock on his captive's face.

'Here. Here is another,' he said, handing Chaplin a photo of his elder son, George, on the day he'd gone up to university, and another of the younger boy, Blake, taken in a London restaurant somewhere. The Circle's research team had done their homework well.

Zamani handed him the rest of the photographs and sat back in his chair to observe his reaction. The Foreign Secretary fumbled to hold on to them. His mouth was half open and his lips were moving, but he had nothing to say. Pathetic.

'I can see that you care about your family,' Zamani said, with mock concern. 'Of course you do. Why wouldn't you? You are a family man like me,' he said, waiting for this to be translated before continuing. 'But you should know something.' He raised a finger in warning. 'We have people in your country.' Chaplin looked up sharply. 'Yes, yes, we do,' Zamani said. 'Clever people. Dangerous people. So I would advise you, Foreign Secretary, that you should do exactly as we tell you. And then maybe, when all of this,' he gestured to the cage, 'is over, maybe, just maybe, they will come to no harm.'

Chapter 86

10 Downing Street

'THIS ABSOLUTELY CANNOT get out. Is that clear?' The PM handed back the grisly photograph to the National Security Adviser, as if he wanted nothing to do with it. 'I mean that,' he added. 'The public must not get to hear of this.'

It was late in the evening, long after the rest of Whitehall had finished for the day, as they stood in a small huddle next to the window, upstairs in the Terracotta Room at Number 10. Above the doorway hung an incongruously garish pink neon sign that said *More Passion*, a gift from Tracey Emin to the Camerons. Inside, sombre portraits of past Prime Ministers stared down from the walls as if in disapproval at the grim image being passed around. Sent through from the embassy in Dubai, the photograph appeared to show Geoffrey Chaplin's finger, slightly crooked, and caked with dried blood that had congealed around the white of the severed bone. Attached to the photograph was a classified MoD document marked 'Chaplin, G. – PID'. Proof of Identity.

Sir Charles Bennett, Britain's National Security Adviser, had had to be summoned from a dinner at the Travellers Club in Pall Mall when the message had come through to the Foreign Office's Global Response Centre. Minutes later, the PM had listened, ashen-faced, as Bennett had told him this was so appalling, so

336

disgusting, so completely hideous that he had needed to share it in person with the PM. The Prime Minister had decided that only one other person in Downing Street should be privy to this photograph: Jasminder Singh, his PA.

The PM listened as Bennett came to the point.

'We have to decide, Prime Minister, if we share this with Washington.'

'No! Absolutely not!' The PM's response was instant and emphatic. 'The White House needs no further encouragement to launch a strike on Iran, and this,' he pointed at the photograph, 'could be just the excuse they need.' The PM walked over to the Georgian window that looked down on Horse Guards Parade, now dark and deserted. Despite the late hour the curtains at Number 10 had not yet been drawn and he rested his fingertips on the bullet-proof pane as he digested the latest horrible development.

'They're going to kill him, aren't they?' he said quietly, still facing the darkened parade ground, his back turned to Bennett and his PA. 'They're going to slaughter him, like a bloody sacrificial lamb. Well, I won't have it, d'you hear?' He whirled round, the strain and exhaustion visible on his face. 'Where are we on this rescue mission? Can't we speed things up?'

He saw Bennett check his watch. '*Astute* is entering the Strait of Hormuz as we speak, PM. The SBS assault team are onboard and she'll be on-station by morning. We've got the suspected location nailed down, we just don't have the man on the ground there that SIS keep promising. I'm chasing them, believe me.'

'And the Iranians?' The PM's brow furrowed.

Bennett let out a short sigh of exasperation. 'They're chasing their tails, quite frankly. They don't seem to have a clue where Geoffrey's being held and we're certainly not about to tip them off. They won't react well when they find out we've gone in and done the job ourselves.'

The PM nodded thoughtfully and gazed down at his shoes. 'No, I imagine not,' he replied, then looked up briskly. 'Well, keep me informed and make sure that photo doesn't get out or the press will be all over it.'

Jasminder Singh put up her hand before Bennett had had a chance to reply. She held out her iPad for them to see what was on the screen. 'It's got out already,' she said. 'This just came through from Press Office downstairs.' The screen showed a grab from the front page of *The New York Times*. There, only partially pixel-lated, was the amputated finger of Britain's Foreign Secretary. And the bold headline beside it read simply: 'Iran Horror for Powerless Britain'.

Chapter 87

Qeshm Island

IT WAS PAST two by the time Luke pulled up in the stolen Nissan to near where he'd left Tannaz. The moon had vanished behind the clouds and he had the lights off and the window down, the night breeze blowing in. Using what little ambient light was left, he had navigated his way across the rough ground, steering between bushes, dodging the lighter patches in case they proved to be soft and treacherous sand. He had expected, at any minute, to hear the wail of sirens behind him, but there had been none. Luke had been careful. He had inched slowly away from those low, silent buildings, first steering the truck in one direction, then dog-legging off at a right-angle to retrace his route back to Tannaz.

Just before he had reached her, he had stopped the pick-up and checked his phone. The battery was down to 26 per cent, and there was a single SMS message, from Angela: *Call this ASAP*, it had read, then a number with a 973 prefix. Someone had answered after just one ring and Luke had recognized the voice immediately. 'Chip!'

He remembered Chip Nuttall from their operational tour with 40 Commando in Afghanistan. He'd also been one of the instructors on Luke's selection course for the SBS. A hard bastard, with a sense-of-humour bypass, as he recalled. Luke was not at all surprised when he had learned Nuttall had made it all the way to commanding the SBS.

'Callsign Quebec are inbound,' he had said flatly. Straight to business, no time for preliminaries. 'ETA first light. What's your status?'

First light? Dawn? Jesus. He was almost out of time. Callsign Quebec? No one had thought to tell Luke that designation but it could mean only one thing: the SBS assault team were on their way to Qeshm within hours.

'I'm around ten clicks out,' he had replied. 'I'm mobile but I've got one injured civilian with me.'

'Then dump him,' Nuttall had told him.

'*She*'s Echo Sierra's daughter.'

A moment of silence, and then: 'Who the fuck's Echo Sierra?'

Luke had detected the exasperation in Nuttall's voice. Like him, he couldn't have had much sleep since the kidnapping. But so much for codenames. It seemed the wonders of Whitehall machinery had thrown up different names for the same individual. Echo Sierra might have been MI6's name for Tannaz's father but it meant nothing to anyone outside Vauxhall Cross.

Luke had sighed. He might as well blurt it out. 'Karim Zamani,' he'd replied. And if anyone was listening out there, he'd thought, there goes our operational security.

'Still dump her,' Nuttall had said. 'The extraction team will take you and the hostage. In a RIB. There won't be room for extra baggage.'

Something inside him had bridled at this. Tannaz wasn't extra baggage. He thought of her as brave, beautiful and in distress. And without her help he'd probably be strapped to an interrogation chair in Evin Prison by now. His response had been instant. 'No. I need her for this phase. She's part of the plan.'

'If that's your calculation, fine. But I'm not making any promises.'

Yes. Just as he remembered, Nuttall was a hard bastard. 'I'm running out of battery,' he'd said, which was true. 'When callsign Quebec is ashore patch me through on what this means. Out.'

He found Tannaz sitting hunched up and shivering, her face covered with wet sand where she had lain on the ground and tried to sleep. He helped her to her feet. 'How's the ankle?' he asked. 'Can you walk?'

She groaned as he put her arm around his shoulders and helped her to the truck, its engine idling, then up into the passenger seat. She hadn't said a word so far. Luke climbed in on the other side, reached across and turned up the truck's heater full blast. Pushing her hair back from her face, she gave him a weak smile. He rested his hand briefly on her arm. 'Tannaz, you remember the plan, right?' He scanned the track ahead as he put the vehicle into gear and moved off. Tannaz did not respond.

'Listen,' he continued, 'we've got four hours max before they find out this truck is stolen. Make that three. In that time we need to get ourselves across this island to where your dad is, hide the truck and ourselves. We'll follow this track until we reach a proper road and then we need to head south.' He braked, narrowly avoiding a deep rut. Tannaz was jerked forward. Bracing herself against the dashboard, she glared at him. The truck had no seatbelts.

They drove on in silence until they reached what looked like a metalled road. All was quiet. Luke stopped the pick-up and checked his phone. Battery level 21 per cent. Damn. He glanced at Tannaz, who was staring out of the window, lost in her thoughts, then clicked on the link to the digital map Trish Fryer had sent over. A pulsing dot indicated the last known location of Karim Zamani, when he'd made a call from his private mobile. Next to it was '4.8 km'. Turning off the phone, he eased cautiously out onto the road and switched on the truck's sidelights: 4.8 kilometres. That wasn't far. Suddenly it was real. They had come all this way from that alleyway in Tehran to the approaching showdown with Zamani. His gut told him it wasn't going to be pretty. He'd had enough experience with the SBS to know that a lot of blood would be spilled. He might not have a choice in the matter, but he didn't want Tannaz around when that went down.

He looked at her. She was so completely out of place here. Her head lolling to one side and her eyes closed, she looked like she was falling asleep. He reached over and gently touched her cheek. She must be exhausted. Maybe Nuttall was right and he should dump her, for her own sake.

Luke drove on. They passed a rusting sign, barely caught in the truck's sidelights: Gas Company Road. Must be a souvenir of pre-revolutionary days, long before sanctions. They were coming into a village, silent and sleeping, a scattering of low, sandy-coloured, flat-roofed buildings, punctuated by date palms and traditional wind towers from the days before air-conditioning. Luke felt his senses go into hyper-alert. If they were stopped now, he didn't think they'd be able to explain what they were doing driving across Qeshm Island in the early hours of the morning.

And then they were through the village and there was another sign on the right-hand side of the road. In Farsi and in English. 'Namakdan Salt Caves 1 km'. Christ, they were nearly there. He needed to get off the road and out of sight. It would be dawn in three hours. He drew to a stop, killed the lights and woke Tannaz.

'*Che khabar?*' she muttered drowsily. 'What's up?'

'Bumpy road,' he told her. 'Hold on.'

Luke swung the Nissan off the road and jolted them towards a cluster of date palms. Then he backed the vehicle between them as far as he could. It was the only cover he could find and it would have to do. Tannaz yawned, stretched, and rested her head on his shoulder, dozing off again. Luke switched on his phone and accessed the map. The pulsing dot was almost bang in the centre of the screen. The figure in the corner read '550 metres'. He was in position.

Chapter 88

Namakdan Salt Caves, Qeshm Island

GEOFFREY CHAPLIN WOKE to see a large man approach the cage. What time was it? Before dawn? Early morning? The middle of the night? He had no idea.

Deprived of his watch and imprisoned in the subterranean cave, he had lost track of time and place. The air smelt stale, of salt and diesel oil, and from somewhere out of sight he thought he heard the faint chug of a generator.

He had slept fitfully since the unpleasant encounter with that vile individual who'd not only threatened him but also his family. Thanks to a handful of pills one of the guards had given him earlier, the pain from his mutilated hand was now reduced to a dull but insistent throb. He remembered reading an FCO briefing paper that claimed the Iranian population was addicted to painkillers.

But this newcomer didn't look as though he'd come to help. Just the opposite. Thick-set, stubbled and with a scarred cheek, he appeared to be carrying a tape-measure.

Chaplin winced as he sat up. 'Hey,' he called. The man studiously ignored him and continued his conversation with the guard. Moments later, the cage door was opened and the big man stepped inside.

'Excuse me?' Chaplin repeated with all the strength he could muster. 'I have some questions.' Again, he was ignored as the scarred man moved about, taking a series of measurements.

'You! I'm talking to you!' Chaplin shouted. This time the man reacted. He lunged at Chaplin, and swung his hand back as if he were going to hit him in the face. Chaplin recoiled, holding up his bandaged hand to protect himself. Laughter erupted round the cave.

Things went quiet for a while, but then other men began to arrive. Some carried assault rifles while others hefted spars of wood, coils of rope and what looked to the Foreign Secretary like a carpenter's tool-kit. The light was poor as it dimmed and flared in time with the generator, but he felt compelled to watch. They appeared to be building some sort of stage. When their work was done, a portrait of the late Ayatollah Khomeini, the godfather of Iran's Islamic Revolution, scowled down at Chaplin. Alongside it, they had unfurled a green banner emblazoned with a script he couldn't read. But if the ayatollah's stern gaze was discomforting, what really alarmed him was the sight of a video camera on a tripod.

Chapter 89

10 Downing Street

BRITTLE. BRITTLE AND caustic. That was the first thing that struck Sir Adam Keeling about the atmosphere in the Terracotta Room at Number 10 when he walked in late that evening. The PM had taken off his tie, which lay beside him on the sofa, like a coiled snake. Bottles of Hildon water stood untouched on the table. There were four other people in the room: the Prime Minister's PA, Jasminder Singh – she gave the MI6 Chief a nervous nod as he came in – Sir Charles Bennett, the National Security Adviser, Nigel Batstone from the FCO, of course – this was all happening on his turf – and some military type he didn't recognize. As he took the last remaining chair, Keeling noted that Bennett had barely acknowledged his presence as he leaned forward to address the room.

'The ultimatum expires in just over six hours,' Bennett said, his voice curt. 'We are fast running out of time.'

'And still no response from them?' said the PM.

'There's no one to respond to,' Bennett replied. 'They've left no return address and that's deliberate, I'm sure. Their demands are completely unacceptable. We were never going to pull our forces out of the Gulf and they know that. And now we've got the Americans to worry about. They're itching to get stuck in.'

'Can't we stall them?' The PM was leaning forward, his head turning from one to another, as if searching the room for answers. 'Perhaps I should make another call to the White House.'

'I'm afraid we're well past that point now, Prime Minister. Our defence attaché's just been on the line from Washington. He says they've moved their own assault team to an airbase in the Emirates. They're just waiting for the word from the White House and they'll be in the air. Christ, they could drop onto Qeshm Island before our team's even got ashore.' He looked around for a reaction, eyebrows raised, lips pursed.

Keeling was tempted to interrupt but thought better of it. He knew he had come to this meeting with a weak hand. They were going to ask him if Luke Carlton was now in position on the ground to bring in the rescue team, and the bald truth was that he didn't know. In the end it was Batstone who raised a hand.

'Yes, Nigel?'

'Look, I'm not a military man,' said the senior diplomat, loosening his tie as he spoke, 'so you'll have to forgive me if I don't quite follow this. But what exactly is the problem with the Americans going in at the same time as us? Aren't we all on the same side here? And isn't there supposed to be something called "deconfliction" between our forces and theirs?'

'The problem,' said the military type, 'is not deconfliction.' Keeling recognized him now, the Chief of Joint Operations, but he was damned if he could remember his name. 'The problem is that the Americans have made it very plain to us that if they're going to hit Iran they'll go in big. That means total suppression of air defences, electronic counter-measures, offensive combat air patrols up and down the coast, neutralization of IRGC command and control centres. We're talking "shock and awe" here. So we could forget about getting Geoffrey Chaplin out alive.'

'Good grief,' said Batstone. 'That sounds like Gulf War Three!'

'Exactly. With all that that entails. Mining the strait, missile attacks on the US 5th Fleet, ballistic missiles fired at Bahrain and Saudi. It will make the Desert Storm campaign of '91 look like an *amuse-bouche*.'

Batstone turned visibly pale. 'But – but that is exactly what the hardliners want!' he protested. 'It will set us back years.'

'And it'll shut the Strait of Hormuz,' added the Chief of Joint Operations drily. 'Which is why *Astute* has been making full speed through it.' He paused to look at his watch. 'The assault team from Poole should be beaching on Qeshm in exactly three hours' time.'

Bennett turned to Keeling. 'Let's bring you into this, C,' he said. 'Is your man on the ground ready to guide them in?'

Keeling felt the eyes of everyone in the room on him, the PM squinting at him from his position on the sofa. 'Absolutely,' he assured them, without hesitation. 'He's close by the Qeshm caves and he's getting local assistance.'

'Well, that's reassuring,' replied Bennett. 'Because we're entering the endgame now, and if there's one thing we can't afford it's any last-minute cock-ups. Good. I knew we could count on you, Sir Adam.'

Chapter 90

AT PRECISELY 0432 hours, Tehran time, HMS *Astute* crossed, ill-egally and undeclared, into Iranian waters. It was not Commander Ben Wallis's first foray into that forbidden territory and the same could be said for his Executive Officer. Neither man had ever spoken of such covert operations since. They stood side by side in the control room, comrades-in-arms, casting a critical eye over the hum of activity taking place. Wallis had ordered the submarine's speed cut from 15 knots down to five, and they were now creeping stealthily towards the still-dark coast of Qeshm Island. Every one of her ninety-seven crew, from captain to cook, had been briefed on the dangers of this operation. It was not just the SBS assault team, preparing to exit the sub into the unknown, who would be in peril. The entire vessel was trespassing in the sovereign waters of a hostile state and the thought of being blasted by a high-velocity torpedo or the sub's hull ruptured by a high-explosive depth charge and sent to the bottom of the ocean was never far from their thoughts.

At sixteen kilometres out from the shore Commander Wallis ordered *Astute* to come up to periscope depth. He ordered his XO to conduct an all-sensor search of the surrounding seas, a combination of visual, sonar and electronic sweeps using her tactical mast, an electronic periscope. Wallis had served long enough to remember the old manual periscope sliding greasily down into the control room with its twin grip handles, *Das Boot*-style. Those days were gone. On that state-of-the-art nuclear sub, with its non-hull-penetrating optronic mast, the Officer of the Watch no longer needed to peer through a periscope. Instead, he could use the digital camera sensor that extended unobtrusively from the submarine's fin to perform a 360-degree sweep above the surface. The resulting images, captured with a minimal risk of detection, could be studied at leisure in the control room.

'How's it looking?' Wallis asked, taking out his spectacles from a top pocket and peering at the first of the images to appear on a screen. It was a blank mass of grey, with no telltale white blips that indicated a vessel.

'All clear, sir.' The Officer of the Watch kept his eyes on the screen in front of him. 'Looks like we have a window.'

Aft of the control room, in the crew's quarters, Captain Barkwell and his assault team were running through their final checks. Personal weapons, ammo, comms, special weapons and breathing apparatus. Sixteen SBS operators had dropped into the Gulf of Oman the previous night. Only eight would be going in on the assault. The remainder were the back-up team, every bit as important, and deployed to extract them, quite possibly under fire, once the mission had been executed. Still, Barkwell reflected, it was never easy being the ones left onboard as your mates went in on the first wave.

He looked up as a figure appeared, framed by the bulkhead doorway: Lieutenant Commander Jess Pearson. 'Captain wanted you to know its ten minutes to egress,' she told them briskly. Some of the operators nodded thanks, others carried on with their checks. Barkwell acknowledged the warning and looked at his team. He knew the presence of a female officer would, for some, have been an unwelcome reminder of the wives and girlfriends they'd left behind. Knowing the immeasurable risks they were about to face, some might even have wondered if Jess Pearson was the last woman they would ever set eyes on.

Little was said as Barkwell and the men turned their attention to their scuba gear. Working in pairs, each man checked the other's kit: tank air pressure, valves, rubber seals, fins. Then, on Barkwell's command, they moved off in single file, following him out of the submarine through a lock-in/out hatch, and into the cylindrical dry dock shelter secured to the hull just behind the fin.

Barkwell paused briefly. This was the team's first sight of the SDV, the Swimmer Delivery Vehicle, the customized minisub that would take them in underwater, covering the last crucial few kilometres to the coast of Qeshm.

Weighed down by their equipment – each man was carrying as much as the craft would allow – they took their places, one behind another, in the tiny compartments of the minisub. All but two carried the C8-CQB assault rifle, with its ambidextrous controls and flash hider, as their personal weapon. Of the others, one hefted the team's support weapon, a belt-fed Minimi light machine-gun, while the other carried the most unusual weapon of all. In preparing for the mission, Barkwell had requested a rifle that could drop a man at nearly two kilometres, and the Director of Special Forces had pulled some serious strings to get him one: a CheyTac M200 Intervention – a sniping rifle with its own inbuilt computer.

But, weaponry apart, what Barkwell's team would need above all else was speed and guile. They would need to get in, overpower the enemy, grab the hostage and get the hell out. Fast. This wasn't rocket science. Linger too long on the objective and they would soon find themselves surrounded by overwhelming numbers, and when their ammunition ran out, then what? Extraction under fire? In the Islamic Republic of Iran, with its 934,000 men and women under arms? That was unlikely to end well.

Barkwell connected his mouthpiece to the minisub's centralized breathing apparatus and his team did the same. It would become their 'lungs' for the journey to shore. A voice buzzed in his ear, coming through on the high-frequency underwater comms. *Astute*'s Executive Officer was speaking to him from the sub's control room. 'Standby, standby!' came the command.

Then, with no further warning, Barkwell felt the chill of the seawater through his neoprene drysuit as it swirled around his feet and raced up his legs, submerging him within seconds. The XO had opened the rear door of the dry dock shelter, flooding it to allow the minisub to float out into open water. Barkwell gave the pilot up front a signal and they moved off under their own power. Behind them, *Astute* was already returning to depth and slinking southwards to extract herself from Iranian waters.

As they headed towards the shallows, Barkwell went through the eventualities. What had he missed? What had he forgotten? What if . . . ?

As the minisub picked up speed and ploughed on through the pitch-black sea, Barkwell's thoughts kept returning to the letters he knew he might soon have to write.

'Dear Mr and Mrs So-and-so, I am writing to tell you about your son . . .'

Chapter 91

SOMETHING WAS UP. Chaplin could sense it. Cold, frightened, hungry and in a lot of pain from his mutilated hand, Britain's captive Foreign Secretary sat on the damp and filthy mattress and observed the activity around him with growing alarm. Since his cave had been measured, the banners erected and the video camera set up, he'd watched as his guards fussed over the camera, making adjustments, testing the microphone and even peering at him through the viewfinder. And someone – he hadn't seen whom – had placed a bouquet of what he was sure were plastic roses at the foot of the portrait of Ayatollah Khomeini. No one was telling him anything.

Geoffrey Chaplin wished more than anything in the world to be delivered from this evil. The pain of the forced amputation nine hours ago had numbed his normal powers of reason. Right now, even death didn't sound too bad an option. Just anything but this. Stripped of everything except the lice-infested boiler suit, he felt more abandoned and helpless than ever. Why wasn't anybody negotiating his release? All his early hopes of rescue by British or American Special Forces had dribbled away into nothing. And his hand still hurt like hell. It came in waves: sometimes it was almost tolerable but at others his hand seemed to be on fire.

Footsteps crunching on the cavern floor caused Chaplin to look up, and he flinched. Coming towards him was the man who'd threatened his family. The way the others deferred to him convinced the Foreign Secretary that this was indeed the man in charge. Those cold eyes and that cruel mouth. Yes, he was the one, and Chaplin's spirits sank even lower. There was something about him that struck Chaplin as extremely dangerous, as if he simply lacked the normal human capacity for love, mercy or pity.

He felt the man's gaze on him. The interpreter stood slightly to one side, listening intently as his commander began to speak.

'So, Mr Foreign Secretary, it is time for me to explain myself.' The man waited patiently while the interpreter translated. 'I am an officer in what I think you like to call our Revolutionary Guards.' Chaplin thought he seemed almost avuncular at that point, a benign relative trying to decide what to give his nephew for his birthday. But when Chaplin returned his gaze and looked up into the man's face he saw nothing that gave him any hope to cling to. It was as if there were no soul behind those eyes. Something very bad was coming his way.

'You believe in one God, yes?' Zamani asked.

'I do.'

'And you pray to your God?'

'That,' replied Chaplin, with more aggression than he felt, 'is my affair.'

'Of course,' Zamani replied. 'But you pray to Him?'

'Yes, I do. Look, what is this all about? I think it's time we came to some arrangement.' Right now, he'd sign anything, any deal they put in front of him, anything to put an end to this misery.

'Then I should urge you,' Zamani said, 'to pray to Him now. Because very soon you, Mr Chaplin, you are going to make history.' He waited again while his words were translated. Geoffrey Chaplin looked from the interpreter back to his master. But Karim Zamani had already turned his back on him and walked away without another word.

Chapter 92

Qeshm Island

FIVE HUNDRED AND fifty metres. Luke sat behind the wheel of the pick-up truck and stared at the number displayed on his phone's screen. He was thinking about what it meant. Karim Zamani and his vicious kidnappers were somewhere out there in the dark, just over half a kilometre away. So was their prisoner. Five hundred and fifty metres to the spot where this was going to end, one way or another. Whatever went down in the next few hours would determine everything: the life of Geoffrey Chaplin – if that poor man was even still alive – the stability of world oil supplies, and whether a crippling, costly war in the Gulf could be avoided. What happened to him and Tannaz seemed almost irrelevant. But he, Luke Carlton, was bloody well going to play his part in this. He had not gone operational all the way to Armenia, Abu Dhabi and across the length and breadth of Iran just to sit back now as a bystander. It was time to deploy Tannaz.

Luke gently eased her off his shoulder. 'Tannaz . . . hey, it's time. You've got to wake up.'

'Mmm,' she murmured, her eyes still shut. 'What time is it?'

'Five thirty. It'll be light soon.'

'Too early.' She settled herself more comfortably but Luke lifted her off him until she sat up straight.

'No, it isn't,' he told her. 'Tannaz, you've got to phone your father. Find out where he is, and tell him you're coming to join him. This is what you wanted to do, remember?' *And it's what I need you to do. The plan depends on you. So please don't back out now. I need you to separate your father from the crew he's commanding for long enough to get Chaplin out.*

She was suddenly wide awake, eyes open and looking around her. Luke couldn't help but feel for her. It was less than forty-eight hours since she and her family had discovered their husband and father was about to become a national pariah, pushing the country to the brink of war. Yet this pampered twenty-two-year-old university student somehow believed she could talk him into giving up his whole operation, maybe even releasing his captive. It was absurd. But if that was what would take him, Luke Carlton, right to Zamani's doorstep, then fine. He just wasn't going to tell her about the SBS assault team who must be fast approaching now.

He held out his phone to her: 18 per cent battery left. This would have to be brief. Tannaz looked up at Luke as she took it. She didn't say a word.

'*Baba? Manam . . . Tannaz*. Father, it's me . . . Tannaz.' She used the plaintive, little-girl voice of someone half her age. Luke listened, straining to catch the odd word of Farsi that he knew. Then she stopped. She looked down at the phone, perplexed, frowning. 'He hung up on me.' She looked across at Luke, her expression incredulous.

'I'm sorry, Tannaz. That's tough.' He waited a moment. 'So where is he exactly?'

She shrugged.

'You didn't give away where we are, did you?'

Tannaz scowled at him, insulted. 'No! Of course not! I just told him I was close by. He told me . . . he told me not to call him again. It was like he was talking to a stranger. It's like he's not my father any more. What do we do now?'

Luke knew exactly what he had to do now, but how to explain it to Tannaz? 'I need you to wait here,' he told her, taking both her

355

hands in his. Hell, she had a sprained ankle and he knew she wasn't going anywhere. 'I shan't be long.'

'But why? Where are you going?' she demanded, catching his arm as he turned, holding on to him. His heart went out to her. She'd been so cool and confident in Abu Dhabi, in London and Tehran, but that had gone. They were in Iran, her country, he was the stranger – and yet he felt responsible for her.

'I'm just going to scout out the lie of the land,' he told her, jumping out of the pick-up and closing the door quietly behind him. To the east, just over the horizon, he could see a faint glimmer of grey in the sky.

Luke skirted the edge of the palm grove and climbed down into a shallow gully where a broad white band of salt crust met the mud brown of the desert. He took a quick look around him – all clear – and brought up the rolling map on his phone. It showed him to be on the edge of the valley floor and precisely 420 metres to Zamani's last-known position. This would be where he would rendezvous with the incoming rescue team. It was nearly first light and time to make contact. From somewhere behind him he could hear a vehicle, the first he'd heard since they'd arrived on the island. Sounded like a jeep, moving fast. Luke kept his head down and waited.

Silence, just the whisper of the pre-dawn breeze. Then he heard it again. The revving of an engine and a vehicle travelling at speed, growing fainter. He hoped to God Tannaz hadn't done anything foolish, like trying to follow him. No, with that ankle she was immobile.

He waited another minute and, hearing nothing, began to retrace his steps back to the palm grove and Tannaz. Stepping into the clearing where he'd left the pick-up, he froze. The Nissan had gone, and Tannaz with it.

Chapter 93

Under Iranian waters, off Qeshm Island

THE COLD. IT crept up on you, seeped into your bones, made you shiver inside your drysuit. Even after all the training – whether in Poole, Cornwall or Norway – the cold took Chris Barkwell by surprise. This Swimmer Delivery Vehicle, the black, underwater minisub, might look like it had come straight out of a James Bond movie but the reality was a lot less glamorous. His assault team – 'the swimmers' – were mostly big men and the compartments, comprising four pairs of seats, one behind another, sealed in with a sliding overhead hatch, were tiny. Barkwell felt numb and cramped and he knew it would be just as bad for the others – there was barely enough room for them, let alone their kit. And to make matters worse, there was the perpetual fear of detection. Crawling along at eight knots, just above the seabed, they would be a sitting target if Iranian coastal defences picked them up. At least there were no air bubbles to give them away – the boffins had thought of that. Each man was using a 'rebreather' device, his expelled air contained and recycled. It did not taste good.

Barkwell checked his watch for the third time. Fifty-four minutes since they had emerged from *Astute*: they must be getting close now. He spoke through his mask microphone to the pilot sitting up front on the right. 'How long?'

'Ten.' The answer crackled back, picked up by the whole team on their underwater headsets. Poised and ready, Barkwell ran through his action plan for the hundredth time. Did he have all the assets he would have wanted for this mission? Absolutely not. Could it still be done? He knew not to ask himself that because they were way past the point of no return now.

At 0535 hours it was still dark as the pilot brought them up to periscope depth and steadied the minisub against the current. There was a console between Barkwell's knees and he used it now, extending the minisub's periscope and making a 360-degree scan through its infrared optics. Behind them, there was nothing but ocean. Ahead, however, a sheer escarpment towered over a rocky beach and a line of low foliage. He held his breath. He could see no thermal signals bouncing back, no sign of life. He breathed out. Thank God. It looked like the intel prep was spot-on: the beachhead was deserted.

Barkwell gave the order and the pilot put the minisub down on the seabed just ahead of the shoreline, settling onto the sand and shale. Each of the hatches slid open and the team emerged as one, feeling their way with gloved hands in the dark, negotiating their way out of the submersible, the bulky rebreathers on their backs, weapons sacks in their hands. Barkwell checked each man was ready, then gave the signal to move off, kicking out with their fins just below the surface, dragging their bulky flotation sacks behind them.

Barkwell was first onto dry land. Like some primordial creature emerging from a swamp, he hauled himself ashore and immediately flipped down his night-vision goggles to check the beach was clear. Dawn was approaching. Within a minute the whole team was ashore and drysuits were being peeled off, cached beneath rocks or buried alongside their heavy rebreathing apparatus, fins and masks. Sitting back on his heels, Barkwell checked his GPS. He heard his signaller squat next to him and proceed to set up the team's encrypted communications with Bahrain. They were in dead ground, hidden from detection by the sheer

358

sandstone escarpment, but with dawn approaching they needed to move fast.

'Any word on that agent, callsign Victor?' Barkwell asked him. The intelligence agencies had promised to have someone in place to guide them in. So where the fuck was he?

The signaller shook his head, still listening through his earpiece, then clamped a hand over his ear.

'Boss! We've got trouble. There's an Iranian drone airborne. It's nine K out and it could be heading this way.'

Traversing the dawn sky high above Qeshm Island, the Iranian Navy drone's all-seeing infrared eye scanned the terrain below. Down on the beach, Tash, Barkwell's radio operator, looked at him with concern. 'Bahrain say it's a Shahed. It's wings clean.'

Barkwell knew what that meant. US Navy 5th Fleet headquarters in Bahrain had confirmed it as a Shahed-129, one of their pilotless aircraft reverse-engineered by skilled Iranian technicians from a US drone downed on the Afghan border. 'Wings clean' meant it was unarmed, which was of little comfort to Barkwell if it meant their mission was about to be compromised.

'What's its status?' he demanded.

Tash spoke briefly into the mic then gave him the thumbs-up. 'Bahrain says she's moved on,' he relayed. 'We're clear to proceed.'

Another glance at his GPS, then Barkwell signalled to the team. A last-minute check of their weapons and kit, and the patrol moved off, their boots making little sound on the damp ground. They followed a route prepared by geospatial cartographers back at Task Group HQ at Poole, enabling them to take maximum advantage of dead ground so they wouldn't be seen.

'One K to the caves,' Barkwell told them. He was worried now. Only three hours left before the ultimatum expired: it would soon be daylight, and with it, they'd lose the key element of surprise. With Chaplin's life hanging in the balance, he knew that every minute counted.

They'd barely gone two hundred metres before Tash tapped

Barkwell on the arm and passed him the headset. 'Boss. They need to talk to you. Bahrain are patching through callsign Victor.'

It was the SIS man, the 'agent' they'd been promised to guide them in. *Good. About bloody time. He's probably spent the night in a comfortable bed while we've just flogged halfway across the Gulf.* Barkwell kept moving, holding the headset close to his ear with his left hand and cradling his rifle with his right.

'Go ahead,' he told him.

'I'm in position. Four hundred metres south of the objective,' the SIS agent replied. 'You've got two Bravos guarding the entrance. Light weapons. Two vehicles.'

'Roger that,' Barkwell replied, his voice low. Two enemy sentries should not be a problem. 'Can you take them out?' he asked.

'Negative,' the agent replied. 'They're armed. Looks like Tondar MP5s. I'm armed with fuck-all. What's your ETA?'

Barkwell paused to check his GPS. 'Six minutes. I was told you're working on a distraction plan. You've got one local friendly with you?'

'Did have. Codename Elixir. She's been taken.'

Chapter 94

Qeshm Island

LUKE LAY BACK against a boulder and silently cursed himself. That one bastard phone call. That was all it had taken. Whatever Tannaz had said to her father in those few seconds had been enough for them to find her. The palm grove was the only obvious cover for miles around. Karim Zamani must have dispatched his goons to come after her in that jeep. Her father was a cruel and vindictive man – it had said as much in his file. He shuddered to think what would happen to her now. Zamani was running a ruthless kidnap operation here in these caves and Luke had to face up to the fact that his distraction plan had failed. So much for using Tannaz to separate Zamani from his team. All he had achieved was to make the mission more complicated.

Luke was beyond angry with himself. He felt sick with guilt. The teams back at Vauxhall Cross and Cheltenham – Angela, the targeting officers, the analysts, the codebreakers – had invested so much in this moment. And then there had been the time away from Elise, the false identity, the lies and the subterfuge. Never mind the disastrous trip to Armenia and the chase through the frozen gorge, the risks he had taken in Iran, the checkpoints, the near escapes, the betrayal, going on the run through the swamp.

And there were those who'd risked so much for him – like gentle, dope-smoking Farz and, of course, Tannaz. And all for what?

But he needed to snap out of it. Self-pity wasn't going to help Chaplin or Tannaz. He checked his watch: 06.05. No sign of the incoming SBS team yet and it was getting dangerously light. Peering out from behind the boulder, he could just make out the entrance to the caves on the other side of the valley. Nearby a truck and a jeep – the one that had snatched Tannaz? – were parked. There was no sign of her. In fact, there was no sign of anyone other than the two guards patrolling the area. The minutes passed agonizingly slowly. Then, from across the valley, he heard an engine cough into life. He could see movement at the caves. The jeep was on the move. And it seemed to be heading straight for him.

Chapter 95

ANGELA SCOTT WAS worried. Nail-bitingly worried. Just before midnight she had been summoned, along with the others, to the ops room at the Special Boat Service base down at Poole. It was now 02.45, the rescue mission was about to go live, and officers from MI6, the Ministry of Defence, the Foreign Office, GCHQ and Joint Intelligence had been squeezed into a small room in a well-guarded camp in Dorset. One of the wall-mounted monitors linked to the SBS Commander, Chip Nuttall, at his forward-mounted headquarters in Bahrain. Another showed the control room onboard HMS *Astute*, while a third live-streamed a satellite feed from the RAF Sentinel spy plane patrolling the skies just south of Qeshm Island. On the largest screen, eight green dots moved jerkily across a murky landscape, each dot a member of the SBS team as they moved inland.

Sir Adam Keeling had been patched through and was listening in. The PM had gone to bed, asking to be informed the minute there was any news.

Inside the tense ops room Angela stared at the spot on the monitor that showed Luke's last-known position – just over four hundred metres from the entrance to those bloody caves. By now he was supposed to have joined forces with the incoming SBS

363

assault team to enter the caves together. So where was he? His last transmission had said Elixir had been taken. By whom? And why the hell hadn't he got them both out of harm's way in time? But for Angela, the worst thing was that no one else in the room seemed to give a damn. The assault team were on the ground and steaming in to execute the rescue of the Foreign Secretary. That was all anybody cared about. She had shared her concerns with Trish Fryer, to no avail.

'I'm sure he'll be fine,' Trish had replied breezily, without even taking her eyes off the screen. 'Probably just run out of battery. I wouldn't worry about him, Angela. That boy knows how to take care of himself. Ah,' she said, pointing at the screen. 'Looks like they're nearly at the cave.'

Chapter 96

Namakdan Salt Caves, Qeshm Island

LUKE CARLTON WAS in considerable pain. His arms had been yanked behind his back and his thumbs tied together with white plasticuffs. His left eye was swelling where they'd hit him and there was a dull ache in his midriff where he'd taken another blow to the stomach from a rifle butt. Worst of all, there was the vomit-inducing nausea caused by having been kicked right in the balls. The bastards had waited until his arms were immobilized behind his back before delivering the *coup de grâce*.

Special Forces operatives were trained to go to extreme lengths to avoid capture. And that training had kicked in the moment Luke had spotted the jeep heading in his direction. He'd taken evasive action but there had been nowhere to hide. The palm grove was the first place they'd come looking for him so he had chosen a different course. Moving fast and low across the sandy, rock-strewn terrain, he had stayed close to a protective ridge. He'd thought he might have made it. His mistake was to raise his head to take a look, only to find himself staring down the barrel of a sub-machine-gun, so close the man with his finger on the trigger wouldn't have failed to miss. Luke had run out of options.

After that things had happened with terrifying speed. He had heard a noise behind him, then taken a crippling blow right between the shoulder blades as something hard – probably a rifle butt – knocked him down. Dazed, he'd tried to rise, but he'd felt a knee pushing into his spine as his arms were pulled up behind him and his thumbs secured. Hauling him to his feet, Zamani's thugs had enjoyed softening him up, then dragged him to the waiting jeep. A short, jolting ride at breakneck speed, still with a machine-gun pointed at his head. Arriving at the caves, hands had grabbed Luke and pulled him from the vehicle. A gun barrel prodded him in the back, and he stumbled towards the dark, gaping maw of the entrance. After the beating, his body ached with every step, but he tried to think clearly. Why hadn't they blindfolded him? That was odd. *Because they're not planning on me coming out of here alive.* That must be the only possible explanation.

Pushing, pulling, prodding and jabbing him with the muzzles of their weapons, the two guards propelled Luke down an ever-narrowing tunnel. The only light came from the torch held by the man in front. He felt the drop in temperature and a dampness that clung to his skin. There was a cloying, unhealthy smell in his nostrils. Jesus, what *was* this place? The moving torch beam gave glimpses of dripping stalactites of white rock. Salt? Calcium? He looked around as they propelled him deeper into the cave system, looking for escape routes and hiding places even though his situation appeared hopeless. *It's never hopeless, remember that. You haven't come this far just to die in a cave. Keep working on a plan.*

He could hear voices ahead now, getting closer, and there was a dim yellow light, the sort given off by hurricane lamps. He shivered as the temperature dropped. They turned a corner, his feet slipping on the slimy surface, and Luke found himself in an underground chamber. His eyes searched for a sharp edge that he could use to cut the plasticuffs that bound his hands behind his back. *Keep thinking, keep planning.* Suddenly there seemed to be a lot of people around him, all armed, all bearded or stubbled, some in military uniform, some in scruffy civilian clothes. As he was pushed through the throng, someone ruffled his hair and said something in Farsi and they all laughed. Then a space cleared in front of him and his eyes settled on an old cage, its bars rusted brown with age, and inside – hunched on a filthy mattress – a dishevelled, grey-haired figure nursing a bandaged hand. Jesus! Beneath the dirt and grime he recognized his country's Foreign Secretary. It was Geoffrey Chaplin.

Luke tried to pull away from his captors. He wanted to rush over to Chaplin and tell him he'd be okay, that the hostage-rescue team was inbound right now, that all he needed to do was keep his head down when the shooting started. But he felt an iron grip on his shoulder as he was forcibly turned around. The cavern fell silent but for the hiss of the hurricane lamps. An unshaven, bespectacled man was looking up at him. Luke knew exactly who this was. He was looking into the face of Karim Zamani, his nemesis. And he had a terrible feeling that Zamani knew exactly who he was.

Chapter 97

Qeshm Island

SPREAD OUT EVENLY, at ten metres apart, moving softly and silently on their rubber-soled boots, the eight members of callsign Quebec moved quickly up the gully. They were travelling light by their standards. No mortar team to give them fire support, no heavy breaching equipment, only the most basic survival rations and enough ammunition for a single sustained firefight. Their orders were explicit. Go in covert, go in fast, locate the hostage, eliminate the threat and extract to the shoreline as fast as possible. Avoid getting into a firefight with regular Iranian or IRGC forces at all costs. The hostage-takers – and the hostage-takers alone – were the only 'hostiles' who should be engaged. As soon as news got out that Britain had mounted its own rescue mission on Iranian soil things could spin rapidly out of control.

Such a geopolitical fallout was not Captain Chris Barkwell's concern. His more immediate worry was that there was no sign of the agent supposed to guide them into the caves. Callsign Victor had fallen silent.

'Fucking spooks,' he said to Tash. 'Try to raise him again.' Hidden from sight of the caves, the team had reached the rendezvous point now and the MI6 man was nowhere to be seen.

'Nothing?' he asked Tash.

'Not a thing, boss.'

Too bad, no time to waste, they needed to crack on. Barkwell made a snap decision. 'Smudge.' He spoke into his head mic and waved over the sniper with the CheyTac Intervention rifle. He pointed to a slight rise above them. 'Get yourself into position up there and be ready to take out the two sentries.' Then he turned to his signaller. 'Tash. Time to jack up the ECM. On my command.' The world of electronic counter-measures had always been a mystery to Barkwell but never, for one moment, did he underestimate its importance. Jamming the enemy's comms at exactly the right moment had the effect of electronically blinding the opposition. He knew it could mean the difference between success and failure.

The CheyTac M200 was a very different weapon from those carried by the rest of the team. With its telescopic sight, its bipod at the front and extendable stock at the rear, it was significantly larger and more powerful than their lightweight C8 assault rifles. Back in Oman, Corporal 'Smudge' Thompson, callsign Quebec's sniper, had carefully wrapped the rifle in camouflage netting, disguising its distinctive form and metallic sheen. Not a single centimetre of its surface would reflect the light and give away their position. It took him a little under two minutes to get himself into the right firing position. Clear line of sight to the target, no silhouetting to reveal himself to the enemy, plenty of cover on either side.

When he was ready, he turned and nodded at Barkwell. On the officer's reply, Smudge chambered the first round into the breech and tucked the weapon tight into his right shoulder. The M200 was a high-tech, high-velocity, long-range precision gun but it was operated with an old-fashioned bolt action and a magazine that held just seven rounds. But they were big rounds. At .375 in calibre, the projectiles could take off a man's arm at two kilometres out. At just 420 metres range, Smudge was confident he was not going to miss. He squinted through the scope, controlling his breathing, and when the moment came, he didn't hesitate. The first round hit Zamani's sentry square in the centre of his chest, blasting a fist-sized hole through his back and slamming him against the side of the truck. He died instantly. The other man had no time to react. Smudge's hand was a blur of speed and controlled motion as he worked the bolt to load the second round and squeeze it off. The rest of the assault team heard the muffled cough as the muzzle suppressor did its work, and for a second time the buttstock recoiled into Smudge's shoulder. With a supersonic muzzle velocity of 884 metres a second, the bullet hit the second sentry just above his right eye, removing the rear part of his skull on the way out.

Thirty seconds later the team was on its feet and moving fast across the valley over open ground. The rescue mission had begun.

Chapter 98

Namakdan Salt Caves, Qeshm Island

KARIM ZAMANI LOOKED as if he were going to explode with anger. With his arms bound behind his back and still in the firm grip of the thugs who had seized him, Luke stood his ground as Tannaz's father let forth a stream of vitriol. He could see a blue vein pulsing on the man's temple and there was a sheen of sweat on his face. Since his tirade was all in Farsi, Luke only understood one word – a name: Tannaz.

As Zamani's outburst ended, he backhanded Luke across the face. He grimaced and tasted blood. The guards around Zamani weren't laughing now. Stern-faced, they stood as if awaiting orders. *Play for time, Carlton. The rescue team will be here any minute.* Luke watched as Zamani took a step back and shouted over his shoulder. Moments later, he heard boots on the rough cave floor and two more guards appeared, dragging a diminutive figure between them. Tannaz. She was hobbling, obviously in agony, her hair demurely covered with the ragged blue shawl he'd picked up in Bandar Khamir what felt like a lifetime ago.

It couldn't hide the livid purple welt on her cheek. She'd been hit and hit hard. He felt his blood begin to boil. Their eyes met, for just a second, before she meekly bowed her head. It was enough for him to see the fear in her face. Luke couldn't begin to imagine what it must be like to realize that the man you'd grown up loving as a father was no longer your protector but the very opposite.

Luke hadn't spoken a word since he'd been seized – he'd taken his beating in silence – and refused to show any emotion. But inside he was screaming. It wasn't the pain of the blows that had been meted out by Zamani's people – he'd been trained to take such treatment – it was the terrible realization that what had happened to the girl was his fault. If he and Tannaz had never met she would be safely across the border and out of the country with her mother and brother by now.

Movement shook Luke out of his reverie. A timid-looking man had stepped forward from behind Zamani. He coughed quietly, almost politely, before addressing Luke in heavily accented English. 'Mr Zamani he says that you have dishonoured his daughter and his family. You are a Zionist spy and an enemy of the Islamic Republic of Iran. And he says that now you must pay for your crimes.'

As the man stepped back and resumed his place, the two guards pulled Tannaz forward. She bit back a yelp of pain and Luke broke his silence at last. 'Zamani, for fuck's sake! Leave her out of this!' he shouted. 'She's done nothing wrong.'

They ignored him. Instead, he watched with mounting horror as Karim Zamani reached inside his jacket and withdrew what could only be a long knife in a leather sheath. Zamani went up to his daughter, seized her arm and jerked her towards him. After his earlier outburst he now spoke so quietly that his words were almost inaudible. But what he said was enough for his daughter to break into sobs and shake her head. 'No, Baba,' she kept saying.

Slowly, almost sensuously, Karim Zamani unsheathed the knife, its blade glinting in the light of the hurricane lamps. He grabbed Tannaz's hand, forcing it open, then closed her fingers around the handle. He turned to face Luke, smiled hideously, then pushed his daughter towards him.

A stillness had descended over the cave. It was as if there were only the three of them there – Luke, Tannaz and her father – surrounded by a low murmur of voices. Zamani's men were mouthing prayers. And above them, scowling down from his giant portrait, the face of the father of Revolutionary Iran: the late Ayatollah Ruhollah Khomeini.

Chapter 99

Outside Namakdan Salt Caves, Qeshm Island

THE BODIES LAY still and prone on the dusty soil where they'd fallen. Two SBS operators hurried forward. A quick thumbs-up, and the rest of the patrol moved cautiously up to the cave entrance. Two more minutes, and they'd cleared the two vehicles and established that no further hostiles were lurking behind the rocks. Barkwell peeled back the grey Velcro covering on his watch: 0655 hours. Still time, just. Crouching, he turned to the team's signaller.

'Deploy the Black Hornet,' he ordered.

Tash removed the grey-and-black nano-drone from its waterproof case, checked the charge, then launched it into the early-morning air. Out in the open, the whir of its motors was inaudible. Inside the caves they'd have to be more careful but the drone's minute size and three hi-res infrared cameras made it perfect for the job at hand. Suddenly alert to the possibility of Iranian surveillance drones, Barkwell ordered his team into the mouth of the cave complex. There, he and the signaller hunched over the monitor, noting every twist and turn of the route ahead. Then, suddenly, he saw it.

'Stop!' he ordered. 'Freeze it.' He pointed. There was the silhouette of an armed figure.

'Range?'

'One zero eight metres,' Tash replied. 'But that's to the Hornet. He's another twenty metres plus beyond that.'

Barkwell didn't hesitate. 'Okay. Let's move in and take him out.'

As the nano-drone was recalled and packed away, Barkwell and the assault team prepared to enter the Namakdan tunnel complex. The acoustics changed the moment they entered the strange subterranean world of dripping, saline stalactites. Every sound echoed and was magnified. Using their night-vision goggles, the SBS operators moved in file, navigating their way along the wet, salt-encrusted surface. Fifty metres in, Barkwell held up his hand and signalled his sniper forward. Up ahead a tiny red point of light moved and flared in the dark: someone was smoking. Smudge manoeuvred himself into a firing position. He'd already chambered a round in the CheyTac rifle and now he levelled the barrel down the tunnel. Once more the precision rifle coughed as the heavy bullet slammed into the sentry's chest. The sound of him collapsing seemed to reverberate down the darkened tunnel. The team exchanged glances. Had that been heard deeper in the cave system? Had they been compromised? They waited for a few precious seconds. But they didn't have time to find out. From the darkness came a cry of despair. A woman's scream.

Chapter 100

Inside Namakdan Salt Caves

TANNAZ'S CRY HAD torn through Luke. Pulling against the plasticuffs that bound his hands together, he tried to shake off the men who held him. He was nearly out of time. The two individuals at the centre of this whole crisis – Geoffrey Chaplin and Karim Zamani – were practically within touching distance yet he was powerless to act. He had reached his objective, in this dank, depressing cave, but not in the way he had planned. Instead of deploying Tannaz, using her as a tactical weapon to separate and isolate her father, he had blundered into the spider's web and dragged her with him. And this was the end of the line. Because what he was looking at now could have no good outcome.

Tannaz stood in front of him, her eyes glistening with tears. She was still beautiful in her distress. He wanted to hold her, to reassure her that it was all right, that it had been his fault, that somehow he could find a way out of this. But he could do none of those things. Luke Carlton was not in control. In her hand she held the blade her father had placed there. It had become obvious what was expected of her. The shawl had fallen from her head and her whole body trembled as Luke held her in his gaze.

'I can't . . .' she sobbed. 'I can't do it.'

Her father shouted at her and again she shook her head. Luke's mind was racing. *Where the fuck was the rescue team? Why weren't they here?* He had to do something. These could be his last moments on Earth and he was damned if he'd go down without a fight. He'd take one of these bastards with him.

It was then that everything seemed to slow down. Luke looked on with a growing sense of shock and horror as Zamani, his face twisting into a snarl of rage, snatched the knife from Tannaz and, with his other hand, reached out and grabbed her hair. She screamed as he pulled her head back, brought his arm up and, in a single, shocking motion, sliced across his daughter's exposed throat, severing her windpipe. For a second she clutched help-lessly at the wound as the blood welled out from between her fingers. Her eyes looked imploringly at Luke. Her mouth opened once, as if she were trying to speak, but no words came out. And then beautiful, trusting, life-loving Tannaz Zamani slumped to the ground at his feet.

Chapter 101

Namakdan Salt Caves

THE ROAR THAT Luke heard at the moment of Tannaz's death was one of sheer, animal fury. It came from him.

Tearing himself free of his captors and oblivious of the consequences, Luke hurled himself towards Zamani and, with all the strength he could summon, headbutted him right above the eyes. There was a sharp crack as the shorter man went down, out cold. Moving fast, Luke went to stamp on the unconscious Iranian's neck but he was not quick enough. Guards grabbed him, hauling him back, and he felt the muzzle of a gun jab at his ribs. A large man with a scar down his cheek was screaming abuse into his face. Luke didn't care. He was boiling with rage. On the ground, Tannaz, her limbs still spasming, bled out, a pool of crimson spreading, corrupting the pure white crystalline floor of the cave.

His mind still in turmoil, trying to make sense of the horror he'd just witnessed, Luke felt an enormous pair of hands reach around his neck and force him back against the cage. His head slammed against the bars and he suddenly remembered the British politician, who now cowered in a far corner of his hellhole of a prison.

Still bellowing into Luke's face, so close that he felt the spittle land in his eye, Scarface had him pinned against the cage with one massive hand, while the other reached down to pull out the pistol he had tucked into his waistband. Luke desperately turned this way and that, trying to regain his balance, to get some leverage if only so he could knee the monster in the groin and buy himself a second or two more. He could feel the barrel of the gun grinding against his skull. The hand holding him trembled, its knuckles whitening with tension as the man worked himself up into a lather of fury. Christ, could this really be it? Was this the end? So much unfinished business to attend to, bridges that needed to be rebuilt – and he thought of Elise, her mother Helen, and even his own long-dead parents, the lifetimes of those few he had loved suddenly telescoping into a one-second blur of longing and regret.

When the shot came, the impact knocked Luke sideways, sending him reeling. He felt no pain, only a hot wetness that splashed across his face. Ears ringing, he shook his head and tried to stand. Of course! He'd been hit by the shockwave of a bullet – the bullet that had just taken off the back of Scarface's skull. The SBS had arrived. Covered with blood, bone fragments and the soft pink slime of brain matter, Luke knew he needed to find cover. And fast.

'Stay low!' he yelled at Chaplin, as he hurled himself down. It was then that the firefight erupted all around him. The noise was deafening. Chaplin's captors reacted with speed. They were well trained and well armed, and they returned fire but it was an uneven contest. The flash suppressors on the assault team's C8s masked just how deadly they were. As the red dots of the laser sights found their targets, so the thirty-round magazines were emptied into Zamani's men. Luke pressed himself to the ground as bullets ricocheted around him. Something fell beside him with a crash: a video camera on a tripod, its casing shattered by gunfire.

And then, as suddenly as it had begun, it was over. Ears ringing, his nostrils clogged with the stench of cordite, Luke could hear groaning. It was coming from the slumped figure inside the cage. Geoffrey Chaplin, British Foreign Secretary, who had already gone through three days of hell, clutched at his thigh with a bandaged hand.

'Over here!' Luke shouted. 'Hostage is down!' Still with his hands secured behind his back, he struggled to his feet as eight helmeted figures stormed into the cave. Cradling their weapons, they moved carefully among the bodies that now littered the cave floor.

'Here!' Luke called again, and one of the team rushed over to the cage. Drawing his sidearm from his leg holster, he shot out the padlock and pulled open the door. As he began to work on Chaplin's wound with a pressure bandage, another trooper walked over to Luke and removed his helmet. 'Chris Barkwell,' he said. 'I'm the team commander.'

'Luke Carlton,' he grunted. 'And am I glad to see you guys!' In spite of everything, Luke found himself grinning. He could only imagine what he must look like, covered with another man's gore. 'You cut that a bit fucking fine!'

Seeing the plasticuffs, Barkwell took out his diver's knife and slit the ties. Luke winced as he felt the circulation return to his hands. 'Now,' the SBS officer said, 'we need to get off this island fast. The Zodiacs are inbound and *Astute* is just offshore.' He slapped Luke on the shoulder and turned to go before changing his mind.

'Here,' he said, and handed Luke a Sig Sauer pistol. 'For your own protection,' he added, 'just in case.' Luke nodded his thanks and watched as Barkwell went to speak to Chaplin. God, he felt tired. He wanted to get home, he needed to see Elise and try to make it back into her good books. But he wasn't ready to leave just yet.

Chapter 102

Namakdan Salt Caves

LUKE CHOSE HIS moment carefully. Geoffrey Chaplin, a blood-stained bandage around his thigh and another round his mutilated hand, had been hoisted onto the back of one of Bark-well's team, then carried to the cave entrance and the waiting rescue boats. As the last of the SBS troopers trudged out of the cavern, Luke surveyed the chaos and death they'd left behind. There would be consequences for what he was about to do now, but he would worry about those later. His jaw was set firm as he cocked the silenced pistol he'd been given and walked slowly to where Karim Zamani lay unconscious. There was a plastic bottle of water inside Chaplin's prison that had somehow survived the firefight intact. He went to retrieve it. Standing over the prostrate figure, his legs on either side of him, Luke emptied the contents over the man's face.

Zamani's eyes widened as he came to with a start. He tried to sit, looking around him as he took in the devastation that sig-nalled the failure of his plans. Did he take particular note of the body of his only daughter, drained and pale where she had bled out from the gaping wound he had inflicted? Luke had no idea, but he was going to remind him anyway.

'D'you see her?' he said, pointing at Tannaz's corpse while

keeping his weapon trained on Zamani. The man's eyes flicked from his daughter to Luke and back again.

'She,' said Luke, his voice quivering with barely controlled anger, 'was your daughter. So tell me, Karim Zamani, how could you do *that* to your own child?'

Zamani's eyes narrowed and he spat at Luke's feet.

'*Khaak bar saret!* Snake venom!' he cursed, his voice full of bile. They were to be his final words.

The Sig Sauer coughed once, leaving a single neat hole in the centre of Karim Zamani's forehead.

'That,' Luke said, 'is for Tannaz.'

Epilogue

'YOU'VE HEARD THE news?' He tried to calm himself, but he knew he must sound anxious and nervous.

'I have.' A pause, and the chink of a tea glass being replaced on its saucer. Beyond that, the faint roar of city traffic. 'And may God curse every one of those sons of Satan.' The words were spoken softly, but with venom.

'We could do nothing, you know that? The English and their boats, they had gone by the time we got there.'

'We know, Ali-*jaan*, we know.'

'And the Circle?'

'What of the Circle? It is no more. It never existed.' Another pause. 'Do you understand?'

He hesitated for a moment before answering. 'Of course. But . . .'

'But what?'

'But the tunnel. The project. What now?'

'Ah, the tunnel . . .' Again, the pause and the sound of breath being blown over a scalding glass of tea. 'The tunnel has been sealed. You should not concern yourself with that now.'

'You mean it's over? Ended? Everything?' He couldn't help the rising note of despair in his own voice.

'It is never over,' came the reply. The tone was soothing, calm and supremely confident. 'What secrets the tunnel holds will remain hidden until the right time comes. And that time will come, I promise. Remember, Ali-*jaan, sabr talkh ast, valikan bar-e shireen dārad.* Patience is bitter, but it has a sweet fruit.'

Glossary and names

Al-Wahibi, Mazin – Omani shepherd boy in the Wahiba Sands

Askari, Dr Erfan – Iranian Foreign Minister

Bandar Abbas – major Iranian port on the Gulf coast

Barkwell, Captain Chris – SBS assault team Commander

Batstone, Nigel – Director, Middle East and North Africa, FCO

Bennett, Sir Charles – UK National Security Adviser

Black Run – MI6 agent inside Parchin Military Complex, Iran

Bleake, Rear Admiral John – Assistant Chief of Staff, Submarines, Royal Navy

Bravos – military codeword for hostile forces

Buckshaw, Sir Jeremy – Chief of Defence Staff. Britain's most senior serving officer

Callsign Quebec – SBS assault team's radio callsign

Callsign Victor – Luke's radio callsign

Carlton, Luke – MI6 intelligence officer, ex-SBS, callsign Victor

Chaplin, Geoffrey – British Foreign Secretary

dry dock shelter – the casing for a miniature submersible, fitted to the outside of a submarine to allow operators to enter and exit before flooding it with water

Dunne, Craig – Principal Protection Officer, Metropolitan Police

Echo Sierra – MI6 codename for Karim Zamani

ECM – electronic counter-measures

Elixir – MI6 codename for Tannaz Zamani

Farz – friend of Tannaz

Fryer, Trish – MI6 Mission Controller, Middle East

Haslett, Jane – Permanent Under Secretary of State at the FCO, and Head of the Diplomatic Service

Hosseini, Morteza – Deputy for Legal and International Affairs, Iran Foreign Ministry

IRGC – Iranian Revolutionary Guards Corps

James, Clare – Deputy Head of Mission, British Embassy, Tehran

JIC – Joint Intelligence Committee; sets taskings for MI6

Keeling, Sir Adam – Chief of MI6, Britain's Secret Intelligence Service

Leach, Graham – Head of Iran and Caucasus, MI6

Mayhew, Elise – Luke Carlton's girlfriend

Mayhew, Helen – Elise's mother

Mort – friend of Tannaz and Farz in Bandar Abbas

Nuttall, Lieutenant Colonel Chip – Commanding Officer, UK Special Boat Service

Parchin – home of Iranian military/nuclear industrial complex

Pasdaran – informal name for the Iranian Revolutionary Guards Corps

Paterson, Dr Ken – Head of Counter-proliferation, MI6

Pearson, Lieutenant Commander Jess – Royal Navy officer onboard *Astute*

PJHQ – Permanent Joint Headquarters, Northwood, from where UK runs its overseas operations

Poole – seaside town in Dorset, home to UK's Special Boat Service

Qeshm – Iran's largest island in the Gulf

Rizki, Faisal – MI6 Dubai Station Chief

SBS – Special Boat Service; Royal Navy counterpart to British Army's SAS

Scott, Angela – Luke's departmental boss at MI6

SDV – Swimmer Delivery Vehicle: miniature submarine used by Special Forces for covert insertions

Sepah – official name for Iran's Islamic Revolutionary Guards Corps

Vallance, Sara – special adviser to UK Foreign Secretary

Wallis, Commander Ben – captain of HMS *Astute*

Weston, Reg – Regional Security Officer at British Embassy, Tehran

Zahra – interpreter for Iran's Foreign Minister

Zamani, Forouz – Karim Zamani's wife

Zamani, Karim – senior officer in Iranian Revolutionary Guards Corps, MI6 codename Echo Sierra

Zamani, Tannaz – daughter of Karim Zamani, MI6 codename Elixir

Acknowledgements

To the team at Transworld Publishers, including the tremendous sales and marketing people, art director Richard Ogle (another great cover!), production director Alison Martin, my scarily organized publicist Sally Wray, Hazel Orme for the copy-edit (that phone!), Tash Barsby and her parents (for the unexpected Alpine cheer), and my ever-patient editor Simon Taylor. To my loyal literary agent Julian Alexander at LAW, for your calm, professional and expert guidance.

To Rear Admiral Hohn Gower, for sharing just a fraction of your knowledge about the world of submarine warfare. To James Glancy, for your first-hand knowledge of Royal Marine aspects. To Paulo, for your impressive knowledge of VIP close protection overseas. To Richard, Jonathan, Julia M., my Iranian friends and all those who have asked to remain nameless, for your advice on everything from Iranian cuisine to the inner machinations of COBRA.

To Paulo R. and his lovely staff, for keeping me supplied with copious cappuccinos and glasses of Montepulciano while I wrote late into the evenings. To Julie Wimbush, for letting me come and write in your peaceful country garden. And to Amanda Gardner for your patience and helpful suggestions.

Lastly, to the people of Iran. Yours is a wonderful country with a rich and profound culture, superb food and great hospitality, a country that I have been privileged to visit three times. And *Ultimatum* is only a work of fiction!

Frank Gardner has been the BBC's Security Correspondent since 2002. He has a degree in Arabic & Islamic Studies. He served for six years in the 1980s as a Territorial Army officer in the Royal Green Jackets. In 2004, while filming with the BBC in Saudi Arabia, he was ambushed by terrorists, shot multiple times and left for dead. He survived and returned to active news reporting within a year. He still travels extensively. He was awarded an OBE in 2005 for services to journalism and in 2006 he published his bestselling memoir, *Blood and Sand*. His first novel, *Crisis* – which introduced readers to SIS operative Luke Carlton – was published in 2016 and became a No.1 bestseller. Frank lives in London with his family.